Khamariti's Wave

David Evans

LOUDHAILER BOOKS

Other Books by David Evans

Tidal Rage
Shadows of the Deep

To my darling wife Julie for giving me the space and support.

Big thank you to Patricia Freeman, my research assistant and storyline and character editor.

Thank you to Max, Esme, Lex, and Thea.

To David Haviland, trusted editor and publisher.

contents

chapter 1:
The Call of Abu Simbel

On a crisp morning in the third month of 1237 BCE, as the earliest rays of the sun rose above the horizon, golden light spread across the vast desert that bordered the western bank of the Nile.

At the threshold of the monumental temple of Abu Simbel, a solitary figure emerged. Khamariti's silhouette cut sharp against the burgeoning dawn, a presence both commanding and enigmatic, framed by the grandeur of the site.

"Nebit, heed your mentor!"

His voice carried across the encampment, rising above the hammer of chisels and the scrape of stone. It was not merely a summons. It was a command weighted with authority, sharpened by urgency. Men turned instinctively, for when Khamariti spoke, his words bore the gravity of truths that few dared question.

Before him towered the colossal, seated statues of Ramesses II, their faces hewn in stern symmetry, eyes gazing east to meet the rising sun. The stone giants were not decoration but proclamation, eternal guardians of power. Beneath their shadow Khamariti felt the weight of his task: the architect's duty was not only to honour the pharaoh's reign but to craft messages meant for the ages.

The temple walls shimmered with hieroglyphs, scenes of conquest and divine favour chiselled into permanence. Yet among the depictions of gods and pharaohs ran designs of a different kind, quiet inscriptions that only Khamariti understood in full. They spoke to more than worship. They whispered of forces older than dynasties, veiled within architecture.

He inhaled, the air rich with the tang of stone dust and faint threads of myrrh burned at nearby shrines. Every breath felt like communion with the land itself, every step an echo across centuries yet to come.

"Nebit, where are you hiding, boy?" His tone turned from command to impatience, bouncing through the corridors of stone.

Khamariti's appearance matched the dignity of his role. He wore fine linen robes of white and sky blue, a broad collar beaded with colour that caught the early light. His head, shaven against the desert heat, was wrapped in simple linen, both practical and symbolic. His eyes were sharp, calculating, forever weighing angles and ratios invisible to others. To the workers he was a master architect, to the court he was confidant of the pharaoh, but within himself he carried knowledge he revealed to none.

From above, a voice answered.

"I am here, teacher!"

Nebit's form appeared, perched high on scaffolding beside the immense head of Ramesses. An artisan was painting the ceremonial headdress in dazzling hues of gold and blue, colours that glittered even in muted dawn light. Against the vast stone, Nebit seemed barely more than a speck, a reminder of how small men were before the monuments they built.

Khamariti moved with scrolls of papyrus clutched beneath his arm, each one inked with lines and glyphs that few others could read. Around him, the site pulsed with labour: stone dragged by ropes, chisels beating time, drums guiding rhythm. His shadow stretched long across the limestone blocks, falling over men who paused only long enough to bow their heads as he passed.

"Come down. The pharaoh will not vanish if you leave him a moment."

Nebit obeyed at once, nimble down the wooden scaffold, his face flushed with heat and effort. When he reached the ground, Khamariti gestured to the temple's rising form.

Beneath the colossi, the older man spread a scroll across a cut stone block, his voice steady above the noise of chisels.

"Look here, Nebit. Every mark carved into these walls is more than tribute. It is covenant. We are binding ourselves to eternity. The desert will preserve what we build if it is worthy. Long after pharaohs are dust, this temple will speak."

Nebit studied the drawings, brow furrowed. "I see them, teacher, but not what you wish of me."

Khamariti tapped a corner of the plan. "Here, in the south west, you allowed a lesser stone. The cornerstone must be flawless."

Nebit's face tightened. "The block cracked in the quarry. To fetch another will take many moons. I found a substitute from a nearer pit."

Khamariti's eyes narrowed, his tone cutting but not cruel. "We do not compromise with eternity. A flawed stone today becomes ruin tomorrow. These works must endure the gaze of gods, align with the earth's hidden lines of power. That is our charge."

Nebit bowed his head. "Forgive me, teacher. I will order a new block from the original quarry, though it may be many moons before it arrives."

Khamariti softened, his hand resting on the boy's shoulder. "Then let it be many moons. Better delay than imperfection. This temple is more than glory. It is alignment. Every measure, every carving must obey laws you cannot yet name. In time you will understand."

Nebit lifted his eyes to the towering statues. "This is not only the pharaoh's tribute. It is yours. When I walk here, I feel it. The walls beat like a heart. You have built more than stone. You have carved our place in eternity."

Khamariti's gaze lingered on the colossal faces. "Do not mistake vision for divinity. I have walked these sands for many cycles, but this is no mere shrine to pride. Its purpose is greater. One day you must continue it."

Nebit frowned. "Teacher, you sound as if you prepare to leave."

Khamariti looked to the horizon. "Every man's time narrows, and mine is no exception. You must rise beyond apprentice. You must become a master."

Their words were broken by a sound like thunder.

A block, vast and heavy, slipped from its rigging above the entrance. The ropes screamed as fibres tore. Men shouted, reaching too late. The stone plunged.

The crash shook the ground. Dust burst like smoke. Screams tore through the haze. Bodies lay broken beneath the slab, limbs twisted in ways no healer could mend.

Nebit's voice cracked through the chaos. "Help! Over here!"

Khamariti was already moving. His eyes did not linger on the horror but searched the angles, the levers, the ropes still dangling like dead snakes. "Together!" he commanded. "Lift!"

His voice cut through the panic, sharper than the breaking stone. Men gathered, shoulders braced, hands raw against rope and wood. They pulled as one, straining until their jaws locked and blood ran from torn palms. The slab shifted, grudging, as though mocking their effort.

Beneath it, a cry rose, faint, human. They heaved again. The block rolled an inch. Enough. Hands reached in, dragging a man out, his chest crushed, his breath a ragged whistle. Another came free, blood pouring from his leg where bone jutted white.

Khamariti's commands changed, urgent but precise. "Bring honey. Myrrh. Wine. Hurry!"

They obeyed. Jars cracked open. He pressed honey into wounds, sticky and golden, sealing torn flesh. He poured wine laced with myrrh into cuts that gaped like mouths, the men's screams biting into the air as the liquid burned clean. Aloe-soaked cloths were laid across fevered skin, cooling where fire seemed to spread through veins.

His movements were swift, practiced, as if he had rehearsed this scene a hundred times in silence, waiting for the moment chaos would test him.

Several hours later and still tending the injured Nebit knelt at his side, face pale. "Teacher… are you well?"

Khamariti did not answer at once. His gaze drifted past the wounded, past the block still red with blood. His eyes were clouded with something heavier than grief.

"I mourn for our men," he said at last. His voice was low, steady, carrying more weight than the fallen stone. "But there is more. This loss feels familiar. Like a thread unravelled once before. It is as if the ground itself shifts again beneath us."

Nebit froze, unsettled by the tone, by the distant look in his master's eyes.

Khamariti's words clung to the air like smoke after fire. Not just a warning of stone and labour, but of cycles that turned beneath earth and sky, waiting to strike again.

chapter 2:
Race Against Time

Maplewood University stood in the centre of Toronto like a fortress of scholarship. Its oldest buildings were carved from pale stone that had seen a century of snow and sun. Newer glass blocks stood beside them, reflecting the towers of the city skyline. Students hurried across the wide lawns, their breath turning white in the early morning air.

Inside, behind oak doors polished by generations of hands, the conference chamber waited. Its walls carried portraits of the university's most revered scholars, their eyes following every gathering with stern approval. A long mahogany table dominated the centre of the room, polished to a mirror sheen.

Lex Mullin entered, his boots quiet on the floorboards, though his arrival drew every eye. He knew the setting was not designed for him. He was a man of the field, more used to desert sand and sea salt than panelled walls. But today, his future, and theirs, was being weighed.

At the head sat Dr Eleanor Vance, chair of the department. Her presence carried authority in every line of her posture. To her right sat John Mills, the financial strategist whose every word was measured against a ledger. To her left, Professor James Langdon, arms already folded in doubt. Dr Sarah Mings, younger, sharp-eyed, and thoughtful, sat a little apart, her pen poised.

"Professor Mullin," Vance began, her voice calm but edged with steel. "The Chester coins have been appraised. The Fitzwilliam Museum has offered three and a half million pounds. After the landowner's share and the recovery costs, Maplewood receives one point three million. A substantial success."

Lex Mullin inclined his head, unsure whether she meant it as praise or a warning. At six foot two, he cut a figure that would have looked confident in any setting but this one. The boardroom's glass walls reflected him back in fragments, tall, tidy, a little too formal for his own comfort.

He had come to Maplewood University two years earlier, seconded from Harvard on a research exchange meant to last six months. He was supposed to deliver guest lectures on ancient metrology, write a paper or two, then return to Cambridge, Massachusetts. Instead, he had stayed. He had more chance of chasing a lifelong dream, Atlantis, here at Maplewood than he ever would have at Harvard. The North Atlantic finds, the sonar anomalies, the buried arcs that defied geological logic, each had drawn him further in.

Now, standing under the cold lights of the finance wing, he wondered how long before they realised that his real work had nothing to do with coins or grants.

"I'll see that the funds are distributed accordingly," he said, his New York accent softened but precise, every syllable shaped by years in academia. "Though I'd suggest setting aside a portion for the next survey phase. There's more beneath Chester than anyone's yet mapped."

Vance's eyes narrowed slightly. "Always more with you, Professor. Just be sure your ambitions stay within the University's remit."

Lex inclined his head. "I'm glad the university's gained from it. But the coins aren't the treasure. The true worth lies in the Roman site itself. That discovery gives us a chance to rewrite what we know about Britain's history," he said in his clear New York-English accent.

Mills allowed himself a tight smile. "One point three million is not bad for rewriting history."

Lex did not return the smile. "That is why I am here. I am asking Maplewood for half a million Canadian dollars. It will fund the next expedition."

The words landed like stone dropped into still water.

Mills's expression soured. "Half a million? Do you think we are a bank? The university is already stretched thin. We cannot throw money at every dream you conjure."

Lex met his gaze without blinking. "Dreams? As you just said, I brought this institution one point three million. Tell me, Mr Mills, how much did your office generate this year?"

Colour rose in Mills's cheeks. He opened his mouth, but Vance lifted a hand. "Enough. Professor Mullin, what is this project?"

Lex drew a breath, steadying himself. "Atlantis."

Langdon gave a short, derisive laugh. "Atlantis? We are gathered here for this. Plato's allegory dressed as research?"

"I know your view, Professor Langdon," Lex said evenly. "You call it myth. I call it memory. Plato described a civilisation erased by cataclysm, rising seas, earthquakes, a wave that swallowed an empire. His texts are not idle stories. They are accounts. And I mean to prove it."

Langdon leaned back, disdain etched across his face. "Reckless nonsense. You risk the reputation of every one of us for a fantasy."

Sarah Mings's voice broke in, measured and calm. "Professor Mullin has delivered results, time after time. I do not know if Atlantis is real, but if there is even the smallest chance, Maplewood has a duty to explore it."

Lex seized her words. "Exactly. This is not speculation. It is an opportunity. If I am right, Maplewood will not just be another university. It will be the place that changed civilisation's story."

Langdon's voice cut like a blade. "And if you are wrong, you drag us into ridicule. You gamble with our standing for your own obsession."

Lex's reply was calm, but each word struck home. "You never leave your textbooks, Professor. You bury yourself in safe theories and let others risk failure. That is not scholarship. That is fear."

Vance raised her hand again. "This will not become a duel. Professor Mullin, you will submit a full proposal. Evidence, reasoning, budget. I will present it to the board."

Lex's jaw tightened. "I took this post with the understanding Maplewood would back me. I have brought results, recognition, funding. If you cannot follow through, I will take this project elsewhere."

The silence deepened. Sarah spoke softly, almost reluctantly. "We owe it to the university to consider the possibilities."

Vance inclined her head. "Agreed. The proposal by tomorrow morning, Professor Mullin."

Lex gathered his papers, his voice low but steady. "You shall have it." Then he turned and left, the eyes of dead scholars watching his back.

Months later, the setting could not have been more different. A lecture hall, bright with lights and heavy with anticipation, was filled with donors, scholars, and reporters. The air carried the hum of expectation.

Lex stood at the podium, energy alive in his stance. He was no ordinary academic. The scuffs on his boots spoke of expeditions through jungle and desert. The faint lines on his face marked days under harsh suns and cold stars. He was not here to teach. He was here to lead.

"Thank you for being here," he began. "We stand on the edge of discovery. For centuries, scholars dismissed Atlantis as myth. But myths often hold truth. I believe Atlantis lies waiting for us, beyond the Pillars of Hercules."

The words stirred the room. Some leaned forward, hungry. Others crossed their arms, sceptical. Lex pressed on.

"This is no dream. The geology supports it. Rising seas, volcanic upheavals, shifting plates. Civilisations have fallen before. Why not one more, lost to time?"

He gestured to the team seated behind him. "I am not alone in this. I have gathered some of the finest minds from across the world."

He turned to the first.

"Thea Eva," Lex said. "A PhD student in marine geology, also trained in computer software. She holds a second degree in palaeontology, a rare pairing that lets her trace the life of the seas from fossil to fault line. She is a diver, a pilot of submersibles, and an engineer who can turn theory into practice."

Thea stepped forward. She looked plain at first glance, her glasses hiding more than they revealed, yet the poise in her stance told another story. Her voice carried the slow drawl of South Carolina, vowels softened and stretched, but every few words caught slightly, the faint hitch of an old stutter that had never quite left her since the car crash that took her parents. "S-sir, it's a pleasure," she said simply, her tone both respectful and firm, her Charleston accent gentle but unmistakable.

Lex moved on.

"Max Keeper," he announced. "Volcanologist and seismologist. His research at Mount Etna set new standards for the study of active fault lines. He comes to us from Liverpool University."

Max rose with easy confidence. His leather jacket was at odds with the academic setting, and his grin carried something roguish. Handsome, dark haired, he looked more like a front man of a band than a man of science. Yet when he spoke, the soft Liverpool accent softened the edges of his words. "Glad to be here," he said, and the sincerity in his tone left no doubt about his purpose.

Lex's gaze shifted again.

"And Esme Miller," he said with respect. "Egyptologist, linguist, historian. A graduate of Vancouver University, Canada. She is sharp witted, and unafraid to test every assumption. Her insights connect the myths of Atlantis with the records of ancient civilisations. She brings the past into the present."

Esme rose, a light scarf looped at her throat, the fabric catching the movement as she turned. Her blonde hair framed a face both striking and composed, the kind that drew attention without asking for it. Her eyes were sharp, curious, and alive with quiet intelligence. When she spoke, her voice carried an effortless clarity, calm, assured, and touched with that easy confidence that came from years of guiding discussion. There was warmth behind it too, a spark of charm that softened the authority in her tone, and for a moment the hall itself seemed to lean in to listen.

Lex spread his arms to them all. "This is our team. Archaeologists, geologists, historians, explorers. Together, we will find Atlantis."

A journalist raised his hand. "Atlantis is fiction. A story by Plato. Why waste your time?"

Lex's reply was ready. "So was Troy. Until Schliemann uncovered it. Legends hide truths. And when we find Atlantis, history will never be the same."

The words rang across the hall. Those who believed felt fire in their chests. Those who doubted felt unease. And Lex knew, whichever side they stood on, they would remember this day.

Tomorrow, the team would leave for Spain. The search would begin.

chapter 3:
The Summons of Destiny

Khamariti faced the royal envoy, his brow taut with unease.

"I have injured men here," he said, gesturing toward the labourers being tended by temple healers. "What summons can outweigh their lives?"

The envoy did not blink. His stance was rigid, his tone crisp with the authority of the throne. "Great Pharaoh Ramesses II demands your immediate return. That is reason enough."

The words struck like a hammer. Khamariti inclined his head, the gesture measured, but the weight of the command pressed hard upon him. For weeks he had planned to remain at Abu Simbel, guiding the last stages of construction. To be summoned so abruptly could mean only one thing: change was upon him. Whether in court or cosmos, unseen forces were tightening the net of his fate.

He looked once more across the temple grounds, at fractured stone and fallen men. His heart sank. Something in the order of the world had shifted.

At the edge of Aswan stood his modest refuge. His main home was in Thebes, yet for many moons this had been his dwelling while he worked on Abu Simbel. It was no palace and no shrine, but a place of rest, its walls lined with shelves of scrolls, maps, and relics. Here his restless search for knowledge found a harbour.

He turned to Nebit, his apprentice, voice low with urgency. "In my quarters lie two scrolls. On them I have drawn two families. If I do not return, hide them in the secret chamber of the monument. This is not a request. It is your charge."

Nebit stiffened, startled by the gravity in his tone. "Yes, teacher. But who are they, to deserve such secrecy?"

Khamariti's expression softened. "They were once my entire world. They are long gone, but their memory burns brighter than any stone I carve. Abu Simbel may carry Ramesses's name, but these hidden names will be my true legacy."

He thought of Merit, his current steadfast wife, of Nefer and Menna, his beloved children. Their lives anchored him, even as shadows gathered on the horizon.

"They are everything," he told Nebit. "But there are truths you are not ready to bear. For now, you have my instructions. Keep your word."

The envoy inclined his head, impatience measured but clear. "We must depart. The Son of Ra waits."

That afternoon, Khamariti and Nebit walked the site one last time, studying the twin temples cut deep into the cliff. Shadows lengthened as the sun sank low, burnishing the stone colossi with molten gold.

At the riverbank, the royal barge awaited. The Dawn of Aten lay ready, its cedar timbers glowing in the last light, its prow carved into the disc of the rising sun. Oars rested like wings, sails furled, canopy draped in painted linen.

The Nile air was thick with the scent of earth and water, timeless as Egypt itself.

"As I have told you before," Khamariti murmured, "something is amiss. I fear I will not return."

Nebit's face creased with worry. "I pray for your safe return, teacher. I cannot complete Abu Simbel without you."

"You can," Khamariti said firmly, though warmth touched his voice. "You must. The plans will guide you. You have grown into more than an apprentice. In five years, you have become my ally. Trust your skill."

Nebit bowed his head, swallowing his fear.

The Dawn of Aten slipped into the current, bearing him northward.

The voyage from Abu Simbel to Thebes was no mere journey. It was a passage between worlds. By day he watched fishermen casting nets with wary eyes, traders shouting prices with one hand never far from a blade. Temples lined the horizon, their columns silent witnesses to centuries of prayer and ambition.

By night he sat alone at the stern. The constellations wheeled above, bright, and cold. The river's rhythm carried him in silence, each bend heavy with memory and foreboding.

He measured the distance not as kilometres, but in cubits, six hundred thousand common cubits of river, a measure that felt more like eternity than span.

After ten days Thebes rose on the horizon. Smoke curled from hearths, temple pylons pierced the sky, and the city's hum reached across the water like a living thing.

The Dawn of Aten eased into harbour and settled against the stone berth. Lines were thrown, the hull drawn snug. From the quay, a clear voice carried over the water.

"Master Khamariti," the envoy called. "The Great Pharaoh sends his palanquin."

The conveyance awaited, borne by handpicked bearers, its canopy rich with dyed linen. It swayed through the streets, past vendors, and guards, through crowds that parted at the sight of Pharaoh's architect.

Then, home.

At the threshold stood Merit, her figure framed in the first light. Menna clutched her hand, her small face half-hidden, then breaking into a smile as she recognised him.

Khamariti's chest ached. He leant forward, arms wide. Menna burst free, running, her laughter cutting through the dawn. He caught her, lifted her high, kissed her cheeks.

"My little goddess," he whispered. "Look how you have grown."

But his eyes lifted over her head, meeting Merit's. Relief glimmered there, but also something darker.

"Where is Nefer?" he asked.

Menna's answer struck like a blow. "Mother says he is playing with the gods."

Khamariti froze. His arms tightened around her. Merit stepped forward, her face drawn with grief. "I have the worst news, my husband."

The words hollowed him. He lowered Menna gently to the ground, searching Merit's eyes. The tracks of tears stained her cheeks.

"What happened?" His voice was barely sound.

Merit's gaze drifted east, to the Per Nefer, the House of Beauty where the dead were prepared for eternity. "Our son is gone."

The storm broke inside him. He dropped to his knees, his cry tearing from his chest, raw and desolate, echoing against the stone walls.

Later, beneath the frail glow of an oil lamp, Merit spoke. The bronze bowl sat upon an alabaster stand, its linen wick drowning in a shallow pool of castor oil. The flame shivered, throwing long shadows across the courtyard wall, light too fragile to warm the night, yet cruelly bright upon her grief-worn face.

"It began with a swelling in his mouth," she whispered, her voice thin as reed paper. "At first, I thought it nothing. He said the bread had cut him. I used honey to soothe it, but the badness took hold, in his gums, his teeth, deep beneath the skin."

Her hands trembled as she gripped her robe. "I tried every remedy I knew. Crushed lotus root, pine resin, salt, vinegar, myrrh. Nothing stopped it. I even pulled five of his teeth, one by one, to drain the pus beneath. He screamed, Ra forgive me, he screamed, and still the rot spread."

She faltered, her voice breaking. "His jaw locked. His breath grew shallow. I could feel the fever burn through him. I held him as he slipped away, and the gods did nothing."

She turned toward Khamariti, her eyes wet, her voice pleading. "I told you," she said. "I always threshed the wheat thrice for the bread. But it is known, the coarse grain tears the gums, wears the teeth, brings sickness and sometimes death. I did it for him. I did everything I could. And still they took him."

Khamariti steadied himself, the oil lamp's flicker trembling across his face. The bronze bowl hissed as a drop of oil spat from its linen wick, the flame bowing low before rising again with stubborn life. His hands pressed into the dust, eyes glinting like molten gold.

"Curse you!" he cried, voice cracking through the still air. "Curse you for this cruelty, for the design that binds love to pain!"

The words tore into the night like a wound. He was not calling to Ra, nor to Osiris, nor to any god carved in stone. His fury was older than prayer, aimed not at heaven but at the earth itself, the living world that birthed and buried with the same hand.

He rose to his feet, chest heaving, eyes blazing with a kind of savage grief.

"You, who make the river rise and the grain grow," he shouted into the darkness, "you who promise life only to feed it back to the soil, why must your balance demand blood? Why must you take the gentle before the wicked, the innocent before the cruel?"

The sound tore through the courtyard and broke into silence. Merit knelt beside him, her hands shaking, tears spilling down her cheeks. The scent of castor oil and burnt linen hung heavy between them.

Khamariti turned, his fury spent as swiftly as it had come. He drew her into his arms, holding her as though the act alone could bar the gods from taking more. Her sobs broke against his chest, small and ragged.

"Merit," he whispered, his voice rough. "You were a good mother. None of this was your fault. Nature is cruel. It always has been. It culls a portion of the living so the rest may endure."

The ground seemed to shift beneath him. The lamp guttered low, its flame bending in the draft like a spirit losing strength. Shadows crawled across the wall as the courtyard sank into silence.

Above them, the stars watched in cold indifference, ancient, perfect, and deaf to prayer. This was not his first family, not his first loss.

chapter 4:
A Quest Through
Ancient Waters

The Mediterranean lay calm, a sheet of shifting blue beneath the September sun. Cutting across it was the *Marine Explorer*, a Spanish research vessel built not for comfort but for discovery. On the bridge stood Captain Ronan Rodrigues, Portuguese by birth, his hands weathered yet steady on the wheel. He had spent a lifetime chasing the deep, first as a geologist, later as a commander of men. Risk sat easily on him, as natural as the salt in his beard.

The ship was more than steel and circuits. It carried echoes of Spain's maritime past, forged anew in metal and wire. Cranes whispered when they swung, winches moved with oiled precision, and the bridge glowed with patient screens. It was a vessel built not for show, but for endurance, for answers hidden far below the surface.

At the quay in Cádiz, the team stood ready. Lex, Max, Thea, and Esme gathered with their bags stacked at their feet, eyes straying often to the horizon where the Rock of Gibraltar rose, the ancient Pillars of Hercules. The air carried diesel, gull cries, and the slap of tide against stone.

Rodrigues strode down the gangway with a broad grin. "Professor Mullin, very good to see you, my friend," he said, the words touched by the smooth lilt of Lisbon, each syllable careful, almost musical.

"And you, Captain," Lex answered, clasping his hand.

The captain's gaze swept the group. "Fresh minds. The sea likes that." He paused at Esme, raising one brow. "Any of you lack sea legs?"

Esme lifted her hand half in jest. Rodrigues reached into his pocket and produced a paper bag, handing it to her with a wink.

"Quem vai ao mar, avia-se em terra," Rodrigues said, the words rolling like surf off his tongue. He who goes to sea must prepare on land.

He fixed the newcomer with a steady look. "No passengers here. If the pull hits you, use this and come straight back. Out here, we all carry our weight."

The crew welcomed them aboard with quiet efficiency. Bags vanished into holds, cases stowed without fuss. The chief engineer nodded once, then disappeared below. Thea moved straight to the tether lines, checking lashings on the submersible. Max stroked the sonar array as if greeting a thoroughbred. Esme stood by the rail, breathing in tar, rope, and the scent of distance.

Lex gathered the team around the table, maps and sonar prints spread before them. His voice carried the steady conviction of a man who had weighed every doubt. He told them he believed Atlantis had not been a myth of gods or poets but a real island in the Atlantic, torn apart when a massive landslip struck its flank. The collapse had driven a tsunami across the ocean, erasing the island in a single night. Their task, he said, was not to chase legends but to follow evidence. The first stage of the expedition would be to trace the scar of that landslide, chart its path, and track the direction of the debris. Only then could they begin to uncover where Atlantis had truly stood.

At dawn, the ship slipped free, her bow turning south and west. Their course: the Canary Islands. Waters that had lured sailors since the time of Carthage.

The first days were for systems. Thea's voice rolled through the cabin with that calm South Carolina steadiness, soft drawl, all control.

"B-b-ballast's true. C-comms are clean. Batteries reading green. Manipulators checked. Emergency air tested. Strobes and beacon confirmed," she said, every word deliberate, no-nonsense, but easy on the ear, the faint stutter threading through her rhythm like a scar she'd learned to live with. She spoke as if she'd done it a hundred times and still cared to get it right.

She stopped only when every line was secure. "ROV's clear," she said. It was a tethered submersible built for deep survey. their eyes beneath the waves. "Ten minutes at dusk, then we bring it back."

Thea leaned over the sonar screens, coloured lines flickerin' like fireflies as she laid out the plan. "W-we'll start with the Cádiz shelf," she said, her drawl calm but firm. "Ship moves at two knots, f-five percent overlap, means every scan kisses the last one just enough so n-nothin' slips through. Numbers first, always."

The ship was built for this work. Her hull carried stabilisers, her decks held multibeam sonar, magnetometers, two ROVs, and a submersible for three. The labs were compact and bright, with benches that locked and racks for cores. A floating workshop tuned to the sea.

By the second morning rhythm had set in. Days divided between dives and data, nights between charts and sky. Esme pulled old maps from her case, cross-checking the ink of centuries with modern prints. She smiled at how faithfully the stars still kept their order.

At a briefing Lex tapped a bathymetry sheet. "We chase terraces, ancient shorelines, odd geometry near Teide's lava fans. If the margin slipped, we should see scars. Sample, if possible, record if not."

Rodrigues gave a single nod. "The sea will decide what it shows you. I will keep you on it."

On the third evening the light dulled to pewter. A wall of cloud rose from the horizon, growing as though conjured. Rodrigues stood at the bridge, eyes narrowed.

"Storm off Africa," Rodrigues called, calm as stone. "Bigger than forecast, moving fast. No chance of port. We ride it."

The sky turned hard and grey. First gusts shook the rails, then waves rose into white-topped giants. Hatches slammed shut. Extra chains bound the sub cradle. Esme went pale. Thea pressed a ginger sweet into her hand.

"Keep your eyes on the h-horizon," she said softly.

Lightning split the sky. Thunder rolled deep and heavy. Green water smashed the bow, spray drenching the deck. The Marine Explorer strained and groaned, but Rodrigues's hands never left the wheel. His orders came sharp and steady. The crew moved as one.

Hours blurred. The storm gave no mercy. Rain hit like stones, sand whipped bare skin. Deckhands caught a lifeboat as it tore loose, Max with them, palms bleeding as he dragged it back.

At last, on the sixth morning, the sea eased. The water lay flat as glass. Faces were drawn with fatigue. Salt coated the rails. Relief came in shallow breaths.

"Past the worst," Rodrigues muttered.

A cry split the air. "Upturned yacht! Port bow!"

Even at distance the shape was wrong. An inverted hull, scattered gear bobbing like wreckage cast aside.

"All hands," Rodrigues barked. "Professor Mullin, with them. There may be air pockets. We check. Fast."

Lex stepped forward without hesitation. "I am the most experienced diver. I'll go first."

Thea buckled his harness with quick, practised hands, her jaw tight. She pressed a ginger sweet into his palm before fitting his regulator. "Clean entry, clean exit now. Nothin' reckless, you hear?" she said firmly, her voice catching just once on the first word, the trace of her old stutter softened by years of control, her eyes locking with his.

The sea swallowed him whole. Cold water clamped across his chest as he descended. His torch beam cut a pale cone through the gloom, each particle of silt turning the water into drifting smoke. The yacht loomed above him, a Sunseeker Manhattan 52, once a sleek predator of the sea, now reduced to a tomb.

Lex circled the hull, searching for entry. He found the shattered patio doors at the stern and eased through the twisted frame. Darkness met him inside. The silence was unbearable, broken only by the hiss of his own breath.

Objects floated in slow motion. A cushion, a silver spoon, a child's toy horse drifting nose down. The image wrenched at him, ordinary life, fractured in an instant.

Then came the bodies. Four of them, pressed into a corner by the roll of the yacht. Their clothes billowed around them like broken sails. Lex steadied himself, jaw clenched and checked each in turn. The smallest, a girl of no more than eight. Her hair waved like sea grass. He forced himself to move on.

His torch caught a face. Recognition hit him like a blow to the chest. Crete, two summers ago. A dinner on the harbour, laughter that carried into the night. Promises of diving together again. The Campbell family. James Campbell, one of the finest divers of his generation. His wife, their two children. Friends. Gone.

Lex shut his eyes for one long breath, the regulator rattling between his teeth. He forced himself to document what he could, every movement precise, every second heavy with grief. Then he pushed away and began the long ascent.

He surfaced hard, water sheeting from his face. He clung to the ladder, lungs burning. The regulator came free, and his voice was hoarse with salt and sorrow.

"The Campbell family," he gasped. "All gone. No survivors."

"Quem nasce para vinte não chega a trinta," Rodrigues murmured, his voice low and steady, the cadence of the old tongue carrying a weight the sea itself seemed to echo. He who's born for twenty will never reach thirty.

He didn't smile when he said it. His gaze stayed fixed on the dark horizon, where the waves folded over one another like pages in a book no man was meant to finish. "Some lives," he added quietly, "are written short from the start."

The deck fell silent. Esme turned sharply, shoulders trembling, her eyes shining. Max's hands curled into fists, raw skin tearing further. Rodrigues lowered his head, lips pressed tight.

A marker buoy was set. The position relayed to the coastguard. The sea rolled on, vast and indifferent.

But Lex wasn't done.

He descended again, driven by a gnawing compulsion. The hull held no more air, no more life. Yet as he swept the forward cabin, his light caught something wedged between the beams.

A shard of black stone, not part of the yacht, not of any known wreck. Its surface was carved with lines too exact, angles too clean, as though it had once belonged to a greater design. When he touched it, the texture was slick, almost metallic, yet warm under his glove.

Lex's heart hammered. He knew it was no part of the Sunseeker. No part of any modern craft. James Campbell must have carried it from one of his dives. Perhaps even as proof.

The shard glowed faintly in his torchlight, etched with patterns like wave crests frozen in stone.

He turned it over once more, the weight uncanny in his palm. One thought rose above the grief, sharp and undeniable.

This could have come from Atlantis.

Later, Rodrigues found Lex at the rail, the security lead watching the buoy drift astern.

"You know sailors," Rodrigues murmured. "Some will call this an omen. A family lost on our line, after the storm."

Lex's jaw tightened. "Do you believe it?"

"I believe the sea," Rodrigues answered. "But omens weigh heavy if men believe them. Keep watch. Doubt creeps easiest after loss."

Lex nodded once. "Tomorrow, omen or not, I'll bring the bodies home."

chapter 5:
The Labourers Deceit

While the workers of the House of Beauty tended his dead son, Khamariti stepped into the hush of the cemetery, grief pressing like a stone on his chest. Among the silent chambers of the Necropolis, he marked the niche that would publicly hold Nefer, a tomb cut from old rock. A small honour granted at the pharaoh's word.

Through tears and exhaustion, he carved the sealing slab himself. Two days of labour left his hands raw. In its centre he cut the name: Nefer, son of Merit and Khamariti, a mark meant to stand until the desert turned to dust. Around the name he set prayers and offerings, at Merit's insistence. If rites were fit for a pharaoh, they were fit for their child. He chiselled each line with a reverence that was both holy and unbearable.

The stone offered honour but no comfort. Its permanence mocked the fragility of breath. Khamariti, who had made mountains speak for pharaohs, learned the cruel truth of his craft. Stone endures, but it cannot hold a child's laughter.

At dawn, head shaven and linen dark with mourning, he stood as a messenger from Ramesses II stepped across his threshold. Five hired mourners waited in the street beyond, their wails ready to carry the news through Thebes.

"Ramesses II, Beloved of Ma'at, has decreed the full seventy days," the emissary said, voice low. "The period begins with your return, Master Khamariti."

Khamariti inclined his head. "Carry my respect to the pharaoh. His grace touches my heart."

Seventy days. Not an empty span, but the measured cadence of embalming and prayer, of body made ready and spirit fortified for the journey. He held to the rhythm. He went daily to the House of Beauty where the artisans worked with reverent hands. In quiet moments he smoothed Nefer's hair, cradled him beyond the embalmers' gaze, a wordless communion between father and son.

Under orders and out of love, he gathered grave goods. Amulets and jewels to protect, the Eye of Horus to ward off malice, shabtis to labour in the fields of reeds. He mixed ritual with tenderness, placing scrolls from the Book of the Dead and simple toys beside them, hoping the sight might ease Merit's pain if not alter fate.

Merit's voice steadied itself and gave him purpose. "Gather the Coffin Texts and what he loved. Place them with him, that he may find joy and guidance." Her eyes were hollowed by sorrow yet held a core of resolve.

Ramesses sent sustenance and gold. Loaves, honey, fine cuts of meat, and the images of Osiris, Anubis, and Isis, set to guard and guide. Khamariti added a model boat with his own hands, a vessel to bear a small boy across a celestial Nile.

Late one afternoon, as heat thickened and shadows lengthened across the fresh cut stones, Khamariti caught a movement that did not fit. A labourer he had known for years, deep in hurried speech with a thin man wrapped in linen too clean for the work. Thebes knew that shape. A thief who haunted the edges of market stalls and funerary corteges. Hands touched briefly. Something passed.

Khamariti felt the old cold rise. He had learned the soundless language of glances and palms, as surely as he read the lines on temple walls.

That evening, under pretence of reviewing measurements, he called the labourer to his quarters. An oil lamp breathed and the room smelt of incense. The man stood just inside the door, eyes hunting for safe ground.

"Tell me about your friend from the market," Khamariti said, voice even.

"He is no friend, master," the man stammered. "Only a talker. He wished to know of your work."

"Does curiosity require him to linger by the gate of my son's tomb?"

The labourer's face cracked. "It was foolish talk. He spoke of riches. I told him nothing. I swear it."

Khamariti's gaze did not soften. "The things in that chamber honour the dead and aid their passage. Whoever violates it draws down the wrath of the living and the curse of the gods. Hear me clearly."

The labourer bowed and bobbed, relief at the reprieve writ plain. "I will avoid him. I will speak no more."

Words would not unmake greed. That night Khamariti began the other work. For the next seventy days he slept scarcely more than two hours in any turn of the moon. He set watch where eyes could not see. He measured the slab's seat and the way it would speak if moved. He turned grief into a plan no one would think to name.

The procession came with the first light, the scent of myrrh in the air and ancient prayers carried on low voices. Ramesses walked at its head. His presence honoured the dead and bound the living. It did not lighten the weight in Khamariti's chest.

Under the shade of old trees, the final rites unfolded. The sealing stone slid home with a cold finality that took his breath. He, who had given the pharaohs their facades and taught the sun to enter halls on appointed days, could raise no edifice to span what had been torn from him. The desert's monuments looked small in the face of one child's absence.

"Your loss is our loss," Ramesses said, robed for mourning, courtiers, and priests at his back. Khamariti bowed his head. "You bless us with your presence, Great Pharaoh."

Merit stood beside him, grief carved deep and quiet. Menna clung to her skirts until the pharaohs knelt and took the child's hand.

"Your brother will play with other children in the next field," Ramesses said gently. "The gods will care for him."

Menna sobbed, the pure sound of a wound that reason cannot touch. It cleaved the air. Ritual held, but the heart did as it pleased.

When the prayers fell to whispers and the last offerings were laid, the family stood alone with their new, hard truth. Thebes blazed around them in carved splendour. It meant little.

Khamariti vanished after the interment and did not return for three days. Merit, tended by a servant, moved through her own storm. Their griefs could not touch.

The labourer and the thief waited two weeks. Precision would be their shield. They found a stonemason and bought his silence with a rich share, a fifth of whatever lay behind the door. The mason crafted a twin for the sealing stone, measured to the finger breadth. A clumsy copy would betray them at once. They would not allow it.

They chose a cool night. Tools wrapped in cloth, footsteps counted and recounted, oil lamps trimmed low. The mason's chisel struck with certainty. The original slab came free with barely a whisper. The copy waited to be bedded in its place when the work within was done.

They passed into the antechamber, eyes already on the gold of Osiris. The floor lay strewn with rushes. Their weight pressed where Khamariti had planned.

"Where is the body?" the labourer breathed. "Where are the tributes?"

In the dark beneath the desert, Khamariti's design woke. He had built a defence as exact as any temple. The antechamber fed a heavy door whose lock was a puzzle cut into its own carving. The door spoke to plates set underfoot. Touch what should not be touched, and the stone would decide.

The instant their boots touched the pressure plate, the mechanism stirred.

The door slammed with a boom so violent it seemed the earth itself had struck. Dust rained from the lintel, choking their throats. Then came the deeper sound, a grinding from the walls as hidden stones rolled into place, sealing the side escapes one after another. Each thud was a verdict.

The chamber fell still. Not the stillness of peace, but of a grave being sealed.

The men froze, their torch flames wavering. Eyes darted to the walls, to the ceiling, to one another. The air grew thick, every breath a theft from the next man's lungs. Somewhere in the dark, sand shifted, a dry whisper like something alive.

"We are finished," the labourer cried, panic tearing his voice. He stumbled backwards, hands clawing at the stone as if he might scrape a way out with his nails.

The stonemason dropped his torch. The flame died on the floor, plunging half the chamber into shadow. The sudden dark was worse than the walls. Their hearts pounded against the silence, against the stone that seemed to lean closer with every breath.

Someone struck the sealed door with a hammer. The sound came back dead, swallowed whole, as though the stone were laughing at them.

"No," the labourer whispered, shaking his head, sweat carving paths through the dust on his face. "This is no door. This is a tomb."

And in that moment, they all knew, Khamariti had built not just a trap, but a judgement. The chamber itself was watching. Waiting. "Find us a way out," the thief hissed at the mason, fear punching holes in bravado.

The stonemason, whose hands had shaped walls for nobles and pharaohs, turned in the cramped light. His face was pale, lined and suddenly old. "They call me a master stonemason" he said softly, glancing at the sealed door, "but there is only one master here."

He ran his fingers across the join, felt the weight of the design in the stone itself, and shivered. "He made this trap. This is not a tomb for a boy. It is a snare for men like us."

Silence thickened. Then frenzy. The thief and the labourer clawed at the joints with bare hands, blood running down their wrists. Dust spiralled in the lamplight. Metal rasped, stone answered with cold indifference. Their fire guttered. The air grew thin and hot.

"There must be a way," the thief gasped.

The labourer gave no answer beyond the sound of failing strength.

At first light Khamariti returned as he had each morning since the sealing. He paused at the slab, listening with his fingertips where the stone met its bed. He did not need to hear the muffled echoes to know his design had spoken. Markers he had set told their tale.

He walked a little way down the slope to a scatter of ordinary stones that matched the hillside. He bowed his head. "Now you may rest, my son," he whispered, and the breeze took the words.

Beneath those unremarkable rocks lay the chamber he had cut in secret. Its walls bore simple hieroglyphs. The floor held toys. The small, wrapped body rested where no thief would ever look, in a room the world would not see.

chapter 6:
The Nile Bleeds

In the two years since the earth had claimed the young life of his son, Khamariti's heart had been shrouded in a sorrow so profound it felt as though even the sun hesitated to rise. Ramesses II, in an act of compassion rare for a pharaoh, had granted him four months of reprieve, time to mourn with Merit and their surviving daughter, Menna. Yet grief, like stone, left its weight long after the rituals had ended.

One evening beneath the star filled sky, Ramesses was struck by a vision. In the silence of Thebes, the god Amun, fused with Ra, revealed himself as Amun Ra, the majestic embodiment of creation and sovereignty. The vision spoke with a voice like thunder rolling across eternity: build a temple in Thebes, a gateway to the afterlife, a structure so vast that even Abu Simbel would seem small before it.

The next day, Ramesses summoned his architect.

"Architect," Ramesses declared, his voice resonant with command, "I have been granted a vision. Draft for me a temple so magnificent it will eclipse Abu Simbel. My armies march east even now to secure the wealth, gold, silver, precious stone, which will feed this work."

Khamariti bowed deeply. "Great Pharaoh, Abu Simbel is not yet complete. It is the monument to your queen, Nefertari, and a testament to your divine stature. I beg leave to honour that promise before turning to the next."

The pharaoh's eyes narrowed, but his voice was calm. "Did you not tell me Nebit is now skilled enough to finish the work?"

"Son of Ra," Khamariti answered carefully, "Nebit has talent, but Abu Simbel was born of your love. It would sit ill with me to depart before its completion."

Ramesses leaned forward on his throne, his gaze unyielding. "Your place is here, with your family, after all you have endured. Abu Simbel nears its end. The gods have spoken. You will build my temple, the Ramesseum."

The words left no room for doubt. Khamariti bowed his head, his voice steady though his heart resisted. "Pharaoh Ramesses II, I will do as you command."

For eight moons, Khamariti laboured over designs by lamplight, his stylus scratching late into the night. Each line on papyrus held not only opulence for his pharaoh but secret alignments with the hidden currents beneath the earth, magnetic ley lines, invisible yet powerful. Few would understand, but he would not abandon what knowledge his race had entrusted him with.

At last, the day came when he stood before Ramesses in the palace of Ma'at. Courtiers filled the chamber, priests lined the walls, and incense curled through the air as Khamariti unrolled his designs.

"Great Pharaoh, Son of Ra, Living Horus," he intoned, "this temple will serve as both a house for Amun and a funerary temple for your eternal reign. Its foundations I have shifted onto bedrock, away from treacherous sands."

The papyrus revealed vast pylons, soaring obelisks, and colossal statues of Ramesses himself. Reliefs chronicled his victories, at Kadesh and against the Hittites, etched into stone for eternity. A sanctuary, the House of Life, would guard Egypt's wisdom.

When the model was unveiled, even Ramesses fell silent. The statues, the courtyards, the pylon gates, all promised to outlast empires. For a heartbeat, Khamariti thought he glimpsed tears in the pharaoh's eyes. Later he would tell Merit: "In that moment, the so-called god-king looked unmistakably mortal."

"Name your needs," Ramesses said at last, his voice softened but resolute.

"Pharaoh, this work will demand five thousand labourers, artisans, quarrymen, and scribes. They must be fed with bread, beer, and meat. Their toil must be dignified, their spirits sustained. Without it, even the strongest will falter."

"How many seasons?" Ramesses asked.

"Many, Great Pharaoh. Enough moons to see a child grow to manhood. Yet if the gods grant it, the Ramesseum shall endure beyond all reckoning."

Ramesses smiled grimly. "My armies have returned from the Hittite lands with gold and silver. The sinews of your vision are secured. And Nebit, he shall return from Abu Simbel to aid you. But appoint a successor there worthy of your standards."

Khamariti bowed. "Your wisdom lights our way, Son of Ra."

The site chosen lay close to the Nile, the river that had fed Egypt since time began. Barges brought stone, cedar, and bronze along its waters. Amara Al Fahil, the logistics expert, coordinated supply lines with the precision of a general.

Nebit, eager yet cautious, walked the foundations with Khamariti. "Teacher," he said, "the river floods each year. Will not the waters undermine our walls?"

Khamariti nodded. "The Nile is both ally and adversary. We will cut deeper foundations and shore them with granite. But more than water, I seek what lies unseen, the currents beneath the earth."

Nebit frowned. "Magnetic forces again?"

"One day, you may understand."

But the Nile grew restless.

One morning, Nebit came running. "Teacher, the river has slowed. The fish are dying. People say the gods are angry."

Khamariti strode to the riverbank. The crowd pressed close, their eyes wide with fear. Fish floated bloated on the surface, the water sluggish and foul. Within days, algae spread, choking the current until the river itself turned red as blood. Women wailed, priests raised their hands to the sky, and rumours spread like fire.

"It is a sign!" cried one man. "The gods curse us for building on sacred ground!"

"No," Khamariti said firmly, though the people scarcely listened. "Water finds its own path. This is blockage, perhaps a landslide upstream."

Still, whispers grew. Some said Amun Ra punished Egypt for pride. Others claimed the work of the Ramesseum had offended Osiris. By the seventh day, panic gripped Thebes.

High Priest Ankhwennefer entered the throne room, his robes whispering across the polished stone like creeping dusk. He bowed low, but the motion did not soften the steel in his eyes. For years he had watched Pharaoh turn not to him, the chosen voice of the gods, but to Khamariti, the architect. Each counsel sought, each answer given, was another wound, another insult that festered.

He rose from the bow with his voice edged in accusation.

"Great Pharaoh," he intoned, heavy with scorn, "the Nile, our eternal lifeblood, runs red as if with blood. Fish rot upon its banks. The fields lie withered. Famine crouches at our gates. The people whisper of divine wrath. They ask if the Ramesseum itself has angered the gods."

His gaze slid, almost involuntarily, to Khamariti. The man stood silent, composed, as though he knew truths hidden from men, truths beyond his years or any library of scrolls. Ankhwennefer's lips tightened. He could not name it, but he feared it: knowledge that was not of this time, and a Pharaoh who listened more to an architect than to the gods' own high priest.

He lifted his gaze, dark eyes gleaming. "And all trace their fears to one man, the architect who builds as though he were himself a god. Khamariti. Always at your side. Always your chosen. I have warned that his designs mock the will of the heavens. Perhaps now the truth is clear. His works do not serve the gods but defy them. And it is we who pay the price."

The words hung in the air like a curse.

Ramesses turned to Khamariti. "Speak, architect. Has your foundation harmed my river?"

Khamariti stood tall though the weight of the court pressed upon him. "No, Great Pharaoh. We cut only rock. The cause lies upstream. It is no curse of the gods but the way of nature."

Murmurs rippled through the hall. Priests frowned; courtiers exchanged wary glances. Ankhwennefer's eyes narrowed, not in open challenge, but in suspicion.

Ramesses lifted a hand for silence. "Then find the truth, Khamariti. If the Nile itself rebels, Egypt falters. And I will not see my reign undone by river or rumour."

The high priest fell to his knees, arms raised high. "Great Pharaoh, I beg you, act now, cast Khamariti aside before further pestilence strikes Egypt. The omens speak, and they are dark."

chapter 7:
The Rising Hope

The studio lights burned clean and bright. Channing Reeves, lead anchor, sat behind the glass desk and read to camera with the unruffled poise that made him a household name.

"Raymond Hope's rapid ascent to the White House is being hailed by some as a masterclass in political strategy and religious diplomacy. At forty-seven, with his distinctive blond hair and lean frame, Hope has become a symbol of unity for religious communities far beyond his evangelical Protestant base. In a move without modern precedent, he has won support from Jews, Muslims, Hindus, Buddhists, and even some secular groups, presenting himself as a unifying figure in American life."

Reeves paused, his gaze steady.

"His rise did not happen by chance. It was built from a decade in the Senate and broadcast sermons that ran every week across the country, drawing millions. His vision is a return to what he calls a more obedient and devout America, where moral clarity and public safety take precedence, and fear of divine judgement shapes personal choices."

He leaned a fraction closer.

"Yet that vision has sparked fierce argument. Hope presses for a larger prison system and harsher sentencing, more Bible in schools. He argues these measures will pull the wayward back to righteousness. His uncompromising stance on the death penalty has split the nation. For some it is justice restored. For others it is a lurch backwards."

The camera widened to reveal two guests at his left.

"Let us bring in our commentators. Jason Tully, veteran strategist, and Amanda Blackwell of The Washington Post. Jason, what explains this rise?"

Jason Tully's tie was immaculate, his smile practised.

"Hope's rise reads like a political thriller. A decade in the Senate taught him how to stitch coalitions, how to speak to the country's deepest instincts. Call it faith fuelled politics if you like, but it is also clinical strategy. He has the Catholic vote locked, won not just through doctrine but presence, rhetoric, ritual. And the Jewish vote is secured by his unwavering, unapologetic support for Israel. In a fractured political landscape, Hope has made cultural conviction a turnout machine, particularly in the South and the Bible Belt. Where others offered policy, he offered recognition. People who felt unseen by Washington saw themselves in him."

Blackwell did not wait. Her voice was calm and precise.

"Hope's rise is not just political, it is ideological. Beneath the outreach sits a single moral frame. He courts many faiths, yes, but the project advances one doctrine. That may electrify a base, yet by definition it marginalises others. Add in a vast prison expansion, brutal sentencing laws, and an unwavering death penalty, and you are not looking at unity. You are looking at control."

Tully tapped a finger once on the desk.

"Control or stability? The country has been rudderless. He offers certainty, and certainty crosses party lines. Look at the breadth of his endorsements. Rabbis. Imams. Business leaders. Even some atheists who like clear rules. Roosevelt was a disruptor too."

Blackwell did not blink.

"Roosevelt expanded rights. Hope is narrowing them. He is pushing the boundary between church and state in a way we have not seen for decades. He speaks with a pastor's cadence from a future president's podium. That should worry everyone."

The camera drifted back to Reeves, who brought the segment to a smooth close.

"Raymond Hope inspires and alarms in equal measure. If he wins his first hundred days will tell us which instinct proves right."

🐦

Election night unfolded like a carefully laid liturgy. Hope waited in his Washington headquarters, surrounded by aides, donors, and a constellation of religious leaders who had stood alongside him throughout the campaign. He had insisted the screens remain off until the count was nearly done, a small superstition folded into his otherwise iron routine. When the door opened and Sean Riley, his chief of staff, stepped through, the room fell quiet.

"Three hundred and two," Riley said. "Thirty-two above the line."

The cheer built and broke over them. Hope climbed onto a chair, lifted a hand, and brought the room to heel.

"Thank you," he said, and the room obeyed. "In our first hundred days we will restore morning prayer in state schools, not as a sectarian act but as a national discipline. We will strengthen legal protections for the unborn. We will mark national days of prayer and reflection. And we will fund what we ask of our citizens."

Applause rolled again, but he was not finished.

"The first practical step," Hope said, letting the words settle, "is to end Sunday working."

Silence tightened.

"Scripture is clear," he said. "Six days for labour. One day kept holy."

He let the citation hang in the air, then allowed a flicker of humour to cut the tension.

"Exodus says it clearly," Hope remarked, his tone light, almost mocking. "Keep the Sabbath holy or face death, Exodus 31:14, Exodus 35:2. Numbers even tells of a man stoned for gathering sticks." He gave a short laugh and waved a hand as though brushing away the words. "No, I don't plan to put anyone to death for breaking the Sabbath. Not at present."

Laughter rippled across the room, nervous, strained, a sound that pretended to be relief. Hope smiled with them, but behind the smile was steel. Those who listened closely understood, the warning had been spoken, the joke only a veil.

Power turned quickly in the new administration. Directors of the FBI and CIA were removed within days, replaced not with neutral veterans but with loyalists steeped in Hope's language of moral order. Boards were reshaped. Advisory councils were rebuilt in his image. The word in town was simple. You could stay if you believed.

Beneath the victory rhetoric, something heavier moved. Hope had long told himself he was chosen. That belief settled now, bone deep.

On Hope's instructions, Riley drafted letters to every college, university, and corporation receiving federal funds, reminding them that continued support was now tied to a clear expectation: all research and teaching must reflect a Christian worldview. Even institutions abroad, such as Canada's Maplewood University, found the directive in their inbox, the message blunt and without room for debate.

The email from Whitmore University landed in Lex's inbox while he was cataloguing sonar logs. He skimmed the sender line, then opened it and read twice before calling Thea over.

Dear Professor Mullin,

I write to outline immediate changes to federal funding that affect universities receiving United States grants.

Revised priorities: agencies now prioritise projects aligned with approved religious or ideological viewpoints, including religious history, moral philosophy, and sciences framed within designated ethical lenses.

Conduct codes: institutions are expected to adopt strict moral and ethical codes mirroring those priorities. These extend to student behaviour, staff responsibilities, and extracurricular life.

Accreditation: accreditation criteria will incorporate adherence to these standards.

While your project is not directly affected at present, continued eligibility requires that activity remains congruent with the guidance. Please review attachments and outline any adjustments you deem necessary.

With thanks,
Dr John Hartfield
President, Whitmore University
Attachments followed: policy extracts, accreditation notes, a checklist that read more like an oath.

Lex exhaled. "Thank God we are based here and not in America," he said, passing the tablet to Thea. "This president intends to rule the academy with a doctrinal stick."

Thea scanned the memo, jaw tightening.

"H-he will not stop at the border. Maplewood and plenty of Canadian universities rely on United States grants. If he can pull levers there, he will try to force his agenda abroad. We will feel this."

Lex nodded once. "Noted. For now, keep our work immaculate and our data unimpeachable. We have an ocean to map."

The legislative calendar turned to Hope's drum. The Senate Majority Leader, a public disciple of the new president, raced a Sunday ban through committee. Economists warned of spiralling losses. Governors protested. The bill passed anyway.

Hope stepped to the lectern that night. He read from prepared notes and then pushed them aside.

"Order is mercy," he said. "The Sabbath restores order."

Reporters shouted questions. He did not take them.

Days later, in a televised address from the East Room, he chose a different text and spoke it in a voice drained of heat.

"Slay those who bow before false gods," he intoned, citing ancient law as if it were administrative code. "There is one God, the God of Abraham. We are, and must be, a God-fearing nation. I will ask the Senate to recognise the Christian and Jewish faiths as the nation's foundation. All other religions may be practised, but only in service to that truth."

The sentence fell like iron. In the streets, the first marches swelled. Synagogues and mosques filled with people who came to pray and to plan. Civil rights lawyers threaded themselves into coalitions that had not spoken in years. Cable news split in two, one half blessing, the other bracing.

In the Senate, the bill did not move at once. Constitutional lawyers spoke to cameras about the First Amendment. Staff churned drafts and redrafts in rooms with no windows. The country stood on the fault line, feeling the tremor before the break.

Reeves returned to air with a panel of constitutional scholars and former officials. His tone was cool.

"Tonight, the White House says it is exploring a national religious framework, while critics call it a frontal assault on the First Amendment. We are joined by—"

The segment ran hot. A former Solicitor General said the proposal could not stand. A governor warned that federal funding would be used to punish dissenting states. A minister, invited to defend the plan, spoke about unity and moral repair. Reeves kept the temperature down and the questions sharp.

After the break, Reeves closed with a monologue pitched to the centre of the country.

"Elections bring new priorities. They do not unwrite the Constitution. The weeks ahead will test not only institutions but citizens. The tone of this presidency is certainty. The duty of the rest of us is clarity."

Lex watched a clip of the address from the mess table and felt the shape of a new world forming at the edge of his work. Thea sat opposite, arms folded, eyes still on the funding memo in her mind.

"It is not just p-politics," she said. "It reaches our lab benches. Our fieldwork. What you can ask a student in a seminar. What you can publish."

"Then we remain who we say we are," Lex replied. "Open methods. Open data. No corners cut. If a storm is coming, we do the work while the sky is still ours."

He pushed the tablet aside and pulled a map toward them. It showed the shape of the seafloor, light blue for shallow areas, deep black for the trenches. In the corner, a silent screen carried new updates.

They leaned over the map, studying the ocean. The ship hummed beneath them. Somewhere above, the world kept moving.

chapter 8:
Frogs and the Fall
of Pi-Ramesses

The court held its breath.

High Priest Ankhwennefer's accusation hung in the warm air of the audience hall, thick as incense. Khamariti stood motionless, eyes lowered in respect, jaw set in quiet defiance. Courtiers edged closer to the columns, as if stone could shield them from whatever would break next.

Ramesses II raised a single hand. Silence fell as if dropped from a height.

"Enough," he roared, voice even, the steel inside unmistakable. "This architect is a loyal servant. I have heard him. I believe the Ramesseum has not angered the gods."

Shamed, Ankhwennefer pressed himself flat against the floor, words of apology spilling from his lips though his heart seethed. In the dust at Pharaoh's feet, he vowed deeper hatred still, loathing Khamariti all the more for the public humiliation he was forced to endure.

Ramesses studied Khamariti, weighing reason against dread. "You may be right," he said at last, the words edged with doubt. "How long will this affliction on the Nile endure?"

"Great Pharaoh," Khamariti replied, careful and clear, "until we know what set it in motion upstream, I cannot say. But I urge you to order extra bread and olive oil for the people while the fish are spoiled."

"That will strain our stores," Ramesses said, glancing at his scribes.

"It will save lives," Khamariti said. "And we may yet face worse. The river is a living thing. When it changes course, all Egypt feels the pull."

Ankhwennefer lifted his hands, eyes raised. "Son of Ra, let us pray. The people need the sight of you in petition to the gods, not the cold talk of engineers."

Ramesses cut him off with a small movement. "No more. There is other business. I will hear no further on the red river today." He turned back to Khamariti, almost gratefully. "Tell me about the progress on the Ramesseum."

That night, standing at the bank with Nebit, Khamariti watched the red waters of the Nile glimmer under moonlight.

"Teacher," Nebit whispered, "the people say the gods bleed. The high priest will not rest, Pharaoh or no Pharaoh, until the blame falls on you. Do you not fear it too?"

Khamariti set a steady hand on the boy's shoulder.

"Fear clouds the mind. The priest spends his life on the gods, but I doubt he believes what he preaches. He seeks power. Power can make a man rich, or it can destroy him. I do not fear him, Nebit. I fear what he might do in the name of the gods. This river is more than myth. It is a vein of the earth, and something has choked its heart."

Yet even as he spoke, a weight pressed inside him. He could not shake the thought that his apprentice might be closer to the truth than he dared to admit. For the first time since he had built for Pharaohs, Khamariti felt as if the Nile itself were watching him.

A week later, under a sun that turned the desert to hammered gold, Thebes gathered to lay the first foundation of the Ramesseum.

The procession moved like a painted frieze come to life. Musicians piped and beat small drums. Priests brought oil and bread and flowers. Workmen stood in ordered ranks with their tools. The pharaoh approached in a blaze of linen and gold, the ceremonial spade carried before him. The ground had been measured and marked, blessed with perfumes, cleared of stones. Dust rose and settled, rose, and settled, as if the earth itself breathed with the great assembly.

Ankhwennefer stepped forward, white robes catching the light. He lifted his staff and began the invocation, voice deep, rhythm ancient.

"O Amun Ra, Lord of the Thrones of the Two Lands, Father of the Gods. We set our hands to sacred earth. Let it carry the weight of a house worthy of your name and of your servant, Ramesses. Make our foundations as enduring as the firmament, our stones as steadfast as the river that gives us life. Dwell in these courts for all ages."

The crowd bowed as the prayer flowed over them. A stillness followed that felt complete enough to last forever. Then Ramesses took the spade.

He paused at the market place and looked across the gathered faces. The air itself seemed to lean towards him. He drove the blade down. Dust rose in a pale curl. It was done.

A faint vibration brushed the soles of feet. Someone murmured. Someone else told them to be still. The tremor came again, stronger. At the river's edge a ruffle ran across the flat water, as if something beneath had turned over in sleep.

The first frog leapt from the reeds and landed on a polished stone with a wet slap.

Then the river let go of its secret.

Frogs boiled out of the red Nile water in their thousands, launched from mud and reed and shadow. They climbed the bank in a rolling, rippling mass, poured across the packed ground, spilled over the oil jars, onto the altars, up the very legs of the officiants. The neat geometry of the ritual fell apart under the living flood. Croaks rose in waves, layered and relentless, swallowing the chant, drowning the pipes, turning ceremony to noise.

For a heartbeat Ramesses did not move. The sun flashed on his headdress. A frog struck his chest and slid down the linen, leaving a damp track.

Khamariti stepped close enough to be heard. "Great Pharaoh, we should return to the palace."

Ramesses nodded once. The gesture travelled outward and became motion. Guards closed around him and shepherded him through a path made with the sweep of shields and boots. People began to push back, first in confusion, then in fear, then in panic. Priests wavered, devotion at war with disgust, then snatched up what holy things they could and fled.

Ankhwennefer stood rigid with his staff, the tendons in his hands white. Frogs clambered over the carved wood as if enthroned there. He tasted bile. This was desecration in its raw state, a shriek against order.

He turned and found Khamariti's eyes. No words passed. His glare said what his mouth dared not: this is your doing.

Sanctuary did not hold.

By the time the pharaoh reached his palace, frogs were already there. They filled the fountains, blackened the steps, freckled the thresholds as if the gold itself had broken out in a rash. They slid beneath chests and chairs, vanished, and reappeared in folds of embroidered fabric, dropped from rails with soft thuds onto marble. Courtiers yelped and shook their sleeves; eunuchs grabbed baskets; servants moved with aprons tied high and faces set grimly, scooping and tipping, scooping, and tipping, as if the problem could be solved with labour.

The sound was the worst of it, a ceaseless rasping chorus that coiled through corridors and lodged in the skull. These halls had once carried the weight of royal decrees. Now they carried something far more unsettling, a relentless, mocking symphony of wet croaks. The noise overlapped and echoed until it became a single, suffocating presence.

The frogs were everywhere. In courts and kitchens. In noble beds and funerary urns. The floors shifted underfoot. The walls seemed to breathe. Servants slipped and cursed. Water jars stank. Bread bins moved.

At first, they tried to drive them out. Then to burn them. The tide only swelled. Shallow pools frothed with movement. Farmlands vanished beneath a writhing carpet. Crops were crushed. Canals blocked. Wells polluted. Children wept, trapped beneath the weight of the creatures that now shared their beds.

By night, the croaking intensified. Sleep withered. Fear spread like mould. The priests called it divine judgement. The elders whispered of famine. The young spoke of madness in the dark.

And still the sound endured, like laughter caught in the throat of a god.

Beyond the palace walls, Thebes fared no better. The marketplace drowned beneath a living flood of frogs. Bread stalls vanished under heaving green bodies, loaves scattered and ruined. In the temples, the floors gleamed with slime, each step squelching as frogs leapt across sacred stone. A foul stench rose from crushed carcasses, curling through the streets in thick, suffocating waves.

From their doorways, people stood helpless, watching the swarm breach their homes, frogs tumbling over thresholds that had never been crossed before.

Ankhwennefer came at last to the pharaoh and bowed so low his brow touched stone. "The gods have been roused," he said softly. "If the Ramesseum offends them, abandon it. Spare Egypt the next sign."

Khamariti held his ground. "Ramesses, beloved of the gods, you will not be remembered for river scum and frogs. Your monuments will outlast this. We are caught in the teeth of the river. We must endure and plan."

Before the pharaoh could answer, a councillor hurried in and threw himself to his knees.

"Son of Ra," he said, voice catching, "I bear news from the Delta. Your capital, Pi Ramesses, is in peril."

Ramesses' patience thinned to a wire. "Do not test me with riddles."

"Great Pharaoh," the man stammered, "weeks ago the Nile rose without warning. The surge came like a wall. The west wall of the city, the one raised under Nekhem Sut, gave way. The river took it. The flood broke through into the streets. The harbour is gone. Much of the city is drowned."

The chamber pulled in around that still point. Ramesses' gaze swung to Khamariti.

"Nekhem Sut built that wall to stand until the end of days," he said, each word clipped. "How does stone betray its master?"

"Great Pharaoh," Khamariti replied, "allow me to bring the records."

Ramesses flicked his fingers. Go.

Khamariti returned with a roll of cracked papyrus and bent to place it on the floor. Servants hurried to sweep a slick mess of frogs to the side. The document uncoiled with a dry sigh.

"As you know I was not stationed at Pi Ramesses through the years of its raising," Khamariti said, voice steady but measured. "I was Second Architect, beneath Nekhem Sut, who held full command of the works. At that time, I oversaw alignments at Karnak and later at Abu Simbel. Still, I submitted drawings for the city's plan, its temples, its barracks, even the harbour district."

He let his hand rest against the carved column of script. "I asked leave to survey the ground before the foundations were poured, especially the western boundary. That land is unsettled, caught between drifting desert and the pull of the river. But Nekhem Sut refused me. He kept the site under his seal alone."

What Khamariti never voiced was what he had already uncovered. Even with the walls barred to him, he had stolen time at the edge of the site. There he saw iron chisels twitch in his men's hands, felt compasses falter as though gripped by an unseen current. Bowls of water shivered on their own, their surfaces broken by something deep below. He realised the earth itself carried force, magnetic veins hidden in the stone. If guided with precision, angles, alignments, chambers set just so, it could be gathered and directed like a silent river.

And Nekhem Sut had sensed Khamariti had another agenda. That was why he denied him entry, not from pride alone but from fear. Fear that the younger man's vision stretched beyond mortar and walls, into mysteries no architect should command.

Khamariti lowered his hand. "I was denied the foundations," he said quietly, "but not the earth beneath them."

He looked up. "He said my remit was design, not oversight. He refused to let me near the foundations. He made it clear I was not to be involved in the engineering of the defences."

The pharaoh's eyes narrowed, ancient calculation stirring. "You imply negligence?"

"I imply nothing," Khamariti replied, bowing slightly. "Only that I asked to see the truth beneath the stone and was refused."

Ramesses held out his hand. Khamariti placed a second scroll upon the first. The seal on it bit into the pharaoh's palm. His own sign. He broke it, unrolled the sheet, and read. Recognition slid over his face like shadow across water. Time had blurred the reason, but the wax had kept its memory. He had seen this once. He had set it aside.

Ankhwennefer made the shape of sorrow with his mouth and kept his eyes down. "This tragedy is not yours, my lord," he murmured. "It began with Nekhem Sut and Khamariti's failure to survey the structure."

Ramesses looked as if he might strike him for the comfort. He did not. He turned to the envoy.

"How bad," he said. "Say it plainly."

"Very bad," the man whispered.

"What does that mean?"

Khamariti answered instead, voice steady. "If the west wall fell, the flood would have pulled the port defences with it. The riverbanks would be torn. The channel would seek another line. In carving it, the river will have cut a new branch and left the old bed to silt and stink. Enough time has passed. The city will now sit away from the flow. The Nile has abandoned it."

"How far?" Ramesses asked, quiet as ash.

"Nearly two iteru, Great One. A full day's march for your soldiers, perhaps more if the ground is soft."

The number entered the room and found its mark. Ramesses whispered it back, as if repetition might make it smaller. "Two iteru."

He saw it then: the long straight avenues lined with statues of his own face, the palace with its painted courts, the frescoes of victories, the storehouses and the armouries and the barracks, the harbour mouth bristling with ships, the cranes and ropes and shouting men, the long curves of grain barges sliding into their moorings. All of it built on a promise that the river had now revoked.

"Send riders," he said, voice striking like a hammer. "A full detachment. Use whoever remains in the barracks if they survived. Secure what can be saved. The throne. The statues. The treasury. The royal archives. Move it all upriver."

The general bowed without a word and vanished into the dust.

Ramesses turned to the high priest. "Where is Nekhem Sut?"

"Near Thebes," Ankhwennefer said, voice careful. "He lives quiet."

"Not for long," Ramesses said. "I declare a Proclamation of Guilt. Strip his tomb. Give it to a worthier man. Impale him. Leave his body to the desert and its carrion."

Khamariti opened his mouth and closed it. Mercy would break against that order like water on rock. He bowed instead. There was nothing useful left to say.

The frogs rasped on. A servant dropped a basket and cursed. Somewhere outside, a hawk called over the river.

Khamariti gathered the scrolls and held them close. Others would mourn palaces and ports. He mourned something no one else would notice. Beneath Pi Ramesses, beneath all that stone and paint and noise, ran lines of the earth that most men never felt. Currents that ordered things. Energies old as the first dawn. Moving the city had torn it from the bed it should have rested on. The moment had gone. The chance to harness what lay below was lost, perhaps for an age.

Ramesses' face emptied of heat and filled with weight.

"Nekhem Sut," he said into the room, as if the man were present, "you raised a great city and built a flaw into its heart. You told me it would last. Now the waters laugh at your boast. Your silence convicts you. Your absence shouts it."

He turned away and stared towards the west where the sun fell on the desert. "Here we stand," he said. "Witness to decay. Proof of trust misplaced. A legacy undone."

Work did not stop at the Ramesseum. It could not. The pharaohs order was law, and the law was build. Yet everything changed. The crowd that had sung at the foundation laying now spoke in whispers. The craftsmen went about their tasks with jaws set hard. Priests moved through the lines of stones and sprinkled water and muttered prayers with an urgency that had not been there before. A city had fallen. The river had turned away. Frogs still hid in the shadows and started when light reached them. The sound had faded to the edges but did not leave.

Khamariti revised the foundation plans by lamplight, cutting deeper, binding stronger, knowing well that stone alone could not still the fear. Nebit came late with lists of men and grain. They said little. They did not need words to measure the distance between what they intended and what the world had become.

Ankhwennefer watched from the shade, his face smooth as pottery from the kiln. He had not forgiven Khamariti. He had simply changed the shape of his vengeance. The people needed a reason their hearts could hold. If the Ramesseum rose and brought calm in its shadow, the architect would be lauded. If the river sent the next sign, the people would be ready to name the one who had angered heaven.

Ramesses sent orders north for the salvage and south for more stone. Messengers ran the river roads, sandals kicking dust. Scribes wore down reed pens on new lists. The palace smelled of rush mats drying and crushed bodies swept into heaps and burned.

At dusk, Khamariti stood alone where the first stones would soon settle. The air had cooled. A faint breeze moved from the river. He closed his eyes and felt for the lines beneath his feet, the quiet pull that had guided him to this exact place. It was still there, steady as a drumbeat under the noise of the day. Something could yet be made that would answer the age, not just the man. But time was a narrow door.

Behind him, footsteps stopped. Nebit's voice came quiet.

"Teacher," he said, breathless. "News from the north. The riders reached what remains of the harbour, just silt and mud now. The river has changed course, exactly as you warned. They will recover what they can."

Khamariti did not blink. "Have there been burn victims?" he asked. "Severe injuries, but no visible fire?"

Nebit hesitated. "The barracks. Five hundred soldiers. Burned to death. But there were no flames. No smoke. Just charred bodies."

Khamariti closed his eyes. He had feared this.

The energy vault had been buried beneath the barracks. He knew because he had designed it.

He nodded. "Have the men rest in shifts. Instruct Amara to double the ropes at the river wall. Bring whatever statues and carvings you can salvage. I will repurpose them for the Ramesseum. We cannot afford a single failure now."

Nebit swallowed. "And the high priest?"

"Pray with him," Khamariti said, weary and wry. "It costs us nothing."

He looked at the mark he had made in the dust where the first column would stand. He drew a single line across it with his sandal. The line meant nothing to anyone else. It told him everything he needed to remember.

𓅓

In the weeks that followed, reports from Pi Ramesses arrived like blows. Streets reeking with stagnant water. Painted walls peeling like scabbed skin. Reliefs of the pharaoh triumphant smeared with river mud. Grain stores spoiled. Workshops drowned. The docks a memory. Those who lived moved upland with what they could carry. Those who died were left where the flood had set them down. The river did not mourn. It took a new shape and went on.

Ramesses did not go north. He would not see his crown city in that state. He poured his will instead into the Ramesseum. The faster it rose, the more certain the message. The kingdom was not undone. A great house would stand where the river still flowed strong. The gods would see and remember.

Ankhwennefer set rites at dawn and dusk, and when frogs fell silent in a court, he claimed the silence as a sign that prayer had prevailed. When frogs rasped again at midnight, he said the gods were testing perseverance. He spoke with a gentler voice now, yet every word pressed his case. People needed meanings. He provided them.

Khamariti kept to his drawings and his stones and the quiet sense of the earth beneath. He slept little. He ate when Nebit put food in his hands. He kept a tally of the things that could be controlled and the many more that could not. He did not speak of the currents that lay under Pi Ramesses, now broken in their grid. He stored the loss in the place where a man keeps pains that will be useful later and will not be allowed to rule him in the present.

One evening during this plague, as the sun dropped to the colour of copper, Ramesses came without escort to the marked ground. He stood beside Khamariti and looked towards the river where boys were hauling lines and singing to keep time.

"The river moves where it wishes," the pharaoh said, almost to himself.

"It does," Khamariti answered.

"And yet," Ramesses said, "we persuade it sometimes. With walls and channels. With prayer and sacrifice."

"Sometimes."

Ramesses turned to him. The mask was off for a moment. The man beneath the god was tired and furious and afraid of leaving less than he intended.

"Build my house," he said. "Build it so that even if the river forgets me, the stone will not."

Khamariti bowed. "I will."

He watched the pharaoh walk away into the lengthening shade. Then he knelt and pressed his palms to the dust. Under his hands the ground answered with its quiet pulse. He breathed with it until his own breathing matched the beat. When he rose, the world had not changed. It felt more possible to face.

The frogs rasped on in the drains. The Nile rolled past, indifferent, and necessary. The lines beneath the earth waited to be met with stone. The city to the north sank slowly into mud and memory. The Ramesseum to the south began to rise.

chapter 9:
Breadcrumbs of History

No one spoke. Only the slap of small waves on steel and the faint rattle of rigging in the breeze. A ripple of whisper moved along the deck, the kind that clings to bad luck. Someone crossed themselves. Another touched the rail and kissed their fingers, a small rite against whatever had followed them from the deep.

Rodrigues gave a single nod, spare and final. "We do it right," he said. "Respectful. No errors."

They did it right. Lex and Thea made four descents, each slower than the last. They moved through the yacht like a chapel, torch beams steady, hands careful. They eased the bodies from the overturned world and brought them up one by one. The deck crew stepped forward without being told, faces set, voices low. Even Max, who usually filled silence with words, said nothing.

When it was done Rodrigues called the coastguard in Casablanca, Confirmed their position and what they had found. There would be a day's wait. Until then the dead had to be kept from the heat.

"In the cold store," the captain said. "Wrapped, separate, covered. It is the only safe space."

The chef exploded. A compact man with a heavy brow and a cross at his throat, he seemed to swell with anger. "The dead should not share space with food," he muttered, then louder. "They should not. It is wrong."

"It is a ship," Rodrigues said, his tone gentler than most expected. "We use what we have, yes? I will seal the door. No one brings food in or out until the transfer. You have my word, my friend."

The chef pressed his lips together. He made a small sign in the air, then turned away. The argument was not won, only put down for later.

"The hull is torn open," Lex said quietly. "Looks like the storm ripped straight through them."

Rodrigues crouched low, eyes fixed on the torn hull. "More likely a reef... or a piece of seabed torn loose in the storm," he said quietly. "Wrong place, wrong time. They are not the first to die on this coast, and they will not be the last, meu amigo."

Lex leaned closer, his hand lifting a dark fragment from the debris. "I think Campbell was diving, possibly searching for Atlantis. Look at this shard. The markings could be inscriptions. It's not from this yacht, I'm certain of it."

Rodrigues studied it, his brow furrowed. "You may be right, Professor," he said after a moment. "I will call a few contacts, see where his boat has been. I am not a man who believes in ghosts or spirits, but I have learned to respect the sea. And the sea, she has her legends. One says Atlantis, like the tomb of Tutankhamun, carries a curse of its own, yes?"

The hours stretched. The Marine Explorer carried a strange stillness, as if she too felt the added weight. Lex drifted to the rail and stared at a line where sky met water and told him nothing. Behind him the crew worked at the pace of respect, not bustle. Thea stood with Esme on the aft deck, both quiet. Max busied himself with lists and straps and labels, as if order could blunt a blade that had already fallen.

The coastguard cutter came at last, its blue light harsh against the clean morning. Voices stayed low. There were touches on shoulders, nods, a hush that lay over both vessels while the transfer took place. Paperwork was done on a battered clipboard. Rodrigues signed and signed again. Then the cutter turned away, a white wake briefly stitching the two ships together before it unravelled.

No one cheered when they got back under way. There was nothing to celebrate.

As they drew near the coordinates, the mood shifted. Sadness did not leave; it stepped aside and let purpose pass. The sea felt watchful, as if it recognised people who had come not to take, but to listen.

"You know, Lex," Max said with a grin, "you've got that look again, like you're about to find Atlantis under the sofa cushions. Let's run the scan first, eh?"

"The currents will carry most of it south and west," Rodrigues said. "We should have a clean field off Tenerife and Gran Canaria. La Palma too, once we get there."

"Or it will s-settle exactly where we need to look," Thea said, tapping a pencil against her lip.

Lex lifted his head. "We work with what we find. The aim is unchanged. We are hunting the mark of an event that altered this basin. Not a legend. A mechanism."

Esme, pale but steady, leaned in. "Working theories?"

"The obvious is plate movement," Lex said. "African and Eurasian plates grinding, opening the gate at Gibraltar. Five million years and some, the Atlantic poured in. But I do not think that breach happened without help."

"S-seismic trigger," Thea said.

"Seismic, volcanic, both," Lex replied. "This arc is volcanic by birth. The islands are young, steep, given to sudden change. Mass wasting," he added.

Max nodded. "If the western face of Cumbre Vieja goes, it'll drop millions of tonnes of rock straight into the ocean. A wave'd run across the basin like a whip crack. The geometry backs it, nasty business if it ever happens," he said, falling back into his soft Liverpool accent.

"And the past?" Esme asked. "Did it happen before?"

"That is what we test," Lex said. "Not a myth of a city. The signature of a slide, or a chain of slides, and the marks such a wave leaves in sand and rock far from the source."

They launched the submersible at first light. The sea lay flat as if exhausted by its own weather. The vessel slipped beneath without drama, a shiver of bubbles, a taut line, a patch of ruffled water. Inside, Thea's voice was calm in their headphones, the practised sing song of depth, orientation, light.

The beams picked out the floor in cones of pale gold. Shapes came into view that were not grand, a shard with a lip formed to pour oil, a fragment of handle with a groove worn smooth by fingers that had never imagined this future. A bronze ring, corroded to a green that looked almost soft. A handful of fasteners. Small things. Honest things.

Thea's tone lightened each time a trace of script showed on a broken surface. Her stutter, faint when calm, began to return in little bursts of excitement, the words tripping over one another as if her thoughts were running faster than her breath. She never speculated beyond what was there, but the satisfaction in the simple fact of finding ran clear in every halting, joyful word.

They did not find anything that would make a minister crow into a camera. But even a quiet haul required time and care. Back on deck, they rinsed and labelled and set each piece in its place. The chain of custody felt ceremonial. It always did, and it always should.

The Marine Explorer put in to Lanzarote long enough to fuel and take on food and fresh water. Men with ropes and shoulders made the ship fast. Baskets of vegetables came aboard. So did crates of water, coils of line, cartons of bolts and tape and gloves that would be used up and forgotten the instant they did their job. No one bought souvenirs. No one felt like it.

They left again the same afternoon, ran down the coast, and squared away for a week of mapping. The sea gave them nothing large. They swept grids with patient stubbornness, watched returns, adjusted plans. On the sixth day they turned east for Fuerteventura and found something that would matter to someone else. Half a hull, Venetian by the joinery and the ironwork, lying on her side as if sleeping. Thea documented the position. Rodrigues made a call. The Spanish authorities thanked them in careful words and asked for coordinates and images. The team sent what they had and moved on. A chapter added to a different book.

At Tenerife, Lex called four days of shore leave. He made it sound like strategy. It was also kindness. The crew scattered with reluctance, as if they might break a spell by stepping on land. Then the spell broke anyway. Sun warmed them. Music got into their bones. Street markets moved like a tide of colour. Spice stung the air. Fish smoked on open grills.

Thea stopped repeatedly at stalls selling rocks the way some people stop at stalls selling scarves, lifting each piece as if listening to it. Max ate with the glee of a man too long on tinned food and discipline, then laid waste to a bottle of sharp white wine and laughed more than he had in weeks. Esme spoke to anyone who would talk. The stories had soft edges and bright centres, tales passed from grandmother to mother to daughter, from old fisherman to boy with his first net.

As dusk pooled in the streets, Max vanished with a grin and a promise to be back for cast off. He was, just, eyes raw, hair damp, face lined with good humour and regret. The others pretended not to notice.

Seven weeks from Cadiz they stood off La Palma. The island rose from the sea like a dark shoulder, the spine of Cumbre Vieja lifting into cloud. Lex called the team to the bridge. Excitement sharpened his voice and made them stand straighter.

"This is the place," he said. "We work here for six weeks."

"What makes it different?" Max asked. His curiosity always arrived first.

"The western flank," Lex said. "Steep. Cut by old scars. The record shows partial failures. They do not read like small events. The geometry says a very large mass could move."

"No proof it has," Max replied, a flick of challenge in his tone.

"Absence of evidence is not evidence of absence," Lex said. "We have not looked in the right places with the right tools. That changes now. If there was a wave that washed the Atlantic clean from one shore to the other, this could be where it started."

"What d-depths are we looking at?" Thea asked, already leaning over the chart, her stutter edging back as excitement crept into her voice.

"From a few hundred metres to more than a thousand," Lex said. "The slope drops quickly. From true floor to crest, the summit rises almost two kilometres. It is a tower."

"I ha, have taken the sub deeper," Thea said. "We can work it."

"What about me?" Esme asked, bright as a blade.

"You go ashore with Max and meet Santos, your guide," Lex said. "Handle the formalities, then spend the day with him. Stay close, no wandering too high. I want you both back on board tonight for debrief. Max, keep your eyes on the crest. Fresh photographs of cracks, vents, anything that hints at movement. Radio, phone, portable unit. Stay clipped to the guide's rope. No heroics."

Esme shrugged. "I hear and obey. Lucky me, I get to spend some time with Max." Max grinned.

"I want to set small arrays on the base of Cumbre Vieja," Max added. "Short-term seismic and pressure sensors. If the island is humming, I want to hear the song."

"Do it," Lex said. "That is enough for today. Rest. We move at first light."

Dawn lifted from the horizon, the deck silver with dew, the sea flat as glass. Then the world changed its mind.

A shudder rose from below, as if a giant fist had struck the keel. The ship jolted and settled. A second tremor followed, sharper, sending cups sliding across a table and a spanner ringing against a bulkhead. The third robbed the crew of breath, the hull groaning, rigging clattering. Someone cursed and then muttered an apology to the air.

"Hold on," Rodrigues said. Not loud, but every ear caught it.

They bent their knees and spread their weight, sailors born to the motion. The tremors faded as quickly as they had struck, leaving a silence that felt more like a warning than a reprieve.

Esme gave a faint, knowing smile. "Guess this island isn't exactly rolling out the welcome mat," she said, her tone light but edged with dry humour.

"Noted," Thea replied, one hand steadying a monitor. "Add to list: island with opinions."

Lex's palm rested on the chart, as though he might calm the earth beneath the water. "Status?"

"Engines sound," Rodrigues said, listening with his whole body. "No leaks reported. No damage on first check."

"Then we continue," Lex answered. "No bravado. No fear. We do our work."

Nose to stern they searched. Nothing beyond an unlatched cupboard and a broken plate. Laughter rose too quickly, sharp with nerves. Then rhythm returned. Work steadied the hands, and the ship found her course again.

Rodrigues's voice came from the command room, tight with excitement he was trying to tame. "I have something. Repeat, I have something."

They crowded the screens. The sonar showed lines where lines had no business being. Not a single clean slope, but terraces. Not random scatter, but organised collapse. A cliff cut into steps by an event and then softened by years.

"That is a s-scar," Thea said, no doubt in her voice. "A big one."

"It runs for kilometres," Rodrigues said. "Look here, and here. Multiple benches. Not one fall. A series."

"Then we get Max to map it," Lex said. "Full sweep. Overlaps. No gaps. If we are right, the pattern will be in the data."

They worked all morning, moved the ship with patient precision, laid down lines as neat as a weaver setting warp. The image sharpened. What had looked like noise resolved into form. A long tongue of slide debris, an apron that thickened and then thinned into the deep. Pits where blocks had punched down. A curve where the edge had pivoted.

Thea traced a fingertip on the glass. "This is where the m-mass let go. This is the run out. The energy must have been enormous."

Rodrigues tapped a cluster. "Block sizes. We can estimate volume.

Esme and Max were already in the launch with a local guide." Santos, a lean man with a kind voice and hands that tied knots without thought. They slipped out of the small harbour and turned along the coast. Above them, the black wall of Cumbre Vieja rose, its ridges scored by past eruptions, its flanks veiled in pine and dust.

They beached near a faint track where roots gripped broken lava. Santos led them up a slope that climbed into trees, each step crunching on pumice and ash. The air carried the smell of sulphur, sharp under the resin of pine.

Max paused often, notebook in hand, eyes tracing the slope. He had studied mountains, mapped ridges, catalogued eruptions, but here the scale pressed in. Fractures like scars ran across the earth. New flows overlapped older colours layered like pages in a book. A single ridge could hide dozens of stories, and each might end in collapse.

""This mountain," Max murmured with a crooked grin, "ain't one problem, it's hundreds, queuein' up polite as you like, all waitin' their turn to ruin my day," he said, his accent curling through the words.

Santos glanced back, his expression unreadable. "La montaña nunca duerme," he said softly. The mountain never sleeps.

By late afternoon Max radioed in. His voice carried a clipped edge through the static.

"Lex, I've spotted fresh fractures near the base," Max said. "Small ones, runnin' parallel with the slope. Santos reckons the vents've been restless these past few months."

"Send images," Lex ordered.

He did. The frames came sharp and immediate, white steam in thin threads, new ash powdered across his gloves, loose gravel where crust should have been firm.

"Do not go higher," Lex said at once. "Mark the sites and get back. Before the light fails."

"Already turning back," Esme replied. Max gathered his equipment. "No heroics. We'll be on deck before sundown."

They descended fast, dust lifting under their boots, the mountain watching with the silence of something that remembered. At the waterline, the launch rocked in the surf. Santos steadied it with one hand while Esme climbed in, her mind still caught in the maze of fissures and faults. Complexity. Fragility. A giant waiting to break.

The run back was smooth. The *Marine Explorer* rose out of the dusk ahead, steel against the fading horizon. As they neared the ladder, Esme looked once more at the ridgeline. The air was still, the mountain dark, as if nothing stirred at all.

Then it came. A low groan, deep and resonant, rolled out from beneath the island. The sea itself shivered. The launch trembled under her feet.

Esme's hand shot to the gunwale. "Santos, she's bitching"

He only nodded, eyes fixed on the looming bulk of Cumbre Vieja.

On deck, Lex gripped the rail, watching the ripples spread. His jaw set hard. "The mountain just welcomed us," he said.

And for the first time, the team felt the promise of tomorrow was not discovery, but survival.

chapter 10:
The Unholy Swarm

Across fields and courtyards, in alleys and temple courts, people watched the oddities of nature and felt the ground shift beneath the old assurances. Ritual fires burned; prayers climbed into the hot air and went unanswered. The priests spoke, the oracles pronounced, but the river kept its crimson stain, and the frogs had already made a mockery of sacred places. Despair, like dust, settled on every surface.

Khamariti did not have the luxury of despair. With Nebit at his side and a workforce spread from quarry to kiln to rising wall, he set the foundations for the Ramesseum and fought day by day to keep men at their tasks and fear at bay. Work carried its own discipline. He used it.

The next plague did not roar. It ticked and buzzed. Lice hatched in folds of unwashed cloth. Flies swarmed in clouds that found eyes, mouths, and wounds with precise cruelty. The sound rose and fell, a constant tremor in the air. Men tied cloths over their faces and cursed, then laughed at the futility of it, and cursed again. The pests were everywhere, turning the camp into slow torment.

Khamariti reached back into the memory that had served him in tombs and deserts, and into the small store of herbs he always carried. He remembered what warded and what soothed. He stripped bitterness from wormwood and bound it with oil. He crushed mint and sweet rush for their sharp scent. He boiled acacia pods until the water thickened, strained it, and stirred in honey and juniper until the paste held a warning smell. He rubbed it into the crooks of his elbows, behind his knees, under his hairline. The flies fell away from him like dropped veils.

"Do as I do," he told the men. He showed them where to smear the paste, how to stroke it along seams of tunics and around ankles. He showed the women how to hang garlic at doorways and to burn myrrh in shaded corners, so the smoke drifted across thresholds. He did not speak of gods. He spoke of what worked.

The routine spread. At dawn, men lined up at the gate to dip rags into the thin mix kept warm on coals. Children laughed at the bitterness on their wrists, then lifted their arms for more. The air took on a new smell, sharp and green, and the flies loosened their grip. Not enough, but enough to stand and breathe and work.

Even so, sickness rose. The river had killed its fish and left rot along the banks. Men scratched until their skin broke; bites became sores. Cattle grew dull-eyed and fell. Panic followed.

Khamariti climbed a stack of stone and called his people to him. Behind him, the quarry gaped like a wound in the slope. The half-raised pylon stood as a forest of timber, all angles and ropes and promise. Men and women gathered until the yard was full.

"Listen," he said, and the murmur stilled. "The river is not angry. It is unclear. Fish have died, and the water breeds what feeds on death. We saw this in ditches; now it is everywhere. Frogs came because the river drove them out. Lice and flies came because the frogs died. That is the chain. If we cut the links, the chain breaks.

"Wash with boiled water. Boil it twice if you can. Do not drink from the bank. Eat bread cooled from the fire; eat nothing raw. Tend the cattle that still stand. Burn what is dead. Bury what you cannot burn. I will ask the Pharaoh for grain. I will trade for oil. We will keep the work alive. If fear leads us, it will lead to ruin."

The words steadied hands. For now, that was enough.

He did as promised. He went to market, traded trinkets, offcuts, and a craftsman's eye for what others wanted. He returned with carts of barley, onions, and amphorae of oil. He gave them out himself until men stopped bowing and took the food with shy gratitude that sat just this side of pride.

Then he went to court.

The great hall shimmered with heat. Torches flared even in daylight. Courtiers turned their faces towards favour like flowers to the sun. Ramesses II sat tired and terrible, the weight of too many burdens braced on his shoulders. Khamariti knelt only when he must, speaking with the courage of a man who had nothing to sell but truth.

"Great One, the men who lift your name work without strength. The river, which is life, has run foul. We ask for grain. Not forever. For now."

The Pharaoh's gaze was a blade. It softened when it met Khamariti's steadiness. "You ask for what the whole land asks."

"I ask for those who build what the whole land will honour," Khamariti replied. "If the builders fail, the Ramesseum fails. Your glory requires their bread."

At last, Ramesses raised a hand. "Send grain to the works. Give them loaves. Oil their lamps. All who labour in my name shall eat."

It was done.

In the shadows, High Priest Ankhwennefer watched with cold eyes. He had once been forced to abase himself in the dust before Khamariti. The memory burned. The architect had shamed him not with insult but with reason. It was the worst kind of defeat. He would not endure it twice.

He began to preach against him. Not by name, but in shadows shaped to fit. "The Nile is sick," he told the faithful. "The gods speak, and some call it chance. Beware men who lift stone higher than prayer. Beware those who put their names where a god's name should be." Fear needs little food to grow. He fed it, morsel by morsel.

Boils came. Merit worked tirelessly, calm, and skilled. She boiled water, made honey poultices, bound wounds with linen. She taught wives and daughters to tend gently and change dressings often. Pain eased. Men who had never bowed before priests wept in gratitude at her hands.

Weeks stacked like bricks. The city learned to move within its grief. Children still ran when the heat dropped. Lovers still met in doorways. Bread still rose. Lamps still burned. The work went on.

Then the sky dimmed.

At first it was like the onset of a sandstorm. Then it became a mass. Then sound.

The locusts struck.

They fell on palms, stripped vines, flattened barley. Men lit smoke pots, beat the swarms with branches, but the insects poured through. Green died. The sound of them was like heavy rain, a hiss that filled ears and would not stop. By afternoon the trees stood bare, crops razed, fields crawling with the living churn of wings and bodies.

Khamariti shouted orders. Cover the bins. Seal them with clay. Guard them in shifts. Drive livestock into sheds. Net them. Keep smoke at every door.

The locusts thudded against stone, crawled under tunics, tangled in hair. Men laughed grimly because there was nothing else to do. They worked until arms burned, then stepped back for others.

By evening, the swarm thinned. It lifted as if mocking them, turned dark and strange in the sinking sun, then moved on. Silence followed for a heartbeat.

Then the storm came.

Rain crashed from a sky that should never have held so much. It fell in sheets, pounding rooftops, hammering mud streets until the earth gave way. Alleys became rivers, pulling carts, timber, and tools into the surge. Priests raised their hands to the heavens in vain. Scribes who had measured the Nile for decades stood with blank faces, their numbers useless. Labourers broke and fled, leaving half-built walls and shattered scaffolds behind them. The exodus thinned the cities.

Khamariti stood in water up to his ankles, watching men abandon the camp. He could not blame them. He could not spare them either.

The flood carried more than mud. In the quarters of the poor, where pits had long been dug for sewage, the water rose and spilled. Egyptians had stored their sewage in clay-lined hollows or stone channels meant to hold it until the river reclaimed it. But now the storm did not wait for order. The pits burst. Filth poured into the lanes, washing against walls, carried out into the Nile itself. The stench rose sharp and sour, choking the air, a mix of rot, dung, and stagnant water.

Men pulled scarves over their mouths. Children gagged. Even the animals shrieked and bolted, their hooves thrashing through the mire. The city seemed to melt into its own refuse.

Khamariti thought of Pi Ramesses, drowned when the river had shifted its course and swallowed the royal city whole. He thought of the Axis Core buried beneath it, the work of his own hands now hidden by flood. Perhaps this storm fed on the same buried power. Perhaps the Nile itself had turned against them.

Merit came, soaked, children at her side. "We've moved the sick to the north store. I need men to carry amphorae of grain and oil. I need fire kept alive. I need the door held shut when the waters come."

"Take them," Khamariti said. "Nebit, with her. Choose men who bend and lift again when they drop."

They moved. That is how people lived through what they should not: they carried, they bound, they held the door.

Night fell early. The rain drummed without pause. A wall gave way. A cart clattered into the current. Somewhere a priest shouted until silence claimed him. Khamariti counted the beats between lightning and thunder, telling himself there was logic in it. He did not fully believe. He needed to say it anyway.

In the small hours, the rain eased. Fear gave way to resolve. At first light he sent men to patch what could be patched, to rescue the weak, to check lines and pits. At the site edge, the foundation markers still held. Defiance. He allowed himself to see it that way.

By midday, the rain returned lighter. People scooped their alleys back. Children floated boats.

A runner brought word: the empire was faltering. Ports failing, labourers leaving, traders gone.

"And we?" Nebit asked.

"We build," Khamariti said simply. "We build in the rain, in the sun. Until we are told to stop. Then we build the reasons not to stop."

By evening the storm's first fury had passed. The fields lay stripped, a patchwork of stalks and bare earth. The city stood scarred but not broken, walls dark with rain, roofs patched with hurried repairs. Smoke from damp fires drifted low, carrying the sour bite of ash and rot.

Ankhwennefer whispered more poison in the corners, his words slipping like oil into ears hungry for blame. He named Khamariti, turning loss into suspicion.

Merit moved through the wounded, binding arms, cleaning cuts, her voice calm. To the young girls she gave not only herbs but steadiness, teaching them chants to keep their hands from shaking as they stitched torn flesh. Her presence was a balm against the ruin.

Nebit returned to the records. His reed pen scratched against papyrus, counting what had been lost, what seed might still be saved, which canals still carried water. His work was not for hope but for survival.

Ramesses sat in the dim glow of torches, his shoulders rigid, his face carved in shadow. He did not flinch from the tally set before him. Land gone. Harvest gone. Men gone. Still, he chose, line by line, grain for soldiers, grain for families, rations cut to keep the army fed. Painful choices, made without pause, for the burden of the throne allowed no delay.

And Khamariti climbed the scaffold to look out across the wet land. The stars returned. He rested his palm on stone and felt the faint tremor that ran through every block when the earth shifted. The rope of fate was drawn tight. He could not yet see where it led. Only that he must follow it.

"Tomorrow," he whispered. "We begin again."

chapter 11:
Race Against Time

By dawn the horizon burned in bands of orange and rose, the sea breathing slow against the hull. On the forward deck, where the boards held the night's cool, Professor Lex Mullin gathered his team.

They faced him in the slant of early light, their eyes sharp and alive with the promise of a beginning that felt heavier than most. Lex let silence stretch before he spoke.

"This is where it begins," he said. His voice carried across the water, low but certain. "No gambles, no second chances. Take your time. Do it safe. Do it right. What we uncover here will change everything."

He turned, his gaze steady on the faces of his colleagues. "Today we divide again. Esme, Max, you will go ashore with Santos. As Esme discovered yesterday, he knows these slopes better than anyone alive. Work the ridge line of Cumbre Vieja. Track the faults. Mark fresh scarps. Note any creep or signs of old collapse. Draw it. Photograph it. Log it. Nothing is too small."

Lex looked next to Thea. "You and I take the submersible. We make our descent today. We chart the chamber beneath the basalt shelf. We bring back some evidence."

Thea nodded once, her face pale but resolute.

Lex raised a hand. "One rule above all. Communication is constant. No dead zones, no silence. The mountain will not forgive mistakes."

The group broke, each to their task. The air was cool still, but it carried the promise of heat to come.

Esme adjusted the strap of her satchel as she followed Santos upward. The path cut into ash and pumice, sharp under their boots, the slope steeper than it looked from the sea. Above, the spine of Cumbre Vieja stretched, scarred with lines where past eruptions had torn it open.

Steam rose faintly from fissures, the breath of a volcano that never truly slept.

Max carried the drone pack, the weight pressing through his shoulders. His shirt was already damp with sweat. Since leaving the boat he had spoken little, his thoughts locked on numbers, probabilities, the cold geometry of the mountain. Every few minutes he stopped, lifted his eyes to the slope, scanned the horizon, then bent to jot quick figures into his notebook before moving on again.

Santos kept the pace steady, neither too fast nor too slow, letting the younger ones match his rhythm. His boots found paths without hesitation, steps measured, certain. "The mountain changes every season," he said without looking back. "New tracks open, old ones vanish. The ground splits, the streams carve fresh lines. You have to read it like a book that never stops rewriting itself."

Esme stopped, crouched, and brushed her fingers over a crack that sliced through the trail. It was narrow but deep, the edges sharp. "Fresh," she murmured.

Max was already kneeling' beside her, lowering' a probe into the fissure. The small screen blinked. "Temperature's up. Bit of movement underneath," he muttered. "Nothin' catastrophic, just means she's alive."

Santos glanced back. "Alive is enough."

They pressed on. At the ridge crest the view opened wide. To the west the Atlantic stretched endless and blue, deceptively calm. To the east the island's villages clung to terraces, white walls bright against the black soil. From here the team could see both worlds, the fragile line where lives were lived and the vast ocean waiting beyond.

Max unfolded the drone with practised hands and sent it aloft. The small craft lifted smoothly, its rotors humming as it steadied against the wind. On his tablet the feed came alive, a rolling sweep of rock, ridge, and sea. He guided the drone higher, mapping the land below with patient arcs.

From above the fractures were clearer. Grey scars cut through darker stone, lines of weakness etched by centuries. Max leaned closer to the screen, his finger tracing one fault that angled hard toward the sea.

"There," he said, voice low. "Movement's trendin' west. If that flank gives…" He didn't finish, he didn't need to.

He stopped. The rest did not need words. The image of the mountain falling into the Atlantic spoke for itself.

Esme caught the look in his eyes. "If Atlantis lay on this side of Gibraltar, how long before a tsunami struck?"

He hesitated, numbers flickering behind his eyes. "Hours," he said at last. "Maybe less, that's worst case."

Santos spat into the dust, an old islander's sign against ill fortune. His voice was flat. "Mountains don't give warnings. When they go, they go."

Beneath the waterline, Lex and Thea prepared the submersible.

The craft sat like an insect of glass and steel, its dome gleaming under the morning sun. Lex checked each system with ritual care, oxygen mix, ballast calibration, thruster response. Thea mirrored him, her hands precise though her lips pressed tight.

The hatch sealed with a low hiss. The vessel tilted, then slid from the cradle into the Atlantic. Darkness closed around them as the sea swallowed light.

For long minutes there was only the hum of motors and the groan of water against the hull. Lex kept his hands firm on the controls. The descent dial ticked downward: twenty metres, fifty, a hundred.

Then the seafloor rose in the beams of their lamps. Basalt cliffs loomed, jagged, pitted, cut as though by blades of fire. Between them yawned a black maw, the entrance to a chamber carved not by nature but by something else.

Thea drew in a breath. "It's real."

Lex guided the sub into the opening. The walls closed in, then widened to reveal a cavern vast enough to swallow a cathedral. Stalagmites rose like teeth. Pools shimmered with trapped air, silver mirrors under their lamps. And in the centre, half-buried in silt, lay shapes too regular to be natural, arches, pillars, fragments of masonry.

Thea's hand rose to her mouth. "G-god…"

Lex steadied the craft, his pulse quickening. He reached for the camera rig and set it recording. Wonderful nature," he whispered. "Extraordinary"

They edged closer. Symbols glimmered faintly on stone blocks, eroded yet still visible. Triangles, circles, spirals, patterns that spoke of design beyond chance. The markings echoed one another with purpose, a language cut into the stone by hands long gone.

Lex drew a sharp breath. The lost part of the mountain above began to speak again. He hoped it would point him to Atlantis.

On the ridge, Esme stood with the wind tugging her hair. She watched Max work, watched Santos mark fissures on a worn map. The drone's feed showed fractures spidering further than expected, some reaching perilously close to villages.

She looked west to the sea. The water glimmered, endless, patient. It was waiting.

By late afternoon, the light on Cumbre Vieja turned copper. Esme, Max, and Santos had climbed to a flat shoulder on the ridge, where a cluster of pines clung to black rock. The ground was uneven and fractured, but it gave them space enough to pitch camp.

Santos moved with quiet economy, driving stakes into volcanic soil and tying lines as if he had lived his life on these slopes. Esme unrolled maps and sketches, weighting them with stones to stop the breeze from scattering them. Max checked the drone batteries one last time, his screen flashing with the jagged outlines of fault lines traced earlier in the day.

When the tent was secured and the fire coaxed to life in a circle of rocks, they gathered close, the heat welcome as the evening chill crept down the mountain. Esme spread her sketches across her lap, her pencil marks tracing fractures like veins across the page.

Max leaned in, setting the drone screen beside her. "Look," he said, tapping the glowing display. "Parallel lines layered flows, each one angled toward the sea. The mountain's practically writin' us a warning."

Santos stirred the fire with a stick, his face shadowed in the glow. "Warnings only matter if someone listens," he said quietly.

Esme's gaze drifted up toward the ridge, where thin curls of steam rose like secrets from the rock. "This place isn't just one problem," she said quietly, her Canadian lilt smooth and certain. "It's a thousand.

Every crack's got a story , and every one of them ends the same way, downhill."

They fell silent. The fire popped. The breeze shifted, carrying the smell of pine and sulphur. For a long time, they listened to the mountain's stillness, each of them aware it was the kind of stillness that carried weight.

As darkness closed over the ridge, Santos threw another branch on the fire. Sparks spiralled upward, vanishing into the night. Then, without warning, the ground gave a low, guttural tremor. Stones shifted under their feet. The firelight wavered.

The three of them sat rigid, listening to the earth grumble beneath their camp, knowing the night had only just begun.

chapter 12:
Fire and Fury

Ramesses II stood on the steps of his palace and watched the horizon burn. At first the flames had been no more than stray sparks, clinging to the broken remnants of homes already battered by plague and flood. Now, under a hot wind, the sparks had become a living force. Fire ran the fields, crossed canals as if water did not exist, and climbed the walls of villages with a will of its own.

Houses of mud brick that had endured generations collapsed in moments. Temple yards filled with smoke. What crops had survived shrank to black husks, the promise of the Nile turned to ash. Ramesses heard the cries even at this distance, carried on the wind, not only fear but the tired despair of a people who had been sick, hungry, and now faced a final trial.

As the fire raged, the sky shifted. Clouds rolled in from the west, black and green, swollen with a fury no man could master. Forks of light tore through the heavens, splitting the darkness, each strike followed by a crack that shook stone walls. The wind died in an instant, the air heavy, pressing against skin like a weight. For a heartbeat, the world seemed to pause. Then it fell.

Hailstones the size of fists rained down, striking with the sound of stone on stone. They shattered reeds along the riverbank, snapped branches from trees, and split roofs already weakened by fire. Walls cracked. Tiles flew like shards of pottery. Animals bolted in panic, goats bleating, horses screaming as ice pounded their flanks, driving them to the ground. Blood mixed with water in the streets.

The fire fought back. Embers rose on the storm winds, carried high and flung across the city. They fell into crowds, glowing red in the smoke. A spark brushed a man's robe and in an instant, he was aflame, his screams drowned in the roar of the storm. A woman tried to drag her child to safety, but a burning reed mat struck her back and fire consumed her hair, her tunic, her flesh. People fell thrashing, their bodies turned into torches where they stood.

A bolt of lightning split a tower in two. Stones cascaded, burying men and beasts alike. The ground shook with the impact.

The canals, the lifelines of the city, were black with floodwater mixed with sewage burst from clay pits. The filth poured through alleys, spreading the stench of rot. Hail beat it into foam that clung to skin, choking those who slipped beneath it.

Khamariti staggered to higher ground, his sandals sinking in mud that only hours before had been a street. Around him men tore at their burning clothes, their cries rising above the thunder. A boy tried to run but a hailstone struck his head, and he crumpled at once, lifeless. His mother fell across him, keening until another ember set her veil aflame.

The sky itself seemed at war. Fire and ice raged together, a storm that mocked the order of creation. The city was no longer a city but a theatre of ruin, streets flooded with sewage and blood, roofs blazing like torches, smoke pressed down by the weight of the storm.

The wind shifted again, howling now, as if the heavens themselves were tearing apart. The storm gave no answer, only ruin.

Ramesses staggered as the first stones struck the palace walls, the noise like a thousand drums. Armies he understood. Rebellion could be met and broken. This had no face and would not bow. Heat rose from the fire while shards of ice bit into the land. It was as if the heavens themselves had turned against him.

The storm moved on, but its ruin lingered. When the fire died and the hail ceased, darkness rose. Not night that follows a setting sun, but a deeper thing that seeped into streets and courts and fields and stayed. Days passed and the light did not return. People moved like shadows. Temples stood black and cold. Obelisks loomed like grave markers for a kingdom that had lost its lamp. Whispers travelled easily in the dark: the gods had turned their faces away.

The pharaoh felt the change in the way people looked at him. Awe had thinned. Hope waited on the edge of collapse. He called for his high priest.

Ankhwennefer stood below the throne steps and bowed low. His voice trembled, then steadied.

"Son of Ra, the gods have shown me hard truths. The plagues, the fire, the hail, the darkness, they do not only strike our fields. They show the cracks in our rule. The loyalty of the people frays. In the streets they speak of your fall as their salvation. The empire teeters. Only you can pull it back."

Ramesses did not answer. The priest read the silence and pressed on, dropping to his knees.

"Act now, Great Pharaoh. Do not let this be the end of your line."

Later, in the courts at Karnak, Ankhwennefer gathered priests and noble counsellors beneath high columns. He had chosen his words and tempered them like metal. His tone was smooth, cool, exact.

"The gods call for sacrifice," he said. "Not blood, but humility. Khamariti must be cast out, sent beyond their favour. Only then will Egypt find renewal. The Ramesseum is not devotion. It is Khamariti's pride. The gods despise pride."

He paced the paving between the pillars.

"It is the architect who bends the Nile, who cuts harbours where none should be, who dares to set the order of creation to his own design. The plagues are the shadow of his arrogance. The gods have spoken. The guilt lies there."

He watched faces. Death would be too bold to demand. Exile would do. Exile would wound and would please those who needed a target. Exile would keep his own robes clean.

"The gods call upon you, Mighty Pharaoh," he finished softly. "With a new architect, the Ramesseum would be cleansed and endure. The fate of our civilization rests in your hands."

The chamber held its breath.

That evening Khamariti came at the summons. He knelt and pressed his forehead to the floor. When he rose to speak, his voice was steady.

"Great Pharaoh, let me seek the source of these plagues. If I fail, my life is yours. Grant me this chance, for the years I have served, for the houses I have raised in your name. Grant me this one request."

The quiet stretched. Even the torch flames seemed to wait. Ramesses looked at the man who had turned his will into stone.

"The priests speak as one," he said at last. "They say this is not chance, but punishment. They say your hands defiled holy ground, that you have bent the river, and that the gods demand you be driven into the desert."

He looked past Khamariti at nothing. "I hear their fury. I feel their eyes on me, hungry for a judgement that is easy to speak and hard to carry. Yet my heart resists. You are not only my architect. You are the mind that makes eternity visible. Without you, my dream is dust."

He straightened.

"I will not cast you out in disgrace. I will send you on a mission. You will leave Egypt, immediately, but not as a broken man. Go beyond our borders, into lands the priests do not name. Find what has stirred the heavens against us. Bring me the cause and we will silence their charges. Do this, and we will raise the Ramesseum not as pride, but as defiance. A house even the gods will have to notice."

Khamariti bowed. "As the Son of Ra wishes."

The words were formal. Inside him a storm turned. It was no exile, and yet it was. It was a burden heavier than any pylon.

At dusk he stood at the gate of Thebes beside his chariot. Merit and Menna sat in a small cart close behind, faces solemn. He looked once more at the skyline: the tall needles, the carved giants that seemed to breathe. This had been his life's work. Now it stood at a distance, dim in a world that had forgotten daylight.

Merit searched his eyes for comfort he could not give. Menna held her mother's hand in both of hers. Khamariti took the reins and felt the weight of his order. A city, a people, a ruler, had set their hope upon what he would find.

In the long shade of temple columns, Ankhwennefer watched. Two cloaked figures stood with him. He spoke without moving his gaze from the gate.

"Jalil. Haroun. Follow him. Do not let him return."

The men slipped into the alleys and were gone.

Khamariti climbed to the chariot board. For a heartbeat he hesitated. The last light of the day touched the tips of the obelisks and then went. The wind off the desert carried a faint, sour taste that spoke of old fire and new trouble. There was no time to read it.

He flicked the reins. The horses took the bit and pulled. The city fell away behind them. The voices of Thebes thinned and vanished. The desert took their sound and kept it.

Above, the first stars pricked the sky, hard and clear. Khamariti kept his eyes on the line of road and the space where it met the dark. In that space lay the cause of Egypt's pain, or the end of his name.

Behind him, unseen, the spies kept pace, silent and patient.

The night closed over the plain. The wheels turned. And with the chariot that carried him out of Thebes, the fate of Egypt moved into the unknown.

chapter 13:
The Ridge

By dawn the ridge was washed in bands of orange and rose, the Atlantic below them breathing slow against black cliffs. Mist clung to the pines and carried the sour trace of sulphur.

Esme pulled her pack tighter across her shoulders, the straps biting where the climb had already worn at her. Max adjusted the drone case, his eyes scanning the slope as though the ground itself might move. Santos walked a pace ahead, steady, and sure, the rhythm of a man who had lived half his life on this mountain.

They paused at a break in the trees where the ground fell away to bare rock. The island stretched beneath them, folded ridges running like scars to the sea. From here the scale of Cumbre Vieja revealed itself, not as a single peak but as a chain of wounds.

"We mark everythin'," he said, half to himself. "Cracks, vents, scarps, nothin's too small."

"Look at this," he murmured. "Parallel fractures runnin' all the way down the slope. They're not old, they're pullin' the same way."

Santos crouched, running his fingers over a narrow fissure where steam drifted. "This ground is young," he said quietly. "Still writing itself."

They worked in silence for a time. Esme sketched, Max flew the drone across the ridge, Santos marked sites with strips of cloth tied to branches. Each fracture, each vent, seemed to tell a story, and every story pointed downhill, towards the sea.

By mid-morning, the sun had burned through the mist. Heat pressed against them, the rock beneath their boots radiating warmth like a kiln. Esme wiped grit from her hands and looked out to the horizon, where the ocean spread wide and unbroken.

For a moment she saw not water but the image of waves, racing in trains across thousands of miles, crashing into coasts that had no defence.

She closed her notebook. "If Lex is right, one slip here does not just take us. It takes everything in its path."

Santos tightened the strap on his pack. His eyes went to the ridge above, where thin smoke curled into the sky. "The mountain is listening," he said. "We had best watch our step."

The ground under their boots gave a faint vibration, almost imagined, then steadied again.

Esme froze, heart catching. Max shot her a glance but said nothing.

They all knew what it meant. The mountain was not silent.

And the day had only just begun.

"We need to get to the other side of the ridge," said Santos.

The island breathed beneath them. A faint roll passed through the slope, stones clicking underfoot. Santos paused, head tilted. "Do not let the stillness fool you," he murmured. "Cumbre Vieja sleeps with one eye open."

The ground gave a faint shudder under their boots. Dust drifted from a ledge above.

Max glanced at Santos, then at Esme, a half-grin tugging at his mouth. "Well, she's wakin' up polite today," he said. "Just stretchin' her legs, that's all. If she starts talkin' though, that's your cue to run."

Esme walked at his shoulder, her pack a tidy promise of work: chisels, hammers, parchment and charcoal, compass, telescope. Max followed with the seismic kit balanced across his back, each step deliberate. Santos carried the quiet necessities that buy time if the mountain holds you longer than planned: tents, stove, water, food for three days.

Esme stopped where wind had scoured ash from basalt, crouched, and sketched a seam of crystals catching the sun, proof of old heat and slow cooling. Max set a probe to measure ash depth; the readings scrolled like the earth's pulse.

A cinder cone rose on their left, rim raw against sky. A whisper of steam slipped from a shaded crack. The sulphur tang lingered at the back of the throat. Max logged coordinates and eased a probe into warm ash. Esme traced distant slopes with her telescope, marking hollows and buttresses where the mountain had given way before.

"If we keep moving, we'll crest the far ridge by afternoon," Santos said. "We camp below. The wind is kind there when it chooses."

They climbed in silence, falling into the rhythm mountains demand. Heat rose from dark rock, breath shortened. Esme stayed alert, eyes quick to note powder where new fractures had met air, scratches where stone had dragged stone.

At a shelf overlooking the flanks, Santos pointed to ash crisscrossed by cracks, thin, parallel, too neat to be chance. Esme laid her hand across the largest. Heat. A faint breath of air. The mountain exhaled.

They pushed along the ridge, narrow in places, the drop on either side sharp enough to catch the breath. The footing demanded full attention. A gull wheeled below, the strange inversion making Esme's stomach shift. She steadied herself with work: sketch, note, measure, confirm.

A scarp appeared, a blunt headwall where a mass of ash and cinders had once torn free. Esme recorded the drop and traced the fan of frozen flow below. Max shot photographs and set poles for scale. Santos kept his eyes on the horizon, as if listening to the mountain more than watching it.

A tremor rumbled, not heavy but clear. Stones shifted downslope, then stopped.

"Mid-slope movement," Max said.

"Noted," Esme replied. "Stay clear of the edges."

By noon, they reached a broad saddle where wind played in gusts. Santos chose the campsite, sheltered by a low rise and scrub. He set water to boil with the ease of long habit. Hot tea became civilisation in a cup.

"Looks like you're mapping the island's bones," Max said with a grin.

"I'm just noting its patterns for you," Esme replied without looking up.

"Patterns show how it dances," Max said.

They pressed on in the hard afternoon light. Old flows knotted the slope, ash clinging in drifts. Balance and patience carried them across a narrow spine. Below, another collapse sprawled across the flank, old, but telling. Esme traced its arc and compared it to Thea's sonar prints: drop, run, deposit. She marked bearings.

"Some lines run through the whole body," she said. "If a fault steps here, the flank could go as one."

By late light, they reached the crest. Wind lifted Esme's hair, cooling sweat. She raised her telescope and studied the slope: ledges scored by old falls, shelves where debris had run, a scoop shaped to catch the next slide. She sketched fast, noting angles and mass. Max set the last flag.

"What d'you reckon?" he asked.

Esme tilted her head, a hint of a smile playing at her lips. "I think this mountain likes to rehearse," she said, her tone light but sure. "The trouble comes the day it decides to perform."

They looped back by a safer line, avoiding sharp scarps. Twice the ridge trembled beneath them, small shivers. Santos altered their path each time without a word. Esme trusted him.

They reached camp at dusk. The stove flared. Tea poured. Max dug out a biscuit and guarded it like treasure. Santos told a shepherd's tale under the first stars, a story without a moral, then leaned back into the slope. Max fell asleep mid-note. Esme sat with her telescope resting on her knees, watching the Atlantic hold the last of the light.

She thought of Thea and Lex. At first light they would dive in the submersible. The mountain had shuddered more than once today. Esme's worry was not for herself. It was for them.

Far below, the sea kept its counsel.

chapter 14:
A Plague of Silent Cradles

The desert wind scoured their faces as they left Thebes, the chariot leading and the cart following in a plume of dust. Hooves struck the hardpan like drums, beating out a tempo that never slowed. Day burned. Night bit. What had sounded like a mission in the throne room became an ordeal measured in sun and sand and the scratch of thirst in the throat.

Khamariti drove the chariot with one hand and shaded his eyes with the other, reading the dunes as a scribe reads a scroll. The horizon shifted and shimmered, lines of heat folding over one another until nothing looked fixed.

At night he kept the fire small, no higher than his knee. He slept in slices, blade across his lap, ears tuned to every shift of sand.

Merit curled in the cart with Menna, the blanket drawn high under the girl's chin. The child slept hard at dusk, then stirred with questions when the desert grew colder.

"Why are we leaving?" Menna whispered one night, her eyes wide and shining in the firelight.

Merit's hand smoothed her daughter's hair. "Because your father knows the way. He will take us where the gods still smile."

Menna turned to Khamariti, her small voice carrying in the silence. "When do we come home?"

Khamariti knelt, brushing his calloused fingers across her cheek. "The river never loses its way," he said gently. "And we follow where it flows."

"But rivers change," she pressed.

His eyes lingered on hers, and for a heartbeat he did not answer. Then he smiled, faint but steady. "Even when they change, they still reach the sea."

On the third night the stars were sharp as flint chips, the cold cutting through wool and skin alike. Khamariti lowered the fire to embers. His hand froze. A shape moved along the ridge above. Then another. Then three.

"Men," he breathed.

Merit stirred, pulling Menna close. "You saw them?"

He nodded once. "Not beasts. Men."

Sand whispered as figures advanced along the crest. Khamariti stepped away from the cart and into the open, placing himself between his family and the ridge. He raised the blade, so the starlight caught its edge.

The men paused, measuring him.

Behind him, Merit's voice trembled but did not break. "Khamariti...?"

"Stay with her," he said without turning. His stance widened, blade steady. "They will come for me first."

He mounted, nudged his horse forward and rode toward them, spear butt thumping against the chariot rail. Sand slid under hooves. He stopped within the ring of their fire and let its light show his face. The man in front had a face carved by wind and years. Scars. Eyes like chips of basalt.

They faced each other in stillness. The desert gave no need for wasted words.

"I seek peace," Khamariti said at last, his voice steady. "You seek silver to feed your men. I have little coin. I have this."

From his robe he drew a small statue, a god cast in gold, its surface worn smooth by many hands. Firelight caught it and flared, a gleam against the night.

The chief's lip curled. "Trade? We take."

"You could," Khamariti answered. His eyes did not waver. "It would be a mistake."

He lifted a parchment next, its seal thick and red, the mark of Ramesses bright even in the dark. "I carry the pharaoh's will. If I do not reach Pelusium, he will know. He does not send merchants when men vanish. He sends soldiers."

The chief's gaze flicked to the seal. The men behind him shifted. Khamariti did not move.

"You could kill me and sift my bones into the sand," he went on, quieter. "You could take the gold. But the army will follow the trail you cannot hide. They will find you. They will not bargain."

Silence held. Fire hissed. The chief's fingers eased off the blade at his hip.

"And what do you offer for our favour, pharaoh's man?" he asked.

"The statue now," Khamariti said. "And at Pelusium I open the grain stores. Enough for a moon. You will guide us there. You will keep us alive on this road."

The chief spat in the dust. "There is no grain," he said. "There is plague."

"There is grain," Khamariti answered. "I hold the seal."

Another long look. The desert weighed his words and found no tremor. The chief's jaw set.

"Mark me," he said. "If your promise is wind, we cut your throats and vanish into the earth."

"As it should be," Khamariti said, and reached for the man's hand. Sand ground between their palms.

"One more thing." He turned his head, eyes on the dark beyond their fire. "Two men follow me. Spies. They have coin for the road and sharp knives. They are a day behind. Send riders. Take their silver. Without silver, shadows fade."

A slow smile cut the chief's face. "You bargain like a desert man." He nodded once and lifted two fingers. Three riders rose without a sound and moved into the night.

They rode at first light. The desert is not empty for those who know how to listen. It creaks. It sighs. It remembers. The nomads moved in a line, silent but for the soft crunch of sand and leather. At noon they drank from skins and shared dates that stuck in the teeth. At dusk they made small fires and ate without talk. Menna laughed once when a lizard ran across the tent rope, then slept with her hand locked around her mother's fingers.

By the fifth day the sun burned as if it had drawn nearer. Words grew curt. Tempers frayed. Even the horses bowed their heads, too wise to waste strength on defiance.

On the sixth day the riders returned. They carried a pouch heavy with coin and a torn strip of cloth, frayed from a cloak. They claimed they had spared the spies, driven them astray, sent them stumbling in the wrong direction.

The chief gave no reply. He had lived long enough to know when a tale was false. And Khamariti knew as well: men of violence do not brandish blades for show.

Pelusium rose from the flat like a promise, walls and towers lifting out of dust, masts bristling along the quay. Relief flickered and died in the same breath. The city moved, but its movement felt wrong. Faces turned away too quickly. Doors shut without sound. Priests burned incense at corners where no shrine stood. The air tasted of smoke and something that lived under the tongue. Fear.

Khamariti did not allow himself to slow. He took the nomads straight to the royal granaries, stone walls, copper locks, guards with spears and tired eyes. He held the seal high until it caught the sun. The doors opened. The grain smell rolled out like breath from a warm beast.

The nomads loaded in silence. When the last sack sat high in their carts, the chief stood close. "You kept your word," he said.

"I meant to," Khamariti replied.

The chief's eyes softened when they fell on Merit and Menna. "Keep moving," he said. "The city is sick."

It began at sunset.

One scream. Then two. Then a thread that could not be untangled, voices pulling others out of houses, faces pale in doorways. Clouds layered until the sky looked like a bruise. Priests ran with bowls of smoke that did not hold their smell. A woman swept the threshold of a house no one had crossed since morning. The bristles lifted ash and streaks of blood. The air shifted; all knew something was wrong. The priests had urged them to sacrifice lambs, mark their doors, believing it would spare them. It did not.

It came fast. Quiet. A spark hidden in rags, spreading like breath across the city. By midnight, the streets sounded like both battlefield and festival, shouts of fear, cries of mourning, the wail of flutes carrying funerary songs. Smoke from fires hung low, heavy as grief.

In their chamber Menna burned. Her skin glowed red, her eyes glassy with fever. The rash climbed her throat like dye soaking through linen. She turned restlessly, each movement weaker than the last.

Merit sat close, cloths in her hands, cooling her daughter's brow, changing them as fast as she could. Her voice never stopped. Prayers, fragments of lullabies, promises whispered to still the tremor in her own hands.

"Khamariti," she said, her voice breaking. "What do we do?"

He had no answer. He had stood before kings, argued with priests, built wonders in stone. None of that mattered in this small dark room where a child lay dying. This was not for the first time, nor the second.

"Pray with me," she said, her words thin with fear.

He closed his eyes. He tried to form the old words, but they broke on his tongue. Silence was all he had left.

"You gave up," she whispered, still stroking Menna's damp hair. "You turned away, and now the gods turn their faces from us."

The words struck like a blade. He bore them without reply, his chest tight, his throat raw.

Menna stirred. Khamariti bent close, his lips almost at her ear. "When we go home, we will plant a tree," he whispered. "You will shake it bare before the fruit is ripe. I will chase you across the garden."

Her lips moved faintly, the shadow of a smile.

Her chest rose once. Fell. Rose again. Then it stopped.

The silence rang louder than thunder. The room seemed to tilt, the world unmoored.

Merit's cry broke the stone walls. It was not a sound of this earth but of something torn from it. Khamariti held his daughter's still body, and for the first time in all his years, the builder who had shaped monuments felt himself collapse. They washed the child's body in boiled water, hands trembling, tears mixing with steam. They wrapped her in linen cut from Merit's best gown. Merit kissed each fold as she bound it. Khamariti tied the cords, hands clumsy, his chest hollow. Together they carried her to the burial ground the city had set aside for children. Too many lay there already.

Khamariti lowered her down. Merit knelt and pressed her cheek to the small bundle until a guard touched her shoulder. She did not look up. She did not release. Khamariti lifted her gently, the way one lifts a broken thing, and guided her back.

That night they sat in silence, Merit folding and unfolding a dress that would never be worn. When dawn came, she whispered only one word. "Why?"

"Because the world is the world," Khamariti said.

"You believe in nothing," she said. "What will hold you now?"

"You," he answered, voice raw. "And the work I have yet to do."

Merit turned her head away. "Then work," she said. "Find the thing that did this. Tear it out."

"I will."

Dawn crept grey across the city. No song rose with it. No chant from the temples, no cry of merchants, no call of labourers on their way to the fields. Only the sound of weeping carried through the streets.

Khamariti stepped out with eyes hollow from the night. His robe still smelled of fever and ash. Merit did not follow. She knelt by Menna's grave, rocking, her voice a low murmur that answered only her grief.

The streets were swollen with death. Doors stood open, linen bundles laid at their thresholds. Faces covered, bodies waiting to be carried to the river. Families crouched beside them, some in silence, some wailing until their voices cracked. The air was heavy with smoke from funeral pyres lit too soon, the sharp stink of oil burning with flesh.

Children lay still in their mothers' arms. Men who had carried stone in the heat of the day now lay as light as broken reeds. Dogs prowled the alleys, whining at the smell, snapping at scraps where they dared. The city, once loud with trade and laughter, had become a place of mourning.

Khamariti walked among them, his hands slack at his sides. The builder, the planner, the man who could measure a wall by sight and tell if it would fall, none of it had prepared him for this. He had no tools to lift the weight of loss.

At the riverbank, he stopped. Barges floated low with the dead, rowers moving without word, eyes fixed on the water. Priests stood ready in white robes streaked with soot, casting words of passage over the bodies before pushing them to the current.

He thought of Menna. Her chest rising, falling, then still. He had whispered of trees and games and home, but she had left him with nothing but silence.

Khamariti looked to the horizon, where the first light turned the river into a blade of bronze. He had built for pharaohs, argued with priests, mapped the heart of mountains. Yet here, with the Nile carrying its dead in silence, he felt himself no more than dust in the hand of a storm.

And still he knew, this grief was not his alone. The city itself was broken, a body of stone and flesh, bleeding out before his eyes.

Pelusium breathed like a wounded animal. Priests burned incense. Parents wailed. Doors shut too fast. But life, cruel and stubborn, crept back in. Boys bartered onions. Women washed thresholds. The sun pushed through smoke.

Khamariti walked the streets as if in a dream, his heart cut open, his steps pulled by duty. He wrote to Nebit, asking for maps and names of men who knew the far coasts. He sealed the message with the pharaoh's mark.

Merit stood at the door, cloak tight. "Where are you going?" he asked.

"To sit with her," she said simply.

"You must go," she added, her tone a command. "Find the source. End these plagues. Bring back something that feels like justice."

He bowed his head. "I will."

She walked out without another word.

Khamariti remained alone. He set his hands on the table edge until his knuckles went white. Then he let go, and for the first time since childhood, tears came without shame.

Pelusium carried on. Grief and grain. Smoke and silence. The world turned, and a father wept.

chapter 15:
Beneath the Surface of Time

Off the coast, the Marine Explorer held station over a long, slow swell. Storm repairs were complete, stores were dry, and the crew moved with the ease of people who knew one another's habits and left space for them. At first light Lex and Thea had slipped into masks and fins to read the rock where shore met sea, teasing out the usual crumbs of passing centuries, a sherd of amphora clay, a thick handle from a lost jug, an iron nail with a skirt of rust. Interesting, but not their quarry.

Back aboard, Thea ran still frames, then pushed the latest sonar to the main screen. Greys and blacks washed into meaning beneath her finger.

"Max is r-right," she said. "These scars are old. Step, drop, slide, drop again. A pattern."

Lex nodded. "The island fails to the west. If a flank went, it went that way. If we read the deposit, we can read the scale."

Captain Rodrigues watched the screen, eyes narrowed, judgement withheld. "Then go and read it," he said. "Second mate, prepare the submersible. Fresh comms lines. I want a clean connection."

"Aye, Captain."

Thea checked the submersible the way a musician tunes a favourite instrument, by touch and by ear. No frayed line, no tired seal, no salt crust lurking in a seam. Inside the small sphere she ran ballast, trim, life support, lights, thrusters. The panels woke with the pale glow she liked. Lex strapped in, tested his headset, and let a stillness settle that always steadied the people around him.

"Take us down," he said.

The winch sang. The cradle released. The sea closed over the canopy and turned the bright morning into a silver disc, then into a lighter shade of black. The surface voice in their earpieces was strong and calm.

"Explorer to Delta. Reading you loud and clear. Depth ten metres. All green."

"Delta to Explorer. Copy. Commencing west sweep."

They fell through colour into absence, green to slate, slate to clear dark. Thea brought up the forward lights and carved a tunnel out of nothing, silt lifting and settling like breath. Fish wandered past with the ease of creatures who have seen storms and outlived stories.

The slope steepened. Thea felt the pitch change in her feet before she saw it on the line, a pilot's intuition sharpened by years. She trimmed the thrusters and let the craft slide along the angle as if stroking the flank of a sleeping animal.

"Scarp thirty degrees off the b-bow," she said. "Drop in twenty metres."

Lex leaned over the display. "Old headwall. Look at the run out. Wide debris field."

They worked a grid with the kind of patience that earns discoveries. Thea set near neutral trim. Thrusters whispered. Lex logged blocks the size of houses, torn and tumbled, set now in silt like things that had grown there. Faint channels cut by long gone currents crossed the plain, the seabed's memory written in mud.

A tremor ticked the hull. Thea laid her palm on the panel and felt vibration translate to skin. It eased.

"L-local," she said, pausing to steady her breath before finishing softly, "nothing heavy."

The nav screen flickered. Numbers lagged, then caught.

The sea moved.

It came as a draw, a small tilt within the water. Silt lifted and turned their beams from black into thick grey. Thea lifted the nose and fed a little power. Comms cracked.

"Explorer, confirm stability," she said.

Static, then Rodrigues, distant. "We see a— ah— small— return. Say again, Delta. Your signal is—"

The line hissed and cleared and hissed again. Thea switched to the redundant channel.

"E—ex... explorer," she managed, the word catching hard in her throat. "W-we're... we're getting inter— interference."

"Copy. Stand by."

The ocean did not. The slope above loosened. A sheet of sand peeled and ran. The movement set other movement. The seabed sighed. A low pulse moved through the water like a drumbeat too low to hear.

Something large rolled out of the dark above. For an instant it was only mass. Then the lights bit a smooth, weathered face, a boulder the size of a cottage turning with the slow grace only weight in water can manage. It came indifferent, a falling moon.

"Thea," Lex said. The rest was unnecessary.

She dipped the nose, lifted, rolled a fraction to port. Small moves, timed to the water. The boulder filled the world, too slow to be real and too fast to escape.

""H-hold... on," she forced out, the strain in her voice clear as she fought the stutter under pressure.

It slid past with the breadth of a hand to spare. The sub rang like a bell. Turbulence punched them down. A cable screamed, a clean metallic tear. Thea corrected with both hands and felt the craft accept the change.

Amber strobed. A thin line of blood moved down her brow. She ignored it, hunted level by touch.

"Systems," Lex said, voice deliberate and even.

"Power holding. Life support steady. Thrusters one and two responsive, three sluggish, four dead. Main comms lost. Auxiliary crackles. Antenna likely severed."

Outside, in their light, a line flicked and fell away, a cable drawing a sad arc into the silt.

"Explorer, Delta," Lex called. "Lost primary comms. Confirm on backup."

Static. The ghost of words. Then nothing but their own air.

"We assume we are on our own," he said, mostly for himself. He read the stack fast. Pressure good. Battery draw is good. The hull groaned once and settled into its familiar song.

Thea trimmed for the lost gear. Thruster four stayed mute. She flew on three, coaxing the sphere into a sliding compromise rather than a drop.

Above them, stones clattered down one after another, each sounding like metal on metal. Thea guided the sub through a narrow stretch, keeping between the lighter rain and a darker stream where heavier debris moved.

Lex spoke aloud, steady and clear, to cut through the noise. "Depth. Trim. Balance the glide. Lights on. Climb if we can, slow, so we don't strain the hull."

"W-working," she said.

Minutes lengthened into a narrow corridor with no doors. The silt wall breathed in and out. Thea rode its edge. When current tried to take them, she gave a finger's pressure into cross thrust. When a shadow swelled too fast, she slid above or below by the inch the engines would give.

Lex brought the side lights up and found a boundary. Beyond it the seabed smoothed into a plain where fine mud settled as if insisting nothing ever happens here. The wrong thought, perhaps, but it steadied the mind.

"Ease left," he said. "Ride that line west, then arc back. We climb by degrees into water that is not carrying half a hillside."

The craft obeyed in small fits. Pitch centred. Roll eased. Depth counters crept the right way. They reached clearer water. Thea felt the release as a cold ache slip from her shoulders.

"Status," Lex said.

"Th-three thrusters. Power h-healthy. Hull kissed, not cracked. Life support c-content. Main comms gone, backup... unreliable." She drew a shaking breath. "We surface on our own time... and sh-shout."

"Then we make every metre count."

She wiped the brow cut with her sleeve. The bleeding had already slowed. Calm brings its own trap. She kept the mind busy with necessary tasks. That is how lives are kept.

"Professor," she said. "That boulder was not loose sand."

"Older block," he answered. "Set in an earlier slide and held by silt. A nudge, the silt let go, gravity did the rest."

"So, the slope is a stack of old failures pretending to be a wall."

"A fair description."

They climbed by patience. At last, the headset cleared.

"Explorer to Delta, blind call," Rodrigues tried, then the water remembered to be kind. "Delta, we have you faint. Say again."

"Delta to Explorer. We read you. Main antenna lost. Managed a slide event. No material damage. Climbing on three thrusters."

The breath the ship had been holding let go across the bridge.

"We have you by guess rather than line," Rodrigues said. "Broadcast on emergency ping and we will triangulate. Do not hurry. We will be here."

"Acknowledged."

Lex set the ping to a slow pulse to save power. Crude, but true enough to draw a ship to a speck in a moving sea.

"Side feed," Thea said.

Lex looked. On starboard the plain rose into a low swell. Too true for a dune, too straight for a careless flow. Thea angled light. A geometry appeared: blocks in a line, a gap, then a second line offset. Not the work of hands. The work of a mountain that had torn part of itself free and cast it downslope, where it slid and halted and dressed itself in silt. The fossil of old violence.

"Coordinates," Lex said quietly. "This is part of the story. If we map enough of it, the numbers will tell us what's happening."

They edged forward carefully. Fear made them sharp. Awe made them sharper still. Both held them to the task.

At one hundred metres, darkness turned to a colour that is not colour. At seventy it warmed. At fifty the sea had depth like green glass. By thirty they could have flown by ambient light.

"Five degrees up," Rodrigues called. "We are one cable to your north."

"Copy."

They broke the surface in a skin of spray. The swell tested their balance and let them go. Thea held the nose to current, slipped them out of the wake of something heavy that had fallen, and kept her hands moving in the small dance that stops a small craft becoming a past tense story.

"A-autopilot off," she said. "Manual. Thrusters balancing."

"Propulsion?"

"Strained, n-not broken."

"Tell me what you need."

"Watch the boards. Call a-any spike."

He watched. Depth, pitch, internal pressure, draw. All sliding from the wrong side of yellow towards green. He reached for the med kit and passed butterfly strips. She set them without looking away from the glass. He taped a nick on his scalp. Thirty seconds later the blood lost interest in both of them.

They looked at one another and did not need to speak.

They went back down.

Lex pulled a spare acoustic transducer from the toolkit, spliced it into the damaged feed, and realigned the mini-sub's antenna array. Static cleared. He keyed the transmitter and called the marine explorer above. Manoeuvrable. Continuing mission. On the bridge, Rodrigues swore in Portuguese. It is a captain's right when careful scientists decide to extend a dive after the sea has thrown a hill at them.

The trench opened like a mouth. The sub slid along its rim. Floodlights cut cones through suspended silt. Ridges and scarps rose and fell like the skyline of a ruined city. The water still wore the earlier tremor. Long slow heaves tried to pull trim off centre.

"F-forward," Thea whispered. "Look."

The beam touched a wall of shadow and resolved. Blocks the size of houses stacked and sheared. Slabs tilted like broken stelae. Furrows ploughed into clay by something that had slammed across it with impossible weight. The largest slab split into three plates like a cracked altar, each the length of a stadium, edges raw where they had bitten into seabed. Streamers of cobbles lay behind it, the signature of run out.

"It is as if a mountain was torn from itself and thrown into the deep," Lex said, not for poetry but because the simile framed the numbers he felt building.

Thea eased the light to a low angle. A curve revealed itself, half buried. Another, matching it. A rib. Another. A cage of bone set in the cooling skin of lava.

"Sea mammal," Lex breathed.

"Long gone, thousands of years possibly," Thea said softly. "Caught in the flow, d-drowned, entombed in lava."

The ribs were wide. The spine curved like a drawn bow. You could guess at fin structure where moving stone had been gentle enough to sketch. It did not need a name to do its work. It dated the flow.

"We need sam-samples," Thea said. "Date the crust that sealed it and we p-place the event."

"Carefully," Lex said, eye on the damaged manipulator. The earlier hit had stiffened the elbow. The arm answered the test with a judder.

"One chance," Thea said.

She extended the arm by centimetres. The claw kissed stone. The sub accepted the offset with a slow roll. She froze, let it settle, shaved a sliver from a crusted edge. The chips hung a heartbeat, then drifted to the intake. The vacuum whispered and took them in.

Again. Shave. Catch. Draw.

Lex watched the seam where the arm housing met hull. The joint complained, then obeyed. Thea skimmed the edge of the fossil's tomb without touching bone, like a thief who had taken a vow not to smudge the art.

"Last pass," she said. The claw took a thicker flake, the vacuum pulled, and she retracted the arm one patient inch at a time. It squealed at the end and stuck.

"That is enough," Lex said. "We document. We verify. Then, perhaps, a gin."

"Some dive," Thea said, eyes still on the ribs. "Not just r-rock and water."

They took photographs with thief speed. Panoramas of the cracked slab, flow lines, cooling crust, fresh fractures bright against older brown. For scale, a measure stick set by suction. Ten minutes. Twelve. Lex tapped ascent.

They climbed with care. The damaged thruster laboured. The compensators grumbled. The dials slid the right way and grey light gathered, thicker and thicker, until the surface broke over them like torn silk.

The cradle's lines sang. The hatch bolts hissed. Frigid air struck their faces. Thea blinked into wind and found her hands shaking only when the buckle slipped twice. The third time it yielded.

Rodrigues waited, rain jacket snapping, expression between relief and rebuke. He took Thea's forearm first and squeezed once.

"Next time you argue with the seabed," he said, "bring a larger ship."

"Under advisement," Lex said.

"Report."

They gave it on deck, the sea a heaving witness, crew leaning in. No lecture. Edges only.

"Massive slide s-scar," Thea said. "Not slump. Failure. A m-massive body of rock."

"Volcanic origin," Lex said. "Chemistry will confirm. Structure says the flank went as one."

"What scale?" Rodrigues asked, last night's wine long gone from his bones.

"Kilometres," Thea said. "One slab runs nearly t-two thousand metres. There are others."

Lex looked to the horizon. "Enough to move oceans."

The word that never stays dead rose in the space between them. Atlantis. Lex shook his head, almost smiling at himself. "We do not name myths. We make measurements. The samples will speak."

The lab was a narrow cathedral of instruments, sieves, scopes, humming boxes that tame chaos by forcing it to repeat. Thea moved like a conductor, gloves and tweezers and labels. Lava chips went under magnification. Vesicles bloomed across the screen like bubbles in glass. Texture logged, colour, void fraction. She weighed the first chip to the milligram and set the machine to build a bracket, not a miracle, just patient physics.

"We will not get a single clean date," Lex said. "We bracket. Old enough, not old enough. We aim."

The machine hummed. Numbers scrolled. Thea's face took on the look some call prayer, though she would not.

"Cross check mineralogy," Lex said, splitting duties. Thin sections under polarised light. Crystal habits to tell cooling. Thea prepped a second fraction to prove the first had not played tricks.

The chime, when it came, was a single bright note. A curve rose and levelled. Thea leaned so close her breath fogged the screen. Lex stood shoulder to shoulder.

"Well," he said.

She ran the verification twice, then with the second sample. The same rise, the same fall, the same settle, that quiet click when numbers fit their teeth into a lock.

"It i—i-is ancient," Thea said. "Old enough to move oceans. But n-no walls, no towers, no t-trace of a people. This is not a lost city."

"How old?" Lex asked.

She loaded it. The curve rose, fell, settled. The number belonged to a wound older than records, older than lighthouse keepers and newspapers. Older than Rome.

Lex closed his eyes and saw a map breathe. Coastlines emptying and returning with a roar that ran from horizon to horizon. He opened them again. Thea was already typing the report, backups across drives, then mirrored again. She is not someone who trusts a single copy.

"Captain," Lex called.

Rodrigues appeared. Lex handed him the printout. The captain did not try to make it smaller.

"What does it mean?" he asked.

"It means the mountain fell before anyone thought to carve it into history," Lex said. "Best estimate puts it around three thousand years. Back in the age of the Pharaohs."

He pressed the radio. "Max, Esme, the deep fault is real. The signal runs under the island. I need you to hold position and confirm it on the ground."

Static cracked before Max's voice came through, clipped and steady. "Copy that. I will need to come back down for the ground penetrating radar. Santos can give me a hand. Without it we cannot test the fault line properly. Esme wants to stay on the ridge, she does not fancy the climb down and back up."

"Copy."

No one dared imagine what the dawn might carry.

chapter 16:
Death Without Dignity

The knock came at dusk. Three slow raps, a pause, then one more, as if the messenger feared the answer. Khamariti opened the door onto a figure grey with dust and travel. The man bowed without a word and held up a sealed scroll. The wax bore the falcon and sun disc of Ramesses II, dulled by sand but unmistakable.

Khamariti broke the seal. The hand was hurried, strokes pressed hard as if against a shaking table. The words were spare. The meaning was not.

The firstborn of Pharaoh was dead.

He read the line again. Dead. Taken by the same scourge that had moved through Pelusium like a shadow with teeth. The room tipped and levelled. For a moment he saw not the child of a pharaoh, but Menna, laughing in sunlight, hoop rolling ahead of her in the courtyard, calling for him to watch. The picture flared and went out like a lamp starved of oil.

"Tell your master Nebit I have received his word," Khamariti said at last, his voice heavy. "Return in three turns of the sun, and I will set my instructions in writing."

The messenger bowed and went, feet whispering down the stone steps into failing light.

Silence folded back into the house. Death had taught the walls to hold their breath. Khamariti crossed to Menna's sleeping mat and crouched, fingertips lightly touching the weave as if touch alone might lift her back from absence. There had been no rites. The physicians, choked by numbers, urged speed over ceremony. The city dug deep pits, threw lime and earth, and named nothing. He had watched the trenches fill, listened to the thud of shovels and the small sounds people make when they try not to make any sound at all. Something in him had cooled to iron.

If the rites so dear to Merit were denied, memory would not be. He would keep her name. He would carve it deep into the marrow of his years, beside the others he had lost, carrying them forward long past the span of men, until even his own name was nothing but dust.

He stepped into the street.

Pelusium had been colour and noise. Barges at the quay, hawkers calling, Roman glass bright as fish, Phoenician dyes staining fingers blue and violet. Now the air smelt of lime and damp earth. Doors hung open on empty rooms. Dogs lay in shade and did not lift their heads.

He went to the river.

The Nile moved like a thought through the city, broad and unknowable. Green films drifted where current slowed. He watched water push against quay stones and thought of the sick who drank and the healthy who were not; of lines on maps where death thinned as the river thinned; of salt, of heat, of the strange seasons; of life so small no eye could see it and yet large enough to empty a cradle in a night.

The city was crowded with gods, chiselled into walls, painted on lintels, raised high in gold and granite. None had come. None had answered.

He did not speak their names. Better to keep his breath than waste it on stone.

He went home when the lamps along the quay were faint coins in the haze. Merit sat in the inner room. She had been quiet since Menna died. Not the quiet of sleep, but the quiet after a lamp is put out. She moved like a shadow. She ate when he placed food before her, drank when he pressed a cup to her lips. At night she lay beside him and watched the roof beam cut the square of the window.

Words had failed her. Then work had failed her. Then even silence had fallen short. There are griefs that will not be held.

He sat with her now. They did not speak. The quiet had length and weight.

When the oil burned low, he rose for another jar. Her hand closed on his wrist.

"Leave it," she said.

He sat. Her fingers trembled, then steadied. "Do you remember," she asked, "the night you made my ring?"

He smiled despite himself. "You scolded me for the hammering."

"I scolded you for the hour," she said. A faint spark there. "It was almost dawn."

"The ring would not sit," he said. "It wanted to be oval."

"It is oval," she said.

Their eyes met. The spark went out.

"I am tired, Khamariti."

"So am I."

"Not of the day. Of the weight." She paused. "It has crushed me flat."

He took her hand. "We will stand," he said. Even as he said it, he knew the words were a rope that would not hold.

Her fingers tightened once. Then loosened. "Sleep."

He waited until her breathing deepened. Then he went to his table in the outer room, where parchment lay in ordered stacks, covered in figures and little diagrams, columns running like narrow roads. He bent to them, grateful for lines and measures that did not change when a heart did. He read until words blurred. He pressed thumb and forefinger to the bridge of his nose and closed his eyes.

He told himself she slept.

He told himself nothing.

He slept at the table.

He woke to a small absence. Weights were missing from the kitchen wall. A clean square of plaster shone where they had hung, catching first light.

The air changed shape. He was standing before he knew he had stood. His steps carried him through the door, across the street, down to the quay without command.

On the coping, near the steps where Menna had sat and kicked her heels, a ring lay in the half-light. Oval. He did not need to touch it to know the warmth of the metal or the shallow file marks hidden on the inner band where he had corrected a fault a lifetime ago. Beside it, under a pebble, a scrap of scraped bark.

He lifted the stone and read. Only a few words.

Forgive me.

It is too much.

I go to where our children wait.

He held the scrap and the ring and stood with the river at his feet and the sky beginning to colour at the edge. Sounds arrived from far away. A man calling to a barge. A jar set down on stone. The small pop of a fish at the surface. He sank to one knee and set the ring to his lips and did not weep. Some griefs burn the tears before they fall.

When the city woke and men came with poles and hooks, he did not go. He would not watch the river give back what it had taken. He sat in the inner room, the ring on the low table before him. Hands folded, he watched the square of light creep across the floor, slide, then vanish.

A man came to the doorway and stood with lowered head. "We searched," he said quietly. "We did not find her body. Sometimes the Nile keeps what is offered."

Khamariti did not look up. He spoke to no god. He spoke to no one.

The men returned and stood in the doorway with the stiffness of those who carry duty with kindness. He thanked them and sent them away. He washed the floor, made the bed with fresh linen, and set the ring on the lintel where a hand would brush it by habit.

Then he went out.

The trenches beyond the south gate were deeper now, their edges whitened with lime. The men who worked there no longer met each other's eyes when they lifted. It made the weight easier to bear.

Khamariti did not go closer. He did not need to.

He set his hands on the river stone again. The surface was cold, polished by centuries of flow, yet it gave him no comfort. His strength faltered. The weight of loss pressed heavier than any block of granite he had ever raised.

At last, his knees gave way. He sank to the earth, the dust rising around him. His voice broke loose, raw, and unshaped.

"Nefer!" he cried. The name of his son tore from him like a wound reopening. "Merit! Menna!"

The sound carried over the lime pits, echoing against the walls as if the stone itself bore witness. The workers froze in their toil, their heads bowed, unable to look upon him.

Khamariti's hands struck the stone once more, but softer now, almost a caress. His words spilled out into the air, not to the river, not to the gods, but to the family who would never answer.

He set his hands on the river stone again. After a time, he spoke aloud, not to the water or the air.

"There are no gods," he said. "Only earth and water and air. If we do not learn them, they will break us."

The words went out, struck nothing, and fell.

He went back to the table. The work waited.

He began with what he knew. Death clung to the river's edge. Where Nile water gave drink and fish, children died in swathes. Where fish were fewer, illness still came, but the shrouds were fewer. Inland the hand moved slower. The smallest fell first. The maps drew the same truth his ears had heard at markets and wells. The pattern spoke.

He wrote: Not wrath. Nature.

He sent for physicians and scribes. They came hollow-eyed, yet they came. The low room filled with them, the narrow window framing a hard square of river light at noon. Khamariti unrolled his sheets and spoke without flourish. One by one they offered their condolences for Merit and for Menna.

"The river gives, and it takes away" he said. "We have sung it since our first songs. But she gives by rules we do not understand. This year the flood came early, heavy. It laid a red veil. From that veil something rose and travelled. It rode the air at child height. It went from water to mouth, from mouth to bed, from bed to shroud."

They shifted. Some watched the door, fearing a priest.

An older scribe cleared his throat. "You ask us to deny the hand of the gods."

"I ask you to see what stands before you," said Khamariti. "If you will not say it, I will write it and seal it. One day, when the river runs green again, someone will read and know they were warned."

A grey-templed physician raised a palm. "What must be done?"

"Boil water. Salt the wells. Do not eat fish. Keep the children from slack water. Bread and oil until the heat breaks."

A younger scribe frowned. "We can say these things, but the people will ask why their offerings cannot shield them."

"Because gods do not lift jars," Khamariti said.

The silence after was long enough for each to hear his own heart.

"The priests will denounce you," the elder warned. "Heretic. Stones will follow."

Khamariti closed his eyes. He felt Merit's hand grow cold in his. He opened his eyes, and it was gone. "Then we will not shout," he said. "We will whisper. In kitchens. At wells. In courtyards where mothers share salt. Whispering will save more than shouting ever could."

No one argued.

They left in ones and twos. Khamariti stayed. He wrote letters, sealed with his own mark. He made lists of markets where women bought millet and figs, of bakers' lanes and public wells, of places where a whisper could become law. He lit the lamp as light failed and took up a fresh sheet.

"Nebit," he wrote, "friend of my house. Fate has taken Merit and Menna. I give you these words not for grief but for purpose. Tell the pharaoh that I mourn with him. A father is a father, crown or none, and no crown rules the grave."

He pressed thumb to brow until the bone ached, then wrote on.

"I have watched this scourge. It follows the river. It rises with heat. It lays a red veil, and from water to mouth, from mouth to bed, from bed to shroud. This is not wrath. It is nature. If we learn its course, we may step aside. If we will not, it will count us and move on."

He paused. The reed hovered.

"Ask the pharaoh to send word to Phoenician captains. I must take passage to Byblos and Sidon and further if the weather permits. The western sea keeps old stories. They speak of great water where none had been, and of land broken and swallowed. If I am to defend what we raise, I must see what the ocean remembers."

He stared at the line. Another door opened in his mind, a stair leading down to a cool dark he knew by other names. He did not go down. Not yet.

"I will need a charter with the pharaohs seal for the magistrates of Tyre and the elders of Byblos," he wrote. "Safe conduct. The right to ask questions where questions are not welcome."

"I do not abandon my oath. My heart remains with Egypt. My steps must carry me elsewhere, but the feet are Egypt's feet."

He sealed the letter, then added a line Nebit would understand:

"I pray you are preserved. May the truths you trust and the truths I seek hold you both."

He called a trusted runner and pressed the waxed sheet into the man's hand. "This leaves tonight," he said. "Sleep no more than two hours at noon until Nebit has it."

The runner nodded and vanished into the narrow lanes.

Khamariti stood in the doorway and let the cool air move across his face. Somewhere a woman sang a low song with no words. He set the ring back on the lintel and let his fingers brush it as he passed, a habit given new purpose.

He slept, not well, not long.

Dawn came thin. He rose before it brightened, ground barley, warmed water, ate standing. He filled a skin and walked the alleys where women queued at wells and boys bent over grinding stones. He spoke as he had promised to speak.

"Boil it," he said. "Salt your wells. Do not eat fish for a little time. Keep the children away from the river. Bread and oil will carry you through."

Some stared. Some frowned. Some nodded. A woman said, "My man says the gods are angry." He answered, "Let your man boil the water for two weeks, then tell me what the gods have done." She smiled despite herself. He moved on.

By noon he had walked half the quarter and repeated himself until the words felt like stones he carried in his mouth. It was a good weight.

At the quay, the steps where he had found the ring were hot underfoot. He stood and looked over water where boats slid and turned like ideas. He set his palm on the warm stone and closed his eyes.

"Merit," he said so softly only the stone heard. "I will carry you into the work. When I speak at a well, you stand beside me. When a child lives because a jar boiled, you live."

He drew back his hand and turned away.

He climbed to the roof that night and lay on his back, arms tucked under his head, watching the stars. He had used these same points of light to set the lines of temples and fix doorways so that the mid-year sun lay on an altar at the breath the singers struck their note. The stars had not moved. He had.

"Three families," he said into the dark. "Three."

The word hung, then thinned.

"You place this burden on me," Khamariti cried to the sky, his voice ragged, uncaring who might hear. "I will bear it. But grant me one kindness. Teach me through stone, through map, through water. Let me find what is behind this. Let me spare the cradles."

A faint wind crossed the roof. A bat stitched the air over the parapet. Far away a drum sounded twice, then once more, the city's way of counting a death.

In the morning, he would send more letters, and then he would walk to the captains' quarter and trade the pharaohs seal for a berth. The Nile would carry him north, and the sea beyond would answer if he spoke its language. But first, he had to wait for the Pharaoh's seal and permission.

He closed his eyes and saw a coastline he did not yet know, an ocean breathing, a mountain falling, a wall of water born and spent. He opened them to the small square of the world he could touch. The ring was under his hand on the lintel. He pressed it with his thumb, once, as if sealing a promise to stone.

Egypt breathed in dust and sorrow. The river moved on. And Khamariti, emptied and unbroken, began to gather what he needed to follow the water where it led.

chapter 17:
The Journey Beyond
the Pillars

The tent stilled before the words were finished. Tarak held his tally stick in the air as if it might catch the next sentence and hold it steady.

Nadir stood with dust caked in the lines of his face, breath torn thin from the run. He carried no sack, no water skin, only the weight of his news.

"They are dead," he said. "Jalil and Haroun. Cut down. Clean kills. Left for carrion."

Reed pens stopped. A murmur rose and failed.

High Priest Ankhwennefer looked up from a papyrus and let the silence settle on its own. "Dead," he repeated, voice flat. "So soon. How many hands did it?"

"No more than two, Holy One," Nadir said, bowing. "Arrows first. Blades to finish. A warning. They moved like wraiths. No trace left."

Ankhwennefer rolled the scroll and fastened it with an ivory slip before setting it aside. "Jalil and Haroun were never meant to close the circle. They were only watchers at the edge. Lesser men." His calm voice carried the sharper cut. Then he raised his hand.

Two figures left the far shade as if the canvas had breathed them out.

"Now," the High Priest said, "the true blades take their places. Khamariti carries knowledge older than pharaohs, knowledge the throne covets but cannot command. Strike him from the earth. Egypt's survival rests on this."

Seneb and Thirsu bowed once and were gone into heat.

Three months of waiting. No omen worth the clay it was scratched on. Only the hiss of the river and the slow creep of light across a room that held more absence than air.

The runner came at last.

With Nebit's seal came Ramesses' authority. Tribute was sent, courtesies exchanged, and the doors of Phoenicia opened.

Khamariti read the letter twice. He pressed the seal to his lips, folded the sheet, tucked it into his robe, and rose.

He packed instruments first. A knotted cord, a plumb line, a plane table. A bag of pegs. A small brass disc cut with circles he had learned by heart. Reed pens and ink cakes scraped bark for notes on decks wet with spray. He lifted the ring from the lintel and hid it deep in his belt with gold coins.

He left the door open behind him.

At the quay he found a captain with salt in his beard and the dry smile of a man who had lost count of landfalls. The man studied the pharaohs seal, looked up, and nodded once, palm open for the coin promised by the letter.

"Byblos first," the captain said. "Then we listen to what the sea says."

Seneb and Thirsu reached Pelusium too late. The sickness had crossed the delta ahead of them and laid its hand on the city. They entered at dusk beneath a gate with no guard. Door leaves hung open. Flies stitched black threads in the heat. A pot rolled across an empty court and came to rest against a fallen stool. From the alleys came the cough that does not stop. Linen strips tied to doorposts had browned at the edges. Smoke drifted from braziers where herbs had burned in panic. It could not sweeten the air.

Seneb pulled his scarf close. "This city is death."

"And yet he passed through," Thirsu said, eyes weighing shadow and sound.

Seneb and Thirsu searched for signs that no plague had made. Boot marks pressed into dust. A scuff along a lintel. Pitch smeared across a length of rope. At the cistern they found rushes abandoned in haste. In the market, a scribe's tablet lay half buried in mud, a single word cut before the hand had failed.

At the river steps, a coin loosened a woman's tongue. "The Egyptian," she said, "the one who walked as if he measured the ground. He left after the burning. Buried his child, lost his wife to the Nile. Then a Phoenician hull carried him off. Byblos bound."

Seneb and Thirsu traded a look. Their quarry still lived, and the chase had only begun.

Beyond the low wall they found the patch of turned earth. Thirsu set his palm on it and closed his eyes for a breath. "He did not flee," he said. "He does not know we track him."

Seneb glanced at the city, where lamps guttered like stars smothered in smoke. "Pelusium could not hold him. Nor his families death." He tied the cloth tighter. "North."

They withdrew to the desert fringe and watched the city subside. Only when the last pyres cooled did they move again, leaner, harder, taking the same road Khamariti had taken. Towards cedar and coin. Towards the sea.

Byblos rose through heat shimmer and gull cry, masts like a forest, cargo stacked in neat pyramids, the air rich with cedar and tar. Khamariti stepped ashore into a world of braided tongues and clattering money.

A man waited beyond the gangplank, silver hair over sharp eyes, cloak the colour of storm water, rings that told their own journeys.

"Master Zamurus," the captain said, saluting the dock.

"Khamariti," Zamurus greeted, taking the Egyptian's forearm with a sure grip. "You come with a Pharaoh's blessing and with the respect of my trade. My house is yours."

He meant it. His estate sat back from the water behind vine-veiled walls. Basins fed by channels. Cedar beams carved as if grown that way. Wealth without apology. He fed his guest before he asked the real question. Later, on a terrace that looked down on the harbour lights, he nodded towards sea.

"You entered a city that should not recover so fast," he said. "Flood, then a second, heavier. Storms built in an hour. Ash in the rain." He let the words sit. "Egypt's year of pestilence was not alone."

He waited. Men keep their hardest sentence to last.

"The captains bring back strange accounts," he said at last, voice lower as if the sea might be listening. "Coasts torn as if cut by a giant blade. Harbours shifted, whole inlets swallowed, charts now make lies. Black rain, far west, ash that stains the water and poisons the catch. And always the same warning: the Pillars. Trouble rides those currents. Ships vanish. Storms rise without cause. What waits beyond is not the sea we knew."

"I need those captains," Khamariti said. "Your scribes. Any tablet that names a river boiling, a mountain breaking, a sea that climbed where it should not."

"You shall have them."

Mornings belonged to mariners who tasted wind. Afternoons to traders who read scarcity and glut. Evenings to scholars who poured oil and memory into margins. A veteran called Elias came with skin burned to leather and eyes like struck flint. He stood with Khamariti on the terrace and spared his words.

"Beyond the Pillars," he said, looking where two shoulders of land reach for one another, "noon went dark. Ash sifted like snow. The sea drained until the bed lay bare. Then it came back with a roar and tore the land. After, even the water tasted wrong."

Khamariti heard the pattern under the tale. River. Sea. Mountain. Fire. Air. Not the anger of gods. A sequence. A chain. He stayed three months and filled pages until the reed bit at the edge of his hand.

When the last sheet dried, he closed the book and looked across the lamp glow at Zamurus. "I need a hull that does not flinch at horizon," he said. "Men who can ride trench winds and land where the sea says no. Not along coasts. Through. Beyond the Pillars."

Zamurus' expression hardened, almost insulted when Khamariti reached for gold. "You have my friendship," he said. "Do not cheapen it with coin. You will have your ship, your crew, and men who see profit where you seek knowledge. You will open the world, we will open routes."

He clapped for a servant. "Send for Imbu."

The man who entered moved like a predator that had learned patience and discipline. Dark as coal, tall, shoulders cut for battle. Scars spoke as truth, not show. His eyes made one measured sweep of the room, unhurried, missing nothing.

"Imbu has kept me breathing more times than I care to count," Zamurus said. "He will keep you breathing beyond the Pillars."

Khamariti offered his hand. "Not master to servant," he said. "A man with a willing to learn and a man willing to teach. You will call me teacher."

Imbu's grip was firm. "I serve the path," he said. "Today it runs through you. Behind you are blades we cannot see, but I feel. Ahead are waves that will try to erase their own shape."

"Imbu has a sense for danger, it's a gift from the gods" said Zamurus.

"Then walk with me," Khamariti replied. "And when your sense warns, pull me back."

The harbour became a ledger of action. Contracts inked. Sails patched or new. Stores laid in: water, grain, dried meat, oil, resin, spare cordage and nails, wax tablets, and reeds. Words would matter as much as rope.

At dusk, Zamurus walked the quay with Khamariti. "There," he said, pointing to a cedar hull with a high prow and lines that promised speed and endurance. "Thalassa's Gift. Crew of fifty. Ten fighters who can hold a deck. Craftsmen who mend sail, timber, or bronze before the tide turns. The rest trade as fiercely as they row. Captain Abdiel brings men and cargo home from waters that try to unwrite their rules."

They met Abdiel on deck, lamplight across forearms roped with work. He studied Khamariti as if measuring a piece of timber before setting it into place.

"Beyond the Pillars," Abdiel said, "water can walk."

"I know."

"Wind there forgets what it did an hour before."

"I know."

"A line on a map is a lie after a mountain moves."

"Yes," Khamariti said.

"Then we will get along."

Byblos was stone and loyalty, but silver can still open a narrow door. For the right price, a servant whispered what should have stayed in the walls. Three months of preparation. A date at dawn.

Seneb and Thirsu became other men. Rough wool. Salt in speech. Dock filth ground into faces until they were the colour of work. They studied the watch list of the Thalassa until they could wear it like borrowed clothes. Forged tokens did the rest.

But a ship bound for the Pillars keeps a tight count. Every berth named. To slip aboard, two men would have to go missing.

They found them in a tavern near the quay, sailors drunk on coin paid before a voyage men feared. Thirsu drew them into an alley with the promise of more. Seneb followed, quick and certain. The struggle was brief. A cut to silence a shout. A blade under the ribs to make sure. They hid the bodies in refuse where rats already worked. By dawn, the city's filth would finish the task.

Clothed in the dead men's tunics, they walked back to the harbour with tokens ready. The security guard checked the marks, gave their faces a glance, and waved them on. Schedules ask fewer questions.

When the watch changed on a smaller dock, they stepped onto Thalassa's as if the deck knew their feet. By the time lines were thrown free, they had vanished into routine, hauling and coiling, learning names that were no longer theirs.

Hunters, hidden in plain sight, waiting for a breath that would open a day.

Khamariti made no speech. "I go because I must," he told Zamurus. "I return if I can. If not, let what I write be enough."

Dawn laid a silver blade across the harbour as Thalassa's leaned and slid out to open water. Zamurus stood on the breakwater, cloak pressed to his legs. He raised a hand once. Khamariti answered with a palm and turned to sea.

Two days out, the water changed its mind. Colour deepened. Swell grew longer. Birds thinned. Abdiel held the tiller with a set jaw.

"Feel that?"

"A pull," Khamariti said.

"A river under the sea, "Captain Abdiel replied. "It goes where it wishes."

On the third dawn, land blurred ahead, two stone shoulders reaching for one another across a throat of water. The Pillars men draw when they mean enough.

Lashings were tightened. Frayed lines checked and checked again. Imbu paced the deck end to end, a warning in motion.

"Now," he told Khamariti, voice low. "If the sea tests us, it is here."

A stain spread in the west. Not cloud. A haze that dulled edges and swallowed distance. The sea under it moved with the wrong kind of patience.

Khamariti set his hand on the rail. The frame held steady. The men did not. He understood.

The wind shifted. The sail cracked, then steadied. The strait seemed to breathe in and out. At the bow, the water dimpled as if something large turned below.

"Hold her," Abdiel said, voice steady as iron. The crew leaned with all their weight.

They entered the throat of the passage. Every sound grew sharp. The timber groaned. Men sucked breath through their teeth.

Three long waves lifted them, each higher than the last. The third carried wreckage, reeds, logs, even a goat adrift. A jar struck the hull, spun once, and was gone.

Khamariti's eyes fixed west. Smoke smeared the horizon where sea and sky met in false peace. Above it, the blue fought to hold its ground.

"Beyond," he said. None asked him to explain.

Ash began to fall, soft and dry. The sea darkened to the colour of iron.

Imbu stepped close but gave him space. "I can read people," he said. "I see you carry old secrets and fresh wounds. When trust comes, tell me your story."

"In time," Khamariti said.

Below deck, two new hands worked the ropes as if born to them. Seneb kept to rhythm. Thirsu listened. Between the beat of water and the creak of timber, they counted the steps of the Egyptian who wrote by lamplight and slept as little as men at war.

On the fourth night at sea, watch turned. A coil dropped. A lantern swung. A figure halted by the companionway and stood very still, measuring.

Not Khamariti.

Imbu.

Seneb's hand hung where a blade could be. Thirsu's gaze did not shift. Imbu's eyes passed over them and did not stick. He went on, weight placed like a man who expected the deck to test him.

Thirsu let out a breath. "Not tonight."

"Soon," Seneb said.

"If the sea does not draw its own blade first," Thirsu answered.

A gust took the sail. The hull leaned and recovered. From the bow came Abdiel's short laugh, the kind a man gives an old enemy when the ground is even for once.

West of the Pillars the water wore history. Lines of darker blue crossed lighter, current on current, as if two rivers ran in a single bed. The ash haze thickened at noon and thinned at dusk. Sometimes the sun bit through as if behind old linen.

Khamariti worked without theatre. He sketched the shape of waves, the set of swells against the boat's line, the tilt of birds that rode air without effort then vanished when the air changed mood. He noted where drift gathered and where it fled, where the sea smelt of rock, where it smelt of rot, where a faint sulphur hung like a warning.

At night he lay on the deck with his hands folded under his head and watched the stars. He had set great cornerstones by those points of light. Now he used them to hold a thought steady while the sea tried to pull it away.

Imbu watched him and watched the crew. Twice he eased a quarrel aside with a word rather than a fist. Once he moved faster than thought and caught a man by the belt when a loose line tried to take him over the side. He said little and missed nothing.

Seneb and Thirsu learned the steps of work and hid in them. They were hands when hands were needed, shoulders when weight mattered, voices when the chant must carry a long pull together. They ate at the same board and spoke the same simple jokes. They built the shape of belonging.

At dusk on the sixth day, the ash thinned and the sky ahead opened a hand. Far to the south a smudge lay low on the sea. Abdiel watched it for a long time, then shook his head.

"Not ours," he said. "Swell wrong. Leave it."

Khamariti kept his eyes on the west. He could feel it more than see it, a slow draw in the bones of the ship, as if something out there took breath.

On the ninth day the sea changed again. From deep grey to a cold green that caught and held the light like glass. The swell flattened. The wind fell away until the sail hung without opinion. The only sound was the slap of small water against cedar.

"Dead ground," Abdiel said. "It does this before it remembers itself."

Khamariti stood at the bow, the ash flakes turning to nothing on his tunic, and knew they had crossed some line that charts could not hold.

"Beyond this," he said, "we meet the place the stories were born."

"And the men who made them," Imbu said quietly, eyes on the two new hands who worked a little too well for men who had only just joined a crew.

The sun fell red into the haze. Night came like a door on old hinges.

The night folded around the ship. The crew worked on, though every man felt the weight of what had passed. Seneb stood apart, silent, watching, learning.

chapter 18:
The Hunt Beneath the Sun

Khamariti stood at the bow of the Phoenician ship, salt wind in his face, Africa falling behind in a blue haze. The voyage itself was grand enough, but it was the hidden pattern beneath it that held his eye. Trade and whispers moved together. Ports were not just harbours. They were doors.

Abdiel, the captain, had lines carved deep by salt and seasons. He smiled often and revealed little. His ledger of risk and favour seemed etched into bone. Every delay carried a value. Every detour forged a bond or burned a bridge. Cargo was coin. Favour was better. Khamariti sensed the man traded not in goods but in possibility.

At each port Zamurus's agents moved like old roots through new soil. Letters changed hands. Seals kissed wax. Bales shifted. So did promises. Khamariti watched with a scribe's hunger, listening for the one note that mattered: knowledge.

The cargo above deck looked ordinary, spices, ingots, cloth. The holds beneath told a truer story: sealed jars of medicines, scrolls bound in oilskins, fragments of lore gathered from storms and shorelines. His heart quickened each time the gangplank struck wood. Goods passed, and stories bled.

He and Imbu moved together in this world. In alleys they shadowed agents through the steps of negotiation: harbour master first, guild chief second, then the quiet figure with no office who somehow blessed or blighted every deal. It was a web of names, woven tight. Khamariti read it as he read walls; Imbu listened with a guard's caution.

Their friendship sharpened quickly. Lines and angles met blade and shield, and between them grew trust. They argued as men argue when respect underpins the words: over the strength of walls, the right curve of a bow, whether bitter seed boiled in milk cured fever or only delayed it. Their worlds were different, yet the edges fit.

The Pillars of Hercules rose ahead, stone shoulders straddling the strait. Beyond them stretched an ocean that had shaped myth. Here Zamurus's agents drew longer breaths, their purpose clear. They were not only trading. They were planting anchor points for a future not yet mapped.

The coast of Mauretania received them with markets loud with goats, copper, and salt. Ships from the sunrise carried respect. Agents traded fine cloth and tools for meat, spice, and fragments of local truth. At each port, one of their own remained ashore, leaving a root for the next voyage.

Khamariti asked his question a hundred ways. He spoke to the old men who mended nets in the shade, to women gutting fish at the quayside, to boys who knew every shoal and current better than a scribe knew ink.

"In the last Inundation, and the one before it," he asked again and again, "did the world break? Did floods come? Fire? Stone falling from the sky?"

Priests would not answer such things. They bound disasters into ritual and silence. But fishermen remembered. They spoke of nights when the sea rose without warning and claimed whole strips of shore. They told of fire that had moved across the waves as if the water itself had burned. They told of ash that fell soft as dust yet killed the river for months.

The answers varied in detail, but they pointed always in the same direction. Northwest of Agadir, where the headlands stood like broken teeth. There the sea had climbed the land. Villages had vanished. Fields once fertile now lay buried under silt and salt.

The south had watched and counted. Every boat that went north carried fewer hands back. Every family lost cousins, brothers, children to the hunger of the coast.

Khamariti listened to them all. His mind set the fragments together like stones in a wall. What priests ignored, what scribes would not write, the fishermen knew. And the shape of their memory pointed to a truth deeper than rumour, something in the earth itself had moved.

One evening an Amazigh elder came to them where the surf licked the strand. His robe flapped in the wind. Time had cut furrows into his face. He spoke a tongue Khamariti did not know.

Imbu tilted his head and answered in deep tones. "The speech of the Amazigh. My people are of his line. Old, deep."

The elder crouched and drew in the wet sand. Islands like beads in a rough arc. He pressed each name into earth, eyes fixed on Imbu.

"Tamazirt N'Wurgh," Imbu said softly. "Land of the Sun — a place of endless light where life bows to fire."

"Tafukt Taneggarut, Island of Fire. A heart that roars beneath the earth, the gate to the underworld."

"Asif N'Imurig, River of Streams. Valleys that cradle water, a land that stirs the sea."

"Arganij, the Argan Isle. Hard soil, hard grace."

"Adrar Ufella, the High Mountain. Peaks and ash, a land that whispers of creation and ruin."

Centuries later, travelers would call these the Canary Islands, Gran Canaria, Tenerife, La Palma, Fuerteventura, and Lanzarote.

The elder lifted his gaze westward. "Look from Agadir to these islands," Imbu said. "That line shows the truth you seek."

Khamariti bowed low. To Imbu's astonishment, he answered in Amazigh, fluent, respectful. The elder's eyes brightened, then softened with age.

His words chilled the sand. "When Teide roars, fire storms, and ice fall. The earth remembers."

Khamariti copied the map onto papyrus while Imbu tried his own hand at the script, learning the marks. Their bond deepened in silence.

Then the air shifted as they returned to the Thalassa.

A ripple of wrongness. The whisper of feet through sand. Bronze glinted, the cruel curve of a blade.

"Stay low," Imbu murmured.

Thirsu broke from the palms, weapon descending. Imbu rose like stone given breath. He caught wrist and elbow, twisted, and hurled the assassin sideways. Sand jumped. Thirsu spat blood, circled again, dagger flashing for the ribs. Imbu met him with forearm and fury, driving him back as a lion drives jackals.

In the trees, Seneb watched with predator's patience. Every movement told him more than words. This was no mere guard. This was danger itself.

The clash raged. Bronze rang. Breath tore. Thirsu feinted high and cut low. Imbu turned the blade with his forearm and stepped inside.

His sica rustled free, a curve of steel honed to a whisper. He let the promise of it speak and saw doubt pass across the other man's face.

Desperation twisted Thirsu's hand. His second dagger flashed in the light and spun through the air. Imbu felled him with a huge blow to his temple.

Khamariti turned too late. Steel bit his side. He cried out, his linen splitting as blood spread warm across his ribs. He staggered, one hand clutching the wound, the other braced against the ground.

"Teacher," Imbu called, his voice raw with fear and rage. He crossed the ground in two strides. Dropping to one knee, he tore off his own cloak, pressed it hard against the wound, and bound it tight. He scooped sand with his free hand, packing the fold to slow the flow. The grit turned red almost at once.

He lifted Khamariti from the dirt and held him close, keeping his body between the wounded man and the open ground. His chest heaved with breath, but his eyes never left the tree line.

The air had changed. The wind still blew from the sea, but another presence clung to the grove. It was colder, heavier, a weight that pressed on the skin.

Khamariti gasped against him. "He aimed for the heart," he whispered.

Imbu's grip tightened. "Then he missed."

Still, he kept watching the trees. The shadow of Thirsu's intent lingered, as if the man's hate had not died with the throw. The grove felt alive with it, a silence thicker than storm.

"Another," he breathed. "Watching."

Seneb melted back into shade, satisfied. He had seen enough. Imbu was a lion. Lions required snares, not blades. Patience would deliver the prize alive. Knowledge, power, Egypt itself.

Imbu's voice went hard. "Coward. Show yourself."

Only palms swayed. Only the hiss of the sea answered.

Thirsu writhed in the sand, broken but alive. "Mercy," he gasped. "I will speak."

Imbu planted a knee on his shoulder and stripped the knives from his hands with clean movements. He turned him and bound his elbows with wet cord so the skin would bite if he strained. Then he stood and let the silence do its work.

Khamariti braced himself and rose to one knee, colour gone from his mouth, breath tight. He refused the offered arm with a glance and steadied his hand against his ribs.

"Name," Imbu said.

The answer came with a crooked smile. "You know my name."

"Say it."

"Thirsu."

"Who sent you."

"The High Priest," Thirsu said at last. "Ankhwennefer. He thinks your master will burn Egypt if he walks where he wishes."

"He's my teacher not my master. What are your orders."

"Byblos," Thirsu said, voice low. "The rich man's ship carries many shadows. I learned the ropes so we could walk among them."

"You were not alone."

"I always work alone." A beat. "But there is another."

"Who."

"Not for me to say."

"Then you die alone," Imbu said, and let the words sit as if setting a bowl of water between them.

Thirsu's eyes slid to Khamariti. "Do you know what you are to these men? They think you are a torch. They think you will set fire to the names in the temples and call that light."

Khamariti's reply was steady. "Truth is light."

"Truth is a blade," Thirsu said. "It cuts the hand that holds it."

Imbu drew the sica, the curve catching dusk. "How many on the ship. Names."

"Enough," Thirsu muttered.

"Answer."

The calm in Imbu's tone drained the warmth from the evening. Thirsu's lips thinned. "A warning, then. Water Hyenas."

"Who."

"A baker in a lane by a dye house. A man who sells nets but never touches fish." He swallowed. "And others. Raiders. The ones men call

Water Hyenas. They have learned there is coin in the plenty. The ship tempts them."

"Describe them."

"Fast boats," Thirsu said. "Narrow, low, driven by scores of oars. A leader named Zarek commands them. He watches the strait. He casts nets of fire and takes men alive if they look rich enough to sell twice."

"How do they find ships along this coast."

"Signals. Fires on the ridges. Riders on the tracks above the sea. Your trader is seen long before he knows he is seen."

Imbu let the weight of that truth settle. He glanced at the papyrus spread before them. A single drop of blood had fallen from Khamariti's side, bleeding the ink like rain, but the line of islands still held.

Khamariti's breath was thin. "Do not kill him," he said, forcing the words through pain. "Thirsu has failed. Let him carry the shame. No more blood."

Imbu's eyes did not leave the man on the ground, wrists bound, chest heaving with shallow breaths. "Teacher," he said quietly, "I would never again go against your word. But an assassin is not a rival. He will not stop because he has failed once. If he rises, he will strike again. And if he strikes again, it will be at your back."

He cut Thirsu's throat, then lifted Khamariti to his feet. The architect's eyes were clear, though pain scratched at the edges. "We go to the boat," Imbu said. "You will not walk far."

"I can walk," Khamariti said, and managed three steps before the world pressed down. Imbu took the weight without asking and carried him the rest of the way.

They reached the longboat at the last light. The mother ship rode easy in the lee of a low headland. Abdiel's lantern on the foremast blinked twice, paused, blinked twice. The reply. The line was ready.

Imbu set Khamariti in the boat and packed wet sand against the keel so the rollers would catch. He heaved and pushed and rocked until the next small swell helped him launch. He waded to the waist, then climbed in and took the oars.

The sea lifted and lowered them without malice. The gulls turned once and settled again among the palms. Imbu kept his eyes on the lantern. The men at the rail took the painter and pulled them alongside.

"What happened," Abdiel said.

"Later," Imbu said. "He is bleeding."

They rigged a sling and hauled Khamariti to the deck. The crew made space without being told. Imbu carried him to the cabin under the quarterdeck. He stripped the tunic from the wound, cleaned what he could with wine, then water, then wine again. The cut tracked under the ribs. Not deep enough to kill by itself, not quickly, yet there was a tremor in his breath that made Imbu think of men who had died on smaller wounds when the flame took their blood.

He pressed a clean pad to the seam and bound it firm. He chewed willow bark and set it between Khamariti's teeth, then gave him a little water. The pupils were slow to move. The pulse jumped like a trapped bird.

"Stay," Imbu said, as if the word were not a command but a friendship.

Khamariti's eyes flickered. A ghost of a smile changed his mouth. "You carry me as if I am your child," he whispered.

"You are my charge," Imbu said. "You put your name in my hand."

Khamariti's eyes closed. His breath ran thin and steady, a thread of air that seemed hardly enough to keep a candle alive. Imbu set himself to watching. He had watched over wounded men in mountain passes and reed marshes. He had learned the way the air changes when a man is leaving. He listened for that. He listened for something else he could not name.

On deck Abdiel walked the rail and back, counting wakes and wind and time as if they were coins. In the cabin the lantern made a small circle of light. Khamariti's breath steadied, then faltered, then steadied again. Sweat gathered at his hairline. The colour in his lips drained, returned, and drained once more.

At some hour when even the gulls sleep, Khamariti began to murmur. No word was clear. The sounds were slow and old, like river water rolling under driftwood. He shifted and the bandage darkened a shade. The cords in his neck loosened. The tremor in his breath eased.

Imbu leaned forward, forearms on knees. The lantern made small light on Khamariti's hands. There were scars there he had not seen, fine white crescents at three knuckles, a short silver line across the heel of the palm, the trace of an old brand pressed lightly as a test. The skin along the ribs had begun to tighten. The blood that had soaked the linen had slowed to a mist. No fever took him.

Imbu sat back and let the question have its full shape. He had seen men die of less. He had not seen this. A man takes a blade near the lung, breath like a guttering lamp, then eases into a different air and wakes on the other side of night as if a mountain had shifted its weight from his chest to the floor.

He said nothing, only watched. Between one breath and the next he knew, with a certainty that did not need words, that the man he had chosen to follow was not as other men. Not a thing to fear. Not a thing to worship. A thing to hold as one holds a small flame in a wind.

Toward dawn, Khamariti's eyes opened. Not all at once. The pupils found the lantern and narrowed. He lay still, as if listening to his own body. Then he turned his head.

"You stayed," Imbu said.

"How long."

"All night."

Khamariti's fingers found the bandage. He pressed lightly and nodded once. "Your hands are good."

"Your blood is strange," Imbu said.

Khamariti might have made a joke and chose not to. "We have work," he said.

"Then you will live long enough to do it."

Khamariti rose, slow but steady, and stood at the rail when he reached the deck, colour back in his mouth, eyes clear. The men fell silent without knowing why.

"Anfa," he said, naming the old port they would reach when the headlands fell away. "Then the long run south."

"You should lie down," Abdiel said.

"I have lain down enough," Khamariti answered. "We move when wind says move, not when fear says hide."

By mid-morning they had made their offing. The sea lay in long slow hills. The cry from the foremast came first as a question, then as a blade.

"Sails. Two, north by east, bearing down."

Abdiel shaded his eyes with one hand and stared out to sea. The light wavered on the horizon, but the shapes held. Dark sails. Oars flashing like teeth. He lowered his hand and did not need to speak. They had already felt what the eye now confirmed. Ships were coming.

Long low hulls. Banks of oars moving like the legs of a centipede. Prows carved to cruel points. Men in two lines, shields ready, helmets blackened with pitch. A strip of cloth at the prow snapped in the breeze, painted with a hyena's grin.

Water Hyenas mark.

"Stations," Abdiel said. "Lines clear. Keep her moving. No panic."

Men set buckets of sand by the ladders. Jars of water went to the galley door. The spare yard came forward to stiffen the bow. The strong hands took up long spars. The archers checked bowstrings and the resin that would make fire cling if fire must answer fire.

Imbu tied a strip of cloth around his right wrist so he would feel it when the air turned to smoke. He checked the balance of the sica and the weight of a short spear. He touched the bandage at Khamariti's side with the back of his fingers, a question.

"It will hold," Khamariti said.

"You will keep behind the mast."

"I will keep behind the mast until the wind changes," Khamariti said, and the corner of his mouth moved.

Abdiel eased the sail and edged the course to steal a small advantage from the sea's long breath. It was not a gamble. It was a conversation with time.

From the war boats came the deep drum that set the oars. It thudded across the water, slow then quicker, a heart that had learned to run. The water between the ships narrowed.

chapter 19:
Seismic Reckoning

Max had wrung every reading he could from Cumbre Vieja. He had flown the drone for a fresh elevation model, set accelerometers along the ridge, logged microtremors through the night, mapped offsets by hand until his eyes burned. The island still refused to give him a clean answer. Yesterday's tremor had cut a new black seam across the flank. It did not match the historic fractures he knew by heart. Real. Recent. Wrong in a way that changed the picture.

The tool he needed to see the hidden rupture was still on the Marine Explorer. The ground penetrating radar would let him trace the first cracks beneath the surface. Linked with the new elevation map and the microtremor sensors, it could reveal how the fault twisted under the ridge. Once he had the lines, Thea could layer satellite scans on top. Data first. Conclusions after. Always.

He thumbed a message to the ship, short and clear.

Leaving 8am, Rendezvous El Pilar. Nightfall. Bring GPR. Spare multi gas cartridges. Extra batteries. Two carriers.

He added a note to Rodrigues about the narrow cuts on the trail. He clipped the radio back to his shoulder.

"We will be back, tomorrow afternoon," Max called to Esme. "Do not move the island without me."

Esme gave him a two-finger salute and forced a grin. "I will leave you a few rocks."

Santos lifted a coil of rope onto his shoulder but lingered, eyes on her. "You know she will not," he muttered.

Max stayed where he was, torn between duty and instinct. "Esme, we should stay. It's not safe for you on your own."

Her expression hardened. "Enough. You both have your orders. Act like professionals, not guards at my shoulder. I can manage a ridge without tripping over my own feet."

Max frowned. "That's not the point."

"It is exactly the point," she snapped. "We do the work. No fuss. No hesitation. Now bugger off".

For a beat neither man moved. Then Santos gave a slow nod and started down the path.

Max followed, still glancing back at her. "Off we go then," he said quietly.

Esme turned away before they could read her face. She had won the argument, but she felt the weight of the ridge pressing all the same.

They took the path towards El Pilar, boots crunching cinder, packs thumping. The pines gave them a breath of resin before the trail rose back into black stone and wind. Within five minutes the mountain kept them for itself. The camp fell away behind a shoulder and was gone.

Esme stood alone on the crown of the ridge and let the stillness come down. It was never truly still here. The island breathed. Steam sighed from thin vents. Heat moved under rock. Far below, the surf combed the old scars at the base of the cliffs.

She clipped a multi gas meter to her chest and watched the bars settle. Oxygen good. Carbon dioxide a hair above ambient in the hollows. Sulphur dioxide and hydrogen sulphide both low. The full-face respirator sat ready on her strap. She had no wish to be clever about air.

She broke camp and set off.

The ridge read like a ledger. Pitted cones opened like interruptions along the spine. Old lava lay in bands of black and deep red. The smooth rope of pahoehoe froze in waves then broke without warning into clinker that cut leather and patience. Thin grasses and stubborn shrubs found purchase where ash had weathered to soil. Steam drifted in white threads and vanished when the wind turned.

Esme worked the way she always did when the past might be close. Ground. Middle distance. Horizon. Pattern first. A crack that ran straight through two different flows meant something older lay beneath. A change in plant clusters meant a change in heat or chemistry. She logged each thing with a grease pencil, backed it with photographs and short bearings, and moved on.

By mid-morning, the light turned hard. The sun carved ridges and gullies into sharp relief so clean the mountain looked chiselled. The south flank fell away to a blue plain that went forever. Somewhere out there old landslide fans slept under water.

She took water in a patch of shade and pressed on.

The first warning was not sound but feel. A sour tremor in knees and ankles like a low note you only notice once it has started. The ground drew a breath. She waited. The tremor rose to a short growl. A line opened thirty metres ahead. It was nothing and then it was a mouth. The seam tore wider with a crack like a mast snapping. A dirty white plume shouldered her vision aside. The meter chirped twice. Sulphur dioxide rising. Carbon dioxide up. She had the respirator in her hands before she knew she had moved. She pulled it on. She pressed the seal with both palms. She watched the oxygen band stay safely green.

She crouched. She counted without hurry. One minute. Two. The plume thinned. The wind edged it off downslope. The bars steadied.

The fissure gaped like a jaw. On the far side she could see only a smear of grey where the ridge should have been. The camp sat four kilometres along the spine. A straight crossing was madness. Gas pooled in hollows. Ash hid teeth. The safer line meant a traverse under the break and a steep climb back to the ridge. Time, she did not have, but risk she would not take.

"Skirt it," she said. "Careful and quick."

She began the descent. She tested each step. She found holds where the old lava wrinkled. She made herself long and low when the slope steepened. She kept the respirator on while the meter stayed jumpy. She lifted it only to brush grit from her lashes when the bars were steady and the breeze held, then reseated the seal and checked it with a short breath. The slope went off like a roof. Every few metres she stopped and listened for small noises that often-meant substantial changes. A tinkle of grit. A whisper under rock. The cough of a crack becoming a line.

Her GPS blinked green at one low knuckle of ridge then died to grey two steps later. Rock did that. She backed up until it pulsed again and took a fix. If the worst came, she would at least leave a coordinate behind.

Twenty minutes bled into heat and stone.

She halted on a small stone outcrop. The ground fell in a clean drop for twenty-five metres, broke into a tilted ledge and a tangle of blocks, then rose again in ribs that ran back to the ridge. The way forward ran under the notch, left across the broken ground, and up. She could go back and risk the gas or lose an hour and commit.

"You have this," she told herself. "One move. Then the next."

She was tightening a strap when the mountain answered.

At first it was a tremble like the footfall of something heavy and far. Then the sound deepened. A grind came up through her boots into her bones. The outcrop shook. Cracks wrote tight lines across the dust. Stones slid. A veil of pebbles hissed past and vanished over the edge. The sea far below hissed back.

"Move."

The ledge she had planned to take sighed and let go. She pressed herself to the slope. Hands flat. Boots flat. Wide as she could make herself. The rock shivered along ribs and thighs. Small pieces came away. She waited for the big break to take her too. It did not come. Not yet.

The shaking eased. Aftershocks ran up and down the ridge like a shuddering wave and then the sort of stillness returned that hides teeth.

Blood trickled along her forearm. A spray of sharp gravel had cut skin in two clean lines. She eased into a crouch, took the small first-aid pouch from her pack, slipped on thin gloves, and worked without fuss. Rinse. Antiseptic. Two broad dressings taped down. Done.

The meter showed a cautious green. The plume behind her had thinned to threads. The slope ahead had changed.

Not the slope. The hill.

Below the notch a fresh opening split the side along a line that had not existed a minute before. The shock had lifted a crust and torn it away to show a seam of old stone beneath. Not a smooth fault plane. A mouth. The breath of the hill had blown out new rubble and dust. In the clearing air her headlamp picked out a low arch under the broken face.

Not natural. Not quite.

Esme stood very still. Her heart knocked against the frame of the mask. Long ago somebody had piled stones there to choke the entrance. Time and tremor had done the rest.

She checked the meter. Oxygen good. Carbon dioxide near normal for open ground now the wind had the plume. Sulphur dioxide low. She eased the mask off, took two careful breaths without it, clipped it back ready.

She marked the find the way she always did. Photograph with scale. A broad arrow scratched on a flat boulder. The mark scored with the point of her hammer so rain could not take it. Time. Partial coordinate from the last fix. One letter E and the date, big enough to read at a run.

She looked back at the arch.

"Far enough," she said. She meant it. She turned to go.

The mountain had other plans.

The second shock gave no warning. No rumble. No grace. It stamped once. Dust leapt from the face of the notch and hung like fog. Far back towards the ridge a heavy thing fell and broke. She climbed the worn stones and stepped through the archway. Into a cavern. Darkness and a cold draught met her face. Stone dropped in slabs and fists across the gap she had come through. Light went. Sound went. The room shrank to a cone of white from her lamp and the thud in her throat.

Esme stayed where she was and did the only things that mattered. She hauled the respirator tight and checked the seal. She watched the bars wake and move. Oxygen adequate near her face. Carbon dioxide heavier near the floor. Sulphur dioxide pulsing low. She kept her head high and breathed through the filter until the panic loosened its grip.

Stillness settled like a weight. The dust sank to a dark haze. She raised the lamp from her chest and swept its light across the broken floor and the raw wall. The last quake had torn the stone aside and cleared what had once been hidden. A gap yawned where no doorway had been. Beyond it, only dark.

She tried the radio.

"Esme to Max. Esme to Santos. Copy."

Only her own voice came back from the speaker. Small. Tinny. Alone.

She took stock. Water enough. Some food. Spare batteries for lamp and meter. A small power pack. Rope. Tape. First aid. The little folding shovel she had never needed until now. The calm her hands always found in tight places came to her. She rolled her shoulders to bleed away the shakes.

The beam caught a line of stone on her right. Tight-set blocks. In one run a smear of pale mortar. Fingers found old tool marks and the shallow polish that a passage earns when hands brush it for years. She felt for a draught.

There. Not much. A cool thread of air, low to the floor, running from somewhere deeper and out through the wreck. Air went somewhere.

"Alright," she told the dark. "I am still here."

She tied a light line round her waist and paid it out. Chalk marks at shoulder height every ten paces. E and the date. She did not rush.

The walls pressed close, forcing her shoulders in tight, then fell away into a low passage that bent left and down. The floor changed beneath her boots, from loose fall to a smooth skin buried under dust. She took a dozen cautious steps and stopped.

Tool marks.

A groove where feet had worn the stone. To her left, at the height of a hand, a row of shallow cups cut into the wall. Lamps had stood here once. She brushed one with her glove and felt something crumble. The brittle ghost of a wick.

She moved on.

The air cooled and thickened with damp. The beam of her lamp ran ahead, found a turn, and climbed a plane of worked stone. A single slab rose in a tight frame of smaller blocks. The face was smooth, deliberate. She tilted the beam low and let it skim the surface until it caught a cut line.

A circle with a triangle inside. The base struck hard, the apex canted slightly left.

Esme froze.

Esme frowned, searching her memory. That mark, she'd seen it before. It didn't belong here. Slowly the name surfaced, like something rising through sand. Nebit. The architect. She remembered poring over brittle scrolls in the Cairo Museum during her Abu Simbel project, his name inked in the margins as if someone had tried to erase it. She'd followed it through other temples too, each time finding just enough to know he'd mattered, and that someone hadn't wanted him remembered.

She pressed her fingertips to the cut. The truth was cold and certain. This was no cave of fire or water. This was shaped. Claimed. Someone had cut this place and left their mark.

The ground lurched.

Stone screamed as the ridge shook hard, throwing her against the slab. Dust poured in waves. Pebbles hammered her shoulders. The floor rolled like the deck of a storm ship.

Then came the roar, deep, final, like the voice of the earth itself. The ceiling split with a crack that shook the air from her chest. Blocks tore free and crashed down in a cascade. The sound was not stone on stone, but thunder trapped underground.

Boulders struck the passage mouth with brutal force, rolling and grinding against one another until sparks spat in the dark. Dust billowed, choking, stinging her eyes, filling her mouth with the taste of lime and grit. The lamp flickered, weak against the storm, and then steadied.

She turned. Where the passage had been was now a wall of jagged rock, wedged tight. No light came through. No sound carried beyond the rubble.

The way out was gone.

chapter 20:
Tides of Deception

“Sails. Two, north by east, bearing down.”

Long low hulls, narrow on the water. Banks of oars moved like the legs of a centipede. No sound carried yet, only a rhythm in the water where blades bit and lifted and bit again. Prows carved to cruel points. Men in two lines, shields ready, helmets black with pitch. A strip of black cloth snapped at the prow, painted with a hyena's grin-Zarek's their captain mark.

He was known only as Zarek. A name that carried more weight than any crown. In the ports of Agadir, along the sun-burned harbours of Byblos, even across the distant markets of Crete, the whisper of his title was enough to still conversation. Some said he had once served as a sailor in the fleet of Ramesses II, a Maltese helmsman who turned his back on his land and found his fortune in the lawless channels of the western sea. Others swore he had drowned twice and come back, salt still clinging to his eyes. None agreed on his past, but all agreed on what he became.

He called his band the Water Hyenas. Not thieves, not cutthroats, but men and women broken by the world, bakers, servants, fishermen, slaves. Zarek took them from the gutters and taught them to fight as wolves fight the night. Under his command they learned the sea as a weapon: the wind as ambush, the tide as trap. He drilled them like soldiers, fed them like kings, and promised them spoils instead of salvation. When his ships came out of the fog, it was already too late.

He was a big man, shoulders like quarried stone, hands thick from rope and blade. A scar cleaved his cheek from temple to jaw, the mark of a Nile boarding raid gone wrong. His eyes were pale, like sun-glare on water, and in their stillness lay a promise: mercy was for priests. Evil followed him as shadow follows flame, and yet those who served him spoke of a strange code. He killed without hesitation, but he never betrayed his crew.

He looted temples but spared the poor. He could cut a throat or save a starving child in the same hour, guided only by a creed of his own making, honour among the drowned.

In Agadir his legend grew to myth. He taxed the harbour masters, dictated prices, and held the wine traders hostage to his favour. The Water Hyenas became a fleet, painted black below the waterline, each prow carved with the jaw of a laughing beast. They struck merchant convoys from Cadiz to Sardinia, vanished before the alarm bells finished ringing, and melted back into the labyrinth of island coves that only he knew.

Those who met him ashore remembered the voice most of all, low, deliberate, with the calm of a man who already expected to die. He wore his scars as trophies, his silence as weapon.

Zarek had never known defeat.

"Stations," Abdiel said. "Lines clear. Keep her moving. No panic."

The crew moved as one. Buckets of sand by the ladders. Jars of water along the passage to the galley door in case flame took hold there. The spare yard hauled forward to stiffen the bow. Strong hands took up long spars. The archers checked bowstrings and the resin that would make fire cling if fire must answer fire.

Imbu tied a strip of cloth round his right wrist, not as a charm but so he could feel it when the air turned to smoke. He tested the edge of his sica, then the weight of the short spear he carried for close work.

He touched the bandage at Khamariti's side with the back of his fingers, a silent question.

"It will hold," Khamariti said.

"You will stay behind the mast," Imbu told him.

"I will keep behind the mast until the wind changes," Khamariti answered, his mouth tightening into something that was not quite a smile.

At the helm Abdiel shifted the rudder a hand's breadth and trimmed the sail. The trader surged, but the effort was vain. The two war boats closed like jaws. Their oars thrashed the sea into froth, driving them forward with brutal rhythm. Spears rose and fell as the men called out in rough unison.

Abdiel's voice carried across the deck. "They are too fast. The wind is ours, but it is not enough."

The trader pitched and groaned as he forced her across the swell, searching for a path that might buy a few more breaths of freedom. For a moment she seemed to slip ahead, sails swollen, prow cutting sharp through the chop. But the raiders adjusted, splitting their courses. One swept toward her bow, the other angled for her stern. The trap was closing.

chapter 21:
First 100 Days

The first hundred days of Raymond Hope's presidency were not a gentle turn of the wheel but a hard swing of the rudder. He arrived with a landslide at his back and set about refitting the machinery of power to match his creed. The moves were swift and deliberate: new heads at the FBI, Homeland Security, and the CIA; a shortlist for the Supreme Court prepared with an eye to reshaping the law for a generation. It was not merely a change of management. It was a new doctrine.

Late one evening in the Oval Office, beneath the stern scrutiny of old portraits, Hope sat with his chief of staff, Sean Riley. A single lamp washed the room in amber.

"Sean, everything is falling into place," Hope said, voice low, almost satisfied. "The new directors are exactly the people we need. They understand the mission."

Riley, who had spent a lifetime weighing costs before gains, inclined his head. "The confirmations were quick, Mr President. That is strength on display. But the Court is different. The nominations will draw fire. Public opinion may turn if we look as though we are remaking the country in a night."

"Controversy is the price of change," Hope replied. "The judges are pivotal. We are laying foundations. If there is risk, it is calculated. Legacies are not built by caution."

They turned to schooling. Daily prayer. New materials. A recast civic and moral frame.

"We are steering the country back to a moral compass," Hope said. His tone left no room for dispute.

Riley did not flinch. "The line between church and state is contested ground. The decision to remove LGBTQ awareness sessions has already polarised debate. The backlash is real."

Hope rose and walked to the window, hands behind his back. "I know exactly what sits on the scales. Real change is never welcomed by those invested in the old order. We lead, Sean. We do not drift."

He paused, choosing the blade and not the club. "Heard plainly, Scripture names wrong and right. Leviticus speaks starkly. We are not a country of stoning. We are not taking lives. But moral injunctions do not cease to have meaning because centuries pass." He turned then, expression set. "We will not mete out death. But if this nation is to be cleansed and set straight, we may have to consider prison for those who make a banner of defiance."

Riley held his gaze. "One step at a time, sir. You have already reversed Sunday trading laws. That alone has brought people onto the streets. If we force criminal penalties on sexuality this term, the reaction could be catastrophic."

Silence hummed in the vented air.

Riley shifted to tactics. "There is another path. We can move a blasphemy bill. It will be contentious, but not as divisive as criminalising private lives. It frames us as champions of faith without fracturing the coalition we need for everything else."

Hope sat again. He laced his fingers, thinking in straight lines. "Very well. Advance the blasphemy bill. And prepare a push for additional prison funding. We will be seen to strengthen order, not simply to preach it."

He added, as benediction, "Second Chronicles promises healing when a people turn from wickedness. We should make it clear we intend to be instruments of that healing."

"The votes look promising," Riley said. "But we pace ourselves. Control is lost when the tempo runs away from you."

Hope nodded, then pivoted with the impatience that often followed his concessions. "Tomorrow, we start on tariffs. Any country that refuses to uphold Christian values will pay at the border."

Riley did not hide his alarm. "Sir, that list includes much of Europe, China, India, half the world. Supply chains will buckle. Markets will slide."

"Markets fall and rise," Hope said, cool and dismissive. "There is profit in both movements."

They stood. Decisions hung in the air like smoke. Riley braced for the week ahead, knowing how the narrative would have to be framed to hold. Hope stared again at the window, where Washington's lights flattened to a haze. They were steering into weather.

In that same weather, a darker current had begun. Under Hope's authority the FBI had opened a covert operation shaped by old ghosts. The new Director, Vic Johnson, Bible Belt surety wrapped in Bureau steel, took the brief as a crusade. Files multiplied. Lives were pulled apart, not at random but by design.

Riley lingered at the door. "There is something else, Mr President," he said quietly. "The Bureau has begun deep background on selected members of Congress. They are trawling personal histories, finances, alliances, especially in the opposition. Traps have been laid. Two congressmen and a senator have already been offered the choice to resign or face scandal and charges."

The words thinned the air. Hoover's shadow needed no recitation.

Hope did not move at first. When he turned from the window, his voice was almost gentle. "Make sure none of this touches us. There must be no fingerprints. We will use cunning and restraint, not brute force."

Riley bowed his head once. The path was set. He would walk it with care.

In the days that followed, the inboxes swelled. It was Riley's job to sift. Among the requests, memos, and pleas from governors and police chiefs were the submissions that funded ambition: research grants, new fellowships, partnerships with universities at home and abroad.

Afternoon sun laid neat rectangles across Riley's desk as he sorted the latest batch. Two tidy stacks: domestic proposals to the right, international collaborations to the left, Canada, the United Kingdom, Singapore, South Korea. He had marked the ones that met the administration's new criteria and the ones that would need guidance to meet it.

Hope came in, jacket off, tie loosened.

"Sir," Riley said, tapping the piles. "These are the current programmes. Home institutions here. Joint projects there."

"Make the criteria clear," Hope said. "It is not only compliance I want. It is alignment."

"Understood. I will call the university heads myself. We will present this as an opportunity to align, not a threat."

Hope paused at the door. "Watch the overseas partnerships. We need them, but they bind us to other people's values. There must be no anti-Christian rhetoric anywhere in work we fund."

"There may be protests," Riley said. "Possibly riots on some campuses."

"Speak to the chiefs of police," Hope answered, without hesitation. "Resolve must be visible. Blackouts on news coverage where necessary. National security orders if editors resist."

When Hope had gone, Riley exhaled once and reached for the next folder. He had learned to live inside these contradictions.

One proposal drew his eye. Broader than most. Thick annexes. A budget that glowed. He laid the summary page on top as Hope returned.

"This one is notable," Riley said. "The lead is a Canadian university, but federal money supports it. The principal investigator is Professor Lex Mullin, New Yorker, Maplewood University, Ontario. Partners at Whitmore University in the Appalachians and Liverpool in the United Kingdom."

Hope skimmed, then looked up. "Any creed hidden in it."

"None on paper," Riley said. "Marine geology, archaeology, they are at sea now, out of Cádiz."

"What is their quarry."

"Atlantis," Riley said. The word landed with a mixture of folklore and ambition. "They say the work is strictly scientific. It may drift into Greek theology in the commentary, but the research itself is sound."

Hope's mouth tilted. "A city of unbelievers struck down, perhaps. As Sodom was. God gives and God takes away."

"Amen," Riley said, because it cost nothing and smoothed much.

"Keep close watch on this project," Hope said. "It is nothing to us if it yields only lectures and papers. It becomes something if it moves the public mind."

Riley nodded. He added a red tab to the folder and placed it at the top of his left-hand stack.

By the week's end the programme of the first hundred days had sharpened to a point. The nominations stood. The blasphemy bill moved to committee. Draft tariff schedules were redrawn overnight at the Department of Commerce. The covert Bureau campaign widened its circle and changed a few careers in the space of a phone call. Police chiefs received crisp instructions couched as national security. University presidents took careful notes and asked careful questions.

Hope slept less and seemed to need it less. In meetings he spoke in declarative sentences that turned discussion into direction. In public he blended the language of restoration with the language of power. In private, with Riley, he listened, pushed, yielded, and then pushed again.

Riley kept his ledger, literal and mental. He tracked votes, headlines, donor moods, the price of wheat and oil, the heat of the street. He stacked his memos so that the most dangerous requests came with a path out attached. He cooled things where he could. He made sure the machinery did not burn itself.

In the small hours, when the building thinned to guards and ghosts, he sometimes thought of Hoover's files and of old lines that had been crossed by men who had convinced themselves that they were saving the country from its enemies. He would stand at the window a moment, then return to his chair and read on.

Hope, for his part, believed he had been sent to place the republic back on its plinth. He quoted Scripture to give shape to his ends and history to give them weight. He could be cold in pursuit of them. He could also be moved. When the letters arrived from parents who thanked him for Sunday rest or from veterans who saluted the new resolve, he read them to the end.

The hundred days closed not with a speech but with a list: what had been done, what had been set in motion, what would not be stopped now even if the hand on the wheel changed. The country felt the shift as one feels a weather front. Some breathed easier. Some could not catch their breath at all.

On Riley's desk, at the very top of the left-hand stack, the Atlantis folder waited with a neat red tab. He lifted it again, as if it were lighter than it had been the day before. Somewhere beyond Cádiz a ship traced lines across a dark sea, hunting an old story. In Washington, another story was being written in bright rooms and long corridors, its pages already heavy with consequence.

chapter 22:
Warriors of the Fiery Sky

The sea had gone glassy in the false dawn. A pale band of light clung to the horizon, neither night nor day, the moment sailors feared most. From the gloom came the hiss of arrows. They cut the air with a sharp whistle, the first volley arcing towards the Phoenician vessel. Shafts struck rail and deck, one clattering from a shield, another burying itself in the mast.

Abdiel growled at the helm. "They are measuring the distance."

The Thalassa's crew moved instinctively, ducking low, shields raised. They were not sailors or traders now but warriors. Years of sailing the open sea had honed them for this moment. Men hauled lines tight, others crouched over bundles of earthen jars waiting for the order.

The second volley came heavier, black shapes falling like rain. One man cried out and pitched backwards, an arrow lodged in his shoulder. The rest held.

"Prepare the firepots!" Abdiel's shout cut through the din.

Leather-aproned sailors ran to the stores. They lifted clay jars filled with pitch, sulphur, and oil, wicked things that breathed fire at the first kiss of air. Hands moved fast, practised, each man knowing his part in the dance. They stood grim-faced, ready to hurl destruction.

On the stern, a chosen few wound slings in slow arcs. The creak of leather grew to a hum, then a whine as they loosed. Firepots lifted into the brightening sky, twisting trails of smoke behind them, and fell upon the nearest marauder.

The first jar burst against planking. Fire leapt up, yellow at the base, orange at the tips, a thing alive. Screams followed. More pots sailed, some striking, others vanishing into the sea in bursts of steam. The battle had begun.

"Steady," Abdiel barked. "Target their deck, make them burn before they reach us!"

Again, the slings sang. More jars lifted, burst, ignited. Enemy decks blossomed with fire. The smell of burning pitch overpowered the brine, choking men on both sides.

Still the water hyenas came on. Long, narrow hulls drove fast across the water, oars biting deep. Black sails strained. Painted prows cut through smoke.

Zarek the Marauder stood at their head, a wolfish grin carved on his face. His men beat weapons on shields, the rhythm carrying across the waves like drums of war.

"Boarding hooks!" Abdiel snapped. "Prepare for the clash!"

The crews braced as grapnels flew. Iron bit wood. Ropes pulled taut. Hulls shuddered together. Planks dropped with a thump. The gap closed.

"Board!" Abdiel roared.

Imbu went first. He hit the enemy deck low, rolling through the legs of the first raider. His axe came up in a rising sweep, cutting through belly and rib. A second man swung down, Imbu met him with a backhand cut that split shoulder from chest. The deck was slick already, men shouting, steel ringing, the stench of fire and blood mixing in the choking air.

Phoenicians poured across behind him. For a moment numbers told against them, raiders pressing hard, blades flashing. But resolve bit deeper than fear. Every sailor who fell left a space another filled. They fought like men who knew there was nowhere left to run.

Zarek's eyes found Imbu. He shoved aside his own men and came straight for him, a broad cutlass in hand.

Imbu turned, meeting him square. Axe lifted, chest forward, no hesitation.

The clash was instant. Zarek swung hard, aiming to cut Imbu from collar to hip. Imbu slipped inside, shoulder ramming chest. The two men crashed together, the impact carrying even over fire and screaming. They grappled, blades scraping. Zarek snarled and drove a knee upward; Imbu twisted, taking the blow on his thigh, then answered with an elbow to the jaw.

The deck cleared around them, men fighting but watching too. This was no longer a melee, it was duel and judgement.

Khamariti, on the Phoenician ship's deck, leaned on the rail, breath shallow. His face was ashen. Imbu's warning earlier still echoed: never trust a calm sea. He gripped the timber, but his strength was lacking.

In the shadows near the foremast, Seneb had waited. The assassin's bow was strung, arrow notched, the moment chosen. Amid chaos, with eyes on Zarek and Imbu, no one would see a shaft meant for the architect. Seneb drew, breath stilled.

Khamariti staggered, his grip sliding from the rail.

The bowstring thrummed, stretched to its breaking point.

He felt it, the unmistakable pull of death aimed squarely at him.

His eyes darted sideways. Seneb. The bow.

The captain seized Seneb by the arm, spittle flying as he roared, "What are you waiting for? Shoot! The man in the rigging!"

Seneb aimed and loosed the arrow, the snap echoing across the deck.

When he turned back, Khamariti was gone.

Zarek struck again, blade flashing. Imbu ducked, answered with a savage hook of the axe. Steel split wood as the cutlass blocked. Sparks burst, smoke curling in their faces.

"You die here!" Zarek spat.

"Then you lead the way," Imbu said.

They closed, shoulder to chest, each straining for the other's throat. Sweat poured, fire roared, men circled but none dared step between. This was survival bound in flesh and steel.

Imbu shifted his weight, dropped a foot back, and twisted with the precision of a man who had fought a hundred times before. Zarek stumbled forward into the lock, his balance gone. In an instant Imbu's arm was across his throat, the corded muscles of his forearm crushing against windpipe and spine.

Zarek thrashed. His nails raked at Imbu's skin, his boots skidding in the blood pooling underfoot. His eyes bulged, veins standing like cords, his breath no more than a strangled rasp. Imbu's grip did not waver. The deck shuddered with the weight of the struggle, men frozen all around as if the world itself had paused to watch.

Then came the crack. Sharp. Final.

The sound echoed above the roar of the sea and the clash of weapons. Zarek went limp, his limbs flailing once before falling slack. Imbu held him a heartbeat longer, then let the body sag, dead weight heavy against his chest.

With a guttural roar he heaved the corpse high into the air. Blood streaked his arms, his face set in a mask of fury and triumph.

Every eye turned. The Water Hyenas faltered. Their blades hovered, no longer certain. For an instant they seemed carved from stone, caught between rage and fear.

Imbu's voice thundered across the deck. "This is your fate!"

He hurled Zarek's body down. The thud rang out like a drumbeat of doom.

Silence spread. One by one their weapons wavered. Knuckles slackened. Steel clattered on timber. The men who had leapt aboard with murder in their eyes now shrank back, their courage gone as if a rope had snapped inside them.

The fight bled out of them.

"Save the raiders ship, it will have valuable cargo!" Abdiel shouted. He pointed to the second ship, flames rising from its stern. The crew needed every hand. Without a pause, Imbu, and the others leapt overboard. Chilly water closed over their heads, salt biting at their throats. They struck out hard, arms burning, the clash of waves against their ears.

They hauled themselves up the side of the second hull where men fought to beat back the fire. Buckets passed hand to hand, chains of bodies throwing water, tearing at burning ropes, cutting sails before the blaze could run higher. Smoke poured across the waves, sparks flying like swarms of wasps.

Soaked, shivering, they joined the line without a word. Fire and sea met on the deck, and for a time nothing mattered but the fight to keep the ship alive.

Those who still lived backed away, palms raised, the smell of sweat and fear heavy in the air.

A third Hyena ship lingered on the horizon. Its crew had watched the fate of the other two and chose to hold back, waiting to see what would follow.

Imbu stood over the fallen, chest heaving, blood, and salt on his skin. He had not only broken a man. He had broken the will of them all.

The Phoenicians seized the moment, binding the wounded and casting the rest into the sea. The ship was theirs. Imbu turned back toward the Thalassa.

But Imbu's gaze turned at once to Khamariti. The architect had collapsed, grey-lipped, half folded to the deck. Infection. Imbu crossed the plank in strides and caught him before he fell further.

"Hold," he muttered.

Khamariti's eyes fluttered open. There was no fear there, only a depth Imbu could not name. Then the lids shut again.

He carried him back across, laying him gently near the mast. The crew gathered, whispering. They had seen Khamariti appear to recover from mortal wounds, now fever struck him. They had watched colour drain from his face. No one thought he would last the night.

Abdiel led the raid on the Hyena ships' holds, stripping them of their treasure and stowing it in his own. By the time the work was done, the third Hyena ship had slipped from sight.

But by morning the architect rose. His step was steady. His voice firm. He gave orders to mend sails, to bind planks, to honour the dead. Men stared in awe. No fever clung to him, no weakness bent him. He moved with the calm of one untouched by death itself.

Imbu watched longest. He had tended dying men, buried comrades, felt their last breaths on his skin. No man came back so quick. No man, save this one. The truth hardened inside him.

Khamariti was not as other men.

The sea rolled easy now, smoke trailing on the horizon where the Hyena ships burned. Yet the stillness carried weight. The crew whispered a new name for their passenger: healer, prophet, perhaps more.

And in the shadow of the mast, Imbu tightened his grip on the axe. He had saved the architect once. He would do so again. Whatever Khamariti truly was, Imbu would be his shield.

The voyage pressed on, but all aboard knew the night had changed them. Fire and blood had written a warning on the water. Enemies still watched from the dark coast, waiting their turn.

chapter 23:
Divine Mandate

The Oval Office lay in shadow, the late evening light spilling pale across the carpet and tracing the edges of the Resolute Desk. President Hope sat motionless, fingers pressed together, his eyes fixed on the sealed folder before him. The room carried the hush of history, its walls thick with the memory of decisions that had altered nations. Tonight, another was about to be made.

Across from him, Chief of Staff Riley and a cluster of senior advisors sat rigid in their chairs. They had seen the president fierce, they had seen him commanding, but rarely had they seen him so still. That stillness unsettled them more than any speech.

Hope broke the silence.

"Tonight, we bring America back to its foundation," he said, voice even yet strong enough to ripple across the room. "Not a foundation of compromise, but one rooted deeply in Christian truth." His hand fell lightly against the desk, a single thud that carried more weight than its sound.

Riley studied him carefully. Hope's rhetoric had grown sharper in recent weeks. Speeches once draped in political calculation now carried the cadences of prophecy. The advisors leaned forward almost unconsciously, drawn by the fire edging his tone.

"It is our duty," Hope continued, "to guide not only this nation, but the world. The time of drift has ended. We stand at the threshold of renewal, a renewal that will restore the soul of America and show others what true leadership looks like."

He rose from his chair, the motion slow, deliberate, his presence commanding the space. He crossed to the tall windows overlooking the White House lawn, and beyond it, the restless capital.

"Our forefathers built this land on Christian principle," he said, gesturing at the view as if it belonged to him. "We will not shrink from that heritage. We will live it. We will legislate it."

He turned sharply back to them. "I have been chosen. This is no accident, no political fluke. It is by divine calling that I lead now. As Moses was chosen to lead his people from bondage, so am I charged to guide this nation through its trials."

Riley exchanged a glance with Homeland Security Director Alvarez. Neither moved. They knew resistance in this room was futile.

Hope's eyes burned with intensity as he began to pace. "Consider the world around us. Climate collapse. Endless wars. Fertile lands falling to sand. Rising seas creeping over our coasts. These are not random misfortunes. They are signals. Catalysts. The Lord is reminding us that time is short."

He stopped, planting both hands on the back of a chair, leaning in. "We are not meant to endure passively. We are meant to lead. America is to be the instrument of renewal."

The words hung like a charge in the air.

On the desk lay a document bound in blue leather: The Proclamation of Faith. More than legislation, it was a manifesto. It ordered prayer restored in schools, mandated Christian symbols in public spaces, and directed public broadcasters to reserve hours for biblical teaching. Its provisions would ignite fury, lawsuits, and protests. But to Hope, it was a sacred script waiting to be spoken aloud.

He signed it with a stroke that cut the silence.

Across the city, networks scrambled. By dawn, headlines ignited: America Returns to God. President Signs Proclamation of Faith. Support surged among evangelicals and conservative strongholds, while fury erupted in universities and urban centres. On every channel, debate burned. America had split along a fault line. Hope, watching from the Oval Office, betrayed no flicker of doubt.

Within hours, the European Union convened in emergency session. The grand chambers buzzed with hurried translation and sharp arguments.

The German Chancellor spoke first. "America is our ally, but we cannot condone this merging of state and church. It sets a precedent that undermines everything we stand for."

The French President leaned forward, voice low but firm. "We must respond carefully. America's influence is vast. Hope is persuasive. If we act, we act as one. United, or not at all."

A draft resolution took shape: a declaration affirming Europe's commitment to secular governance and religious freedom, its language diplomatic but edged. It would stand as a rebuke, even if cloaked in courtesy.

In the White House, Hope pressed further. Envoys were dispatched to capitals across the globe, urging allies to adopt similar religious laws.

"This is a crusade for our time," he told his Secretary of State. "Not a war of swords, but of spirit. A sacred mission."

The results were predictable. Leaders nodded politely, offered smiles for the cameras, but behind closed doors expressed alarm. Few wished to follow Hope down this path. Privately, their language was blunt: destabilising, authoritarian, dangerous.

Elsewhere, in a secure villa on the Swiss border, a quite different meeting unfolded. Around a polished oak table sat twelve figures, magnates of industry, media barons, architects of technology. They held no office, yet their influence rivalled nations. The meeting was chaired by an American magnate called DeWalt.

Hope's rise had unsettled them. Not because of faith, but because of control.

They spoke in quiet tones, their strategy already forming. Funding would pour into global campaigns for diversity, secularism, and pluralism. Films, adverts, social movements, all seeded, all subtle. Protests would ignite without ever knowing their patrons.

"Counter zeal with narrative," said one.

"Flood the networks with images of inclusion," said another.

"And let him choke on the world's reaction."

"A coup," said DeWalt, but the idea was quickly brushed aside.

Weeks later, the capital itself shook. From the Lincoln Memorial to the Mall, a vast rally swelled: Christians, Jews, Muslims, atheists, Buddhists, gay and straight, black, and white. They carried banners of unity, not faith. Their chants rolled like thunder, captured by every camera, streamed to every device.

The air trembled with song and fury. Fires flared in braziers, symbols of resistance.

Hope watched from the Oval Office, the feed flickering across a bank of monitors. For a moment, his reflection in the glass seemed framed by the flames outside.

"Let them protest," he said quietly. "The righteous path is never easy. But it is ordained."

Riley stood behind him, face unreadable. He had seen leaders consumed by conviction before. Conviction was fire; it could illuminate, or it could burn everything to ash.

As night fell in Washington, the president sat alone at the Resolute Desk. The Proclamation of Faith lay open before him, the ink not yet dry. Outside, chants rose like a tide battering the walls of power. He gave the order to call in the National Guard.

But in Hope's mind the board was already set. The pieces were moving. The renewal had only begun, and if there were casualties, which was the choice of heaven, not his.

chapter 24:
Echoes of Agadir

The Phoenician vessel neared the shores of Agadir under the steady hand of Thalassa captain, Abdiel. His crew cast weighted lines into the cerulean depths, probing for reefs and sandbars. The soundings were not merely precaution but ritual, the seaman's respect for the sea's unpredictability. The lines traced the shape of the seabed as faithfully as the stars above traced their course.

Caution slowed their advance but marked them as masters of the mariner's ancient art.

Canoes darted from shore, paddled by children and men alike. Faces alight with curiosity and welcome met the weary crew, a balm after the savage clash with the Water Hyenas. Agadir was not yet the city of stone it would one day become, but already it thrived as a place where desert and sea met in commerce and exchange.

Atlas peaks guarded the land to the east. The Atlantic stretched endless to the west. Agadir's markets smelled of cumin and dried fish, of oil and leather. Adobe walls, baked by sun, held cool rooms within. In the alleys, colours flashed: bolts of cloth, bronze trinkets, polished shell. For Khamariti, the city was a gateway to wisdom. For Imbu, it was proof that resilience took many shapes.

Zamurus's agents busied themselves with trade: Phoenician craftwork exchanged for goat skins, grain, salt, and amber. But Khamariti's eye turned elsewhere. He sought not coin but knowledge. Imbu shadowed him as a shield in a place that welcomed strangers but never ceased weighing them.

Among the scholars gathered in Agadir, one commanded particular respect. Alim, an elder robed in desert hues, fingers heavy with rings etched in old symbols. Age had dimmed his body but sharpened his voice. Beside him moved his daughter, Zarah, sharp-eyed, measured, carrying scrolls and speaking when her father allowed.

Khamariti had studied fragments of Alim's writings. They were precise yet incomplete, as though truths had been veiled by the safer dress of myth. That absence gnawed at him.

When Khamariti and the Amazigh elder finally spoke, it was less a meeting than a contest of veiled truths. In the library's close air, amid leather bindings and oil smoke, Alim spread a parchment across the table. It was no merchant's chart, but a coastline marked with exacting detail. His nail traced a jagged line through Asif N'Imurig.

"The Great Shaking," he said, "tore away land from sea. What remains is fragile."

The murmur in the room confirmed the gravity.

Khamariti leaned close. The map matched fragments he had pieced from fishermen's tales, but fuller, sharper. Alim's words carried the cadence of memory preserved across generations. He spoke of Tafukt Taneggarut, the great fire mountain veiled in cloud; of patterns in the stars that mirrored upheavals in earth and ocean.

"This is no solitary disaster," Alim warned. "It is a reminder written into the bones of the world."

Khamariti felt the invisible weave: lands and peoples linked by catastrophe, their fragility bound to the same forces.

When the others had gone, Alim's voice softened. "I am too old to chase truths across the sea. My bones ache with each step. Promise me only that you will return and speak what you find."

Khamariti studied the elder with steady eyes. He heard not frailty but hesitation, and hesitation was a danger they could not afford. His reply came measured, deliberate.

"You have hidden truths before, Alim. Scrolls scraped and written over. Gods added where facts would have served. You call it duty. I call it concealment. I cannot risk such compromise. You must come with me. No one else holds what you know."

Shock crossed the elder's face. His gaze flicked to Imbu, searching for an ally, but Imbu stood motionless, his expression carved in stone.

Alim's shoulders sank. For a heartbeat he looked less a scholar and more a man cornered. "You would force me?" he asked.

"I would," Khamariti said, his voice low but unyielding. "Because the truth we seek will outlive us all. And I will not see it bound in silence."

Alim's lips parted, then closed. He bowed his head at last, defeat mingled with a bitter acceptance. "Better to be accused of shaping truth than of burying it," he whispered. "But pay attention, this voyage may cost me my last breath. Very well. I will go."

A shadow of calculation crossed Zarah's face. She had long lived with the cost of her father's choices. Now she weighed what his exile might mean for them both.

Preparations began at once. Alim and Zarah were given cabins. Agents of Zamurus stayed behind to plant a trading post, their faces unreadable as the ship's hull groaned free of its moorings.

The vessel slid into open water, its flanks shadowed by canoes. Islanders swarmed close, chanting blessings, hands lifted high, prayers to guard the crew against whatever awaited them.

Alim stood at the rail, his cloak drawn tight against the salt spray. His eyes clung to the receding shore with the ache of a man who feared he would never see it again. The line of land blurred, then vanished, leaving only the endless swell of sea.

At dawn Arganij rose from the horizon, a barren blade of wind and stone. Beyond it the ocean changed. As they neared Tafukt Taneggarut, the sea bubbled with sulphur. Dead fish floated in their hundreds, bellies white in the morning light. From the depths came a groan, a dull rumble like the earth grinding its own bones.

Men dropped to their knees, voices low with prayers to gods of desert, sea, and sky. Fear passed among them like fire through dry grass.

Khamariti turned to Imbu. "And you, Imbu, who do you call upon in such times?"

"My people honour Simbi," Imbu said. "Spirits of water, forest, and air. We give them food and song. They guard us when the world shakes."

Khamariti's gaze held on the volcanic peak ahead, cloud and fire curling from its crown. "Perhaps the earth listens closer to such spirits than to gods who stay silent."

Behind him, Alim gripped the rail, his knuckles white. The chant of the crew rose and fell, but he heard only the rush of the waves and the pounding of his own heart. He knew then, with a clarity that hollowed him, that this voyage was no passage out and back again. It was a severing. The sea was swallowing his past, and he might never walk his homeland again.

The ship pressed on into the realm of the Fire Islands, the sea alive beneath them with warnings.

chapter 25:
Veils of Fire and Mist

The sea had deepened to a darker shade by midday. The men leaned on the rail and stared at the horizon. Out of the haze, sharp peaks cut through the sky. Tenerife rose in an extensive line of slopes that carried the eye upward to its crown. At the summit Mount Teide breathed thin threads of smoke. The wind carried the smell across the water, sharp as flint, bitter as ash.

On the mountain's side a seam of molten rock crept downward. It glowed red against the black slopes, slow yet relentless. Where it touched the sea, towers of steam shot skyward. The explosion of water and fire shook the ship beneath their feet. Columns of vapour rose high and were torn apart by the wind.

The sailors said nothing. Their silence was heavier than words.

Imbu's gaze stayed fixed on the mountain. He watched a boulder tumble, bounce, and vanish into the sea. The ship trembled again. He spoke softly, almost to himself. "It is as if the earth melts. Listen to the hiss when fire touches water."

Khamariti stood at his side, his face calm where others were afraid. "It melts, then it hardens stronger than before. That is its way. Break, mend, endure."

Abdiel had braced himself at the stern. He gave a short command to the helmsman. The ship kept her course along the spectacle but stayed well clear of danger. His eyes stayed flat, his voice without wonder. "A sight to behold," he said. "And a sight to leave."

Evening pressed its weight across the sea. The sky lost its colour and dimmed to iron. To the west another island rose from the water. The sailors gave it a name with unease, speaking low as if not to wake it. Asif N'Imurig. La Palma. The name was not needed. Its dark slopes spoke for themselves.

Three canoes were lowered into the dusk. Each carried three men and packs wrapped in oilcloth. Bread, dried fish, skins of water.

The oars dipped without sound, leaving thin seams behind them. On deck Zarah stood at the rail with Alim.

"Will they be welcomed?" she asked.

"They will be watched," her father answered.

Imbu stood close, watchful, silent. Since Agadir he had left no man in doubt. Eyes that lingered on Zarah soon found other things to look at.

Night settled. Mist slid from the island and stretched across the water. The ship rocked like a creature at rest. In the pool of lamplight by the mainmast Zarah and Imbu spoke. She asked about his home. He answered plainly, without performance. Forests that sang when the wind was kind. Rivers that shifted their paths after floods. He spoke as if setting tools in a line. She listened, then offered small truths in return: how her father wrote shapes in the air before he laid them on parchment, how he mouthed words from languages he would never admit he knew.

Before dawn one canoe returned. The men's hair and beards were beaded with droplets. The bowman spoke at once. "No settlement at the landing," he said. "Black sand. A stream of fresh water. But the air tastes wrong."

Imbu drew a breath through his nose and felt the sting in his throat. "Brimstone," he said.

Khamariti tore strips from his tunic and pressed them into Imbu's hands. "Tie these across your mouth and nose. If the gas is strong it will choke."

By dawn the ship moved along the northern coast. The men stared at cliffs that rose sheer and smooth, untouched by time. Elsewhere the forest pushed right down to the tide, branches dipping into the sea. Birds moved in restless clouds. Nothing else stirred.

At the southern end, the land bared its wound. A ridge rose like a blade. At its base, the sea bit hard. Huge sections had fallen away. The pale scars shone where the skin of the island had split fresh.

Khamariti pulled Alim to the rail. "These faces are young," he said. "Fresh torn."

Alim gripped the wood, peering over. "Not weathered. A fall, sudden, not slow." He laid his charts across a coil of rope and set his dividers. His voice dropped to a murmur. "It is a guess, but perhaps one fifth of the island has gone."

Khamariti's thoughts turned dark. "A mass that size drags the sea down, then throws it back. A wave born like that would strike hardest in narrow waters. Harbours would be torn apart."

Abdiel listened but kept his eyes on the sea. "There is a Mycenaean tale," he said. "A surge that split land at the Pillars of Hercules. It opened the way for the Great Sea. But that was long ago."

Khamariti looked at him. "Then we go ashore. We read the memory of the island."

The party was chosen at once: Khamariti, Imbu, Alim, Zarah, and three steady sailors. They packed bread, fish, skins of water, rope, wooden wedges, two picks, a ladder lashed with planks. Food for five days.

The beach was black sand that squeaked underfoot. A trickle of fresh water slid into a pool before reaching the sea. Mist clung low in the trees. The forest glowed with a green the desert would never understand.

No voices. No dogs. No smoke. Only the sigh of the wind.

They found paths at once. Cleared by hands, not animals. Stones lifted feet above the mud. Steps were cut into slopes so steep even Imbu used his hands.

Zarah touched bark polished smooth. "Hands rested here," she said. "Not long ago." Imbu saw nothing but believed her.

In a clearing they found low walls and broken bowls. Zarah lifted a shard, its edge glazed by fire hotter than any kiln. She set it down with care.

Alim brushed moss from a slab. Tiny grooves ran across it, forming lines and chevrons. "Currents," he whispered. "Not wind. Sea. And here, stars. The same constellations but marked in their way."

Khamariti closed his eyes, mapping knowledge. "Not simple men. They watched and they kept."

The path climbed higher. A grove opened. Wildflowers pushed through old ash. At the centre stood a monolith. Its face was cut with patience.

Light caught the grooves. An island. A line down its spine. A hand pressing. A broken part sliding into the sea. Waves radiating outward.

Zarah covered her mouth. "They saw it."

Alim nodded. His hand hovered over the smaller shapes, figures with arms raised in terror. He pressed his lips together. "They carved this as a warning," he said. His fingers traced the lines of bodies falling, the marks cut deep and frantic. "Many died when the mountain gave way. They carved the dead into the stone so no one would forget how the slope collapsed into the sea."

The ridge trembled. Pebbles skittered. Dust rose.

"The mountain is alive," Alim said.

The climb took them two days. At first the path wound gently among pines and scrub, the air heavy with resin and the sound of wind moving through branches. But as they rose, the slope grew harsh. Loose stone slid underfoot. The ground tilted to cruel angles that forced them to lean into the rock, fingers clawing at holds. Packs cut into their shoulders. Breath came shallow in the thinning air.

By night they found narrow ledges and scraped hollows where they huddled together. The mountain never slept. It creaked and shivered under them, the stone shifting in its sleep. Dust drifted down from above. Pebbles ticked across the rock like beads scattered by unseen hands. Even in the dark they could hear the mountain breathe, long sighs that rolled from deep inside.

The second day was worse. The slope grew raw, stripped of trees. Only black rock and sharp ridges remained, marked with scars from old slides. The sun beat against their backs. Sweat stung their eyes. More than once the ground shifted, sending small avalanches of stone rattling away down the flank.

When the first true tremor struck it came like a hammer blow. The ridge heaved under them, a deep groan rising through their feet. Zarah slipped, the path crumbling beneath her heel, but Imbu caught her arm and dragged her back before she slid into the void. Stones thundered down the slope. A crack opened along the ridge above them and closed again with a sound like thunder trapped in stone.

They pressed on, searching for shelter. Each tremor brought the same fear, that the whole flank might give way beneath them. Khamariti studied the slope, his eyes narrowing. "There will be hollow ground," he said. "This mountain has broken before. The slide leaves scars, and sometimes it leaves caverns."

His words proved true. Ahead, half hidden by a jagged lip of rock, a black hollow yawned. The path led towards it, as though the mountain itself guided them. Another tremor shook the ridge. Stones clattered. The mountain groaned again, louder this time, as if warning them to move faster.

They reached the opening. The cavern mouth gaped wide, cut into the ridge by violence long past. Cool air drifted out, dry and still, carrying the scent of ash and dust. They stepped inside.

The light of their torches struck the walls. Basalt rose in sweeping arcs, frozen waves of black stone. The ribs of the cavern curved like the vault of a temple, vast and echoing. Columns of rock leaned where molten stone had once hardened in place, stilled in the moment of collapse.

Khamariti ran his hand across the wall, the surface glassy and smooth. "When the flank gave way," he said, his voice low, "the slide tore open a chamber. Magma cooled too fast, trapped in motion. The mountain swallowed its own fire and left this behind."

They stood silent, their torches throwing long shadows against the black stone. The world outside trembled, but here in the heart of the ridge they felt both shelter and awe. The cavern was no accident. It was the mountain's memory, carved by fire and collapse, waiting to be found.

Khamariti stopped, transfixed. His voice was low, reverent. "No hand of man could risk such a span. Yet it stands."

He dropped to his knees. Charcoal scratched across bark as he sketched the arches and ribs. "What the mountain built by chance, men must build by design. Here is balance. Here is strength. The pattern of endurance."

The ridge growled above them. Dust fell, but the cavern held steady.

Khamariti looked up once more, eyes shining. "This is revelation."

The ground shook harder. Rocks split from the ridge. The cavern mouth shivered as if alive. Outside, the mountain roared.

They stood on the threshold of the cavern as the island trembled beneath them.

chapter 26:
Asif N'Imurig

The ridge shook until grit danced in the torch light. Then the sound rolled away across the island and left a soft hiss in its place. Ash fell from the roof of the cavern in a thin silver rain. The flame steadied. For a time no one spoke.

Imbu listened with his head tilted, the way a hunter listens for the last footfall. When nothing more came, he lowered his shoulders and looked to Khamariti. Zarah had one hand on Alim's sleeve. The old scholar's breath was short but even. The echo of the quake went on inside the stone like a low drum.

"We go down," Khamariti said. "Slow and sure. Stay to clean rock, not to loose ash. If the ground speaks again, we move for shelter. The stench indicates danger."

They doused the torch until only a coal remained to carry fire. Outside the cavern mouth the air had the taste of a struck coin. Ash lay over everything. It softened the edges of the ridge and filled each footprint as soon as it was made. The world was grey on grey. Only the plume over Teide held colour, a red heart wrapped in smoke.

Imbu tied a cloth across Alim's mouth and laid another over his own face. Zarah did the same. Khamariti wetted the cloths from a skin and pressed them firm. The first steps were cautious. Then the path took their feet, and they found a steady rhythm.

They moved in a line. Imbu went first with Alim on his back. Zarah carried the staff and the packs the old man could not hold. Two sailors took the rest. Khamariti held the rear to read the ground and to check each footfall. He called out hazards in a quiet voice that did not carry far. Loose stone to the left. A crack that ran across the path and then vanished under ash. A root that would trip an ankle. Few words. Enough.

The air scratched their throats. It stung the eyes and crept over the tongue. Sometimes the wind lifted, and they caught the scent beneath the ash. It was the sharp smell of brimstone. It came in a thin thread and then was gone. Each time it passed they tightened the cloths.

They moved past a low wall of rough blocks that had stood before the last fall of ash. The wall was now a soft curve, like the back of a beast asleep. Zarah brushed snow grey flakes from one stone and found a deep carved mark. She traced it with a finger. A simple sign. A hand with the palm up. It could have been a greeting or a warning. She let the ash fall back and covered it.

"Someone lived here," she said. There was no need to add that they had gone.

Far below the sea lay like a sheet of hammered lead. The cove where their ship had anchored was a darker notch in the line of the shore. Smoke did not yet rise from it. The sight gave Khamariti a small lift. He allowed himself one slow breath. Then he moved on.

They crossed a slope where a fall had torn old ground away and left the inside of the island bare. In the exposed face Khamariti read layers as if they were pages. Old ash, then older soil, then a seam of rock, then more ash. He pointed and spoke between breaths.

"The land keeps its story. Each layer a season. This line is a flood. This thick pale bed is a fall of ash from another age. Here, a thin dark strip with broken shell. The sea reached this height once. Then fell away."

Zarah looked and tried to see as he saw. The shapes refused to resolve. Then they did. The story rose from the face and sat plain on the slope. She almost laughed with relief.

Alim heard and smiled behind the cloth. His eyes were bright in his worn face. "Teacher," he said in a voice no louder than a whisper.

A gust came up the draw and made the ash dance. The ridge gave a small sigh. Pebbles went skimming. Imbu flattened a hand to the ground and waited. Nothing followed. He stood again and shifted the old scholar higher on his back.

"Another fifty steps," Khamariti said. "Then a rest and a drink."

They made those steps and came to a shoulder where scrub clung to stone and held the slope against the wind. Here the ash lay shallower. The air flowed cleaner. They took a little water. Zarah gave Alim small sips, slow and careful, and then wiped his lips with the back of her hand. He patted her wrist once and closed his eyes.

Imbu looked to the sea through a gap in the scrub. The cove lay in its notch. The ship rode as a dark shape against the pale wash. Even at this distance he could see a single figure on the quarterdeck who moved from rail to rail, watching the headlands. It would be Abdiel. The sight settled something in Imbu's chest.

They pushed on. The ground fell away in broad steps and then drew tight again to a spine. On the far side the drop was clean. It ran down to a gully where water had once worked, and then to a patch of black sand by a promontory of rock. A hawk crossed the grey air and vanished. No other life showed itself.

They were three turns above the hollow of the cove when the first sign reached them. It was not sound but a shift in the air. The ash carried a new taste—thicker, heavier, laced with smoke from wood and tar. It came in a single breath and then in a flood. It had taken the best part of a day to get down the mountain.

Imbu's head snapped up. He looked through a small break in the ridge towards the sea. A thin line of black rose into the wind. It was far at first. It thickened. It bent inland. Now they heard it as well. Not one sound but many, layered. Men shouting. Oars slapping. A cry that carried a note of alarm and then another. The crash and hiss of flame.

Zarah took a step as if she would run and then checked herself. Khamariti was already moving. There was no need to tell them to hurry. They hurried.

The path fell into a narrow defile. In places ash had drifted into long smooth backs that slipped under a heel. Imbu cut his steps clean. Zarah did the same. One sailor slipped, caught himself with both hands, and came up coughing with ash in his mouth. Khamariti hauled him straight and sent him on with a slap on the shoulder.

They came out on a ledge no wider than a man is long. The cove opened below them. The ship rode at anchor on a short line. Her stern swung to face the mouth of the inlet, then swung back. Men ran on her deck. Two watchmen waved arms from the headland. Three long boats were already clear of the point and were coming fast. Others were further off, but these three would arrive first.

On the lead boat men stood with jars in their hands. The wicks in the necks burned slow. Even from the ridge Zarah saw the pale flash of teeth as one grinned. Imbu felt his grip tighten on the haft of his spear until the wood cut his palm.

The first jar fell short and burst in the shallows. A dark slick spread on the water and caught fire in skipping patches. Buckets flew from Thalassa. Men dashed water over the line of flame and over the place where the slick reached for her hull. The second jar struck the rail and broke. Fire climbed the canvas as if it had waited all its life for this moment. The sail roared into light. The cry from the deck was not fear. It was anger.

Abdiel strode to the rail, stripped to the waist, his chest, and arms black with soot. He pointed to the cable and drew a slicing motion through the air. "Cut," he called, and though the words did not reach the ridge, the order was clear.

Axes flashed. The cable parted. Oars flew out. The ship drove under their push until she kissed sand hard and with a long groan. The shock threw men to their knees and scattered loose gear across the deck. Abdiel did not fall. He was already calling his next orders.

"Buckets to the fire. Slingers to the bow. Hooks ready. Keep the flame wet. Cut what you must. Save the ribs."

The third water hyena boat, hidden until now, striking in the dark while Thalassa lay at anchor, drove straight for the gangplank set to the sand. The men in it gave a long low sound in their throats, the sound a pack makes when it scents blood.

Abdiel left the quarterdeck and took the fight to the seam where ship and shore met. "Javelins," he said, and hands answered him. Light spears flew. The first raider took one through the shoulder and fell back into his boat. The man behind him leaped over him and kept coming.

Imbu drew one slow breath and then set Alim down behind a shoulder of rock. He placed Zarah there as well and put the staff in her hands. "Stay. Guard him," he said. He looked into her eyes to make sure she would obey. She nodded. There was no time for more. He ran with both sailors at his back.

Khamariti did not call him back. He knew what would happen if he did. He took Zarah's place beside Alim for the span of three breaths, checked the old man's cloth and his pulse at the neck, and then looked to the cove again. His mind worked. His hands were still. He chose.

He would go with Imbu. Zarah would hold the old scholar safe. She was not a child.

"Keep him in the lee," he said to her. "If the wind turns, wet your cloth again. If ash thickens, lie him on his side. We will draw the fight away." He took a spear from the nearest sailor and ran.

The slope to the beach was a ribbon of loose stone over hard earth. Imbu did not slow to choose his steps. He picked a line and trusted his feet. A raider saw him coming and turned to meet him with a short spear and a wide grin. The grin ended with a single crack as the axe took him across the temple. Imbu did not pause to watch him fall. He kept moving.

On the deck of the Thalassa, Abdiel met three men at the rail and put all three down with the work of a moment. He moved as a man moves who has no time for waste. There was no flourish. He struck and turned and struck again. Two of his own men fought at his shoulder. One went to a knee with a blade in his thigh and crawled clear. The other took a blow on his arm and kept his feet.

The boat that had tried to block the mouth now laid oars side and threw lines with hooks to the stern of the ship. Hooks bit, held, and men heaved. The stern slewed and opened a gap at the bow. Three raiders shoved their boat into that gap and leaped. The first man looked up to see a lead bullet fly from a sling and heave his brow in. He fell as if a hand had taken his legs at the knee.

Imbu ran and swam until reached the Thalassa and shimmied up the anchor chain. Two hyenas tried to board from a long boat. He had a spear and the habit of seeing where a force goes before it gets there. He let the first man come two steps and then shifted his weight and drove the butt of the spear into the man's shin. The man pitched forward and met the edge of the plank with his teeth. The second made a cut for his ribs. Imbu turned and took the blow across the shaft and felt it bite through to his skin. He stepped in, close enough that the other could not bring his arm back and shoved his palm under the man's jaw. The man staggered. A sailor behind Imbu finished him with a short hook to the throat.

The smell of burning canvas thickened. Flame ran where oil had found new timber. A handful of men formed a line from sea to deck.

They passed bucket after bucket in a rhythm that made no sense to the eye and yet saved the wood. Wet sail was rolled on the worst of the flame and hissed loud enough to kill other sounds for a breath at a time. Steam rose and carried ash with it.

On the far side two boats grounded on a bar. The crews threw themselves into the water to lighten their load and push forward. The sea took their feet out from under them and tumbled them. Slings from the stern found heads and ribs. A jar fell from a man's hands, broke on the gunwale, and threw flame across his chest. He went under and did not surface.

The new leader of the hyenas made a gesture with his hand that was small and exact. Three men broke left. Three broke rights. The rest bunched for the gangplank. Abdiel saw the gesture and answered with one of his own. The men on the bow opened a space and then closed it again like a mouth. They took the first two raiders who made it through and dropped them into the gap. The men behind could not stop and fell over them. Hooks met them there. Wood met bone. The place became red and slick and then still.

For a moment, the air was full of shouting and smoke and the crash of water. Then the sound changed. It turned from a press to a scatter. Men stopped shouting and started breathing in hard jerks. A boy in a raider's boat looked about him with the round white eyes of a goat. He let go his oar. An old sailor on the ship took aim with a stone and sent the boy out of the fight with a neat soft thud.

Imbu reached the stern boat that still held the hooks. He put his foot on the gunwale and made to cut a line. A raider rose under his blade with a knife in his hand. He was quick and low. The knife bit Imbu's side where the cloth had lifted. Imbu grunted and brought his elbow down on the man's neck so that the knife fell away by itself. Then he cut the line, and the boat began to drift. He stood there for a breath with his mouth shut and his teeth tight. Then he set his feet again and looked for the next work to do.

Once again, the discipling of the Thalassa crew overwhelmed the Hyenas. The surviving hyenas tried the headland. The watchmen there had stones and the reach to use them. One raider went down with both hands clapped to his face. Another fell and rolled and did not get up.

Khamariti arrived on the scene and felt the tremble underfoot that said the tide had turned. The hull sucked and settled and then lifted half a hand. Men shouted to one another to hold lines and brace poles. Abdiel jumped to the quarterdeck again and took the helm as if the ship were already at sea. He shouted to cut what was burning loose and to keep fire from the ribs. He called for men to fetch the small spare sail from the hold. He ordered the wounded brought to the lee side to take ashore for Zarah to tend. He did not look to see if Zarah had come down.

Zarah came at a run. She took a roll of honey and clean linen and a knife and a bowl of boiled seawater from a pot that someone had set in the sand. She found the man who had fallen from the rigging. His head was broken and his breath shallow. She cleaned his face, laid honey under the cut to keep rot from the wound and bound it. She spoke to him softly as she worked. Then she went to the man with the blade in his thigh. She cleaned it, pressed her hand above it, and pulled the blade out in a smooth firm draw. He cried out and then he was quiet. She bound him tight and told two men to keep him warm. She never once looked to the fight except when a sound rose that was so new the ear could not place it. Then she looked up, decided it was only a rope under load, and bent to her work again.

A shout went up from the headland. The last of the Hyena long boats that had circled wide came into the mouth of the cove in a hard fast sweep. The men in it bent to the oars, then rose and threw a last jar. It flew true. It would have struck the aft sail and set the last of the canvas alight. A stone met it, neat as a mark on parchment. The jar turned, hit the water, and went out in a puff that was almost comic. Men laughed. The laugh had the tired sound of men who have fought long and at last have won the right to draw a breath without a blade at their back.

Abdiel let the bow swing. He used the lift of the wave to work the hull clear of the soft sand that had held her. Men at the poles heaved as if they were moving a piece of earth. The hull slid. She did not float yet. She moved enough.

The hyenas on the beach looked at the ship and then at each other. There were not many left. One threw down his blade and lifted both hands. A sailor put a spear through him without a word. Abdiel did not call out to spare any man. He did not call out to kill. He called out only the work that would save the ship.

At last, the cove fell quiet. There was the small sound of flame and the bigger sound of water, and the soft deep sound of men in pain. The wind took the smoke. It sent it along the headland and out to sea. Ash still fell. It lighted on faces and in hair. It made everyone look old.

They counted the living and then the dead. Six of the crew would not rise again. Two more would not fight for many weeks. Others had cuts and burns and broken fingers and heads that rang as if bells were being struck inside them. The Hyena's left more bodies than they took away. No man of the raiders remained to boast.

Abdiel went along the rail and laid his hand on the blackened wood as if he were reading the grain with his palm. He nodded once. He did not smile. He called for pitch from the hold and for spare lengths of timber. He sent men to the palm grove with axes to cut straight lengths for makeshift spars. He had the burnt sail rolled tight and the worst of it cut away. He set lines from the bow to the headland to use the lift of the next tide. He did not waste a word.

Khamariti stood with his back to the Thalassa's mast and let his breath come right. He looked to the ridge. From that high place the cavern mouth was a dark tear in the stone. It seemed to watch them. He thought of the ribs of basalt and the clean span that had not bent when the mountain shook. He thought of the cut on the monolith in the grove. The hand pressing on the spine of the island. The broken part sliding. The wave moving out in bands like rings in a pond. The tale set in rock, plain as any script.

Imbu came to him then with a hand pressed to his side. Blood had dried in a dark patch at his belt. Khamariti reached to see the wound. Imbu tried to move away. Khamariti did not let him.

"It is a cut," Imbu said. "It is nothing."

"It is a cut that would be something if you were a fool," Khamariti said. "Be wise instead." He called Zarah. She came with clean linen and honey. She cut the cloth aside with a small knife, cleaned the slice, and pressed the edges together. Imbu did not make a sound. She bound it tight. Her hands were quick and sure. When she had done, she looked him in the eye and smiled once.

The men built a pyre for the Hyena and their own dead at the far edge of the cove. They used driftwood and broken spars. The smell that rose was pitch and meat and the sour note of sulphur that had been in the air since dawn. Zarah turned her face and then turned it back. She did not flinch again.

By noon, the ship looked like a beast that had fought and lived. One sail lay in a wet black bundle on the sand. The forward rigging was scorched and heavy. The rail bore burns and deep cuts. The deck was washed clean of blood but showed dark stains where fire had licked it. Yet the ribs were sound. The keel had held. She would go to sea again if they gave her time and skill.

Abdiel stood with Khamariti and considered the Thalassa's hull. He spoke as a man speaks to another worker over a job that must be done today or not at all. "There are trees here. We have pitch. We have men who will obey. With work she will float. If she floats, we take her off the sand and we hold her in the cove. We mend what we can. If the mountain sends more, we go. It will be many, many moons."

Khamariti nodded. He looked to the ridge again and then back to the ship. "We will do what the sea lets us do. But before we leave this island, I must set down what happened so that it will remain if the island takes us or when we are dust. Not in reed. Not in skin. In stone."

Abdiel gave him a look that weighed time against truth. "How many men would you take?"

"Three," Khamariti said. "The rest should stay with you and do the work on the ship. I have found a cavern high on the mountain. It will give me the space I need to set down the record of this voyage and my study of the plagues."

The afternoon ran on. Men soaked what rope they had saved and pulled it through sand to strip away grit. They drove wedges under the hull and set poles to give the tide a path to lift her. The water rose a little and then a little more. At last, the hull stirred. A cheer started and then died as Abdiel lifted his hand. They worked instead of cheering. The hull rose, slid, and then floated. Lines took the strain. Anchors bit. The ship lay in deeper water, safe enough for a night if the wind did not turn wicked.

They cooked grain in a pot on the sand and made it thin so that the men could swallow it with sore throats. The taste was dull and clean and felt like life. Zarah gave the worst hurt a little fruit pulp she had saved in a leather wrap. She made them drink water even when they said they had had enough. She made them keep warm with blankets from the hold that still smelled of tar. She moved without drama. Men watched her pass and knew they had not yet been left alone by the world.

Abdiel worked without rest for several days.

He ordered the hull sealed tight with pitch and resin until the ship could serve as shelter for the men. The lower deck became crude quarters, dry enough to sleep and eat.

He placed watchmen on the headlands and at the mouth of the cove, their eyes scanning sea and ridge alike. From the wreckage of raider boats, he salvaged what he could, ropes, hooks, blades, and pieces of timber. Then he set his men to the hardest labour.

Axes bit into the forest. Trees fell, were stripped, and hauled to the beach where they were shaped for masts and spars.

A canteen was raised on the sand with tarpaulin stretched over poles, a place where men could gather for food, water, and a measure of order. It was rough work, but under Abdiel's hand the chaos of battle gave way to a rhythm. The cove began to look less like a battlefield and more like a camp that might hold until the ship was whole again.

Khamariti, Imbu, Zarah, and Alim set out with three sailors who would ferry supplies to them without pause. Together they began the long climb back up Cumbre Vieja.

chapter 27:
Ascent Amidst
Awakening Giants

The ridge gave nothing away. It stretched like a black spine under a flat morning sky, ash drifting in pale veils, the air carrying that sour bite that clung to the back of the throat. Max kept one eye on the ground and one on the horizon, the habit of a man who knew a mountain could change its mind between one breath and the next.

Santos moved a pace behind, rope slung over one shoulder, the ground penetrating radar strapped to his pack, the drone kit clipped tight at his side, and the seismograph case patched with tape where the corners had split. They were climbing back, equipment heavy, their thoughts on Esme, still unsettled by the shaking they had felt in the night.

They walked without words for the first half hour. There was no need. The ridge set the rhythm, the breeze made a dry sound in the ash like pages turning in an old book. Now and again a faint hiss rose from a vent when the wind fell still. Far below, the surf combed the cliff base that had seen storms older than memory.

Max followed Santos up the mountain's flank, muttering under his breath. The climb was brutal, a spine of black rock that offered no handholds, just sharp edges and gravel that slid at every step. The air thinned as they rose, each breath tasting of sulphur.

"Bloody hell, Santos," Max grumbled. "You climb like you're chasin' a bus. Some of us weren't built for mountain goat duty, y'know."

Santos only laughed and kept moving, light on his feet. Max felt the burn in his thighs, the sting in his lungs, and still he pressed on.

By midday the following day, the sun struck hard against the bare rock, and heat shimmered across the ridge. A gull wheeled once and vanished into the glare. Santos slowed, studying a scatter of pebbles disturbed on the narrow path. He crouched, eyes level with the stone. Then he rose, silent, and pressed forward.

They reached a ledge where the mountain sheared away, the drop running sharp and sudden to the sea below. Santos stopped there. He raised two fingers and tilted his chin. Max followed the line and saw what he hoped for. A broad arrow cut into a boulder at waist height, the groove struck deep. Beside it, a time, a chalked scrawl of partial coordinates, and a single letter that tightened the chest.

He stepped closer without touching, as if the mark were a butterfly wing. The arrow did not lie. Esme had stood here and left a breadcrumb trail for us. Yet Max's gut turned. The line was too quick, the cut jagged. Not her usual calm hand.

They left the ridge, following Santos's lead down the flank. The slope was steeper here, ash looser, every step sinking half a boot deep. Fifty metres below, the land tilted into a shallow bowl where old rockslides had left broken shelves of stone.

Santos crouched again, scanning. His hand brushed a groove in the ash where a foot had slid hard, cutting deep. He traced the line forward to where two stones had rolled out of place, their fresh undersides pale against the black crust. "She came fast here," he muttered. "Not careful like before."

Max swallowed. He had followed Esme enough to know the difference. She always moved with control, even under strain. These marks spoke of haste, maybe fear. The thought pressed at him, heavier than the pack on his shoulders.

She was not just leaving signs. She was warning them.

Max knelt beside him, heart tight. "She was running?"

"Not quite," Santos said, eyes narrowing. "But she felt something. Shaking maybe. Same as we did last night." He pointed farther downslope where the ash was churned more heavily, each impression pressed deeper than the last. "She quickened her pace. She wanted out of this ground before it spoke again."

Max followed the trail with his eyes, the line angling toward a cluster of darker rock farther below. He felt the mountain's weight under his boots, the memory of its midnight tremor still alive in his bones.

"She knew it too," Santos added quietly. "Whatever we felt, she felt first."

It was not a spectacular wound. No giant chasm. No geyser of ash. The mountain had simply lifted a crust and set it aside like a lid. The slab in front of them stood half shifted within its frame. Dust still fell in fine threads from the edges. Along the base a seam no wider than two fingers breathed a shallow draught that cooled their boots and carried the smell of damp stone.

They pushed on, following the churned trail down to a wall of dark basalt streaked with pale veins. Santos stopped short, hand lifting. "Here," he said.

At shoulder height, carved into the rockface, was a mark. Crude, but unmistakable. A single letter—E—and beside it, yesterday's date, the lines scored sharp with chalk and stone. Below, an arrow gouged into the wall pointed left, deeper into the flank.

Max stepped close, throat tight. The mark was Esme's, her quiet way of saying she had passed, that she still lived when she made it.

Santos's eyes tracked the arrow's line, and his jaw tightened. Where it pointed, the mouth of a cavern yawned half-buried. Rockfall from the night's tremor had collapsed the entrance, sealing the way in with jagged blocks and spilled ash. Dust still clung to the cracks, as if the earth had only just breathed out.

"She went in," Santos said, voice grim. "Before the mountain dropped its teeth."

Max's chest clenched. The arrow was hope. The rockfall was threat. Esme was inside or trapped beneath.

He and Santos braced themselves either side and put their backs to the rock. On a count they pushed. Stone grated in its seat. Dust poured down in a fall of grey. The rock gave a fraction. The seam widened to the width of a finger. They set and pushed again. Two fingers.

They worked in silence for almost an hour, dragging rocks aside, levering slabs, shovelling ash. Dust burned their throats. Sweat cut lines through the grime on their faces. Max's arms shook with effort, but he did not stop. Every stone shifted felt like one step closer to her.

Then three faint taps. A pause. Three more.

Max froze, heart pounding. "Esme…" he whispered.

They worked faster, driven by the sound, until a glove pushed through a narrow gap, grey with ash. Max seized the hand, holding tight, then stopped as the fabric snagged on stone. The edge of her respirator scraped, grit sparking loose. Esme's shoulder wedged in the narrow opening and stuck fast.

"I cannot get out," Esme said, her voice strained but steady. No panic, just control. "The rocks."

"Do not use force," Santos warned, bracing his palm against the slab. "If it chips, the frame will lock."

Max kept her hand tight, feelin' the faint tremor in her grip. "We'll widen it," he said quietly. "We're not leavin' you here."

Her respirator rasped as she drew breath. "The frame is close. If you push it, it will seal."

Max nodded once. "Then we try another openin'. Mark this seam, we'll come back to it if we have to."

He thumbed the radio. "Max to Explorer, copy."

"Explorer to Max, go ahead."

"Explorer, we've located Esme. She's trapped but alive. We'll need a crew up here with tools, not the coppers yet, they're swamped with quake rescues. Move fast and brute force should get her out."

"Explorer to Max, copy. Team on their way. Out."

Santos kept his hand steady on the slab. "We hold what we can until they come. No mistakes."

Max gave her hand a squeeze and managed a grin. "Stay with us, yeah? Help's on the way, though knowin' this lot, they'll stop for tea first."

They chalked the rock, took compass bearings, then moved west along the ridge crown. Twice they found seams that promised a way, twice they ended in dead mouths where stone had fallen and sealed into cement only another quake could break. Time drained in hard minutes.

The multigas meter on Max's strap chirped and settled, chirped again, a nervous bird. The radio cracked with Thea's voice from the water. Pressure ridges were moving from the north like giant hands closing in turn. She warned of a wind shift, air pooling where it should not, and told them what to do when it came.

At last, where a spur bent west, they found it. No doorway, no design. Just a low opening in a fold of rock, hardly wider than a pack. The draught that seeped out smelt of water and of old places.

Max knelt, slid his lamp in, and watched the beam carve a narrow crawl. Ten metres down, it levelled into shadow. There was room for one man if he kept thin and forgot his ribs.

Santos looked once at the seam, once at his chest, then shook his head. "Not me. The stone would close on me like a clam. You can pass."

"Then you bring help," Max said. He wanted to add do not leave me here, but the words stuck. Instead, he unclipped his pack. "Max to Thea, we have an opening. Shallow crawl. Esme is beyond the first slab.

Thea came back clean at first, her voice quick but steady. "C-copy. Wind from northwest at twelve, gusting fifteen, trending steady. Carbon dioxide pooling in the leeward basins, sulphur dioxide low along the crown."

Then the pressure in her tone tightened; words began to catch. "Th-the surge model shows a window of forty minutes before the next p-pressure pulse overlaps your position. Rodrigues has a skiff w-warming. If he calls a turn… you turn."

"Understood."

Santos set his palm on Max's shoulder for the smallest space of a second, a touch that stood for things men did not waste breath on when breath might be in short supply. "If the wind fails, keep her head up," he said. "If the bars climb for carbon dioxide, do not sit to rest. Walk until they settle."

Max slid his pack through the opening and went next, flat on the stone with his arms long and his head turned sideways where the roof came too close. It was like passing between teeth. The rock rasped his ribs and took hair from one forearm where he misjudged a ledge.

Dust fell in lazy threads from the roof and lay on his neck like warm sand. He breathed out and moved forward on lungs that had made themselves smaller for him. When he had breath again, he measured the hollow with the lamp and chose where to put the weight. There were tricks to this that had nothing to do with courage and everything to do with weight and angles. He let those tricks do their work and saved the mind for other things.

Max tried the seam. He turned sideways, pressed his chest flat, and pushed with his toes. The stone did not move. The gap narrowed until it bit into his shoulders. He exhaled hard, tried again, but the rock held him. No way through. He pulled back, gasping, dust coating his tongue.

He slammed his fist against the wall, her hand had disappeared. "Esme!" His voice cracked in the dark. "Esme, answer me!"

No sound came back. Only the faint hiss of ash falling through cracks above.

Santos crouched beside him, face grey with strain. "It will not take you," he said. "You will break yourself before the stone gives."

Max pressed his forehead to the rock. His hands shook with helpless anger. She was in there. He knew it. The mountain had swallowed her, and he could not follow.

The ground shivered again, harder than before. Pebbles rained down, bouncing off their packs. A deep groan rose from inside the ridge.

"Move back!" Santos barked, dragging Max by the arm.

They stumbled clear just as a split opened in the seam, dust blasting out in a choking wave. Max fell to his knees, coughing, his eyes burning.

Then a voice cut through the chaos. Strong. Commanding.

"Max!"

He looked up. Lex and two sailors were striding towards them along the ridge, coat whipped by the wind, face set against the tremor. Behind him the sky boiled with ash.

"Get clear of the wall!" Lex shouted. "It is not done with us yet!"

The ridge heaved under their boots. The mountain roared, as if the earth itself had found a voice.

And the stone at the seam gave a long, tearing crack.

chapter 28:
Voices in the Cavern

Lex stood at the entrance and listened. Water ticked somewhere deep inside. Stone pressed close on either side. Max was at his shoulder, jaw set, trying to look calm.

"Esme," Lex called, steady and low. The name carried down the throat of the cave and came back thin and tired.

Max raised his voice. "Esme!"

Only the scrape of small stones moved. Santos and the sailors worked at the fallen slabs, hands flayed and black with dust. Each rock they shifted opened a little more of the narrow gap.

Then a sound, soft and human.

Max froze. "Did you hear that?"

Lex nodded. They went faster, passing rock hand to hand. The sound came again. Not a trick of the cave. A voice.

"Here. I am here."

Max's breath caught. "Esme?"

"Max. Professor." The words were faint but firm.

Hope pulled them on. The gap widened. Frigid air slipped through it, old and clean, as if kept aside for this moment alone.

"Can you reach us?" Lex called.

A pause. Then Esme again, stronger this time. "Climb in, Professor. You need to see this."

Duty and curiosity pulled the same way. Lex lay flat, slid his arms through, and eased his shoulders past the rough lip. He inched along, one knee, then the other, careful with each move. The earth felt damp and old against his palms. The dark ahead seemed to lean toward him.

His torch was the only light. Its beam searched the narrow throat of rock and found the way, bend by bend. He crawled forward until the passage opened without warning and the floor fell away to a wide shelf. Esme was there, pale with dust, eyes bright.

"You would never have forgiven yourself if you had missed this," she said, a tired smile on her mouth.

Lex rose beside her and lifted the torch. The cavern took the light and gave it back in pieces. A roof soared above them, lost in a forest of stone ribs. The walls curved like the inside of a great shell. Mineral veils hung in folds. Pools lay still as glass. It felt like a hall built by the earth itself.

The beam slid over the nearest wall and found lines cut by a human hand. Figures stepped out of the rock as if woken by the light. Ships. Standards. A man in a chariot drawn at speed. Colours still sat in the carved depths, red and blue and gold that the years had not quite drained.

"My God," Lex breathed.

"Not your god, Professor," Esme said, gentle but certain. "Osiris."

"Egyptian," he murmured, stunned. "There is no proof of an Egyptian presence this far west."

"There is now," she said. "I worked until the battery died. It is unique."

Max squeezed through the breach behind them, his torch flaring as he stepped clear of the rocks. He stopped in his tracks.

"Oh my. Oh my."

"Look," Lex said, turning his beam to the far wall.

The light ran across cartouches and bands of text. The cut of the signs spoke of the New Kingdom. Names sat inside rings. The arm of a scribe held a reed. A young boy reached for his father's hand. A woman stood with a lotus to her nose.

"Nineteenth Dynasty," Esme said. "Rameses the Second. The style fits."

Lex frowned. "Could this be later work? A copy? After the script was read in the nineteenth century?"

Esme shook her head. "No. Come."

She led him deeper along the shelf. The floor dipped and rose. The cold smell of stone thickened. Then the beam struck something that did not belong to the cave at all and both of them stopped.

The statue stood in a basin of shadow, towering above them, twice the height of a man. The carving was flawless. A pharaoh faced forward, young, and unyielding, the tall crown of a god rising in two plumes beside him. The faces were calm, their symmetry absolute. Every line spoke of mastery and purpose, the work of hands that understood eternity.

"Rameses the Second," Lex said, barely above a whisper. "And Amun Ra."

At the base, neat lines of signs ran clear and deep. Esme traced them with the light and read slowly.

"This cavern is dedicated to my Pharaoh Rameses the Second. He trusts in the gods, so I have set their images here."

She paused, eyes on the last line. When she spoke again her voice had changed.

"I have no faith, but I record in the style of the temples."

The words hung in the cold like a veil.

Max came to stand with them, silent. The cavern seemed to listen.

"What does it mean?" he said at last, almost to himself.

Esme turned, the beam still on the text. "It means the hand that made this loved and doubted in the same breath. This is not only a monument. It is a confession."

Lex looked from the text to the walls and back to the statue. His mind ran through dates, reigns, roads, winds, and ships. "The Egyptians did not have the means for such a voyage. Not in the time of Rameses."

"Yet we are here," Esme said. "And so is he."

They moved along the wall again. The carvings shifted from scenes of war to images of family. A man stood tall, his hand resting on the shoulder of a woman. Two children were carved beside them, their faces cut with unusual care, the lines deep and deliberate, as though the sculptor had known them well.

"Khamariti," Esme said softly. "Merit. Nefer. Menna."

Lex turned, the torchlight catching the edge of his profile. "You know them?"

Esme nodded, her eyes fixed on the wall. "I found Nefer's tomb in Thebes. A modest place, hidden away, as if someone wanted to keep it out of sight. The text there named his father, Khamariti, the royal architect."

Lex's breath eased out slowly. "The master of Abu Simbel. The Ramesseum. So many works that carried Ramesses' name but his genius."

Esme kept her gaze on the carvings. "And more. Some believe he designed ways of using water to lift stone, with canals and locks. It would explain what has always seemed impossible, the sheer scale, the precision. He thought beyond brute force."

She fell silent for a moment, but then her voice returned, quieter, weighted with memory.

"A few years ago, when I was working in Cairo, I spent time on Nebit. He appears in scattered records, a pupil from the workshops of Thebes. His name surfaced in fragments, half-faded inventories, a scribe's lists. At first, I thought he was the architect behind some of the lesser works. His hand seemed there, faint but present."

Lex frowned. "Nebit. I have never seen him named as more than a functionary."

"That is what I thought too," Esme said. "Then the head of the Cairo Museum showed me scrolls I had never seen before. They were brittle with age, but the ink still held. They spoke of Nebit not as a master, but as a pupil. A pupil to the star himself, Khamariti. His work was real, but it was only ever under the shadow of the greater mind. The scrolls described him as 'the hand that copies the hand of the master.'"

Lex's brow furrowed as he absorbed her words. "So Nebit was never the true innovator. He was recording, imitating, perhaps preserving. And the true architect…"

"Khamariti," Esme finished for him. "The one they trusted with secrets. The one they allowed to build not only tombs, but hidden places. Places like this."

The torchlight moved again across the wall, catching the names as though they glowed from within: Khamariti, Merit, Nefer, Menna. The family stood eternal in the stone, a reminder that behind the grandeur of pharaohs there were lives more enduring, and a mind that had reached far beyond the Nile.

The sight stopped him cold. His eyes widened at the walls alive with colour, the statues looming from the dark. Then he saw Esme, pale with exhaustion but upright beside Lex.

Relief surged through him. He crossed the floor in a rush and pulled her into a fierce hug. "Thank God, Esme," he muttered into her hair, the words half-choked.

But she stiffened and pushed him back with a shrug. "Not now, Max," she said sharply, her gaze never leaving the wall. Her eyes were fixed on the carved family, her lips shaping names that had slept for centuries.

Max frowned, hurt but silent, his light trembling as he raised it higher. The beam swept across the walls, and his breath caught in his throat. For a long moment he could not speak.

The rock face was alive with detail. Carvings ran in long, unbroken lines, scenes of battles, of gods, of families gathered under the sun. Colours clung stubbornly in the grooves, deep ochres, faded blues, and streaks of gold that still gleamed in the torchlight. Figures seemed to step out of the stone, their faces intent, their eyes carved with unnerving clarity.

His light moved again and struck upon drawings etched in finer hand, schematics, measures, strange alignments of stars. A scatter of hieroglyphs framed them, dense with meaning, some so sharp they looked as though the chisel had been lifted only yesterday. Max lifted his hand as though to touch but stopped, fingers hovering, reverence holding him back.

He turned slowly, his torch catching the far side of the cavern where low shelves of stone held what no one expected. Scrolls, tucked into niches, their ends wrapped in linen gone brittle with age. Parchments pressed flat under slabs, ink still marking their surfaces in tight, ordered lines. Fragments of a library sealed away with the mountain itself.

Max swallowed hard. "This is... mad. There's records here, drawings, a whole archive. Not just some carvings for prayin' at, but proper knowledge. Stuff they meant to last."

The cavern seemed to breathe with him, the weight of its history settling across his shoulders. He lowered the torch a little, voice rough with disbelief. "How could this be here, hidden in the Canaries? And for how long?" "Hydraulics. In that age?"

Esme kept her eyes on the wall. "I think he built things we have not yet found.

They stood before the statue once more. The roof dissolved into darkness above the towering crowns. At their feet, the pool mirrored the image in perfect stillness, pharaoh and gods, bound together in the water's quiet embrace.

"Forget Atlantis, Professor," Max said, his voice echoing off the stone. "You don't need a lost city after this, you've just found somethin' that'll keep the historians arguin' till retirement."

Lex shook his head. "This is Esme's find."

Esme smiled faintly. "History may not remember that. It never does. I am glad to be here. That is enough for me."

Lex drew a small packet from his pocket, cracked it open, and passed Esme two spare batteries. She clicked them into her torch. The beam steadied and grew. The walls stepped closer out of the dark. The signs seemed to breathe.

"Have you read much?" he asked, eyes still moving over the lines.

"Some," she said. "I need time."

"We will take it," Lex said. "Carefully. We touch nothing we do not have to. We grid the room. We shoot the panels twice. We take samples only where the paint is gone." He looked up at the statue. "And we try to be worthy of this."

The mountain gave a small tremor under their feet, a low growl that ran through the stone. Dust sifted from a high seam and drifted down like ash. The pool trembled and stilled.

Max looked at the breach, jaw set. "We keep the others out," he said. "Get Santos down there to alert the authorities, quiet-like. And tell the two sailors to stop standin' about and start haulin' gear. Might as well make themselves useful."

"Good call" remarked Lex

chapter 29:
Climbing the Sulphur Trails

The first light brought no warmth to Asif N'Imurig. The island lay buried beneath a mantle of ash, every ridge and hollow muffled in grey. No birds called. Waves came and went as if wrapped in cloth. Tafukt Taneggarut flared on the horizon and fell back, a distant furnace behind a curtain of dust.

Through that stillness moved four figures: Khamariti, Imbu, Alim, and Zarah. Cloths bound tight across their mouths filtered the ash but made each breath heavy. Their steps left shallow prints that the wind hurried to erase, as if the island itself wanted to deny the living.

Khamariti walked at the front, his eyes fixed on the dark slope above. He carried no weapon, only a staff capped with copper, the metal dulled by the air. To the others it looked like a pilgrim's rod, but he had cut the shaft hollow and filled it with a blend of resin and oil that he believed could mask the worst of the choking fumes.

They climbed the ridge slowly, eyes on the ground as much as the sky, hunting not comfort but means. Khamariti had set a simple charge: find colour, find tools, find a way to make stone speak. What should have been a morning's walk became a day of switchbacks and false crests. Alim refused to be left but faltered first. Age and bitter air conspired against him.

Imbu bent without a word. "Climb on," he said, steady as bedrock. Before Alim could protest, Imbu had tied a sling from spare cloth and lifted him. Two sailors shouldered the bags. They moved on.

By afternoon they reached a shoulder of the ridge above the cavern. The view that should have been triumph was a world without colour. Ash veiled the horizon. Sunlight dulled to a pallid glaze, painting the land in bruised greys and iron reds. Where green had crowned the ridge, only cinders stood.

They settled in the lee of a spur. Imbu eased Alim down. Zarah shared water in small measures. A low fire licked warm lava stones and gave back little heat.

Khamariti stood apart, reading the ground as if it were a tablet. When he returned to the circle of light his face held the decision already made.

"This island will give us what we need," he said. "Not comfort, but speech. Look there." He pointed to a gully scoured by past rain. "Red scoria holds iron, we crush it for ochre. Below, where ash weathers pale, there is yellow from limonite. Charcoal from the burned pines gives black, and soot from our fire the rest.

The dark pockets of basalt may yield manganese to warm the black to brown. Those pale crusts along the fractures, gypsum, and ash lime. We can burn driftwood and shell for lime wash, make a ground for paint. If the sea throws old ore to shore, we may find a green from copper stains, but we do not count on it."

He knelt, sifted soil. "We grind on pumice, smooth with water on flat stone. Bind with egg if the gulls have left nests; if not, fish glue from skin and bone; or sap from the shrubs that still live under the ash. For tools: obsidian flakes for cutting, a basalt pebble for a hammer, reed stems for brushes, hair bound to a twig for fine lines, bone spatulas to press pigment into cut lines so colour endures."

Imbu nodded. "When the wind eases, I go to the shore. Nets and wreckage may have spared eggs, oil, rope. I will bring labour and resin if the trees still bleed."

Alim managed a faint smile. "Even here, you find a temple in the making."

"Not a temple," Khamariti said, eyes on the ash-dark slope. "A record. Iron for blood and earth, charcoal for night, yellow for sun through dust. When the wind forgets us, this will remain."

He swept a hand to the torn flanks. "These scars are not idle time. They are the earth's handwriting, written in fire. The violence that opened this ridge is the same that darkened Egypt. Ash turned day to dusk. Fire became hail. Seas drew back and rushed in. What we called plagues were mountains speaking."

They worked until dusk. Then ash thickened; a new tremor ran the ridge; they went back to the cavern.

Inside, shadows yielded to lamplight and a small fire. For a time, the world outside seemed far.

It did not stay so.

As night deepened, a low rumble spread through the stone. The cavern walls shivered. With a roar that tore the sky, Tafukt Taneggarut erupted anew. Rivers of fire ran. Ash rose in columns that blotted out the stars. Lightning stitched the plume.

The air soured. An egg-stink bled in. Khamariti pressed ash into the layers of their masks. "It will slow the poison."

Khamariti studied the vents by day and by night, watching how the earth released its poison. The ground itself seemed to breathe, long sighs of smoke that left men weak and animals dead. Where others saw doom, he saw rhythm. The mountain did not spit death at random, it exhaled in cycles.

When the first strong surge had come, he had set his mind to a task no one else dared imagine. From timber lashed with bronze he built frames that held slabs of basalt, polished smooth so they fitted tight. He wedged them at the mouths of smaller vents and sealed the joins with clay mixed with goat fat. The crude barrier worked like the stoppers of amphorae. The hiss slowed, the gas held back, and the earth seemed to calm.

But Khamariti was not content with blocking alone. He carved narrow channels from the upper vents, lining them with stone brought down from the cliffs. Through those channels he led the fumes into open pits, where fires of green wood burned. The flames consumed part of the poison, the smoke rising thinner, less deadly.

"Stone, clay, water, and fire," he told Imbu as they worked. "Nothing more. We use the gifts of our age, and we make the mountain serve the living."

A full moon's cycle had passed when the mountain gave its fiercest cry. The ground heaved, and the sky split with sound like the tearing of the world. Fire burst from the summit, not in steady streams but in showers, great balls of molten rock hurled high into the black night. They fell with trails of fire, bursting as they struck the slopes, scattering sparks that raced down toward the sea.

The air shook with thunder as if gods themselves were at war inside the earth. Ash rained down in waves. Even with Khmarti's defences, the smell of brimstone burned their throats. Imbu pulled Zarah close beneath a rough shelter of timber and stone, while Alim shielded his face with his cloak, eyes wide against the glare. All night they crouched together, listening to the roar, the crash, the hiss of burning earth.

Later that night, Alim's cloak lay folded near the fire. His staff was gone. Imbu rose. "I will find him."

He wrapped a cloak, tightened cloth across his face, and stepped into the storm.

The island was a waste of ash and flame. Imbu moved swiftly, reading faint scuffs in dust. Twice he ducked falling stones. Once he pressed flat as a sheet of fire broke across the ridge.

He found Alim half buried, face grey, robe scorched by a fallen rock still warm at the heart.

"Master Alim," Imbu said, kneeling. "I am here."

Alim's eyes fluttered. His breath rasped. "I wanted to see... the mountain speak."

"You have seen enough. We go."

Alim's hand tightened on his wrist. Words came thin and stubborn. "Promise me. Look after Zarah."

"I promise," Imbu said.

The hand slackened. Alim's gaze lifted once to the fiery sky. A small smile touched his lips. "What a thing... to witness." Then he was gone.

Imbu closed his eyes for one beat. When the next tremor struck, he lifted the body across his shoulders and turned for the cavern.

Zarah knew before Imbu spoke. The truth was written in the silence, in the empty space where her father should have been. Her body gave way, and she fell to her knees, the sharp stone cutting through her robe. Sobs racked her, shaking the ash loose from her hair until it fell about her face in a grey veil. She pressed her hands to her eyes as though she could hold back the weight of the world, but the sound of her grief spilled into the morning air, raw and unrestrained.

Khamariti came to her side. He was silent for a time, his face lined with weariness, his eyes dark with loss. At last, he reached out and set his hand gently on her shoulder. His touch carried no strength, only shared sorrow.

"He is beyond suffering," he said softly, his voice rough, almost broken. "We will honour him. His name will not be forgotten."

Zarah lowered her head, her tears tracing streaks through the dust on her cheeks. She could barely draw breath between the cries. "He should be here with us," she whispered. "He should have seen the dawn."

Imbu stood close, fists clenched, unable to meet her eyes. He turned away, staring at the mountain that still smoked, its slopes black and burning, as though the earth itself had swallowed her father. The silence between them grew heavy, filled with the ache of what had been taken.

Khamariti's hand remained on Zarah's shoulder, steady despite the tremor in his chest. His words came low, but with a weight that carried through the ash-laden air. "The mountain claims who it will. But we will give him back to memory, not to nothing. His deeds will stand with ours, carved in stone, carried in the breath of our children. That is how we honour the fallen."

Zarah's sobs eased only slightly, her grief still pouring out, her voice catching as she bowed forward until her forehead touched the blackened ground. In that moment it was not only the mountain that seemed broken, but their hearts with it.

They sealed the mouth of the cavern against ashfall and rationed water. On the second day the skins ran dry.

"I must search," Imbu said. "If I fail, we die here."

A young sailor, Khan, went with him. Only Imbu returned, hours later, gaunt, and grey, carrying two bladders. His silence answered Zarah's question.

Khamariti lit the lamp and drew. Zarah held the light. Imbu ground ochre with soot to make colour. Stone took line: Alim's face, Zarah bowed, the ridge crowned with flame. Below, Khamariti cut signs that set the truth plain, that calamity walked up from earth and sea, not down from wrath.

"Zarah," he said gently, "wash your father. I will preserve what I can."

There was no natron, no oil, no linen of an embalmer's art; necessity gave other tools. Obsidian bit cloth and sinew; fire sealed what could not be saved; resin and ash hardened to a skin.

Khamariti painted on the wrappings with ochre and lime, not only the scarab and the eye, but other signs, curves that returned into

191

themselves, angles that sat like hinges, a circle that seemed to reach past its own arc. As he worked, his voice slipped into cadences that were not the desert tongue. The tones rose and fell with a maker's measure, as if the stone itself were being tuned. He did not lift his gaze to the stars; he lifted it past the mouth of the cavern, to a silence vast enough to listen.

When Imbu and Zarah returned with wood and water, the air smelled of smoke and stone. Alim lay on a slab at the rear, bound and black-glazed, at rest. Khamariti stood waiting, staff in hand, face unreadable.

Let him lay for a quarter cycle of the moon. We will complete the embalming process with what we have available, and then commend him to the underworld " he said.

chapter 30:
Carved in Stone,
Etched in Time

The sound came again from the darkness.

Not echo. Not stone. A living thing.

Khamariti raised his hand for silence. The torch wavered in his grip, its flame dancing across the obsidian walls. Zarah pressed one hand against the rock for balance, the other to her mouth as fear closed her throat.

From the deeper shadows, a shape broke free. It slid into the circle of light.

A feral goat.

Its ribs pressed sharp against the skin. Its coat was dust-caked, the horns long, curling back like hooked knives. Its eyes caught the firelight, pale and frantic. The creature's breath came in quick bursts, steaming in the cool air of the passage.

It lowered its head and stamped, challenging the intruders who had claimed its refuge from the ash and fire above. A single charge from those horns could cut a man down.

Imbu shifted, putting himself between Zarah and the threat. His voice came deep and steady. "Back."

"Wait," Khamariti said softly.

He lowered his staff to the ground. He raised his palm outward in peace. When he spoke, his voice was low and rhythmic, each syllable drawn with care. It was not prayer, not language, but something older, measured tones that carried like music along the cavern walls.

The sound echoed faintly, as if the mountain itself remembered the tune.

The goat's ears flicked. Its stamping slowed.

Khamariti reached into his robe. He drew out a few dates and a heel of dry bread. With deliberate calm he broke the bread into small pieces and scattered one at his feet. The goat sniffed the air, wary, then stepped forward. It ate, never once looking away from the man with the calm hand and the impossible voice.

"Good," Khamariti whispered. Another piece. Then a date.

Zarah had braced for a rush of horns and blood. Instead, she watched the animal grow still, soothed by the strange cadence. Her fear melted into wonder.

When the last crumb was gone, Khamariti lowered his hand and stepped back. The goat flicked its ears, turned, and vanished into a side passage. Hooves clattered briefly on stone, then silence fell again.

The cavern seemed to breathe.

Zarah let out a shuddering sigh. "How did you do that?"

Khamariti's smile was weary and private. "We share the same shelter. Let the mountain keep its old guests."

He raised the torch. "Come. The work does not wait."

The silence broke with the sound of footsteps. Heavy, deliberate.

The cavern became a place of ritual.

Torches smoked, filling the air with the sharp scent of resin. Tools were laid out on linen cloth, bronze blades sharpened to a fine edge, jars of salt, bowls of cedar oil and fish oil, strips of linen cut clean from their stores.

Together they worked. Imbu carried jars from the shore caves, lifted stones to make a flat table. Khamariti prepared the tools. Zarah washed her father's body with water from the spring fissures, her hands trembling as she touched his still skin.

Days passed. The body rested under layers of salt, drying in the cool breath of the cavern. When the time came, Khamariti unwrapped him. The skin was drawn tight, preserved, the features still recognisable.

Zarah wept again, but this time her grief was gentler. "He is still my father," she whispered.

Khamariti anointed Alim's brow with cedar oil. He painted the lids with kohl. He wrapped the limbs in linen, each fold spoken over with low words. Zarah placed a shell amulet on his chest. Imbu laid a carved stone by his side.

At the end, Khamariti bound a dark cloth across his brow. Into it he pressed a thin copper plate. With a chisel he carved four letters into the metal, deep and permanent.

ALIM.

The torchlight made the name gleam.

Zarah touched the plate with trembling fingers. "He will not be forgotten."

Khamariti's eyes were weary, but steady. "No. His name will endure."

The work of survival and memory went on.

At Khamariti's command, Imbu learned the patience of stone. His first cuts were clumsy, his strength too great, the glassy rock splitting under force. He swore once but then slowed. His great hands found restraint. He carved glyphs and faces with thought instead of brute strength.

Zarah gathered colour from the island. Ochres for red, sulphur for yellow, azurite and malachite for blues and greens, soot for black. She ground them fine, bound them with oil and egg white, and carried them to the walls. Under Khamariti's eye, she blended them with care, red thickened with iron dust, blue tamed with soot, green touched with yellow to echo leaves in drought.

"This is not colour only," Khamariti told her. "It is meaning. When you paint your father's face, you bind him into memory."

Her grief did not leave, but it changed. She painted her father's likeness onto the wall, shaping his cheek with tenderness, his eyes with reverence. She wept as she worked, but her tears gave strength to the lines.

Seasons passed. The cavern became their chronicle. Panel by panel the walls filled with scenes no scribe had ever dared to set down. Ash fell like rain. Seas burned red beneath a sky torn with fire. Men fled in terror, their shadows long on the stone.

Imbu worked the hardest. His hands shaped the figures, his chisel striking in steady rhythm, the sound echoing through the hollow dark. Beside him, Zarah mixed pigments from crushed stone and ash, her brushes giving colour to the agony they had witnessed. Khamariti cut signs into the walls, his script holding both record and warning. Together, their labour turned grief into memory, and memory into stone.

Yet sorrow lived among them still. Alim's body had been laid out with care, bound in linen that Zarah stitched with her own hands. A slab of rock had shifted during the mountain's fury, severing one of his fingers. Zarah had found it in the dust, small and broken, but precious. With trembling hands, she placed it gently upon the wrapped form before the final layer of cloth was tied.

"Whole again," she whispered, tears streaking her ash-stained cheeks. "You are whole again."

At the heart of the chamber, they carved a group of three: Alim first, his eyes set on a distance beyond life; Zarah beside him, head tilted as if listening for a hidden voice; Imbu behind, shoulders squared, carrying the weight of their future.

It took a full cycle of the moon. When it was done, Zarah placed her hand on the carved cheek of her father and whispered, "You are here."

The chamber echoed her voice as if the mountain itself agreed.

The walls became their record, their living memory, their testimony to the earth and the gods who refused to answer. Under Khamariti's guidance, he taught them of the plagues, for the plagues came first. Zarah ground pigments until her fingers bled, setting into colour what they had endured. She painted the days when ash blotted the sun and men coughed black until their lungs failed. She drew the nights when fire leapt from the sea itself, red waves breaking against ships until timbers cracked.

Imbu carved beside her, his chisel biting deep into the glassy stone. He gave form to locusts that had swarmed across the island, to storms that had stripped the soil bare, to the seven nights when the sea had glowed with strange light. His great strength made the stone yield, but his patience gave it meaning.

Khamariti moved among them, guiding each stroke, each colour. His own hands cut the lines that mattered most. Symbols older than Egypt, fragments of a code only he understood, began to lace through the scenes.

At first, they looked like small additions to the drawings, marks a careless eye would miss. But together they formed a lattice, a puzzle stitched into stone for those who would come after.

"This is not for us," Khamariti said one night, his torch casting long shadows across the cavern. "It is for the adventurers of the future. They will follow these signs when we are dust. They will find the truth if they are worthy."

Zarah leaned on her brush, exhausted, eyes hollow with grief but lit with a new spark.

"Will they understand?" she asked.

"They must," Khamariti said. His voice carried no doubt. "Or the earth will break them as it breaks us."

The work consumed them. Day after day, moon after moon, they returned to the cavern's heart. Their tools were simple, yet the labour was endless. Cuts of chisel, strokes of pigment, lines of meaning layered upon meaning.

Zarah painted her father's face again and again, tucking his likeness into corners of the wall where the eye would only find him after long searching. Imbu carved channels so fine they seemed like natural cracks in the glassy stone, but when traced by torchlight they joined into hidden symbols. Khamariti laid down geometry with the precision of a master builder, his lines echoing pyramids, river mouths, constellations, and forces unseen.

The cavern grew into a book no scribe could carry, a record that no flood could wash away, they hoped.

It would take more moons to complete than their combined fingers could count. Yet still they worked, driven by grief, by duty, by the weight of what they had seen.

Khamariti did not confine his labour to the cavern. At dawn he would climb the ridge above their shelter, standing where the wind tore ash into spirals. From there he studied the flank of Cumbre Vieja. His eyes followed the lines of fresh cracks, the slant of new scarps, the places where the mountain had sheared as if some vast blade had cut it open.

He carried a rod cut from ship timber and cords knotted to mark distance. He paced the slope with the care of a surveyor, planting stakes where the ground had shifted. He measured angles of descent, the direction of falls, the widening of fissures.

Sometimes he would crouch low, placing his palm flat to the ground. He felt tremors that others did not notice. The mountain whispered, and he listened.

At night he returned to the cavern and spread scrolls of papyrus on a flat stone table. He marked figures with a reed pen, calculations that translated the shape of the ridge into numbers. His hand moved fast, neat, precise. Ratios, curves, and sequences took form.

Zarah once watched him as the torch burned low. His face was set, jaw hard, eyes shadowed in thought. She whispered, "What do you see?"

He did not look up. "I see a wound that will not heal. One day this ridge will fall into the sea. The water will carry its anger across the earth. Cities will drown that have never heard this island's name."

She shivered. "Then why write it down?"

"Because one day, someone must know. If they cannot stop it, perhaps they can prepare."

When the scrolls were finished, he sealed them for the ages. Resin from pine was melted over clay jars, hardening to a gloss that would resist damp and time. Inside he placed his figures, his diagrams, his warnings. Each vessel was set deep in the cavern wall, hidden in niches they cut with Imbu's strength and Zarah's steady hand.

"This is our covenant," he said as the last jar was sealed. "Stone for the eyes, numbers for the minds. Together they may endure long after our bones are dust."

Zarah touched the cool surface of the sealed jar. Her grief was still heavy, but for the first time she felt that her father's death might not be in vain. His memory was bound now to walls and to numbers. His face would watch, and his name would endure, until another age found these warnings.

Khamariti stood, his torch raised. "Come. Tomorrow, we carve again. The work is greater than us all."

chapter 31:
Veins of the Earth

awn barely touched the crown of Cumbre Vieja. Ash veiled the ridge. Wind pushed dust along jagged basalt. Deep inside, stone swallowed every sound.

Lex tightened the strap of his headlamp and crept after the small, steady glow of Esme's torch. The air was metallic and cool. The passage bent twice and then widened without warning. He stopped.

Colour lived on the walls.

Figures seemed to step from the stone, first in shallow cut, then in paint that still held its life. Reds and yellows glowed like banked embers. Blues lay quiet where the light kissed them. Black drank the beam and gave back eyes and oars and crowds.

"This is not tomb art," he said at last. "This is a record. "Said Lex.

The first band told a beginning. Long hulls with square sails cleared a river mouth that could be no other than the Nile. Falcons and lotus opened along the cloth. Oars beat the water in lines so sure they seemed to move. Above, signs ran like narrow streams. Lex caught words he knew. Not yet the sense.

Esme's finger hovered close to the wall, never touching. She read in a low voice. "From the river to the sea, to the western horizon."

Max leaned in on the hulls. "Not ceremony. These ships are built to live beyond sight of land."

They moved slowly along the wall, the story unfolding in sequence. First came scenes of peace, ships heavy with grain, men bartering, women gathering water, voices raised in talk.

Then the tone changed. Fire spread across the stone. Long boats surged forward, their prows carved low like snarling beasts. Hyenas crouched at the bows, their jaws open. Shields lined the rails. Behind them men fell, their bodies cut down in waves. Sails caught flame, curling into smoke. Cities burned beneath the rising plumes, towers lost in the haze.

Yet through it all, one figure appeared again and again. Smaller than the rest, he stood apart, a staff of measure in his hand, and on his brow a crown inscribed with script. "Khamariti," Esme said, and the word seemed to bring the man out of the stone. "He put himself here."

She lifted her torch and moved on. "This chamber is his legacy. He made sure his name would outlast the Pharaohs."

Max stopped at a panel where merchants sat with trays of fish and jars of wine. Robes of Phoenician traders rested beside Egyptian collars. Another panel gave trees cut with such care they could still be named.

"Cedar. Olive. Almond," Esme said softly. "He wanted us to know what moved across the sea. Not only war. Value."

Lex spoke under his breath. "If this holds, then Egyptian ships reached the ocean and traded with Phoenicians in their own water."

Her beam slid to a darker band. They all felt it before they read it. A river thick with fish turned belly up. A swarm of insects black against the sun. Frogs crowding a wall. Families with arms raised under a hail that fell as fire.

"The plagues of Egypt," Esme said. "He carved them all. Not as scripture. As witness."

Lex stared. He had learned those stories from school and stone and priest. Now the man who had raised Pharaoh's monuments had set them here with a different weight. Not as miracle. As memory.

Max had wandered toward a narrow slab near the edge. The markings shifted there , ratios, angles, curves. No gods, no men. The chisel spoke with the precision of an engineer. Then he saw the tubes embedded in the wall, papyrus sealed with resin. He eased the seal on the first scroll with care.

"These are not stories," Max said. "They are measurements."

Lex joined him. The patterns were not star maps. He knew those well enough. These showed cross sections and slopes and noted heights. A triangle repeated with ruled edges.

"This is geology," Max said, and felt odd to say it here. His finger ran along a row of short strokes. "Beds. The angle of rest. Here is the first sign of failure. Here is the base."

"Impossible," Lex said by reflex. "They had no instruments."

Esme swept her torch to the crowned figure again. "He was the instrument. Khamariti read the earth as others read scripture. He recorded the plagues, the wars, the trade. But this—" she raised the light over a field of neat lines and numbers, "this is the warning he left for the future."

"Khamariti of Ramesses," she added, firm now, "the same chief architect who set the axis at Abu Simbel so that the sun would touch the inner statue at the day and hour. The same mind cut this chamber and put the measure of a mountain here."

They stood a long moment, each with a different part of the wall in view, each holding a piece of the larger truth.

Max took a step to a second slab. The same number set sat in three places beside the same mountain sign. The values were wrong to be chance. They were right to be the slope at which a flank lets go.

"They mapped the way this island breaks," he said. His voice had gone small. "They knew it could fall into the sea."

Esme moved on. The tone of the work shifted again. Animals ran in a tight band. Dark cloud laid a lid on the sun. A wave climbed a shore and took boats like toys. The small symbols of frogs, locusts, and welts were there again, not as list, but as echo of older ruin.

"These really are the plagues," she said, then shook her head. "Or the stories you write after flood and ash. It is suggestion, not dogma."

She lifted her lamp. A figure in dark scattered dust by hand. A wall of water rose beyond stones that stood for a harbour.

They went deeper. The roof rose. A sky had been laid there in paint, full of stars, but shifted from the map any sailor would know.

"Not today's sky," Max said. "Older. The slow turn of the pole set back to where it was."

"Precession mapped in stone," Lex said. "That is advanced work."

Max stayed with the numbers. He read neat sets that spoke of height to width, load, and runout. They hummed in his teeth, that small inner ring when values sit where they belong. They sat close to models he had sketched for first year students on a clean white board.

He swallowed. "This is the physics of a landslide wave. If this were a hoax, it would be a clever one written by someone who knows our field notes."

Lex glanced at him. "You think this is recent?"

"No," Max said, still staring at the stone. "I think I'm more afraid of what it means if it isn't real. We'll take samples. Date the ash, the mortar, anything we can. But the writing feels right."

"This place isn't random," Lex said. "It's planned. It's his voice."

Esme swept her light across the walls. It caught a small statue on a low block. A seam barely visible ran under it. Below that, a narrow band of carvings showed boats meeting a cliff, and a simple front that could have been any old temple. But one mark stood out. Small, clear, deliberate. A circle with a triangle inside. The base line thicker than the rest. It sat beside the river, the cliff, and the building face. Almost like a key.

"He's linking places," Lex said quietly. "There's a design that runs underneath all of this. Under Egypt, and now here. A key and a lock."

A low sound rolled through the mountain above. You didn't so much hear it as feel it. Like a door dragging across old stone. Threads of dust floated down. The paintings around them seemed to hold their breath.

Esme lowered her lamp and looked around from wall to wall, as if counting. "We record everything. No one touches any loose pigment. We set a grid across the room. We take two photos of every panel. We only take samples where the paint is already gone. The binders in the colours will tell us how old it is. The soot underneath will tell us what burned the day this was painted."

Max nodded. "I'll start with the cut stones. I want ash from the lines and a small binder sample."

Lex stood for a long time in front of the ships. He moved his hand through the air above a line of oars, careful not to touch. He spoke without turning around. "If this checks out, we've got the first solid record of an Egyptian led trip into the Atlantic that didn't end up as just a story. And we've got the first sign of someone from that time treating a volcano like it was a machine."

Esme gave a small, tired smile. "Get ready for people to hate it," she said. "But it's going to hold."

Max's lamp caught a line of words near the exit, lightly scratched in. He read them to himself once, then again.

"Not a temple," he said. "A witness."

"He wanted this to outlive him," Lex said.

"It did," Esme said.

They started working. Lex drew chalk lines on the floor so the cameras could build a clean grid shot by shot. Max marked sample points with a pencil where the paint had already flaked off. Esme kept reading, voice low, pulling meaning from faded signs, from the tilt of a crown, from the weight of a line.

On the far wall, a row of small alcoves sat under layers of dust. Esme brushed one clear. A jar was inside, sealed with resin that had set to a dark shine. A plain clay disc held the seal, pressed with a mark shaped like a wheel with three spokes.

Lex came over. "Don't break the seal," he said gently. "Take a photo. We'll find the least damaging way in."

Esme nodded. "He meant this to last."

"Stone for the eyes," Max said, "and numbers for the mind."

Esme's light dropped to a panel near the floor. It didn't show ships or cities. It showed a man standing on a ridge with a measuring rod and cords stretched out to stakes. It showed the side of a mountain with cracks drawn in exact lines, each marked with a number. It showed jars like the ones in the wall, a hand placing a scroll inside and sealing the jar with resin.

"Khamariti took his readings up there," she said. "He saw what we see. He recorded it. And he put it in the wall."

Lex felt the echo of dawn shift in him. He saw the ridge and the flanks and the patient hand that had watched them, then cut them here. He saw the mind that had stood under Ramesses and put light onto a face in stone at the day and hour, now standing on a far island and measuring the fault of the earth. The same man. The same craft. The same will to leave a path.

They worked on. The light from their lamps seemed small when the roof rolled away above them. It was enough. The chamber gave up more each time they passed a beam across it. A fisher with a net that had the twist of real cord. A girl with a tray and a smile like a quick mark in ochre. A pair of boys pushing a boat from a strand. These lives were old and yet present, held here by craft and by will.

The mountain spoke again. A slow heave went through the floor. Fine grit sifted down. Max looked up at the roof and then back to his slab.

"We have time," he said. "But not all day."

Santos crackled in the radio. "Professor, wind is picking up. The ridge is calm, but we are seeing small slips around the exit. Nothing big. Be aware."

"Copy," Lex said. "Give us twenty minutes and then call again."

"Twenty."

Esme raised her torch and looked across the chamber with a gaze that counted and chose. "One more thing," she said. "Then we go."

"What more?" Max asked.

"The centre," Esme said. "There is a basin there. I think it holds the oldest piece."

They crossed the room. The floor dipped in a shallow bowl where the rock had once pooled like black syrup and then set. The air felt cooler in the dip. The light slid across the curve and picked out a long shape curled near the far side.

Lex slowed. The shape had the wrong stillness.

They moved closer. Dry skin clung to a rib cage. The skull showed where the face had tightened back to bone. A strip of dark cloth crossed the brow. Near the outstretched hand the smallest finger bone lay separate, clean, and pale, as if cut and placed.

Max swallowed. "A body," he said, soft as a thought.

Esme did not move for a long breath. When she did, it was only to lift her torch an inch and bring the light steady to the band across the brow. A thin plate was set into the cloth. Letters were cut into it with care.

She leaned in, careful to keep her breath from the dust. She read in a whisper.

"A L I M."

Lex felt the name move something in him that had not moved since he had crawled inside. He did not know why. He picked up the severed finger and stared at it for several minutes.

Esme kept the light on the plate. "He is part of the story," she said, very low. "We saw his face on the walls. We read his work in the trades.

Now we see the man kept by the rite Khamariti knew. He is witness too."

She raised the torch again and let the beam travel from the plate to the face and back. The name was there. The cut was clear. Alim. The torch made a thin sound, a small strain like a breath drawn through a reed.

Santos called in the radio. "Professor, we need to let the authorities know if you have discovered something."

Lex gripped the rope at his waist, his torch beam fixed on the carvings. His voice came low but steady. "We are not leaving. Santos, you go back down. Tell the authorities what we have found. Do not wait for us. Max, Esme, we stay here until every panel is studied and recorded."

There was a long pause. Then Santos's voice crackled thin through the radio, the signal breaking on the edges of static. "Professor, are you sure of this?"

"I am," Lex said firmly. "Listen to me, Santos. This chamber is older than anything our history books admit. Its walls carry records of voyages, of cities, of fire and ruin. They show Egypt reaching beyond the Nile, far beyond what scholars will allow themselves to believe. If we walk away now without proof, this place will be swallowed again by ash and darkness. You carry the word. We will carry the record."

For the next hour Lex spoke into the radio, his tone measured, precise. He described every scene as if dictating to the world itself. The order of the panels, the colours that clung to the stone, the tools abandoned in niches, the scrolls pressed flat under slabs.

He explained the figure of Khamariti, carved again and again with his staff of measure, his crown inscribed with script. He spoke of battles at sea, of hyena, prowled ships, of cities vanishing under smoke. He gave distances, angles, the scale of the cavern itself, even the echo of his own voice when it carried through the hollow space.

Santos listened, silent but intent, the radio hissing in his hand as Lex's words became a living map of the chamber. When at last Lex fell quiet, his voice hoarse, the line held its static a moment longer.

Then Santos spoke, calm but heavy. "I have it all, Professor. Every word. I will take it down the mountain and make sure it is safe. But the authorities will close this site down as soon as they get here."

"Not before the world has to see what lies here." Call the harbourmaster first, then the Guardia Civil. Give them the coordinates and the headline only: historical site, sealed chamber, safety risks. Copy?"

Santos nodded, jaw tight. "Copy."

"Drag your feet," Max added. "If you find a café, order two coffees."

Santos managed the ghost of a smile. "Three."

"Good man," Lex said, low and urgent. "You're our witness and our clock. Once you see blue lights, ring twice, end the call."

Santos slung his pack and started down the trail, a single headtorch weaving into broom and rock as evening thinned.

Esme's torch gave one last flicker and died. She had already spoken the name. "Alim," she whispered again in the dark, as if to let it live beyond the failing light.

The mountain gave a deep groan. Dust drifted down like threads of ash. Max's lamp cut a single circle that reached only part of the wall.

"Max," Lex ordered, "keep that beam steady on Esme. Esme, you focus on the inscriptions. Film everything. No detail is too small. Every mark, every figure, every measurement. We need it all."

Max nodded, his face tight but controlled. He began to unpack the camera rig, hands working by habit. Esme steadied her breath, lifting the lens toward the wall where ships, cities, and plagues waited to be seen again.

Lex stood between them, one hand still on the rope, eyes fixed on the chamber as if he could already see headlines and sceptics waiting outside. "We will give them the truth," he said. "Stone for the eye. Numbers for the mind. And no one will ever erase Khamariti again."

Outside, ash rolled across the ridge in pale waves. Inside, the mountain held its silence, waiting to see if the witnesses within were strong enough to finish what had been hidden for three thousand years.

chapter 32:
Byblos Awaits

The harbour wind carried cedar and salt as the Thalassa readied for her return voyage. Sailors moved with practised hands, ropes taut, timbers creaking like a beast eager to stretch.

"Captain," Imbu said, bowing slightly. Hardship had forged respect between them. "Khamariti asks about the stock in the holds. His work in the cavern draws near completion."

Captain Abdiel looked up from where he oversaw lashings. Relief and anticipation coloured his reply.

"It is about time. We have been here for fifty-eight moons, this ship has been ready for six moons."

Imbu's deep voice softened. "You know the man. For Khamariti, time bends to his work."

The captain grunted, though a smile tugged at the corner of his mouth. "Then let us hope his precision weighs in our favour when we stand before Zamurus."

He began to recite the cargo with a merchant's pride and a warrior's reverence.

"Fifty talents of obsidian," he said first. Volcanic glass, razor edged and prized, glinting in its chests, blades, mirrors, tokens of fire and stone.

"Dyestuffs, another fifty talents. Purple, indigo, madder red. Worth more than silver in Tyre."

"Twenty talents of gold and silver, from the Hyena boat." He let the words linger. treasure taken not by force but by fate itself.

"Seventy talents of pumice, to polish stone and soften flesh."

"One hundred talents of exotic wood, for builders and artisans."

"Thirty talents of medicinal plants."

"Forty talents of seeds and cuttings."

He closed with a curt nod. "And enough food and water to reach Byblos."

The ledger was more than a list. It was a chronicle of years at the world's edge, a record of survival, trade, and faith.

Zarah's decision had been final. Her father's body remained in the cavern, wrapped, and mummified, laid among the carvings that bore their truth. Loss and discovery entwined. His spirit belonged to the mountain now.

Inside the cavern, Khamariti lingered. The others had gone ahead, but he turned once more to peer into the dark. His hand found a stone and pressed. A panel shifted, revealing a hidden chamber just large enough to hold a small statue.

From his cloak he drew out a small statue, obsidian, black and polished, carved by his own hand in long hours of silence. It was Imbu's likeness, strong and watchful, yet it held more than form. In its base he had cut signs, a hidden key, a message locked in stone. He knelt and placed it on a ledge near the entrance, the last piece of his craft he would leave in this secret hall.

"I wonder if our work will endure," he whispered. "We have given Fifty-eight moons to this place. The walls hold our hands, our colours, our grief. Yet one day this cavern, perhaps even this mountain, may fall into the sea and be lost to silence."

Imbu stood close behind him, his eyes fixed not on the walls but on a distance only he seemed to see. His face was still, as though he were listening to something beyond the wind.

"I see others," he said at last, his voice deep and low. "Not in our time, but far ahead. Scholars, men and women, standing where we stand now. They hold strange tools in their hands, tools I cannot name. Their presence is shadowed by loss. I feel it like a wound, but I cannot see its shape."

The words hung between them, heavy as the mountain itself. Khamariti bowed his head, knowing the cavern was no longer only theirs. It belonged to time

Khamariti touched his shoulder. "Your gift sees farther than ours. What you speak will come."

Imbu's voice faltered. "Teacher… I have taken Zarah as my wife. But when we return to Byblos, I fear she will be bound to servitude."

"Fear not," Khamariti said gently. "Zamurus owes me as I owe him. He will not enslave her. I have set gold aside in Byblos under his care. With that, and with what we bring, you will have liberty."

Imbu shook his head with quiet defiance. "No liberty. We go where you go."

"Then I must prepare you both."

The Atlantic fell behind. They turned east through the Pillars of Hercules. The first sight of Mediterranean waters hushed the crew, as though they had crossed a threshold in the world itself.

Cadiz offered respite: fresh water, bread, smoked meat. Traders from Mauretania and Iberia filled the port, but Khamariti urged haste. Their journey was not to end here.

Beyond Gibraltar the sea stilled, but unease walked the deck. For three nights Imbu, Zarah, and Khamariti kept to their cabin. Flashes of light slipped through cracks. Sailors whispered of forbidden knowledge. None dared intrude.

When the three emerged, they looked unchanged, yet those with keen eyes sensed weight behind their gazes. Sailors murmured that they had been entrusted with a great secret.

By the time Byblos' coastline appeared, the ship had become legend among her own crew. Tales of storms, fire, and discovery spread in hushed tones.

The city stirred as the Thalassa entered the harbour with Zamurus's flag aloft. Dockworkers paused. Word raced to the noble's house: a ship under his banner, unknown yet familiar.

Zamurus came himself. Age had streaked his beard with grey, but command still marked his stance. His eyes narrowed at the vessel gliding toward him, familiar yet transformed.

The gangplank dropped. Abdiel stepped down first. Zamurus's eyes widened.

"Abdiel! By the gods, you live! Sixty moons I thought the sea had swallowed you."

"The sea tried, Noble Zamurus," Abdiel said. "It did not win. We return with riches, and more."

At the name of Khamariti, Zamurus's heart leapt. He scanned the deck, and there they were. Khamariti, Imbu, alive. Small changes since they left and a woman holding onto Imbu he did not recognise.

Zamurus embraced Khamariti with laughter rolling over the harbour. "You old fox! Did you find what you sought?"

Khamariti's eyes glinted. "I found tales enough to fill many nights. But let us speak after wine and bread. Stories are too heavy for empty bellies."

"Always you keep me waiting," Zamurus said, laughing. He looked to Zarah. "And who is this woman?"

"She is Imbu's wife," Khamariti said simply. "I blessed their union."

"Imbu was always loyal. If she has his strength, you chose well."

Khamariti's voice grew solemn. "Our voyage brought more than treasure. We uncovered truths buried for centuries. Truths that may change not only what we know of the past, but what waits in the future."

He lowered his voice. "And the future I fear will bring turmoil. I will brief you before I depart for Egypt."

But even as Zamurus welcomed them, another set of eyes had marked Khamariti. Seneb. Patient. Watching. He had waited since the island. To kill him there would have been death for himself. But if he did not strike before Egypt, the high priest would flay him alive.

chapter 33:
Master of Misdirection

"Right," Lex said, voice clipped. "We've bought a day. Maybe less. Let's make it count. Once the authorities take this, we're out."

They slipped back into the fissure, past the canvas hung as false rockfall. The passage exhaled cool air, and ahead the cavern opened, an ancient hall shaped by hands that understood stone and silence. Esme's torch cast clean light across the western wall where figures emerged: a man and woman; two children; boats on a wide sea; a god with green skin; a crown like a helm.

Max set the drone case on a flat bit of rock and snapped the latches open. "Power cells're sittin' at sixty percent," he said. "Low-light sweep only. Lex, you want the body cam runnin', or savin' it for somethin' prettier?"

"On." Lex clipped the unit to his strap, felt the vibration as it spooled. "Esme, you lead. I'll prompt, not push."

Esme gave a single nod. Her hair tied back, chalk flags at the ready, discipline set hard against awe.

Max ran the drone along the cornice line, mapping joints, recesses, the soft tick echoing like a trapped insect. Esme's torch fixed on a family panel.

"Khamariti. Merit. Children: Nefer and Menna. Late Ramesside style. The lower cartouches are scorched, not erased. A warning."

"Why scorch?" Max asked, eyes on the drone feed.

"To mark without destroying," she said. "It tells later readers to look deeper. And see here, the restrikes on his title. He claims Abu Simbel, the Ramesseum, Karnak's restorations. But also voyages beyond the Nile."

"Here," Lex murmured.

She traced the boats turning west. "Atlantic waters. And these, hydraulic lifts, canals, locks. Not brute labour. Water raising stone. A manual in carved form."

Lex leaned close. "The ramps were theatre. The real method was hidden."

Esme's gaze burned. "He carved this for memory, not myth."

The drone drifted over another panel, showing three scenes divided by water symbols. In each, Khamariti stood with a woman and children, but their clothes belonged to different centuries.

"Three families," Esme said. "Not one lifetime. Either artistic pride or a claim to something beyond human years."

Max frowned, his Scouse lilt cutting through the chamber. "Maybe it's just a priest showing off. But time travel? That's a tough one to swallow."

"Let's call it misdirection," Lex said.

They turned to a new image. Osiris stood tall, green-skinned and crowned, then softened to human form as Isis and Nephthys knelt beside his body.

"Osiris betrayed, Isis searching," Lex said for the record.

"Khamariti changes the tale," Esme replied. "Osiris starts as something other, armoured, not human. Then he becomes man. It hints the gods were visitors, and men their students."

The idea hung in the air.

Esme crouched beside brittle papyri and unrolled a fragment. It showed figures with long skulls, curved arcs, discs, and flying shapes that were not boats.

"Metaphor," Max muttered.

"Record," Esme said firmly. "To them, this was real."

Lex tried to steady the room. "We name it when we prove it. Not before."

Max's earpiece ticked twice. He froze. "Santos." He checked his satphone. One missed call. No message.

Lex's tone changed. "Blue lights. First warning."

"How long?" Esme asked.

"If he called from the forestry track, give it half an hour," Max said. "Assuming he's not stopped for a brew and a selfie first."

"Then we move fast." Lex's hand sliced the air. "One: wall stitch. Two: server dump. Three: two fragments only. Four: the statue."

They turned. The seated figure loomed ahead, hands on its knees, face worn smooth. A seam ran around the base.

"Named here," Esme whispered. "'He who hides to protect.'"

"Master of misdirection," Max said quietly.

Lex pressed thin papers against the stone. Twice, nothing. On the third try, at the northern corner, the sheet trembled.

"Void," he said.

"Then a chamber," Esme answered.

Cold air slipped through the crack. Max's satphone ticked again. "Fifteen minutes."

Then the lamplight caught something new in the far corner of the cavern. They moved closer, tracing the nearby glyphs, heart, weigh, wake, gate. Lex tapped the plinth twice.

On a plinth rested a black, obsidian gleaming statue. The name Imbu was carved on its side, surrounded by curling glyphs.

Esme's breath caught. "Imbu," she whispered. "I've never seen anything like it."

Her hands trembled as she traced the carved lines. "This isn't just a statue. The markings call it the key to knowledge. It's personal. Khamariti's left riddles, messages, for us to solve."

Lex felt the weight of the moment. His voice stayed even, but his jaw was tight. "Take it."

Esme drew back. "Lex, no. That breaks every code we work by—"

"I know," Lex said sharply, eyes fixed on the figure. "But if we leave it, it's gone. Locked away forever. And everything he meant us to find dies with it."

Max's accent thickened as he spoke. "And if we're caught, then what?"

Lex's eyes turned cold. "Then we don't let them."

Esme slid the statue into her satchel and pulled the flap tight. Her voice was firm, almost clipped. "Take the severed finger too. Thea can carbon-date it for us."

The mountain rumbled. Sirens wailed closer.

Lex straightened. "We have what we came for. Now you run. I'll hold them. Get everything to Rodrigues. Secure the data."

Max stared at him. "Right. So, we nick the statue and a severed finger, while the Guardia Civil hike straight toward us. Perfect."

chapter 34:
Imbu's Second Breath

The dining hall burned bright with oil lamps, their light gilding trophies from far coasts. Zamurus presided at the long table, a farewell banquet set in Khamariti's honour. Imbu and Zarah, though not of noble birth, ate with the ship's officers, their cups refilled, their plates generous.

"Esteemed architect, your presence restores my spirit," Zamurus said, rising with a smile that did not quite hide his concern. "Your tales nourish the soul as much as this feast. Your guidance has brought us riches I could not have secured alone."

He gestured to the goods set out like tribute.

"Fifty talents of obsidian," he began. Volcanic glass glinted in its chests, blades and mirrors, a mastery over fire and stone.

"Dyestuffs, another fifty talents. Colours from sea and earth. Royal purple, deep indigo, madder red. Worth more than silver in Tyre.

"Twenty talents of gold and silver from the Hyena boat." His tone lingered there. Treasure taken not by design, but by fate.

"Seventy talents of pumice," Abdiel added, "to polish stone and soften flesh.

"One hundred talents of exotic wood, for builders and artisans.

"Thirty talents of medicinal plants.

"And forty talents of seeds and cuttings."

Zamurus turned back to Khamariti, softer now. "These are more than goods. They are the promise of renewal trade. For that, I thank you."

Khamariti inclined his head, accepting the grace. "Noble Zamurus, we speak with purpose tonight. First, any word of our pharaoh's health"

Zamurus' gaze darkened. "Ramesses is beset by age. Teeth that torment him. Joints that resist the morning. His vigour fades."

"Then our time is shorter than I hoped," Khamariti said. "I must return to his side. What I bring cannot wait."

"Be wary," Zamurus answered. "As the pharaoh weakens, the high priest grows bold. His reach is long. If Thebes has not heard of your return, it soon will."

"Then we move with care," Khamariti said. "Before I leave, hear what we found."

He spoke plainly. The sea had taught him. The land had confirmed it. Currents, faults, floods. Patterns men had mistaken for wrath. He laid out causes as a mason lays stones, each one set to carry weight without show.

Zamurus listened in steady silence. When Khamariti finished he nodded once. "Your deductions ring true. You pull the veil from fear and show the order underneath."

"Our people see the hand of gods," Khamariti said. "It is the world they know."

"Men have long named storms as anger and tremors as judgement," Zamurus replied. "To search within nature is courage. It strips comfort and leaves reason and will." He raised his cup. "May that courage carry you home."

At dawn the estate stirred. Scrolls and sketches were wrapped. Gifts went back to their chests. With papers that set out his case, Khamariti made ready for the river.

Zamurus had secured a fast boat north to Pelusium. Under a hard blue sky, they ran along the coast and into the mouth of the Nile. Eight days later Pelusium rose from haze, not as ruin but as renewal. Scars showed, yet markets were open, streets alive.

Khamariti took modest rooms on the city edge with Imbu and Zarah. Quiet. Clean. A place to think. That first night a folded note slid under the door.

Come alone. It named a courtyard near the east gate. The mark was Nebit's.

He went at once.

Amara al Fahil waited in the fig shade. "Khamariti," he said, low and urgent. "Nebit sent me. The high priest's circle moves in the dark. This is no shift of statues. It is a remaking of power. Your return to Thebes puts you in the path of a blade."

"What have you heard" Khamariti asked.

"Whispers with teeth," Amara said. "Orders prepared. A pretext ready. They will make you the cause and cut away the cause."

"You advise delay," Khamariti said.

"I advise breath," Amara replied. "The ground in Thebes is not steady. A sandstorm looks like a cloud until it is upon you. Give it time to pass."

Khamariti held his gaze. "Your warning is heard. I will step with care. But return I must."

They parted. Khamariti walked the river path, lights flickering on black water. Halfway to the lodging a figure stepped from reeds, wrapped like a journeyman, standing like a fighter.

"Architect," Seneb said. The voice had a blade in it. "That was your last warning. The high priest forbids your return. You walk toward your end."

Khamariti did not step back. His eyes stayed fixed on Seneb.

"I was ill when last we met," he said. "I saw you raise a bow against me and blamed the fever. You broke bread with us for sixty moons and wore a mask. When the pharaoh hears what you and your master plan, there will be no refuge."

Seneb's smile was thin. "The pharaoh weakens. His body fails. So will his will. The strong will decide."

The knife came fast, a flash of steel.

Imbu had waited for this moment. He had never trusted Seneb. He broke from the shadows at a run. His hand clamped Seneb's wrist and stopped the strike cold. Bone jarred against his grip. Imbu twisted. The knife clattered to the ground.

He slammed Seneb into the mud, driving him down with the strength of a storm. His knee pressed hard between the traitor's shoulder blades. His hand forced Seneb's face into the wet earth.

"You did not pull your weight," Imbu growled, his voice rough with years of anger held back. "Sixty moons you lived among us. Sixty moons of labour of hunger, of storm. Others bent their backs. Others bled. But you, your muscles softened, your waist grew fat, your hands forgot the rope. You drank, you lied, you waited for others to carry you."

"Do not think I ever trusted you. I watched every step, every word. I would not let my teacher walk free without me beside him.

217

If betrayal came, it would strike me first, not him. But to do that I needed you close. I needed you to show your hand."

"And now you have. I drew you out, Seneb. I will not let your poison touch him again."

Seneb bucked and clawed, mud filling his mouth. His body thrashed under the crushing weight, but Imbu pressed harder, smothering the breath from him.

A second knife flashed from Seneb's belt in one last act of spite. He drove it upward blind. The steel struck deep, sliding under Imbu's ribs.

Imbu grunted, the heat of the wound blooming through his chest. Still, he held Seneb down, grinding his face into the earth until the traitor's body stiffened, then went slack.

Only when the fight was gone did Imbu push himself upright. He staggered, blood dark across his tunic. The knife was buried to the hilt.

Seneb lay lifeless in the mud. Justice had come, but its price was drawn in Imbu's own blood.

Pelusium stank of rot and old smoke. In the small room they had taken, a few torches fought the dark. Imbu lay on a pallet, breath shallow, fever sheen rising. The skin around the cut had begun to blacken. Veins stood like cords.

Zarah worked fast. Wine to wash. Cloth clean and boiled. Garlic, hyssop, myrrh. Simple tools, sharp.

"We must drain it," she said.

Khamariti heated a blade until it whispered. He pressed the edge to the wound. Imbu's body arched then shuddered. Dark blood ran. Zarah ground herbs to a paste. Garlic to fight rot. Hyssop to cleanse. Myrrh to quiet the flesh. She packed the cut. The skin hissed. Imbu clenched his jaw. He did not cry out.

"It is not enough," Zarah said. She opened a small jar. Leeches clung to the glass. "These will draw what we cannot reach."

They set them. They swelled. The torches sank lower.

"The poison moves fast," Zarah whispered, fear cutting her voice. "I cannot stop it."

Khamariti knelt beside Imbu, his hand pressed firm against the wound, his face set in calm that did not falter. The air smelled of blood and ash.

"He carried me through storms and fire," Khamariti said, his voice low, steady. "He will not be lost to a coward's blade."

He turned then, his eyes finding Zarah. For a moment he seemed older, worn by the burden of choice. "But to save him, I must act. What I will do will change him. He will still be Imbu... yet not the same. His fate will never be as it was."

Zarah's breath caught. Her hands trembled as she clutched the edge of her robe. "Different?" she whispered.

Khamariti nodded, sorrow deep in his eyes. "I can keep his life, but I must bind him to a path that cannot be undone. If I do this, he will walk with us still but altered. The man you know will remain, yet he will carry something else within him, something that sets him apart."

Silence stretched between them, heavy as stone. Zarah lowered her gaze, tears welling as she pressed her hand to Imbu's uninjured arm. At last, she whispered, "Do it. I would rather have him changed than gone."

Khamariti bowed his head once, solemn. "So be it."

He set his hand upon the wound.

Imbu cried out, eyes rolling back. Foam touched his lip. Zarah turned away, shaking.

Khamariti closed his eyes. His lips moved without sound. The room thickened, as if the air itself held its breath. Torchlight dimmed. Shadows stretched longer than their walls allowed. A hum rose at the edge of hearing, deep, resonant, as if the stones of the floor had remembered a song.

Khamariti's hand shifted, and something unseen pressed deep into the vein. Imbu's back arched, a strangled sound breaking free, then the spasms eased. His breathing steadied, still shallow but measured. The black tide around the wound ebbed. The swollen veins thinned as if retreating from an order given in a language the body had once known and forgotten.

The hours crawled. The low vibration held, the pulse of a second heart under stone. Zarah drifted into half sleep and woke to find Khamariti still at Imbu's side, hand unmoving, eyes shut in a labour that asked no witness.

A pale shaft of day found the shutter's crack. The hum faded. The torches guttered to ash.

Imbu stirred. His chest lifted on a long, steady breath. He opened his eyes and pushed himself upright. Colour returned to his face. The fever had broken. Where poison had blackened flesh, only a pale scar remained, thin as a drawn line.

He looked at Khamariti, bewildered. "Master… what did you do?"

Khamariti drew his hand back slowly. His face gave nothing away. "What was required," he said at last. "Something I had not done before."

Imbu pressed his palm to his side. His voice was thick with disbelief. "I should be dead."

"Then live," Khamariti said, iron hard once more. "Stand and walk. Our road grows darker still."

Zarah stood in silence. She knew she would never speak of what she had seen. She was not certain she could even name it. The cut herbs, the strange powders, the steady rhythm of Khamariti's touch, the low words that sounded more like numbers than prayer, none belonged to the rites of Egypt.

By full light Imbu stood tall. His strength had returned, but something in him was altered. The wound had closed, yet his eyes held a different depth, as though he carried a part of the night within him. He was alive, but his life would never be the same again.

Two days later a river boat took on water and grain at the quay. News pressed from the west. Danger pressed from the south.

They pushed off. The Nile had shed its red stain. Fish broke the surface. Crocodiles warmed along the banks, jaws open, motionless, an old warning that never lost its truth. The current took them south toward Thebes, toward a palace where a great pharaoh waned and a priest sharpened knives with prayers.

Khamariti stood in the bow and watched the river write its old line through green and sand. His hand drifted to the place on his palm that still remembered a hum no ear had heard. He did not look at Imbu.

He did not look at Zarah. He looked ahead, where the work would demand the last of any man.

He drew a breath that belonged to someone older than he was, and the river carried them on.

The high priests spies watched them leave.

chapter 35:
Artifacts and Alibis

The descent from Cumbre Vieja was brutal. Loose pumice slid underfoot, the mountain shedding its skin with every step. The air was sharp with sulphur, each breath heavy with warning. Max led the way, shoulders hunched around a sealed crate that pressed against his ribs. Inside, drives ran warm from the scrape in the cavern, memory fat with scans that could redraw history.

Two sailors who had once clawed through the rockfall to free a path to Esme now carried a different burden. Lex placed into their hands every item of computer gear and testing equipment, bound tight in canvas packs. Under cover of darkness, they slipped away down the trail, sworn to bear the cargo to the marine explorer without a trace, unseen and undiscovered.

When Max, and Esme turned back to the cavern, the world shifted. The air throbbed with rotor blades, and the horizon filled with noise. Spanish authorities swept up the slope, boots striking ash, rifles slung at their shoulders. Helicopters beat overhead, their lights raking the ridge like search beams at a prison wall.

There was no time to run. Voices cut through the smoke as armed men flooded the cavern entrance. Lex stayed where he was, pinned to the rock, hands forced up, searched, rough, fast, without mercy. Torches were torn away, orders barked in a language half-understood.

For Lex it was like losing air itself. They had brushed a world that had waited centuries for eyes to see it, and in a single flash of guns and glare, it was swallowed back into darkness.

Halfway down the slope, Max slowed until Esme drew level with him. His voice was rough, his throat dry. "Heads up. I never told you what's eating at me. The aftershock set gave me numbers I can't square. Phase offsets don't fit any path we'd expect. Either I botched the calibration, which I doubt, or the mountain's inside is built on a geometry I can't yet model."

Esme fixed her eyes on him. "Bad as in collapse tomorrow?"

"Bad as I won't be buyin' any real estate here," he said. "We get off this ridge, and I'll tear those models apart until they talk."

They reached the forestry road just as the moon broke through a low drift of cloud. For ten tense minutes they stayed hidden among the trees, watching the beam of a Spanish Guard helicopter sweep the slope. When the rotors faded, Lex was set down near the clearing. Below, the Marine Explorer's inflatable nudged the shingle, Captain Rodrigues waiting at the waterline, arms folded, a dark shape against the silver sea.

"You took your time professor," he said, and then, at the sight of the satchel and the crate, the edge left his voice. "Aboard. Now."

They rowed in silence, the oars dipping soft into the black water. Each stroke carried them further from the mountain's glow, further from the noise of rotors and shouts that still echoed faint across the night. Santos had remained behind with the authorities on Cumbre Vieja, his figure last seen framed against the ash and searchlights.

A beam swept the slope, cutting through smoke and rock, then passed on, blind to the sea below. The boat slid into deeper dark.

Moments later the vast hull of the Explorer rose before them, its lights muted, its shadow covering the small craft like a shield. They caught the dangling rope ladder and began to climb, fingers raw, knuckles grazed, lungs burning with salt and smoke. One by one they hauled themselves up, leaving the silence of the sea for the steel deck above.

Lex had given the Spanish authorities a single story, flat and careful. He told them of the cavern, of the wonders carved into its walls, ships, battles, gods, and families preserved in ash and stone. But he gave them no more than words. No proof, no images, nothing that could be held against him.

His tone was measured, almost dull, as though the place were no more than a curiosity. Suspicion lingered in their faces, but with nothing solid they could not hold him. In the end, they sent him back to his ship, empty-handed, yet carrying more than they could ever guess.

In the lamplight he reached for Esme's satchel with steady hands. She passed it over, unable to stop the tremor in her fingers.

"You understand what this means," she whispered.

"Yes," Lex said. "And you understand why it cannot be in their hands."

She nodded once. No more was needed.

Max gave a short laugh. "You realise you're in deep with us now, handling stolen goods and all."

They spread the impossible on the table: the finger in linen, the little Imbu whose stone drank the light, the humming stack of server boxes with the cavern's harvest.

Rodrigues closed the hatch and cut to the point. "Madrid will send more men. They will be thorough. If there is anything else, anything at all, give it to me now and I will make it vanish."

"Digital evidence," Max said. "Scans, recordings."

"Upload at once," Rodrigues answered. "Your clouds, then the Professor's. Wipe what you cannot explain. They will take your machines if they can lift them."

"Surely our research—" Lex began.

"It is already online," Esme said, phone in hand. "Rumours everywhere. Some of them ours by accident, most of them not."

Rodrigues' mouth pulled tight. "He had to report the discovery. But yes, in the last hour someone sold the story. It is done."

Thea slipped in, hair tied back, a thumb drive in her hand. "Th-the ridge is sealed," she said. "Geologists, police, soldiers if they can find uniforms. Cairo is pressing for entry. They used the word s-sacred twice in one cable."

"This find is ours," Lex said, heat startling even him. "We will not let others twist it. Upload everything. Back it up twice. In two hours, we meet again."

Rodrigues lifted a hand. "Write clear statements on how you found the cavern. Simple. The same. If you are asked, you read, you do not invent. If anyone falters, the story still stands."

Heads nodded.

They split to stations and worked like a factory of cover and erasure. Clones spun, checksum logs piled, laptops wiped clean. Esme took frame after frame, front, back, glyph detail, worn edges, threads in linen. Thea drafted statements with dull precision that would lull a tired clerk. Max built his seismic map, watched bars crawl, cursed when one failed, then ran it again.

By two in the morning the first plan sat coiled between them. The smallest pieces, the Imbu figure and Alim's finger, went into waterproof housings and then, at Rodrigues' insistence, into the bilge, tucked behind a mess of hose and a sacrificial coil of rope.

An hour later Rodrigues checked his watch, checked the horizon, and made his choice. He ghosted down a rope and slid into water black as crude. The housings bumped against his chest under his shirt. He kicked out into calm, thinking in distance rather than fear. The reef rose as a pale ache just below the surface. He ducked, wedged the cylinders into a cradle of seaweed and stone, brushed sand across the seams, and steadied his breath.

He was back aboard twenty minutes later, hair plastered to his skull, eyes like flint. He said nothing. No one asked.

Dawn arrived thin and pewter. Patrol launches knifed through the chop, white hulls bright with authority. The boarding was efficient and theatrical, boots on ladders, rifles slung but ready, a clipped exchange of courtesy at the rail.

Rodrigues met them with papers and effortless Spanish that sounded, to foreign ears, like administrative poetry. The commandant nodded once, and the ship filled with strangers. Lockers opened, floorboards lifted, bulkheads tapped, computers confiscated.

Three hours later the Explorer looked robbed in reverse, drawers yawning, cushions upended, an elderly kettle dismantled on the galley counter. Only the computers were seized. At the rail, the commandant offered a single condition. "You will remain at anchor until clearance. Do not leave."

"Por supuesto," Rodrigues said mildly.

Engines took the launches away. Silence surged back like tide.

Max let out a breath he did not know he had kept. "Too close."

Esme's hand went to the satchel hidden deep beneath a false panel in her bunk, empty now but heavy with meaning. "Closer than they will ever know."

Lex measured faces for steadiness. "Do not sleep. Work. We publish before the tide turns."

They did not yet know what Rodrigues had done in the dark. They only felt the sudden gravity of reprieve.

By late morning, the cabin had become a war room. Thea, Max, and Esme had catalogued for sixteen hours straight. The work had an edge now, the knowledge that strangers might return with barges and warrants and a mandate to turn the ship inside out again.

Rodrigues ducked in with an update. "Spanish divers went under our keel at first light. More are coming. If anything has not moved, move it now."

Lex gathered them at the table. "As it stands, they intend to inspect again. If you have brought anything aboard, hand it to the captain and forget where it went."

"What about the digital evidence," Max asked. "Scans and recordings."

"Secure everything," Rodrigues said. "Clouds first. Drives will grow legs if they can."

"It is not just ours anymore," Esme said, watching a tide of speculation scroll across her screen. "Some guesses are wild. Some are too close."

The second search came at noon with more men and bigger tools. Barges nudged close. Pumps started. The bilges coughed up their usual stink. Thin wands probed the fuel tanks with a priest's solemnity.

Only when the barges turned away did Rodrigues bring them aft, out of the wind, and tell them where the truth lay sleeping under weed and stone. Relief went through them like a physical thing, legs soft, breath leaving in almost laughter.

"For now," he said, "they are safe."

"For now," Lex echoed.

Night fell like a curtain. The Explorer rocked gently, a cradle with sharp edges. Screens lit the cabin. Outside, a fattening moon stitched a silver zipper along the water.

Lex took the floor. "The scope has widened. The search for Atlantis led us here, but this exceeds any single story."

"It may not," Max said. "The landslide evidence and the Atlantis narratives could be knots on the same rope."

"Test before we d-declare," Thea said, though her gaze stayed on the screen as if it might look back.

"Thea," Lex said.

The wall lit up with colour. Lidar peeled open the slopes, currents showed in pale plumes, the seabed around La Palma glowing like a city from orbit.

"The sc-scars are real," Thea said. "Debris fields too. Last week's quakes stripped s-some cover. We got clear windows. Lava and shell fragments date to about three thousand two hun-hundred and seventy years ago, give or take fifty."

Max exhaled. "Late Bronze Age."

"The lab is decent," Thea went on, "but not the best. University kit will tighten the range. I'm sure it stays in the same century."

"A collapse in the right window," Lex said. "Myth or not, the Great Sea would have felt it."

"My seismics are still off," Max said. "Even after recalibration. The lags don't match a single plane. Could be another cavity under the south flank. Or a network of vents. The core's more complex than any map we've got."

"That," Thea said, "keeps m-me awake. The past is shouting. The present is starting t-to speak."

"Esme," Lex said.

The cavern filled the screen, vivid and sure, like a dream that refused to fade.

"Ramesses," Esme said. "Shown as a god-touched ruler and patron. But the walls point to one mind, Khamariti. His name repeats beside works we know in Egypt, Abu Simbel, the Ramesseum, and in places less expected, Byblos, the Pillars, even here."

"You're certain?" Lex asked.

"As certain as anyone can be, anchored with patrols closing in," she said, a quick smile flashing. "The hand reads Nineteenth Dynasty, but with quirks. A man writing for himself, not a priest. Some lines are like a logbook. Others drift into myth. Noon turned dark. Water foul. It calls the plagues to mind. I need more time to separate fact from symbol."

Thea drew a slow breath, pausing to gather her thoughts and steady her speech. She knew it was magnificent, too magnificent, and the excitement made her tongue stumble. "Th-the w-work... it's magnificent," she managed at last, awe softening the strain in her voice.

"And human," Esme added. "There's a family scene. Khamariti, a woman, a girl, and a boy on a bier. The line shakes with grief. After that, the hand hardens, more exact, more urgent."

A ship rose on the screen, a long hull with a Phoenician curve, sails full, reef lines neat as music.

"Byblos," Esme said. "Zamurus supplied the crew. The deal is clear, profit, patronage, or both."

"Why La Palma?" Max asked.

"Cause," Esme said. "He chased cause beyond the Pillars, through fire islands. He marks Agadir, then a leap, then here, under the name Asif N'Imurig. The journey becomes a record. The record becomes a warning."

"What do you think?" Lex asked.

"I think, from the glyphs and carvings, he was searching for the cause of the plagues, and more besides."

"Khamariti was real," Esme said. "He served under Ramesses. He sailed with Phoenicians. He wrote of a collapse here or near here. He left this to outlast him. And he buried keys. One is the likeness of Imbu we hold. The other is an idea I'm not ready to voice."

"The statue," Max said. "Does it fit a lock?" "Maybe a lock," Esme said. "Or a measure, a scale, a cipher. The grooves on its base match channels on one lintel. It could mean nothing. Or everything."

She clicked forward. Abu Simbel filled the screen, drawn in elevations and sections, the lines so sharp they seemed modern. Next came the Ramesseum, measured with the same precision.

"Khamariti drew like an engineer," Max said, "but painted like a man who'd seen the gods."

"With a trace of the p-physicist," Thea added, pointing to a grid of numbers in the corner.

"In the margins," Esme said, "angles that look like bearings, south and west. And if I read the offset right... home."

Max leaned in, eyes narrowing. "These numbers, some track time, others look like decay curves."

"I thought geology when I saw them," Esme said. "I told myself it was romantic. Khamariti as geophysicist. Absurd."

"Impossible and true," Max said. "He had no instruments, but he had water and the patience to time ripples. If he marked intervals over distance, he had comparison, which is all science is."

Lex paced once. "We are either rewriting a footnote," he said, "or a chapter."

"Both," Esme said. "If we publish only what we can prove."

The room seemed to breathe as one.

"There is one more line," Esme said quietly. "He writes that he honoured gods because the people demanded them, but his true faith was in earth, sky, and stars. He swore those three words would outlast him. They are not carved apart from the text yet, but the vow is clear."

Thea tilted her head. "That sounds lit-literary."

"No," Esme said. "It is human. And more. He was caught between ritual and the fault line. A man who served kings, but whose purpose was greater. He was not just an architect. He was something else.

The first mate filled the doorway, face pale from the hiss of the radio. "Chatter ashore," he said. "Orders have changed. They are assembling a larger team. Expect immediate boarding."

chapter 36:
Sacred Vengeance

Thebes shone and roared as Khamariti stepped ashore. The berths on the river seethed with barges piled high with grain and papyrus. Traders cried glass and faience, scribes haggled for ink and reed. Oxen pushed carts of cedar toward the western bank where the Ramesseum rose like a mountain of intention. Even half born it ruled the light. Columns stood in ordered ranks, scaffold bound like ladders to the sky. Obelisks speared the last fire of the sun. Reliefs in their first cuts ran across the stone, the beginnings of victories that would one day be a wall of memory.

Imbu came to his side, face caught by the glow. "This is your vision," he said.

"With Nebit's hands as well," Khamariti answered. "He was once my student. Now he commands men as I did."

From the shadow of the works a figure walked out with the stride of one who belonged. Nebit bowed, then embraced his teacher. His face was leaner, his eyes brighter, his voice low and quick.

"Teacher, you should not have returned," he said. "The high priest gathers power as Pharaoh fades."

"My path lies here," Khamariti said. "Tell me what you have raised."

"The Pharaoh comes each week," Nebit replied. "He is carried now, but still he comes. He gave me all I asked. Stone. Men. Time. That is why the house rises as it does."

"I must see him," Khamariti said. "Yet the priest will strike the moment I step within reach. Can you place a veil over my steps."

"I have already set mischief among his watchers," Nebit said, a hint of pride in it. "They believe your ship comes in two days. For now, you are safe. I have a refuge for you and your companions."

"You place yourself in danger," Khamariti said.

"Not while the son favours me," Nebit answered. "Ankhwennefer, the thirteenth by Isetnofret, has asked me to design his tomb when the crown is his. The high priest thinks twice before he reaches for me."

Imbu frowned. "Two Ankhwennefers. One a priest, one a prince."

"The name binds them," Nebit said, "but not their hearts."

They vanished into the city's inner streets and entered a mudbrick house near the necropolis where reed mats softened the floor, and a single lamp kept company with the dark. For five days they stayed hidden. Nebit came and went, bringing food and whispers. The city crawled with the priest's men. One watcher whom Nebit had misled was found at dawn with both hands cut away. The message needed no scribe.

On the sixth morning Nebit came early, dust on his sandals and urgency in his voice. "Pharaoh goes to the Ramesseum today," he said. "It is the chance you asked for. A moment off the throne. Fewer eyes."

Khamariti wrapped his head in a coarse wig and wore a simple robe. The plainness was a mask that drew no gaze until he chose to discard it. Imbu walked a half pace behind, a wall that moved.

The city filled the avenues as the royal palanquin approached. Trumpets shivered the air. Soldiers pressed the people back with the easy cruelty of habit. Ramesses came borne high, thin now, the gold bright on his brow, the old will still burning in his eyes. He halted at a tent where a scale model of the temple stood in perfect lines, a dream made small to be understood.

He dismissed his carriers with a flick, and only Nebit and a handful of guards remained. The gaze of the pharaoh fell on the little group and stayed.

"Nebit," he said. The voice was deep and rough with age. "You are not alone. Do my watchers lie or does the priest's quarry stand before me."

Khamariti took off the wig and bowed. "Great Pharaoh. It is I."

For a space, the face of Ramesses did not move. Then sorrow passed over it like a cloud that hides and then reveals the sun once more. "You return and the whispers thicken," he said. "The priest says the plagues ended when you were sent away, that your exile bought our peace. He calls your name a wound in the skin of Ma'at."

"I return with remedy, not harm," Khamariti said. "What struck Egypt was not wrath from the sky. It was the earth and the sea in their old violence. I have followed their signs. I know what we felt and why."

Ramesses shut his eyes for a breath. "I sent you away to preserve you," he said. "Not to seek. The priest would have broken you then. Now my strength is a lamp at the end. The scales draw near. Do not lay on me a truth that would tear the court while I yet breathe."

"Your reign is not weighed by storm," Khamariti said. "It is weighed by the mercy you give and the knowledge you shelter. This is not revolt against the gods. It is wisdom that protects your people when the earth stirs again."

The old man's sight moved past Khamariti to the far line of his own years. "I cannot stand for you now," he said at last. "The priest's circle is stronger than my hand. Leave Egypt. Go to Phoenicia or beyond. I cannot hold you safe."

They looked at one another, the space between them full of the weight of years and work and memory. Then Ramesses turned away. "Go," he said. "Nebit will bring me word. I cannot keep you."

The crowd outside had a mood of weather about to turn. Imbu felt it before he saw the shape. Men slid from the edges of the throng, plain cloaks, quick eyes, blades in sleeves. Servants of the high priest, hunters who knew the crowded street.

"Teacher," Imbu bellowed as he drove into the bodies in front of him. The soldiers braced and pushed back. He broke the line, but the space closed on him like water.

Three men reached Khamariti first. Their grip was rough, and ropes cut into his wrists before he could speak. Temple guards pressed close, spears crossing to block any step toward freedom.

A covered carriage waited in the shadow of a tall date palm, its horses restless, stamping at the dust. The door swung wide. Hands dragged him forward, his sandals scraping stone. He tried to resist, but the ropes pulled tighter. The door slammed behind him with a sound that echoed in the square.

The driver cracked his whip. Wheels jolted over the paving and spun fast, the carriage lurching away. Dust rose thick and brown, rolling over the road, swallowing the sight of it.

Imbu forced his way through human weight and sudden fear, sending men sideways with shoulders and hands. By the time he reached the edge of the square the carriage had gone, swallowed by streets made to lose a man in a breath.

Now the weight of that promise pressed down on Imbu. The palace square fell to whispers as the guards moved. Dust settled where the carriage wheels had cut through. Imbu stared down the track as if his gaze alone could bring it back.

The high priest had made his move.

Khamariti was a prisoner now.

Nebit found Imbu before the sun slid to the line of the colonnade. He pulled him into the shadow under a ramp and spoke fast.

"They took him to the temple precinct," Nebit said. "Not the palace. They will not dare spill blood in the court, not yet. They will question in the House of Life. They will call it concern for order. They will speak of blasphemy with soft mouths."

chapter 37:
Rites of Piety

The echo of the plagues still haunted Egypt. Months had softened memory but not fear. Rivers had run red. Skies had gone dark at noon. Locusts had eaten the green to its bones. Faith, once a rhythm of offering and song, had hardened into chain and yoke. Temples swelled each dawn. Farmers left first fruits. Mothers laid curls of their children on stone. Soldiers touched lips to amulets before they raised a spear. Every mouth asked the same thing. Do not let it come again.

Ankhwennefer thrived in that weather. He stood each morning in white linen, incense drifting like a tame cloud about his head. His voice carried smooth and bright across the courts. He spoke as if he alone could stand between Egypt and ruin. The people believed him. The court needed him. He never forgot the day Khamariti had corrected him before Ramesses. A small cut made deep. It had never healed. He had fed it with prayer and pride until it became a blade.

The grand court weighed the air with heat and breath. Torches shook light on gold. The gods looked down with eyes that caught fire. Ramesses sat high. The frame was thinner now, but the will still sat in the bones. The room waited to be told what to think.

High-Priest Ankhwennefer stepped forward and struck his staff once on stone. "This man returns from exile with a tale that makes a mockery of the gods," he said, pointing, palm open like a judge. "He says the plagues were not divine warning but tricks of earth and sea. He names far islands as the source of our pain. He would trade worship for drawings and words."

Khamariti did not bend. "I have seen those islands," he said, steady, the tone of a teacher instructing a class. "I have stood where the mountain split and hurled rock into the sea. I have watched water run from shore and return as a wall. If the Nile is Egypt's life, then wisdom is its guard. We must guide the water. Build where it cannot break us."

Gasps answered him. To shape the Nile was to touch the work of a god.

"Blasphemy," said the priest, mouth sweet and eyes cold. "He would lift his hand above Ra. More ruin will come if we let him teach."

The room rose. Voices struck voices. Ramesses stood and the noise fell as if cut. "Enough," he said. "You ask for death. I do not forget the walls he raised for me. I grant mercy and judgment together. Serve Nebit for three moons. Finish the drawings for my house. When that time ends, you will die. You may choose the manner and the place."

He looked at the man who had made his visions live in stone. He wished to spare him. He could not. The court and the gods' servants watched for weakness. A pharaoh can bend only so far.

chapter 38:
Secrets Within Stone

The sirens died into distance. The patrol craft flattened their wakes, white scars that slowly stitched back into the grey skin of the sea. The Marine Explorer fell into the old long roll, a ship that had learned how to breathe again.

"Back to work," Lex said.

They gathered in the central cabin. Thea lowered the lights until one screen owned the room. Esme pushed the satchel deep into its hidden cavity and returned with notes and a steady cup of tea. Max checked his recalibrations one last time, fingers moving from memory.

"First," Lex said to Max, "walk us through it."

Max nodded. "Thea's right about the seabed. A huge landslide struck here in the Late Bronze Age, around three thousand two hundred and seventy years ago. But what I need to show you now belongs to the present."

He brought up a seismic profile. Pale bands marched across black, the language of rock taught line by line. He explained the reflections and the logic behind them, pausing when Thea asked for a second look and when Esme asked him to tie colour to depth.

The next image stripped Cumbre Vieja to its bones. An overlay traced the lost mass that had once filled the slope and now slept on the ocean floor.

"This is my best fit," Max said. "Volume might drift, but the geometry's sound."

A darker line appeared. It ran just behind the crest, then down the west face like an old wound that had learned new ways to ache.

"Another fault," Max said. "Saw it on a traverse, checked it with the handhelds. Starts about twenty-seven metres back from the rim, drops near half the flank. Went looking 'cause of Khamariti, Esme read a bit about dodgy ground. His numbers in that scroll line up with mine."

The room went very still.

"Is it m-moving now," Thea asked.

"Slow," Max said. "Not racing, not dead. Can't give you a clock, but I can give you a direction. The old slip ran southwest, this one's edging for deeper water, out west. If it goes, the whole mass drops straight into depth."

Thea looked from the screen to the chart. "Deep water lets a wave build fast and clean."

"Yes," Max said. "Not a forecast for tonight, a warning of what's coming, if we ignore it."

Esme held up a page. "The panel here says the same thing. Khamariti built a cavern, he hoped someone would find it before it was lost to the sea. He knew."

Lex rubbed his jaw. "An Egyptian architect pointed to a fault line we can now measure. What's on the wall matches what's in the rock."

Max switched slides. Two columns of numbers appeared.

"The old collapse was massive," he said. "Somewhere between ten and a few hundred cubic kilometres of rock. Let's say a hundred to keep it simple. At about two and a half tonnes a cubic metre, that's roughly two hundred and fifty billion tonnes of rock on the move. Even a bit of that's like a mountain hitting the sea."

Esme's voice was quiet. "And the wave?"

"In deep water, it moves as fast as a jet," Max said. "About seven to eight hundred kilometres an hour. It would reach other continents in hours, not days. The height depends on the coastline and the tide, anywhere from thirty to a hundred feet. That's not a guess; it's what past data shows. Some areas could flood up to thirty kilometres inland. Others less. Cities built for storms wouldn't stand a chance."

Lex leaned forward. "How long from the moment it fails to the first warning?"

"Not long enough without a proper watch," Max said. "We'd need eyes on that crest, kit that doesn't lie, and the nerve to hit the alarm before the committee's finished its coffee."

"Nem rei escapa à morte," Rodrigues said as he stepped from the shadows, his voice carrying the calm certainty of a man long acquainted with loss. Not even a king escapes death.

He moved closer, the lamplight catching the salt lines on his coat. "Remember that" he added softly. "The crown, the soldier, the sinner, it makes no difference when the tide turns."

"Brilliant," Max muttered, his soft Liverpool drawl edged with dry humour. "We're all doomed then, are we?"

Thea said, her tone softening for a moment before she pulled the conversation back to its weight. "Then we tell the people what they n-need to know," she said, her stutter edging through as focus returned. "Spain first. With d-data and a plan."

Max slid a sheet of paper across the table. "Four tiltmeters on the summit, two more on the west side. Pressure sensors in the bays, sound, and heat monitors along the ridge. If Spain lets me back on the mountain, I'll set them up myself. If not, I'll hand the plan to their team and watch them hold three meetings to agree which end of the cable's up."

Lex read the list and nodded once. "Madrid tonight. Washington after that. Keep it simple. Just science."

Esme leaned closer. "I need to go to Egypt. Not now, but soon. The cavern points toward Thebes and Abu Simbel. If we're going to talk to Egypt about a mountain in Spain, we need to understand how their story connects to ours."

"You are not going alone," Lex said.

"I won't be alone," Esme answered, her voice even.

Lex's reply was steady. "Then we'll be ready."

They split the work without fuss. Thea checked the upload links and sent a careful message to the Spanish authorities.

Max wrote a short report showing where each sensor would be placed. Lex and Esme drafted a letter to the Cairo Museum, asking for a partnership, careful not to reveal what they had found or promise too much. Lex gathered all three into one simple packet, a request for help and nothing more.

Night settled around the ship, steady and calm.

Just before dawn, Rodrigues knocked on Lex's door. His smile was tired but steady. "We've got clearance," he said. "I called in a few favours from my cousin, the Portuguese ambassador to Spain."

Before they lifted anchor, as the first light touched the sky, Rodrigues dived beneath the hull and retrieved the statue and finger bone, both sealed in waterproof bags on the ledge beneath the coral. To the east, the mountain stirred, a thin white plume rose, pale at first, then turning dark.

Max watched the smoke twist upward. "Guess the past's tired of being ignored," he murmured.

Esme stood beside him, eyes fixed on the seam of rising ash. "Then we listen."

The Marine Explorer steadied on her course. Behind her, the island breathed and waited.

chapter 39:
The Gathering Clouds

The swell pressed an old rhythm into the hull of the Marine Explorer. It should have calmed nerves. It did not.

Inside the chart room the air was tense, heavy with unspoken thoughts. Lex spread both hands on the scarred table as if he could steady the ship by will alone. Thea hunched over her screens, eyes fixed with the stillness of a hunter. Esme sat with her notes gripped too tightly, her knuckles pale. Max stared at traces of seismic lines, his jaw set, his eyes refusing to blink.

Lex broke the silence. "The trouble's getting worse by the hour," he said. "If we don't speak first about what we've found, others will do it for us. Social media's already calling us everything from treasure hunters to vandals, thieves, and frauds. I think Santos has been pressured to talk."

No one disagreed. They all knew the truth. The cavern's discovery was too large to hide. Already rumours moved faster than fact.

They set to work.

Thea combed through the seismic images until the layers told a story any audience could follow. She sharpened the colours, pulled back the noise, and left only what mattered: the line of the ridge, the scars on its flank, the threat it carried.

Max rebuilt the profiles, stripping away jargon. He turned his equations into clean words that could carry weight without losing truth. Ratios, angles, stress lines. He practised them aloud until the numbers rolled plain and sure.

Esme recorded every scroll and parchment she photographed and filmed. On her computer, she built a three-dimensional model of the entire cavern, capturing every detail. What she preserved were the brush marks and chisel cuts, the ships, the storms, the plagues, the work of a man who had carved a warning three thousand years before. She rehearsed her presentation like a story, each panel alive, each line of stone a voice speaking across time.

Lex trimmed his closing remarks to the bone. No theory. No excess. Only fact.

By dawn they were ready.

The city of Cadiz rose through haze, its old walls and towers blurred by morning light. On the dock a marquee waited, white canvas stretched tight, cameras already sweating under the lamps. The air smelled of salt and oil. Security lines were strung with tape, ready for the prearranged press conference.

Rodrigues walked them in, calm under pressure, patient with guards and checks. His shoulders carried the look of a man who had walked through storms before, steady no matter how fierce the wind.

Inside, the hall was already packed. Journalists leaned forward over their notebooks. Cameras hummed, lenses trained like weapons. The crowd had come ready for spectacle, ready to doubt, ready to pounce.

Lex stepped up to the lectern, the hum of cameras rising as he adjusted the microphone. "What we found," he began, "is unlike anything we've seen before, a vast cavern carved into volcanic rock, sealed for what may be thousands of years. Inside lies a collection of carvings and relics that could rewrite parts of our shared history. I know there have been accusations, claims of theft, secrecy, even fraud. My own university has advised me against holding this conference. But discoveries of this scale belong to everyone, not to rumours or private interests. We believe it is in the public's interest to show what we've found, to let the evidence speak for itself."

He paused, then turned slightly toward the side of the stage. "Dr Esme Miller will now take you inside that cavern."

Esme took her place at the lectern. The lights dimmed and the first slide filled the screen. She paused a moment, letting the audience take in the blaze of colour. The carving was ancient yet alive, pigments still clinging to stone after millennia. Deep blues, fiery reds, and burnished gold traced the lines of a ship cutting across the waves. At its centre stood Khamariti, his profile sharp, his arm raised in command. The cartouche beside him burned with his name, a mark of ownership and destiny.

Another slide followed. The journey unfolded in a sequence of panels, each one more vivid than the last. Khamariti's ship, built with Phoenician skill, sailed out from Byblos and into open seas. The details were astonishing: ropes twisted with precision, oars biting the painted waters, crew bent to the rhythm of waves. The colours seemed fresh, as if the stone still remembered the sun of the shipwright's yard.

Then came the battle. The cavern walls had captured it in strokes both violent and graceful. Carvings showed sleek figures rising from the surf, their faces marked, their jaws bared.

"These," Esme said, "Khamariti himself named the water hyenas. Raiders who came from the sea. He carved them as beasts, half men, half predator, to mark the terror they brought."

Bronze blades clashed in painted lines. Shields split. Waves crashed in carved relief that seemed to roar even in silence. Flames tore through the ship, painted tongues of red and black rising into the smoke. Beneath the ridge of Cumbre Vieja, the burning vessel was preserved forever in pigment and stone, a monument to survival and loss.

A murmur spread through the room, but Esme pressed on.

The ridge appeared behind the blaze. Those who knew the island sat forward at once.

"Cumbre Vieja," she said. "Their ship burned beneath the ridge you see here. This is a record, not a legend. Khamariti and his Phoenician crew were stranded on the island after the fire. They stayed there nearly five years before they could rebuild their ship and leave."

She drew a slow breath and moved to the next image. The photograph filled the screen with hieroglyphs and painted figures. Pharaohs stood tall in crowns of red and white, their faces sharp with power. Yet the gods beside them were not as expected.

The falcon, the ibis, the jackal. Their eyes were missing. Some had smooth stone where the eyes should be, others were painted with cloth drawn across their faces like blindfolds. Their gaze was absent, their power stripped away.

"Here," Esme said softly, "the message changes. The gods watch no longer. They are blind. Eyeless. The carvings suggest they did not exist, or that they had turned away."

Below, the photograph shifted the mood in the hall. A body lay wrapped in linen, dried by salt and resin. His face was narrow, his hands crossed over his chest. The cloth bore faint traces of hieratic script, prayers for safe passage. The image was stark and raw. A man long dead, yet preserved, his name carried across oceans.

"This is Alim," Esme said, her voice tightening. "An ancient academic from Agadir. His body was honoured, his name remembered. They buried him with some care, his daughter part of the historic expedition. His sacrifice carried weight enough to be painted on these walls."

For a long moment, no one moved.

Below them the story ran on. Lines of plague and suffering, men bent with sickness, priests with arms raised in helpless appeal. No divine gaze met them. No god answered.

Esme clicked forward. The next painting filled the screen. Frogs swarmed across the banks of the Nile, drawn in such numbers that the surface of the river seemed alive. Another slide showed locusts in dark clouds, wings and jaws etched with frantic strokes, fields stripped bare in their wake.

The room grew tense as the story deepened. Hail rained from the sky in shards of white, crushing crops and splintering huts. Fire followed, painted as red streaks that fell like spears from above, the fields left blackened and dead.

And then came the most haunting images. Rows of children, painted in pale tones, their bodies still, their mothers bent in grief. Priests stood in silence, unable to act, their eyes raised to gods that were blind or absent.

Esme's voice dropped to almost a whisper as she moved to the final slide.

Here the carving was different. Simple, almost private. A single figure of a young girl stood beside Khamariti, her name cut into the stone. A line of glyphs ran beneath: Taken in the night of passing.

Esme steadied herself. "This… this was his daughter. The plague that swept through and took the lives of children did not pass his house. For him it was not deliverance, it was loss. He carved her here so she would not be forgotten."

"Khamariti had travelled far," Esme said. "He left Egypt, sailed north to Byblos, and from there joined a Phoenician ship bound for the open sea. He was searching for the source of the plagues that were destroying his land. And from what we've found in the cavern, we believe he discovered it. It's not what is depicted in the Bible."

The hall erupted. Some gasped, moved to silence by the intimacy of the carving. Others shouted in anger, calling it an attack on sacred scripture. Pens scratched furiously, cameras flashed, and voices clashed in outrage.

"Are you denouncing the Bible?" one journalist shouted from the front row, his voice cutting through the noise of the room.

Esme held her ground, her eyes fixed on the screen. "This is not our intention," she said firmly. "This is what was carved into the stone. The record of a man who lived, who suffered, and who told us the truth as he saw it. The disasters were not the work of gods. They were the work of nature itself. This is history, first hand and what we believe to be fact. However, we need to do further tests to verify."

Gasps rang through the hall. She pressed on, but voices cut across her words.

"You are meant to be a scientist, not an enemy of faith," one man shouted, his voice ringing above the rest.

Another journalist stood, his face flushed with anger. "My readers will want to know, are you saying the Ten Commandments don't exist? That it's acceptable to kill, to steal, to covet. You call yourself a researcher, yet you stand here like an enemy of faith, mocking what people hold sacred."

The cries spread. Some journalists slammed their pens against their notebooks, their words already framing headlines of outrage. Others snapped photographs with flashes that lit the tension like lightning.

Esme held her ground, her voice steady. "I am showing you what is carved into the stone. This is evidence. Not belief. Not denial. Evidence."

Lex pushed back his chair, ready to rise, but Esme caught his eye and raised a firm hand. He froze, then sank back down. This part was her battle.

The uproar grew. Some, the minority in the hall clapped and called for Esme to go on, while others shouted her down, their anger turning the room into a storm of voices. The noise swelled until it felt as if the walls themselves were trembling.

Thea leaned toward Lex and whispered, "T-this is a-s- setup. Look at the press row, every outlet's aligned with Hope. The Jerusalem Herald, the Christian News from Holland, the Catholic Chronicle, they've packed the room with his people."

Esme resolute, turned back to the screen and pressed the control. The next slide burst into view.

The painting showed a wave vast and black, carved in sweeping lines that filled the stone. It struck the coasts of distant lands with unstoppable force. Boats shattered into splinters. Houses broke and vanished beneath the surge. Glyphs showed men and women scrambling up steep ground, their arms raised in terror as the sea swallowed everything below.

The hall fell to a harsh silence. Even the loudest voices stilled as the image burned on the screen, a disaster painted in colour more than two thousand years ago.

"Although Max is our chief geologist and will explain this in more detail later," Esme said, her voice steady but tight, "I want to show you the next set of drawings and glyphs."

She pressed a button, and the screen behind her filled with an image from a fragile sheet of papyrus, its edges darkened by time, its centre marked by a bold cartouche. Inside it was a scene carved with astonishing precision: a great mountain split apart, its flank sliding into the sea. Waves rose higher than temples, ships tossed like leaves. "This," Esme said softly, "is a record of a landslide on the island we now call La Palma. Khamariti's hand drew it. He worked out the source of the plagues when the mountain fell."

She clicked forward. The screen filled with the image of the roaring wave, its black crest carved in sweeping strokes.

"The tsunami," she continued, her words carrying across the hushed hall. "It raced across the sea. Not only the islands, but the whole Mediterranean."

Esme pressed the control again. The next slide brought life back to the room. A painting showed men cutting trees on a foreign shore. Axes swung at trunks that leaned with the blow. Others bent over clay jars, filling them with resin drawn from fresh cuts in the bark. Fires burned in the background, smoke curling into the sky.

"They repaired their ship," Esme said. "They used what the island gave them. Timber for planks, resin for pitch. They fought to keep moving, to finish what they began. And while the crew laboured to keep the vessel afloat, Khamariti, with his companion and guard Imbu, and Zarah, the daughter of Alim, turned to the mountain itself. Together they cut chambers from the rock, shaped the cavern, and set the walls with paint and glyphs. What they left behind was more than refuge. It was a temple, a record, a warning for the future."

Details filled the screen. Ropes coiled on the ground. Stone tools sharpened on flat slabs. Men with sweat on their faces, drawn with lines so fine that each stroke felt alive.

"This is not the work of myth," she told them. "This is memory. They built again. They endured."

She clicked forward once more.

Now the chamber itself appeared. The photograph widened, showing the cavern in all its glory. Pillars rose from the volcanic floor, their bases painted in deep greens and blues, lotus and papyrus carved into their stone. The ceiling shimmered with faint traces of gold stars, constellations arranged as they once appeared above the Nile. The walls blazed with scenes of journey and worship, their colours still vibrant in the glow of torchlight.

""This," Esme said, her voice low, "was their temple. Not a place of prayer, but a place to record history. Carved beneath a mountain alive with fire, they left this record hidden in stone, preserved by the volcano itself. It is both tomb and testimony."

The image lingered, vast and silent. The audience shifted in their seats, but no one looked away.

Esme lowered the control and stepped back from the lectern. Her words were finished. She let the cavern speak for her.

The silence in the hall was deeper than any applause, but it broke fast.

Voices rose at once, sharp, and hostile.

"You call this evidence? It is heresy."

"Are you rewriting scripture?"

"Is this science or theatre?"

"Who funds you?"

Cameras flashed, the light harsh on Esme's face. The storm of questions clashed in the air until it felt like the walls shook.

A journalist from The New York Times leaned forward, tie loosened, pencil tapping a steady beat against the desk.

"Your slides are convincing, the recordings too," he said, his voice carrying across the room. "But how do you answer the Spanish authorities' claim that this is just an eighteenth-century hoax, the work of Sebastián de Morales, the court artist who supposedly carved the cavern to mimic the style of Ramesses II?"

The mention of the name stirred a low murmur. De Morales, the eccentric painter-sculptor who, according to legend, had vanished in the Canary Islands while chasing 'the light of the ancients.' The Spanish government had made him their shield, a convenient ghost to hide behind.

Before Esme could respond, another voice rose from the back, a young reporter from El Daario, her accent edged with pride and challenge.

"And what about the tariffs?" she called out. "This morning, President Hope lifted all duties on Spanish exports to North America. Do you think that's just a coincidence, or a payoff for cooperation?"

A ripple spread through the hall. Cameras swung toward her, pens froze mid-note. The question sliced through the air, turning the press conference from inquiry to confrontation.?"

The room stirred. Heads turned. The question hung between politics and science, drawing a murmur that Esme could feel tightening around her like a net.

Lex stood to answer the next question. "Carbon dating will prove the pigments' age. If the Spanish authorities allow us to test, the results will speak. And consider this, hieroglyphs were not deciphered until 1822, when Champollion worked with the Rosetta Stone. In the eighteenth century only a handful of men could even guess at their meaning. To suggest such scholars conspired to create a hoax on this scale is beyond belief."

A second hand rose, sharp. The Post. A woman in dark glasses asked, "Spanish authorities have blocked Cairo's archaeologists from visiting. Do you know why?"

Lex's reply was careful. "We are also barred from returning. We hold the same questions you do. For answers, you must ask Spain directly."

The third question came from the Mail, sharp and urgent. "Do you believe Khamariti's theories of the plagues?"

Lex's tone softened. "He was Pharaoh's architect, a man of vision. His carvings show dead fish in the Nile, frogs swarming the cities, skies darkened with ash, storms of fire and rock. These are not myths. They are natural disasters, witnessed and cut into stone. I find no scientific reason to doubt him."

The tension rose. The Sun struck next. A man with a grin that did not reach his eyes. "I know this was touched on before, but to make clear are you saying the biblical account of Moses and the plagues is false?"

Lex breathed once and held calm. "We speak only to evidence. The Bible was written centuries after the events it describes. The reign of Ramesses was a thousand years before that. Stories grow. We cannot say what is fabricated, only what the stone shows. We respect faith. But we must follow fact."

The room erupted.

"Are you reducing miracles to geology?"

"Are you accusing prophets of invention?"

"Do you understand the offence this causes to believers?"

Esme leaned to the microphone, her voice even. "We are not dismissing faith. We are showing that natural events can be remembered as divine. A flood to one is a punishment. To another, it is geology. Khamariti chose the second."

The storm grew. Questions flew like arrows. Some wanted proof, others wanted blood.

Lex fielded them with patience, always pulling back to evidence. "Carbon dating," he repeated. "Seismic truth. Pigment chemistry. These will decide. Not opinion."

When the pressure grew too sharp, security stepped in, discreet but firm, guiding the team out under a wash of hot lights and restless voices.

Lex stood, his voice cutting through the noise. "Enough. You will have your answers, but now you will hear the science." He turned, steady, and gestured toward his colleague. "Max Keeper, our geologist, will show you what lies beneath the ridge."

The uproar dulled, not gone, but forced to listen. Max stepped forward, calm in the heat of the storm.

He carried no notes, only a laser pointer. The first image lit the screen: a clean profile of La Palma, its ridges traced in sharp lines. He pointed to a long scar running down the volcano's flank.

"This," he said, his voice plain and steady, "this is the second fault. New to us, but not unrecorded."

He clicked, and the next slide appeared. Across the cavern wall, alongside the painted ships and plagues, Khamariti had cut lines of numbers and measures. Ratios of slope. Marks of distance. Angles of strain. It was not prayer. It was calculation.

"Khamariti saw it," Max said. "Mapped it, logged it, even left the receipts in stone. He knew this mountain had a crack in its character, a fault from the same landslip he was chasing."

The room stirred. Journalists leaned forward. Some scribbled furiously, others stared.

Max went on. "Our data says the same, stress lines, pressure build-up, a steady crawl down the flank. Khamariti wasn't guessing; he was warning. The fault's still breathing under this ridge, and if it wakes, it'll rearrange the map for us."

The screen changed once more. A wave model swept across the map, black water racing outward from La Palma into the Atlantic. The hall shifted in unease. No one needed equations now. The image told the story.

"Khamariti left us a message in stone," Max said. "And our science shows he was right."

The silence that followed was sharp, heavy, and full of doubt and disbelief.

🦅

The next two days blurred. Lex and his team had a confirmed booking to present their findings. They left the ship and flew into John Lennon Airport in Liverpool, the rain and fog waiting for them as they landed.

Liverpool greeted them with rain and hostility. Airport was lined with cameras, microphones thrust forward, voices raised.

"Are you blaming Pharaohs for climate change?"

"Isn't this fearmongering?"

"Are you rewriting the Bible?"

"Who is paying you?"

They were not questions. They were stones dressed as words.

At Max's home university in Liverpool, the mood was different. The lecture hall filled not with politicians or pundits, but with scholars, men and women armed with pens instead of cameras, notebooks instead of placards. The air carried curiosity, not confrontation. Here, questions were meant to uncover, not accuse.

Their questions were sharp, but professional. Pigment control. Binder chemistry. Error margins. Artifact context. They probed with knowledge, not fury. This was their battlefield, and they welcomed the fight.

Thea stood first, walking them through chain of custody for every file, every scan, every recording. She spoke with a teacher's patience, her tone calm. Max followed, fielding questions on seismic baselines, on the limits of monitoring tools, on the need for tiltmeters on the ridge. Esme showed fragments of panels. She spoke of the hand of a man who had carved plagues into stone, her voice steady despite the protests outside. Lex closed, reminding them that no theory yet explained everything, that evidence must come before interpretation.

Outside, chants rolled like surf against stone. Protesters hammered placards against iron railings.

chapter 40:
Digital Storm

E sme's laptop glowed in the dim office, its light harsh against the rain-dark window. The cursor blinked over a tide of open tabs: hostile comments, spliced soundbites, hurried think pieces that mistook speed for insight. Every headline screamed the same message: frauds, heretics, liars.

Her thumb scrolled until the words blurred, insults sliding over her like grit on the tide. One window offered a live panel where a pastor in Texas called them "apostles of science who wish to dethrone God." Another was a video clip from a London talk show where a red-faced pundit dismissed their work as "a forgery painted in a cave." Below, a scrolling banner repeated the accusation: the biggest archaeological hoax of the century.

By the window, Max sat forward, elbows on his knees, jaw set hard. His analytical eyes, once bright with discovery, were dulled now by days of attack. He had the bruised look of a man who had wrestled too long with numbers that would not stay still.

"Esme," he said at last, voice flat with disbelief. "You need to see this."

He turned his screen. A new article from The Chronicle of Science pulsed in its headline glow. MAX KEEPER: FEAR-MONGER, FABULIST, FRAUD.

Max paused before reading aloud. "'He cannot read a graph. His alarmist claims have no place in responsible science.'" He closed the laptop. "So, I'm a fear-mongering fabulist now, good company, if you like Galileo."

Esme's mouth twisted. "Fear mongering? We gave them dates, data, margins of error. We gave them the truth, and they set it on fire."

Max's grip tightened on the chair. "Not the data they're after now, it's us on trial."

It had begun with scepticism. They had expected that. La Palma's fissures were ancient, and the island's geology a palimpsest of collapse and renewal. Max had presented a chain of signals that ended in a warning: an unstable flank that could, one day, fall. His warning had not been welcome.

At first, colleagues picked at calibration and scope. The expected jabs. Then the circle widened. Commentators who had never touched a seismograph pronounced the research reckless. Religious leaders filled late-night panels, declaring that human pride was the oldest sin. Then the President of the United States made their names part of a speech about blasphemy and lies.

Thea alone had been spared. She hated that more than any insult hurled at the others.

The office door clicked. Thea stepped inside, hair pulled back, her face pale with something deeper than fatigue. Esme looked up.

"They have not gone for you," Esme said. Her voice was quiet, but it cut.

Thea hesitated. "N-no. They have not."

"Why not?"

Thea's eyes flicked to the rain-streaked glass, then back. Her breath came quick, uneven. "B-because I kept my mouth shut," she said, the words breaking as tension tightened her throat. "You… you denied the plagues, denied the G-god the President of the United States and millions upon millions of others claim to serve."

She tried to steady herself, one hand trembling against the table. "In one of my interviews, they asked if our work contradicted faith. I said no. I s-said text and evidence could live side by side. I even said the flood was part of a tradition m-many still honour."

Esme's eyes narrowed. "And that was enough? One sentence, and you were spared while we were dragged through fire?"

Thea swallowed hard. "Yes. I see it now. And I did not step back into the line with you. I should h- have."

Esme's breath came slow and heavy. "We are in this together, or we are not in it at all. Remember that when the next storm breaks."

She left. Thea stood frozen, the weight of her choice pressing down. She had said the safe words in a dangerous moment, and something in her integrity had cracked.

Unbeknownst to the others, her uncle Gerald DeWalt had warned her himself: Do not dig yourself in too deep.

Three weeks after the Liverpool uproar, the reckoning came. Every university with ties to the United States cut them off. All of them. Lex, Esme, Thea, and Max found themselves out of work in a single sweep.

Thea seemed to vanish after Liverpool. None of them had seen her since, no messages, no calls, not even a trace on the project servers. It was as if she had stepped out of the frame and taken her secrets with her.

The storm had travelled faster than any wave.

The blow came fast and without appeal. Within days every door closed. Universities struck their names from registers, journals withdrew pending articles, and archives revoked passes they had carried for years. Access codes were cancelled. Databases locked. Research grants vanished overnight. For Lex, Esme, Thea, and Max, it was exile dressed as administration.

They gathered in quiet rooms, speaking in low voices of futures that now seemed broken. Esme stared at her notes, knowing no library would host her again. Max scrolled through seismic feeds, cut off from the networks that made sense of them. Thea, always composed, watched her projects sink into silence. Lex said little, but the weight of it pressed against him with every hour. Their work, their names, their lives as scholars had been stripped away.

It was in that silence of loss that DeWalt reached out. His message to Lex was short, almost casual: Meet me in Quebec, if you ever want to work again.

Lex walked through falling snow, the sting of it sharp against his face. Ahead, the Fairmont Le Château Frontenac rose above the city like a citadel. Inside, wealth softened the edges of power.

In a suite lined with dark wood, Gerard DeWalt stood by the window, watching snow spiral past the glass. His presence was as deliberate as the summons that had drawn Lex here.

"Professor," DeWalt said, turning. "Tea?"

Lex accepted. "You know what they say about me. You know why this is an odd invitation."

DeWalt's eyes gleamed. "Thea is my niece. She came to me. My people traced the campaign against you, it was crafted, not organic. You were discredited by design. I am not here to bury you. I am here to see what can be built."

"You can trust him," said a voice from the door. Thea entered, cheeks flushed from the cold.

Lex looked between them. "Wondered where you disappeared to, Thea," he said, his voice low but edged. Then his gaze shifted. "What do you want, Mr DeWalt?"

"Facts," DeWalt said. "And the chance to fund what others fear. I propose a research unit in Vancouver. You and your team lead it. You publish without permission. I will provide cover, laboratories, reach. But first, I need to know what you carried out of La Palma."

Lex weighed the silence, his eyes moving across the table before he spoke.

"We have more than a theory," he said quietly. "We have a statue, black, polished like obsidian. It was found sealed in the same strata as the glyphs. The figure is of a man, broad-shouldered, one arm raised as if in warning. The inscription beneath names him Imbu, one of Khamariti's own."

He paused, letting the words settle. "And we have a bone. Alim, the scholar from Agadir, traced the markings on it to a burial record, a name preserved in glyphs, carved by Khamariti's hand. Together they form a chain that stretches three millennia."

He leaned back, studying DeWalt's expression. "It's enough to occupy scholars for years," he said. "And you already know that —, you've had Thea feeding you pieces since I appointed her to the team."

DeWalt's expression barely shifted, though his voice carried a trace of warmth. "Good. I have already secured a carbon-dating machine in a private lab. You will not wait for permission. And the fault line, you will have my support there as well." He paused, eyes narrowing. "Thea did tell me about the artefacts. I wanted to see if you would admit it yourself. Now I know you are being honest."

Lex leaned forward, voice tight with urgency. "The fault line, Max's models show the slope is unstable. It may hold for centuries, or it may fail tomorrow. We cannot wait."

DeWalt's gaze didn't move. He folded his hands, then gave a slow nod. "I will make calls. Quiet ones." He let the pause draw out before continuing. "For now, you'll prepare for Vancouver. Understand this, it isn't charity. I do not give my wealth away; I invest it."

He rose, pacing slowly toward the window. "We fight the battles right in front of us, Professor, but we plan for the longer wars. You will build what timid universities cannot. You will chase what governments fear to name, the truth beneath history. Plagues, Atlantis. Khamariti. The stories the earth tried to bury."

Lex thought of Cadiz, of Liverpool, of the scar on La Palma's flank. "I will not move without my team."

""Unity," DeWalt said, "is the first defence." He checked his watch, then looked up. "And before you start debating logistics, it's already done. I'm flying your team in. The jet leaves within the hour. Luxembourg. Quiet routes, no customs chatter, no leaks."

chapter 41:
A Sacrifice at Dusk

Nebit leaned low over the horse's withers, urging it faster, the animal's breath bursting into the dusk like steam from a forge. Thebes' walls fell behind, shadows lengthening across the plain, the air still heavy with the scent of barley stubble and hearth smoke. In his belt-pouch the decree lay sealed, but its words already burned his thoughts raw. High Priest Ankhwennefer had ordered Khamariti taken to the Nile and sacrificed before nightfall.

Nebit had read it twice by torchlight in the scribe's chamber, praying that ink might trick him, that the script might shift into something lesser, banishment, mutilation, exile. But it had not. The lines stayed fixed, merciless. The decree was not law; it was execution cloaked as ritual.

Each gallop brought him closer to the village where Imbu and Zarah waited, guardians of Khamariti's hidden scrolls, the only ones with knowledge enough to protect what must not be lost. Nebit's eyes skimmed the fields: a potter stacking cooling bowls, a fisherman mending his net by lamplight, a mother drawing water into a jar. These ordinary motions sharpened into a ledger of all Egypt stood to lose if wisdom died with one man.

He had prepared them for this day. He had warned of sudden arrests, of seals pressed into wax that broke families like reeds. But the high priest had moved faster than even Nebit feared. Too fast.

He pressed his heels again. The horse stretched into its stride, hooves throwing sparks from flint. Behind him the chants from Thebes' temples drifted across the plain, an echo of incense and threat.

On the western bank of the Nile, torches multiplied like fallen stars. Flames licked the breeze, staining the water in wavering gold.

A procession gathered. Guards pressed the people into order. Farmers, boatmen, artisans, none dared resist. Yet the air did not carry the jubilant roar Ankhwennefer expected. It carried grief.

Khamariti was dragged forward, wrists bound, robe torn, dust clinging to his limbs. Once the Pharaoh's master builder, the man who raised Abu Simbel, who charted the stars into stone, now shuffled like a condemned criminal.

Ankhwennefer led from the front, staff in hand, robes white as bone. He expected cheers. Instead, silence pressed against him like a stone wall. Men and women averted their gaze, mothers clutched children close. The quiet stung more than open defiance. It was sorrow, and it soured the taste of triumph.

The barge awaited at the bank, cedar planked, its prow carved into the head of a falcon. On its deck lay a basket of stones, each one cut with symbols of judgement. The guards shoved Khamariti forward and forced him aboard. The timbers groaned under the weight of men and armour.

Khamariti did not resist. He moved with a strange calm, his eyes steady, his shoulders relaxed, as if he had chosen to walk into the trial rather than be dragged. To some in the crowd this calm looked like arrogance. To others it looked like courage. The whispers began to shift with the mood.

Priests in white linen lined the steps of the quay, and among them the High Priest stood with his staff. His guards stepped forward to lay harsh hands on Khamariti, gripping his arms and twisting them back. The architect did not flinch. The murmur of the crowd rose, uneasy, caught between anger and awe.

The High Priest lifted his staff. "Enough." His voice was low, but it carried. The guards froze at once. He looked out over the crowd and felt the sway of it, the shift of hearts. Some were ready to condemn, but many were not so sure. The calm of the accused was undoing their certainty.

Ramesses II descended from the carriage, the copper bells of the horses still ringing with a mournful chime. Half veiled in shadow, his face was leaner now, cut with years of rule and burden. He stood still, silent, a god-king to those who watched. His presence steadied the gathering, but his silence deepened their unease.

The judgement had been given, and the crowd no longer knew what they wished it to be. Khamariti straightened. The torches cut his face into granite planes, his eyes fixed not on the priest but on the river, as if measuring its secrets.

"You will kneel," a guard barked.

"I will stand," Khamariti replied. His voice carried, unwavering.

Ankhwennefer lifted his staff. The first chant rolled across the water, syllables trained to sound eternal, crafted to bind fear into obedience.

"O you who guard the threshold of life and death, receive this sacrifice. Through the waters, restore balance to the Two Lands."

The crowd held its breath, the Nile mirroring torch and moon. Some shut their eyes. Others clenched their fists where no one would see. Imbu was nowhere to be seen.

When the chant faltered, Khamariti spoke. His voice struck like a hammer against silence.

"Remember, Ankhwennefer, pride comes before a fall."

A ripple moved through the watchers.

The priest leaned close, venom low. "Your end was written long ago. The Nile will finish your line tonight."

Khamariti turned his gaze to the people. "I have crossed lands beyond your maps. I have stood before beings you call gods. They are no more divine than you. Legacy is not decrees or temples, it is what we teach our children. You, childless, will leave nothing."

The high priest's lips thinned. "And your family? Gone. If you speak truth, what endures when the line is broken?"

Khamariti raised his chin, his voice steady as the current. "Truth. It does not die with me. It will outlast even you."

The people stirred. Whispers moved like a current through reeds.

Ankhwennefer cut them with a lash of his staff. "Bind him!"

Guards looped rope across Khamariti's chest, around ankles, the knots precise, efficient, impersonal. The largest stone was fastened to his feet, its ash-grey surface glistening. Khamariti watched without flinching. He had taught men to shift mountains with weights and counterweights. Now his own lessons would drag him down.

"You have one moment," the high priest said. "Speak wisely."

Khamariti did not look at him. He raised his voice to the people on the bank. "Build wisely. Teach what you know. Do not be deceived by robes."

The murmur grew, no longer grief alone but defiance half-born.

"Enough!" Ankhwennefer roared, his voice splitting the night. The chant surged to its fevered height, rolling like a storm over the riverbank. Torches buckled in their brackets, flames bending as if the gods themselves had turned to listen.

He raised his arms, eyes wide, veins standing in his neck. "Let the heretic be swallowed! Let his deceit sink beneath the sacred current!"

Then, with sudden violence, he thrust his staff forward. The guards obeyed without hesitation. Iron met flesh. Khamariti stumbled, his chains biting deep, and the crowd gasped as he was driven to the barge's edge. For a heartbeat he stood there, framed by fire and moonlight, before the push came.

He fell hard, the weight of stone dragging him down. The Nile broke open with a single hollow crack, swallowing him whole. Ripples widened, colliding with the torchlight, shattering it into a thousand trembling shards before folding back into calm.

The crowd exhaled as one, a sound caught between grief and disbelief. Women pressed hands to their mouths. A priest dropped his torch. Somewhere, a child began to wail.

Ankhwennefer raised his staff again, forcing strength into a voice that now trembled. "The Nile gives life," he cried, "and it takes it away! Speak his name no more!"

But the words did not carry. They fell dead into the dark, lost to the water that had claimed him.

Ramesses did not move. His face was carved from stillness, unreadable even to those who knew him best. Only his eyes followed the river, the widening rings, the last gleam of flame, until the surface smoothed and Khamariti was gone.

chapter 42:
Truth Under Siege

Gerard DeWalt was not a man who left things to chance. In the weeks since Professor Lex Mullin's research had been savaged across pulpits, newsrooms, and social feeds, he had mobilised his arsenal like a general arranging regiment on a battlefield. Lawyers, investigators, media operatives, each deployed with precision, each move chosen to wound or protect.

The first strikes were swift. Smaller outlets and lone commentators who had gleefully accused Mullin's team of fraud received cease-and-desist notices. The letters were curt and lethal, their message simple: retract or be ruined. Within days, retractions appeared, couched in legal jargon but underpinned by panic. One by one, they deleted articles, apologised, begged obscurity. It was not guilt that drove them, but fear.

The bigger adversaries proved harder. National broadcasters, religious consortiums, political think tanks, they held the line. Their lawyers stalled. Anchors sneered. Commentators wrapped their attacks in righteousness. They had the ear of the President, and that made them bold. Yet DeWalt was relentless. His investigators dug deeper, tracing the smear campaign's origins. What they uncovered led back to corridors of power within President Hope's administration itself. Emails. Leaks. Funding trails. Enough to confirm the smear had been orchestrated, not spontaneous.

When DeWalt confronted contacts in Washington with the evidence, the silence that met him was its own admission. He knew then that he was directly over the target.

But defence alone was never enough. DeWalt launched a counter-offensive. He chose his battlefield with care. His media operatives partnered with the *New York Clarion*, a paper known for rigour and reach. Together they built a story that would strike where Hope was weakest: on science ignored and lives endangered.

The piece ran across two full pages. Its centrepiece was Max Keeper's seismic data from La Palma. Independent seismologists, with spotless records and no stake in politics, had reviewed the findings. Their conclusion was unanimous. The fault under Cumbre Vieja was unstable. Its collapse could hurl a tsunami across the Atlantic, striking the eastern seaboard within hours.

The article did not merely publish Max's theory; it validated it. And it exposed the administration's attempt to bury the data. President Hope's ridicule of Mullin's team was framed as reckless indifference to millions of lives. The Clarion headline cut like a blade:

"White House Ignores Tsunami Threat: Experts Confirm La Palma Fault Could Wipe U.S. Coast."

When the presses rolled, the effect was immediate. Phones rang in capitals across the Atlantic. Networks broke schedules to cover the story. Twitter blazed with graphs, tide models, and the #LaPalma tag. The revelation could not be ignored.

At the daily White House press briefing, Riley braced for questions. His notes were ready, bland deflections rehearsed. But before he could step to the podium, the doors opened, and President Hope himself entered. The room stiffened. Cameras snapped to life. The President's presence shattered protocol; he rarely appeared unannounced.

Hope strode to the podium. His face was set, his voice sharp enough to cut steel.

"This morning's publication by the Clarion is nothing less than desperate sensationalism. A backroom deal with Gerard DeWalt dressed up as journalism."

He dismissed Max Keeper as a "English fear-monger" and Lex Mullin as a "New York fraud dressed as a scholar." He accused the paper of paying "prostituted experts" to invent opinion. He thundered that it was not about science, but power.

A reporter stood. "Mr President, if the story is baseless, why are you here personally?"

Hope's jaw clenched. "Because such lies threaten to erode the foundations of our splendid work. To govern in fear of events that may never come is folly. The timescales of fault lines are for the divine, not for us."

Another voice cut through. "So, you dismiss Professor Mullin's teams discoveries in La Palma outright?"

Hope's eyes narrowed. "Only those archaeologists and scientists in DeWalt's employ would call that cavern genuine. Spain itself declared it an eighteenth-century hoax. Romantic fakery, dressed up for gullible scholars."

The room erupted, questions fired like arrows: on science, on faith, on trade deals, on corruption. Hope's mask slipped; anger poured through.

"If La Palma collapses and the ocean rises, then impeach me," he snapped. "Mark my words, such calamity will not come on my watch. God would not allow it."

He turned, the air vibrating with the force of his fury. Papers trembled on desks as he strode from the room. At the threshold he stopped, eyes burning into Riley.

"I will not allow these people to twist the word of God. I will not have the Bible undermined. Do whatever it takes to silence them. No more claims. No more evidence."

Riley's voice was low. "Do I activate Jones's team?"

Hope's reply came like the stroke of a blade. "You do whatever it takes."

DeWalt's office hummed with screens replaying the press conference. Lex sat rigid in his chair, Esme beside him. DeWalt leaned forward, fingers steepled, expression cold.

"Hope is bleeding," DeWalt said softly. "The more he struggle, the tighter the chains bind."

Lex exhaled. Weariness etched deep lines across his face. "Without you, we would already be history. Discredited footnotes."

Esme's eyes were alight with fire. "Then we don't stop. Abu Simbel. Khamariti left us a trail there. We have to follow it."

DeWalt nodded slowly, the faintest hint of a smile ghosting across his face. "Arrangements are already in motion," he said. "Your letter to the Cairo Museum has been stripped of clutter, pushed through the right hands, and stamped with confirmation. You go."

He leaned in, voice dropping until it was almost a growl. "But we move quietly. Hope's people will be watching, CIA, FBI, whichever suits he's sent this week. They'll be waiting for us to make a wrong move."

He straightened, eyes glinting. "We won't give them one."

The escape began before dawn.

Two vehicles rolled from a Luxembourg basement. Inside: doubles disguised with wigs and prosthetics. Their habits rehearsed until even a casual glance would be fooled. They lived an ordinary day in extraordinary detail: coffee in a familiar café, library study, a walk through the park. The FBI agents logged every movement, confident they were tracking Lex and Esme.

Meanwhile, the real Lex and Esme slipped through service doors, into alleys, then unmarked vans. Their route was scouted, cleared of cameras, timed to avoid patrols. By mid-morning, they were at a private airfield.

A cargo plane waited. Its manifest listed textiles and machine parts. But one steel container inside was fitted with benches, vents, water, enough for two passengers to vanish across the sky.

At 03:47, the plane lifted into cloud. Controllers logged a routine freighter bound for Iceland. The decoys sipped coffee in Luxembourg café. The FBI watched, unaware they were following ghosts.

An unmarked shuttle collected Lex and Esme at a military strip near Cairo. With them was Dr Amirah Zahid, her expression taut, her voice dry.

"Like something from a spy novel," she muttered as they moved through Cairo's chaos: horns blaring, donkeys weaving, soldiers watching with practised eyes.

Their destination was a villa on the Nile, discreetly guarded. From its gardens, the river stretched black under lamps. Inside, tea was poured, its steam curling in the night air.

Lex offered thanks for the refuge. Zahid's reply was crisp. "If we find nothing in Nefertari's statue, this expedition never happened. Egypt will not be made a fool."

"And if we do?" Lex asked.

"Then we prove it. On record. A national crew will film everything. They won't know what they're filming until it's done. But if the evidence is there, no one can deny it."

Esme unwrapped the black effigy of Imbu. Zahid traced its lines with awe. "This is not ornament. It is a master's work. Khamariti himself."

She handed it back reverently. "We leave at dawn. No phones. Only my team. Secrecy above all."

In Washington, the Oval Office seethed.

CIA Director Rotherham delivered the blow. "Our source confirms Mullin and Esme are in Egypt. Abu Simbel."

FBI Director Johnson blustered. "Impossible. My men have them under watch in Luxembourg."

"You were chasing decoys," Riley snapped.

Before they could argue, an aide rushed in. "Sir, CDN broadcast. Now."

Max returned to Vancouver under escort, several of DeWalt's security team shadowing him like wraiths through the terminal. Days later, his face filled the screen in the briefing room, pale from travel, eyes sunken from lack of sleep.

On screen, a gloved Max Keeper lifted a small bundle wrapped in linen. The camera tightened, catching the tremor of the fabric as he peeled it back layer by layer. Inside lay a single severed finger bone, small, precise, its surface marked with faint traces of ochre and age.

The room went still. Even the guards stopped pretending to listen to their earpieces. "A relic," Max said. "Taken from La Palma. Removed, not robbed. A mistake, and one we're finally fixing before someone else claims the moral high ground."

Murmurs rippled through the press. Max raised a hand and continued.

""Carbon dating puts the bone around the thirteenth century BCE," Max said. "Geochem points to the Agadir basin. The remains are Alim's, scholar, explorer, Khamariti's companion. Etchings in the

La Palma cavern show him right there beside the architect. He was part of the mission."

Thea stepped forward. Her tone was calm, contrite. "We extend formal apology to the Spanish government. The finger was already severed when found. I preserved it by protocol. But in the chaos, I failed to declare it. That was my error."

Max unfurled a photograph: the finger bone lying beside Alim's desiccated remains in the cavern. The linen wrappings were ancient, brittle, impossible to fake.

The oval room fell into stunned silence. The image was clinical yet devastating.

"We will return the relic to Morocco," Thea added. "And in good faith, we ask Spain to release the remainder of the find."

The press erupted, questions flying. The world gasped.

President Hope's fury was volcanic. "Arrest him! Artefacts stolen. Make them pay."

Riley countered, voice cold. "Arrest makes him a martyr. Better to muddy the waters. Claim eighteenth-century forgery. Spread doubt."

Rotherham shook his head. "The real danger is Mullin. Abu Simbel. That is where history waits to be changed or used to mislead."

Hope's voice dropped to ice. "Tell the Egyptians to shut them down. Or face consequences."

Rotherham stared at him for a long beat, the room shrinking around the words. "Due to our Christian policies, we have lost influence in many Muslim countries, including Egypt. It would trigger protests. An incident. They want access to the cavern. We don't have the leverage there that we do elsewhere.'"

Hope slammed a fist. "Then what options remain?"

Silence.

But Riley didn't move. Instead, he turned, eyes flicking to the corners of the room. "Sir, the room is live."

Hope stilled. Every word here was recorded. Every syllable a future noose.

Riley lifted four fingers.

Hope nodded once.

Protocol Four.

No voice confirmation. No digital trail. No chain of command. Just action, deniable, and irreversible.

The room was silent save for the ticking of the clock. Riley's face betrayed nothing. But he and Hope both knew: DeWalt had outplayed them. Lex and Esme were already on the road to Abu Simbel, beyond Washington's reach, for now.

chapter 43:
Nefertari's Secret

The convoy rolled to a stop beneath the watchful faces of the rock cut giants. Morning light lifted over Lake Nasser and turned the water to hammered metal. Abu Simbel waited with the old patience of stone. The great seated colossi of Ramesses stared into the desert. To their right the smaller sanctuary of Nefertari for the goddess Hathor held its own gravity. It was less in size yet equal in precision. The mountain face breathed heat as if waking.

Professor Lex Mullin shaded his eyes and let his gaze travel along joints and seams. He had pored over the relocation records from the nineteen sixties, measured the saw cuts in photographs, memorised the stitch pattern of the reassembly. Knowing the facts in a study was one thing. Seeing with his own eyes how a hill had been lifted and laid down again without killing what lived inside it was another.

Esme stepped beside Lex and tied her hair back with a band. The air carried the dry taste of sun-baked rock and the faint tang of the lake.

From the second vehicle, Dr Amirah Zahid, crossed with brisk precision. Her voice cut cleanly through the thrum of engines as she reached Lex, offering a firm handshake and a quick, confident smile.

"Professor Mullin, welcome to Abu Simbel," she said. She turned and began issuing rapid instructions in Arabic. Her Egyptian team moved with well-rehearsed rhythm, conservators marking ground for shade frames, laying cable runs, spreading protective pads across the dig site.

DeWalt stood back, content to let her command. He had bought them time, machines, and silence. The ground, for now, belonged to the archaeologists.

By mid-morning, a canopy shaded Nefertari's statue at the forecourt. The national recording crew, cleared at the highest level, filmed everything without commentary. No voice over. No clever angles. Fixed lenses, wide frames, time stamps on every minute. A record that would stand in any court of opinion.

A helicopter thumped over the ridge and dropped onto the temporary pad in a storm of sand and heat. Rotor wash clawed at the tents and tarpaulins until every rope strained. The noise rattled the valley like artillery. The pilot and copilot clambered out and began to offload crates stamped only with codes and weights. Plain skins for advanced tools.

Within minutes the containers split to reveal the heart of a field lab. A mobile X ray unit. A compact computed tomography trolley. A close-range scanning rig with twin heads on a truss. A long calibration bar studded with targets for photogrammetry. A curtain of ultraviolet lamps that shimmered like a veil of neon when tested.

Engines whined to the west. Three matte-black four-wheel drives tore down from the airstrip, tyres pounding the ground in rhythm. A security team and a doctor rode inside.

Moments earlier, a military transport had offloaded them, men, and crates together, each vehicle stacked with sealed cases, instruments, and rations enough to keep them working for weeks if needed.

DeWalt stepped forward, jacket snapping in the rotor wash. He shook the pilot's hand, then moved along the line of equipment like a field commander inspecting his troops. His nod was brief, decisive, and final. "Get them under cover. We are live."

Lex ran a palm over the smooth casing of the scanner. It was not affection. It was respect. These were the witnesses they would need.

They started where stress and meaning meet. At the base. At the knees. At the crown. The first day was measurement without judgement. The scan rig walked the surface in slow arcs. Reflector targets registered position to the fraction of a millimetre. The camera crew kept to tape marks and never stepped into a frame that mattered. Every cable lay on foam. Every tool sat on cloth. No scratches. No excuses.

By late afternoon, an X ray of the head removed a rumour. There was no hiding place carved in the skull. A void had once existed and had been filled during the rescue and reassembly. Mortar and stone now occupied the space. The image showed careful work done with the best intent of its time.

Disappointment touched Lex for a breath. Esme saw the flicker and closed the door on it before it could grow.

They worked until the light died. Dinner at the safe house above the site was bread, chicken with cumin, olives, and tea. They ate looking over the ridge to the wide water and the temples below like black teeth. Guards walked without sound. Far out on the lake a boat showed a moving constellation of deck lights.

Dr Zahid set the plan in three clear steps. Day two would be a complete three-dimensional surface scan of the base and plinth, including interior geometry inferred from resonant returns. Day three would be verification and careful testing of any discrepancies that presented as voids or cavities. No chisels. No prising. Only imaging and non-invasive light. Anything further would wait until the ministry signed the line, they had left blank on purpose.

The second day delivered what eyes could not. The base looked whole. The scan disagreed. From the level of the knees down to the plinth, returns changed in a way that could only be a hollow space behind a shell. Within that space the pattern was not flat. Small points glittered on the display like stars.

Organic scatter. Particulate signatures that belonged to plant fibre and old adhesive. Not a modern repair. Not a clean gap left by a saw. Something made on purpose.

Esme found a mark on the back of the base where feet could never polish it. It was so slight the light barely caught it. She fetched the small figure of Imbu from its case. On the underside of its base lay a twin of that mark. Not an exact twin. A complement. One raised. One sunk. A sign and its answer.

They brought the ultraviolet lamps to the figure and to the mark. Under that light a thin ring of residue around the line on the statue bloomed a dull green. Old resin. Once flexible enough to seal, now brittle but intact.

Dr Zahid looked to the camera and spoke for the record. She also spoke to any sceptic yet to be born.

"We have a mark on a portable object and a complementary mark on the base. We have a scan that indicates an interior cavity. We will attempt a non-destructive test to see whether the marks engage and whether that engagement changes the state of the seam we believe to be a panel."

At dawn on the third day the site felt as still as an empty church. The crew lit the base with ultraviolet. Conservators stood ready with small bottles of soluble gel and scalpels fine enough to lift a hair. Camera lamps came up.

Esme knelt, the black obsidian figure of Imbu cradled carefully in both hands. She followed the faded instructions from a photograph of a scroll discovered in the cavern on La Palma, drawings that hinted the statue itself was a key.

She aligned the raised mark to the sunken line and pressed. Nothing moved. She exhaled slowly, remembering the marginal note on the ancient image, and turned the figure a fraction clockwise.

From within the stone came a soft, hollow sigh, like air drawn through a reed. The microphone caught little more than wind, but those nearest felt it in their teeth, a low vibration that seemed older than language itself. "Again," Lex murmured.

She turned back a hair and then forward. The sound returned and changed. At the lowest course of the plinth a hairline darkened then closed as if it had never been. She kept the pressure light.

Dr Zahid came in with the conservators and started to work. They did not pry. They softened the old resin with gel so slow and gentle that a clock would look impatient. The scalpel lifted a sliver the size of a fingernail. A bag took it. Another sliver. Another bag. The seam admitted a whisper of air.

Esme studied the photograph again. The image showed a niche cut into the stone, its edges marked with faint chiselled lines. She measured, tried, withdrew, and tried again. Twice the statue refused to fit. On the third attempt, turning the base a fraction and sliding it deeper into the groove, the shape locked. Stone shifted with a muffled thud. The chamber door opened, rising a foot above the height of the average man of the Ramesses period, who stood around five feet six inches tall. The opening reached nearly six and a half feet from the stone floor.

The air that drifted out was not foul. The first scent was sharp and resinous, like forgotten myrrh sealed for centuries. It caught at the back of the throat. Dust followed, dry and thin. The space beyond was black, as if the stone itself had swallowed all light.

There were no carvings on the walls. No prayers, no hymns, no painted gods. The chamber was plain, unadorned, almost austere. But its shelves held the weight of centuries. Bundles wrapped in brittle cloth. Tubes the length of a forearm and the width of a wrist, capped with dark wood and bound with copper clasps now green with age. Scrolls lay stacked in trays, their edges curled but still whole. A scatter of thin wafers carved from bone and wood rested on another ledge, their lines so fine they seemed no more than strands of hair.

Esme's lamp cut across the chamber. The space was not wide, no larger than a small room, but it carried the sense of design. A triangle had been cut into the far wall, exact in its angles, like a measure left as a sign. Beside it, a shallow recess cradled a rod of dark metal, its bands marked by grooves.

Lex steadied himself against the nearest table, breath caught between awe and disbelief. The weight of history pressed down, yet the silence held it steady.

Dr Zahid leaned closer, her voice clipped and precise. "Record all. No cuts. No tricks. Pan slow. Show the hands."

The conservator dusted one of the tubes without opening it. She lifted it gently, tested its weight, and returned it to the shelf. "It could hold papyri," she said. "Or vellum. Or nothing but dust. We will not open it here."

DeWalt waited until Zahid, Esme, and Lex were absorbed in the study of a cartouche. His eyes had already caught what theirs had missed: three tubes set apart from the rest, their ends sealed in dark resin, half-hidden in the corner of the chamber.

He moved with care, steps muffled against the stone. Without a word, he reached for the tubes. They were cool to the touch, heavier than expected. He glanced once at the others, still bent over the carving, then slid the tubes beneath a ledge where no other scrolls or bundles lay. Out of sight. Safe.

Across the chamber, Zahid pointed to a wrapped bundle tied with a dried knot. Her voice was sharp, firm. "That knot goes on record."

They eased the wrapped case onto a cloth, severing the cords and sealing them in labelled bags. The box was heavier than it should have been, solid but not purely metal. Inside, something shifted, a cluster of assemblies locked within.

Esme lifted the lid a fraction. A faint scent of resin and dust escaped, followed by a dull gleam. Within the folds of linen lay a compact frame of bronze and crystal, its joints engraved with lines too fine for the tools of the age.

Lex leaned closer. "That shouldn't exist."

The device resembled a theodolite, but millennia too early, its sighting arms fashioned from gold-inlaid copper, its base marked with the same spiral geometry found at Saqqara and, impossibly, ratios identical to those used in modern optical alignment. In the heart of the mechanism sat a fragment of obsidian carved with concentric circles, one for each star of Orion's Belt.

Esme whispered, "The drawings on the box... it's the first pyramid."

Lex frowned, brushing more dust from the lid. The incised lines resolved into a stepped structure, flanked by symbols of alignment, the eye of Ra, a rising sun, and beneath them, a sequence of numbers cut with almost mathematical precision.

"The Step Pyramid," he murmured. "Saqqara. Designed by Imhotep for Pharaoh Djoser... around 2,670 BCE."

Esme nodded, tracing the engraved tiers with a gloved finger. "That's nearly five centuries before Khufu and the Great Pyramid. This was the beginning, architecture becoming astronomy."

Beneath the drawing, another mark gleamed faintly under her torch: a small spiral enclosed within a triangle. She looked up. "It's not just the pyramid. It's a map of its foundation chamber. These spirals, they're the same geometry we found in Khamariti's cavern on La Palma."

Lex ran a gloved finger along one curve. The instrument hummed faintly, responding to his touch as if remembering its purpose.

Dr Zahid raised her hand. "Enough. Stop speculating. We reseal. We will take the case back to camp in convoy for safety, after that it will travel to the lab in Aswan under police guard. The chamber stays under watch."

The panel slid back into place. Adhesive sealed the join against dust. Logs were signed, times recorded, custody forms checked twice. The wrapped case was carried out and placed in a waiting car, its blue lights hidden, ready to wake.

The chamber returned to its silence, but the scent of resin lingered, sharp as memory.

On the ridge above, something hung in the air. It was not a bird. A lens tracked everything below, feeding images to a windowless room far away. On the screens, the convoy, the people, and the case were all marked. A calm voice gave orders to ground teams: hold position, watch, wait. The time to act had not yet come.

The convoy left the temple and rolled toward the checkpoint. Heat shimmered on the road and dust clung to the air. Three black SUVs moved in line, guards tense, the case held safe in the centre vehicle.

Ahead, a grey flat-bed truck swung across the lane and braked hard. Its tyres spat grit as it blocked the road. Two men jumped down from the cab. They pulled at a strap as if cargo had shifted, bodies bent, hands busy. It looked like a simple roadside delay. Too simple.

At the same moment, a white pickup slid out of a lay by behind them and tucked in close to the rear SUV. Its grille almost touched the bumper. The convoy was boxed, front and back.

The lead guard slowed. Dust swirled. Heat haze shimmered until the road itself seemed to buckle.

Dr Zahid's eyes locked on the men by the flatbed. They were not relaxed like drivers fixing a load. Their feet were braced wide, shoulders tight, eyes fixed on the SUVs. Every line of their stance screamed intent.

She drew breath to shout a warning.

It was an ambush.

One man yanked the strap. The canvas fell away. On the flatbed's bed sat a mounted gun, heavy-barrelled, aimed squarely at the lead SUV. At that instant, the guards' radios went dead. A mechanical voice boomed through a loudspeaker, ordering the convoy to stop.

DeWalt's voice stayed calm. "Five."

A guard flicked a switch. Two small cylinders slipped from the bumper of the centre SUV and rolled onto the road.

"Four."

The men outside cocked their heads. They heard the hiss but did not understand.

"Three."

Lex clutched the case. Esme's hand tightened on his wrist. Dr Zahid froze.

"Two."

The white pickup behind nudged the rear SUV's bumper.

"One."

The cylinders hissed. Gas spread low over the tarmac. Not smoke, but CS gas. It cut at lungs, burned at eyes. The men by the flatbed went down first, clawing at their faces.

The lead SUV, driven by one of DeWalt's security men, plunged straight into the thick chemical cloud. Inside, throats burned and eyes streamed. Lex doubled over coughing, lungs clawing for air. Beside him, Esme's vision blurred to white, her hands groping for balance as the vehicle jolted. The guards shouted over each other, half-blind, weapons raised though they couldn't see a target.

The driver fought the wheel, coughing hard, one hand slapping at the window controls in vain as gas poured through the vents. The SUV fishtailed, tyres skidding on dust and gravel. Through the haze, the flatbed truck appeared without warning, its silhouette massive, its gun fixed dead ahead.

Through the milky air, shapes twisted and shifted, blurred figures, a flash of metal.

The SUV's driver yanked the wheel, tyres screaming. The vehicle skidded sideways, clipping the truck's fender. The impact spun the flatbed off balance. Its rear wheels lifted, caught the edge of the embankment, and the entire truck tipped, crashing onto its side with a thunderous roll. Crates and shells scattered across the tarmac.

Behind them, the second SUV ploughed into the pickup ahead, metal shrieking as steel crushed against steel. In seconds, DeWalt's security team spilled out, weapons drawn, and dealt swiftly with the men inside the pickup.

Only at the checkpoint did a siren rise. The barrier lifted without a word. The SUV with the case drove on, steady in the centre lane, as if the painted lines alone could protect it in a land this wide.

On the ridge, the camera lens shifted a few degrees, then held.

In a dim operations room half a world away, a man with neatly parted hair pressed a switch twice, two short buzzes: No go.

Thousands of miles distant, a phone on Sean Riley's desk in Washington vibrated once. Just long enough to be noticed. Far too brief to trace.

Back at the temple the panel behind the base lay in stillness. Fresh resin sealed the seam, to be opened again tomorrow. Inside, the small triangle cut into stone waited. It remembered where to stand, how to place a rod, and how the light must fall when the reader arrived. It had waited centuries for a hand that could listen.

There was no celebration. The team were too tired. They ate in the shade and watched the river turn. Their voices stayed low. Names threaded through the talk, Khamariti, Merit, Menna, Nefer. Names Esme had read on La Palma and could now almost touch. Names that might lie in ink, only a room away.

Lex set his cup down and turned to DeWalt. "These SUVs," he said. "What have you built into them? I want to know how safe we are."

DeWalt's eyes glinted in the half-light. "I never go anywhere in the world without a doctor," he said, "or a team to protect me. The vehicles are armoured, the tyres run flat, the windows resist more than glass. If they come again, we will be ready."

Late, the safe house windows glinted with the tiny eyes of camera tally lamps. Guards walked their pattern. Far off a motor droned and faded. The night held its breath.

Tomorrow they would lift the seal completely.

Somewhere in that same night a man who prayed too much moved pieces on a board and smiled at a line only he could see.

The stone slept under stars that were old when the first block was set.

The door inside the base had not forgotten its purpose.

It would open in the morning.

And there would be a price.

chapter 44:
Beneath the Resin Seal

The sun climbed and the air warmed as if nothing could ever go wrong. At the base of Nefertari's statue, the conservators laid out clean cloths and set up lamps, bottles, labelled bags, and their small tools. The national crew took their places. Cameras rolled.

They began with the first chamber, the one they had opened the previous day. Resin still clung to parts of the seam. Gel softened what the builders had pressed there to lock out air and water. A sable brush worked it in, pads drew it away, and flakes lifted like onion skin into numbered bags. Slow work, patient work, but the only way to live with yourself when you open a door that can never be replaced.

When the last of the resin lifted, the air shifted. Not colder by measure, but cooler in feel, like a box that had kept its breath for centuries. A faint scent of spice and resin drifted out. The panel eased wider with the gentlest protest. Shelves appeared in the lamplight, lined with tubes and trays. The wrapped case had gone to Aswan, but the cavity still held its order. Dust and pollen drifted into the light and fell back again, uncertain of the new world.

Then Esme's lamp found something more. At the far side of the cavity, almost lost in shadow, ran another seam. Narrow. Exact. Cut into the stone with the same hand. A second door.

Silence spread through the team. Even the guards edged closer. Dr Amirah Zahid gave a single nod. The cameras turned. New cloths were laid. Fresh gel mixed. The brushes began their work again, this time on the seam of the second chamber. Each stroke softened the resin. Each flake lifted into a labelled bag.

They worked until the shadows stretched across the forecourt. Two doors now stood before them: the first chamber open, its shelves revealed, and the second still sealed but starting to yield at the edges. Dr Zahid raised her hand. Enough. The air inside must equalise. The full opening would wait for dawn, when the light was steady and the cool hours could shield what was fragile.

They left the forecourt as the light faded and crossed to the tents set up in the camp beyond the statue. Supper was simple: bread, stewed lentils, olives, tea. The guards took first watch, their rifles across their knees, eyes on the ridge.

At a folding table outside the main tent, Lex and Esme opened their notebooks. The air still held the heat of the day, but the night wind carried a cooler edge off the lake. Lex sketched both seams, the small triangle they had seen on the monitor, and the faint outline of the second panel. Esme wrote her list of the objects by shape and likely material, then set beside each line the questions that mattered. What is it for? Where does it connect? What does the mark demand?

The first shot split the table. It smashed the cup from Esme's hand. The sound came late. The second shot tore through the canvas. The third struck a canopy pole with a dull ring. Guards shouted and dropped for cover. In a heartbeat the quiet evening turned to chaos, men diving for angles as gunfire clattered around the site.

"Down," said Dr Zahid. It was the kind of order that passes through bone.

Lex had been rising when the first shot cracked. A shard of the aluminium frame scythed across his shoulder and bit. He dropped to a knee, swore once, and then said he was fine in the same breath. Blood spread through his shirt as if black ink had been poured into the cloth.

Esme crawled to him, voice steady. "Pressure. Press and breathe." He obeyed because in a collapsing world obedience is simple.

Dr Zahid ripped a strip of cloth, made a pad, and pressed hard. "It is a puncture from the frame, not shrapnel. You will curse me now and bless me later."

More shots. A different rhythm. Short bursts from higher ground. The guards answered and killed the floodlights. Darkness swallowed the yard, broken only by muzzle flashes.

DeWalt slid to the table, radio in hand. "Tango One, immediate assistance."

A voice answered without name or rank. "Heard. Moving."

Esme kept the pressure and said nothing. She knew who would shoot at a team inside a temple. Men who fear paper and ink more than guns. Men who cannot bind what a record becomes.

The fire from the ridge grew ragged, then focused into short strings, then went thin. A low engine came from the dark. It rolled without lights, drifted to a stop, and died. Three figures in dark clothing slid out and moved as if they had rehearsed this ground yesterday. One raised a hand and the others peeled left and right. No shouts. No waving. Only the quiet of men who knew what to do.

The gunfire changed at once. It flickered and went out. The radio in DeWalt's palm spoke like a man who did not waste words. "Two down. One moving north. Perimeter holds."

Dr Zahid exhaled a breath she had not known she was holding. She checked Lex's shoulder. Blood still came, but slower under the pad.

The man the radio called the Doc slid in beside them. He always flew with DeWalt's team as a precaution that had become part of the furniture. He spoke without fuss while his hands worked. He lifted the pad, nodded once, poured water, pressed a fresh dressing, taped, and bound. He placed a tablet on Lex's tongue and raised a bottle.

"Your pulse is angry, not wild," he said. "Lungs are clear. You will live long enough to argue about history."

Esme laughed in a sound that almost became a sob. Lex tried and failed and then tried again and the small success steadied him.

The guards called clear. Floodlights came back with a wash that turned the yard to a stage. Two bodies lay at the edge of the forecourt. A third trail of blood led into the rocks and vanished in brush. The Doc told them to stay. DeWalt went with two men to the fallen and stood a moment with stillness that was not indifference. He nodded to the captain and walked back.

They carried the bodies to the edge and covered them. They checked pockets. Dollars. No cards. No papers. No marks beyond the small scars that rough trades collect. They photographed the faces for a file that would later find no match. They did not keep the bodies. The desert takes what it is owed. The captain, a pragmatic man, folded the dollars under a clip.

"My men will have proper graves," he said. "The money will not go to waste."

Esme knelt by the plinth and traced a smear of blood, then a faint scuff where a boot had slipped. For a breath she pictured a president giving the order, then corrected herself. Fear walks down a chain until a man in a room calls a man in a truck.

Lex did what men do after walking away from death. He apologised, too late. "I am sorry about your men," he told the captain. "I should have said it sooner."

The captain gave a dry smile. "Living men forget the dead when their own blood runs. My men were brave. They will be remembered as such."

Stars returned. Radios crackled in wider circles. Tango One melted back into the dark and left no trace a camera could love. Dr Zahid checked Lex again, told him to lie on his side and to try to sleep. He did not.

At dawn, the seam was ready to give. The panel slid under the mason's hand and the chamber breathed its cool, dry breath. The borescope showed what they had seen the day before. Nothing had been touched. The tubes, the tray, the triangle, the empty place where the case had been.

They lifted the first tube with formal care. Heavier at one end. The cap looked as if a stern word would crumble it. In the lab they would loosen it with humidity and patience. Here it would break if asked to.

They lifted the second tube. Then the third, fourth and fifth. They set them on padded cradles and carried them into a world that had just proved it would break anything if asked.

Esme stared at the tray. Small carved pins. Each had a notch, each was numbered, not with digits, but with marks stepped like stairs. Thin wafers of bone and wood lay incised with lines that echoed the layout grid in the hidden room on La Palma. She did not touch them. She drew their positions while the camera filmed without hurry.

On the inner wall the small triangle waited to be read. The rod with bands and a slot lay beside it as if a reader should know what to do. Esme looked at the figure of Imbu and wondered how many such figures had once been issued to men who could read marks and open doors without breaking them.

Quite a few hours later, Dr Zahid called it a day. The team sealed the cavity to protect it from air and from men. The tubes went to the same car that had carried the case to Aswan. Blue lights slept under the grille and woke as the checkpoint grew near.

In a room far away that had no windows a neat man watched a screen and saw the second convoy move with the same quiet purpose as the first. He told the drone operator to hold high and be patient. He did not like patience. He clung to it.

At the temple DeWalt spoke softly to the camera operator. He asked for the faces of the men who had fallen, and for the hands that carried the tubes. There is a kind of record that makes men careful with lies. The operator filmed with the care of a man who knows an image can be armour.

By noon, the site felt again like a place of work. The air hummed with heat and with that particular quiet that follows noise. Esme took a breath, tasted grit, and told Lex he should be in a hospital.

"I have seen men march three days with worse," said the Doc. "He will not die today if he does not insist on lifting stone."

Dr Zahid stepped out from the shade, her hair pulled back, her eyes sharp despite the fatigue. She had spent the morning on calls, to the ministry, the police, and a general whose cousins still remembered the rescue at Abu Simbel in the nineteen-sixties. Promises were made: a report, a press release. But not today. Today was for evidence, bags, samples, and the people who knew how to read them.

She led the team under the canopy. The camera light blinked red.

"We've confirmed a chamber built into the original geometry of the statue," she said. "The seal kept out water even when the lake rose. We've recovered containers for papyri, a case that may hold a mechanism, and measuring pieces that are clearly functional, not decorative. We were attacked, but we continue. We have no right to stop on the edge of something like this. We move forward, carefully, without arrogance."

Esme stepped closer, holding the small, wrapped figures they had found behind the hidden panel. Khamariti, a woman, and two children, Merit, Menna, Nefer. The carving was exquisite, each detail alive with care. It was more than the work of a master craftsman; it was the devotion of a husband and father captured forever in stone.

Beside it lay another piece, cut from finer stone: a second woman, different children. The story shifted, no longer simple. Lives overlapped. Choices tangled.

Lex looked up from where he was being bandaged. "Your patience brought us here," he said.

"Stop talking," Esme replied, tightening the dressing. "You'll bleed faster if you try to be noble."

He smiled, then thought better of it.

The rest of the day moved with purpose. The case and tubes were locked away in Aswan, under guard and constant camera watch. The chamber beneath Nefertari's base was sealed and braced.

As the sun fell, the ridge swallowed the light. The lake turned from bronze to black silk. Lamps flickered on at the safe house. Tango One took a long drink of water, then melted into the dark. Overhead, the drone's night feed painted the desert in shades of grey and secrets.

In Washington, a burner phone rattled on Sean Riley's desk. He let it buzz twice, then answered.

"We stopped nothing today," said Jones. "If that evidence goes public, it is finished. I lost men. I cannot launch again. DeWalt has his own unit. Ex Navy, ex SAS, something like that."

Riley didn't speak for a moment. The line crackled faintly, a sound like breathing.

"You're an idiot," he said.

The burner phone lay on the blotter like something dead. He looked up at the portraits on the wall, men who had smiled through wars and scandals and thought about the lengths they'd gone to protect the stories they needed the world to believe.

Esme stood at the rail and looked towards the temple. The day lay heavy on her shoulders. The promise of the chamber sat in the night like a charge. She thought of Khamariti and of the neat triangle inside the wall, and of how a mind can speak across three thousand years if a reader brings the right key.

Behind her Lex slept at last, breath even, shoulder bound. The Doc sat in a chair with his feet on another chair and snored like a man warned that tomorrow would need him. Down by the ridge a wind came off the water, moved the date fronds, and carried the faintest tang of old resin from the stone below.

In the morning, Dr Zahid stood at the edge of the tent, her expression tight with disbelief. In her hand was the latest report, its pages smudged from being handled too many times.

"I owe you, Lex and Esme, an apology," she said quietly. "The results are verified, run three times and checked in two separate labs. The linen wrapping dates to about four thousand seven hundred years before the present, around two thousand six hundred and seventy-four BCE."

She looked from Lex to Esme, her voice softening. "That places it within the reign of Djoser, possibly even earlier. Every researcher in the Cairo Museum is perplexed. Nothing in our records, nothing in known Old Kingdom metallurgy or optics, explains this device."

She placed the theodolite carefully on the narrow ledge, its brass frame glinting in the flicker of the torch. Beside it, Esme set down the small obsidian statue of Imbu, the guardian's black glass surface catching the light and burning from within like trapped fire. For a heartbeat nothing moved. Then the theodolite shuddered. Brass spheres shot free from its housing, rising into the air with a metallic hum. They hovered, circling each other, aligning into orbits that shimmered with pale light. The obsidian statue began to glow, its dark surface alive with the reflection of distant galaxies, spirals of stars spinning across the cavern walls.

The brass orbs settled into the shapes of the planets, Mercury, Venus, Earth, each one moving with silent precision. But one sphere refused the pattern. It drifted apart, tracing a strange, looping path through the projection, weaving across the Milky Way and brushing dangerously close to Earth's glowing sphere.

Esme's breath caught. She lifted her phone, filming the vision before whispering, "Max needs to see this," and sent the file as the final light dimmed and the brass spheres fell still.

"How did you know?" Lex asked quietly.

"Something I remembered," Esme said, her gaze still fixed on the statue. "A drawing on the cavern wall."

chapter 45:
Ripples of Fate

The Nile carried the smell of lotus and ash. Its broad current glistened silver where the moon laid a path across it, and the ceremonial barge creaked against the slow pull of the water. Torches hissed in iron bowls, their flames bending in the desert wind. From the banks, the chants of priests rose and fell in heavy waves, the cadence not quite mourning and not quite celebration. It sounded like a lament for both the living and the dead.

On the deck, High Priest Ankhwennefer stood at the centre of a ring of guards. His robe, once immaculate, no longer carried dignity. The fabric clung with oil and incense, heavy against his legs, whipping in the breeze. He tried to wear defiance as armour, back rigid, chin raised, but his eyes betrayed him. Behind the mask of power flickered the truth: he felt the gods withdraw.

Moments before, he had watched Khamariti shoved to the barge's edge, bound in ropes weighted with stones. He had seen the architect vanish beneath the surface, a trail of bubbles rising, then gone. That should have been the end. Triumph should have settled on him like a cloak. Instead, under the cold stare of Pharaoh Ramesses, he felt the ground tilt.

The barge groaned. Oars dipped and rose, steady against the current. Ramesses sat slumped for a moment, then rose with measured effort. He leaned on his sceptre. Firelight touched the deep lines in his face. Age had claimed much of him, his body, his strength, but not his presence. When he raised the sceptre, the chants died. Even the Nile seemed to pause.

Ramesses's voice rolled across the deck, deep and steady, carrying grief and judgement together.

"Khamariti has been taken by the river. The gods have tested us. One death does not cleanse a greater treachery."

His gaze did not waver. It locked on Ankhwennefer.

"The rot has roots," he said. "And tonight, they are cut away."

The priest jerked against the guards' grip. Rage twisted his mouth, making him look less like a holy man and more like a cornered animal.

"I am the high priest!" he shouted. "I am the voice of the gods. You dare nothing without me!"

"You were," Ramesses said, his voice low and heavy, each word dropping like a stone into deep water. "You set yourself above duty. You turned brother against brother, council against throne. You played with the soul of Egypt as if it were yours to command. You betrayed your office, and in doing so, you betrayed the gods themselves. Listen to them now. The crowd cries for your blood."

Ankhwennefer spat at the deck. "If you do this, Pharaoh, you condemn Egypt. The underworld will answer."

Ramesses leaned closer, his jaw cut by fire and shadow. "The underworld has already answered. Storms. Ash. Pestilence. My child, dead. Hunger. I ignored the man I charged to learn the cause. You fanned fear because fear fed your power. Now you will join the river you made into a theatre."

The guards moved before he gave the order. From a wicker basket they drew smooth stones from the riverbank, heavy with judgement. They tied them into the priest's robe, binding his waist, his ankles.

Ankhwennefer's breathing quickened. His lips searched for words, for arguments, for anything that could hold back the tide. None came.

"Mercy," he gasped, the word pitiful in his mouth. "I served you!"

The pharaoh stepped closer to the edge, his shadow long in the torchlight, and turned his words on the crowd. "It will take more than the sacrifice of an architect to appease the gods. They are silent. They do not listen. It is men who must decide Egypt's fate."

The words thundered across the water. For a breath, the crowd stood stunned, weighing defiance against faith. Then the sound broke. A roar rose from the banks of the Nile, rolling like surf. Arms lifted. Feet stamped. The river mirrored their frenzy, torchlight breaking into a thousand shards of fire.

Ramesses lifted a hand. The guards thrust.

The priest stumbled, arms clawing at empty air. He struck the river with a slap and a rush. His head broke the surface once, mouth open, but no sound carried. The weight dragged him under. The water folded over him, smooth and untroubled. Torches cast broken lines across the ripples. The moon shattered into silver fragments. Then the surface calmed, as if nothing had happened.

Silence hung for ten, then twenty heartbeats. Ramesses lifted the sceptre once more. Not as a weapon, but as a staff to keep him steady. He turned toward the riverbank.

People stood as far as the torchlight reached, men with arms folded in sleeves, women clutching cloaks, children hoisted high. The Nile mirrored their faces, breaking them into wavering fragments.

"The high priest is gone," Ramesses declared. "Let it be known. Egypt is cleansed of treachery. Balance will be restored, not with fear but with work that honours earth and gods."

Runners shot from the banks, hurling the message into the night. One toward the city. Another toward the temples. By dawn, Thebes would buzz with the news.

On deck, temple guards bowed their head. A young guard wiped his blade clean on a strip of linen and folded it with care.

Ramesses leaned on the rail. His hand trembled, and he let the sceptre hide it. He stared into the water, no longer as pharaoh but as a man who had sent another to drown. Every command, he knew, left a scar on the soul of the one who spoke it.

"May he meet the judgement he taught others to fear," he murmured.

The oars turned. The barge swung upstream. Lanterns cast ovals of light across reeds where crocodiles slid silently away.

Near the bank, reeds bent then straightened as something large passed through them. A heron lifted one leg, waiting for the ripple to pass.

chapter 46:
Beneath the Sands of Time

Dr Amirah Zahid rested her hand on the cool stone doorway as the last light from the ancient model faded. The small bronze spheres that had moved like planets stopped turning, their glow swallowed by the dark ceiling above. The silence that followed felt alive, as if the chamber itself remembered what it had once been built to show.

Esme exhaled slowly, her fingers tracing the carved wall. "The cartouches link earth and sky," she said. "Three signs, earth, sky, stars. The same pattern we saw at La Palma. The same hand. The same mind."

Lex shifted, his bandaged shoulder aching from the fight the night before. He ignored it. "Khamariti wrote through placement as much as through words," he said. "Each symbol builds on the next, like rhythm in music." He lifted his phone, recording the ceiling. "We've captured everything. The ministry will get a full copy."

On the screen, Max's lab glowed with early New York light. His voice came through, tight with disbelief. "That's no tomb," he said. "It's a model of the heavens, a working map of the planets. The rings show precession, and that red point in the middle. That's not decoration. That's a planet."

Zahid frowned but kept her voice steady. "Models can be deceptive when we let excitement lead the way," she said. "We'll check every frame and compare it with the museum's records before we draw any conclusions." She paused, meeting Lex's eyes. "And for what it's worth, I was wrong to doubt your team, especially after what you proved with the theodolite."

Max hesitated. "Still… I reckon Khamariti brought you back to Abu Simbel to show you that planet. I just don't know why. It doesn't act like any we know. Shows up in our skies again and again, then vanishes, like it leaves the solar system and comes back. Shouldn't be possible, but the pattern's there. It's like a ghost world, here for a bit, then gone without a trace."

The words lingered in the air, heavy as the stone around them.

Night settled. Lamps flickered. Guards walked their routes. DeWalt's eyes found Philips. A nod was enough.

Philips moved when fatigue was deepest. The sentry at the passage slumped on his stool, eyelids heavy. He came like a shadow. From his sleeve he drew a small pistol. A hiss of air. A dart touched the sentry's neck. His eyes widened, then closed. He sagged sideways, breathing slow, as if sleep had claimed him. Philips plucked out the dart and rubbed balm to hide the mark.

From the dark, Thea stepped forward. Her face was pale, the flight's exhaustion still clinging to her. She'd been on the plane with DeWalt's security team. She glanced toward the unconscious guard. "H-he, he will w-wake up?" she asked, her voice low, almost unwilling to break the moment.

Philips smiled faintly. "He will dream. That is all."

Thea expertly removed the resin seal Dr Zahid had set in place days earlier, easing it free without a sound. They slipped inside. The chamber exhaled a cool breath as the air shifted. Their lights stayed low, thin beams sliding over stone. Cameras were positioned wide, their lenses open but blind to the corners.

Philips moved straight to the Ledge. He followed DeWalt's instructions exactly, reaching behind the row where the dust had not settled. His fingers closed on the cache. Three tubes, sealed in resin, smooth and ancient. He lifted them with care and slid them into a satchel lined with cloth.

But DeWalt had told him more. Philips and Thea searched further, eyes running across bundles and trays. In a niche cut close to the floor he found a scroll, its outer wrap brittle, its surface scored with sharp lines. By torchlight, faint schematics appeared, angled shapes, curves, marks of measure that looked more like engineering than prayer. Philips slipped it quickly into the satchel.

Near the scroll lay two spheres, dark and polished, hidden in a recess no larger than a handspan. They felt heavy, too dense for their size. He wrapped them in cloth and placed them with the rest.

Thea brushed dust back with her soft bristle brush, steady hands erasing the trace of intrusion. The shelf looked untouched.

They left without a sound. At the threshold, Thea knelt and carefully reapplied the resin seal, smoothing it back into the joint exactly as Dr Zahid had done before. When the light caught it, the surface looked untouched, the chamber undisturbed.

Philips and Thea were gone. The satchel of scrolls was gone. The tubes were gone, along with several spheres and two small statues.

The guard stirred. His head jerked up, the night air sharp in his lungs. He rubbed at his neck, frowning at a dull ache he could not place. Shame burned hotter than pain. He had fallen asleep on duty.

Muttering under his breath, he straightened on the stool, gripped his torch tighter and promised himself it would not happen again. No memory of visitors. No hint of theft. Only guilt for his lapse.

At dawn, the camp woke to another day. Zahid believed the record whole. Lex thought the work safe. Esme pressed her mirror to stone, tracing faint grooves. The panel gleamed under careful light. None of them knew. Under their noses, history had already been stolen.

chapter 47:
Unveiling the Celestial Map

T he camp felt charged. The statue loomed over them, the air itself uneasy. The museum team worked with the precision of surgeons. Each sealed scroll was logged, measured, photographed in place, then left untouched.

Lex and Esme stood before Max on a laptop screen propped against a crate. Behind him, the New York skyline was a sketch of towers in shadow. His office lights were low. His wall was plastered with charts and maps.

The satellite link flickered, stabilising into the face of Max, the glow of his lab screen casting pale light behind him. Static rolled once, then cleared.

"Energy," Max said, his voice sharpening through the satellite feed. He tapped the centre of the printout pinned to the wall behind him, where three lines met in perfect symmetry. "Here, the battery," Max said, lowering his voice. "The Great Pyramid of Giza. Dead centre of the grid. Every line connects back to it. If this data's right, the ancients weren't guessing, they were maintaining something. A system still humming under our feet."

On the monitor, Lex leaned closer. "Then they're connected," he said, his voice almost a whisper.

"Doctor Zahid, I ran your photographs through the new software," Max said, his voice taut. "I laid the cartouche lines over a global grid." He tapped the wall behind him. Three maps glowed in the screen light.

Zahid leaned in. "What are we looking at?"

"Not ley lines in myth," Max said. "Magnetic points, the earth's field. When I joined them up, it lit like circuitry. This isn't random. It's an electrical grid laid across the planet."

Esme frowned. "How's that even possible? They were built thousands of years apart."

Max nodded. "The Great Pyramid of Giza went up around 2,560 BCE, under Pharaoh Khufu. Chichén Itzá came nearly thirty-five centuries later, about 900 CE. But the maths line up almost perfectly. I reckon the Mayan site could be a backup, an upgraded version of the Giza design, built in case the original system ever failed."

Lex studied the lines on the screen, brow furrowed. "So, they're not separate monuments. They're parts of the same network?"

"I can't say for sure," Max said. "But everything points to a link, two power sources built for the same purpose. One ancient, one renewed."

He nodded. "They're components, each one tuned to the sky, each one storing and feeding. Khamariti was building an engine out of the earth itself."

The projection on the linen shifted in front of them. The red dot flared again.

Zahid whispered, "And the orbit ties into this?"

Max's reply carried the soft cadence of Liverpool. "Yes. The planet triggers the grid. When it passes, the system activates. That is what we're staring at."

DeWalt's arms remained folded. His eyes did not blink.

From the chamber came a voice. "Doctor."

They turned and hurried inside.

On the third shelf, in a niche no wider than a hand, lay a slate square. At first it looked blank. Esme tilted the sidelight until the beam raked across the surface. Fine lines shimmered into view, silver rising from the dark.

Cartouches emerged, not one, but three. Each showed the same figure, Khamariti, his form etched beside three different royal crests. The first was Old Kingdom, the second Middle, the third New. Three dynasties, many pharaohs, three families, separated by centuries. And yet the same man.

Esme's voice broke the silence. "How can the same figure stand beside pharaohs a thousand years apart?"

Lex stared at the stone, pulse quickening. "Because maybe his ancestors, not unheard of the family all doing the same work over centuries."

Zahid's pen hovered above her notebook. "That is not possible," she said, though her tone lacked force.

In the corner of the slate, the familiar triangle of symbols gleamed, same as the orb.

Esme whispered, "It is a key. We need to rethink what we think we know."

"Catalogue it," Zahid said at last, forcing steel into her words. "Photograph it in place. No one touches it."

DeWalt shifted, then let out a low laugh. "Three dynasties, the same face, the same name. And you still hide behind caution, Doctor? At what point does evidence stop being impossible?"

Zahid turned on him, her eyes hard. "At the point where science ends and fantasy begins. And we are not there yet."

DeWalt's smile stayed cold. "We already passed that line. You just refuse to admit it."

The chamber fell silent, the cartouches gleaming faintly in the raked light, as if Khamariti himself listened.

Guards were stationed all around the perimeter. DeWalt had arranged for his men to handle security inside the camp, everywhere except the chamber itself, which would have drawn too much attention.

Terrella and Kiln, members of DeWalt's team under Philips's command, patrolled the outer line. Both moved with casual ease, water bottles in hand, posture loose, but their eyes missed nothing. Terrella lingered near the vehicles, chatting idly with a cameraman while quietly counting the cars under his breath.

Philips stayed close to the chamber, seated on a low rock, one boot resting on a pack that carried far more than just rations. The others spoke in low voices.

Esme wrote from memory, matching each glyph to the photos. Lex watched her, sensing for the first time that the maze ahead was becoming a road.

On the ridge above, two men crouched behind scrub, radios whispering. They were not DeWalt's men. They were not Egyptian police. They were watchers.

Far away, CIA Director Mike Rotherham leaned over the drone feed, eyes hollow. His voice was flat. "Confirm the device. Confirm the team."

The order came down the second line, colder, higher. From Hope himself.

Behind them, on the ridge, the Jones and Clinton in silence around an old-fashioned drone, an outdated, skeletal thing Rotheram's men had hauled from a military cache. It was a relic from another era, the kind Riley had insisted on sending. He didn't want anything that could be traced back to him.

The drone was clumsy by modern standards, its guidance system half-analogue, its stabilisers unreliable. There was no satellite lock, no smart targeting. If it was going to hit, they would have to see the target themselves and guide it manually, line by line.

Two Russian short-range missile had been strapped beneath its belly, a cold war souvenir modified for this single flight. The payload was unstable, the circuitry temperamental.

Jones knelt beside the launch pad, sweat cutting lines through the dust on his face. "If this thing even clears the ridge," he muttered, "we'll be lucky."

Clinton adjusted the feed, eyes fixed on the small, flickering screen. "We don't need luck," he said quietly. "We just need a clear line of sight."

The engines coughed to life, a rough, uneven whine that sounded older than the men who launched it. In the dark, the drone trembled, ready to climb toward a target only human eyes could confirm.

The first missile tore the sky open. Its scream was high and merciless, a sound that froze marrow and made the night itself recoil. A streak of fire cut down through the dark, a rod of flame hurled like judgement.

The impact struck just beyond the outer wall. For a heartbeat, the world paused, then everything was ripped apart. Tents disintegrated into ash. Canvas became sparks. Men were flung like dolls in the grip of an angry god. Two of DeWalt's men never had time to cry out. They were gone in an instant, burned to nothing but shadows on the sand.

Three Egyptian guards, caught in mid step, were blasted backwards. Their bodies broke against stone and lay twisted where they fell.

The camera operator's scream pierced the chaos, thin and human against the storm. Then the second missile hit. Metal vaporised. Cables melted into black rain. Every second of priceless footage, every inch of magnetic tape, every record of their work was obliterated. Lost to fire.

The shockwave thundered into the cliff face. Rock trembled and groaned like a wounded beast. Dust exploded from fissures that had not breathed in three thousand years.

The great seated statue of Ramesses II, the eternal guardian, began to fail. First came a crack, sharp as a gunshot, running across the shoulder. Then the head split. One stone eye crumbled into sand. The mouth collapsed inward, the lips of the god king silenced by the force of war.

And then the impossible.

Abu Simbel itself began to fall. Stone that had endured pharaohs, plagues, and empires now gave way in a cascade of ruin. Blocks split free. Statues shuddered. The earth shook as if Egypt's ancient heart were being torn from its chest.

Centuries of patience undone in a breath. Columns folded. Stone thundered. Faces carved before Christ ground into sand. Lex threw himself across Esme as a chunk of ceiling missed them by inches. Dr Zahid vanished in the smoke, her voice shouting something no one could hear.

It was over in less than ninety seconds.

The desert was scorched. The air stank of cordite and burnt canvas.

And where the chamber had stood, where once gods had looked down with calm indifference, there was only ruin.

Lex pulled himself to his knees, blood on his cheek. Esme coughed, eyes wide. She stared at the statue's shattered torso and whispered, "Three thousand years... gone."

DeWalt did not speak.

He stood apart from them, motionless, fists clenched, staring into the heart of the destruction.

Dr Zahid staggered in circles, her cries raw and incoherent, palms pressed against her face as though trying to hold herself together. Blood seeped between her fingers, dark streaks running down her wrists. Lex caught the glint of plaster fragments lodged in her brow and cheek, cruel shards of the collapsing chamber that had torn into her.

"Doctor, sit down!" Lex shouted, lunging forward. She did not respond, stumbling blindly until he seized her shoulders and pulled her to the ground. The sudden strain ripped through him. His old wound tore open, fire lancing under his ribs. He gasped, teeth clenched against the pain.

Her own cry followed. When her hands fell from her face, Lex saw the damage. Her eyes were swollen and red, thin threads of blood running from the corners. Splinters of stone and dust clung to her lashes like needles.

Esme dropped to her knees beside them, first-aid kit already unzipped, her hands trembling but purposeful. "Morphine, now," she said, voice clipped with urgency. She snapped open the vial and filled the syringe with practiced speed.

Lex held Zahid's arms still as Esme slid the needle into her thigh. The doctor convulsed, then sagged, her breathing slowing into ragged sobs.

"Pressure dressings," Esme muttered, pulling gauze free. She dabbed away the blood, flushing grit and plaster with sterile saline, wincing as Zahid cried out. Lex cradled her head steady while Esme packed the wounds with gauze, taping improvised pads over the bleeding sockets.

Zahid whimpered through clenched teeth, voice fading. "Can't see... can't..."

Lex gripped her hand, firm. "You're alive, Doctor. That's what matters. We'll keep you that way."

And then, as if fate wasn't done with them, Esme's eyes rolled back and she collapsed, the delayed shock finally claiming her.

Behind him, Philps and Kiln were already moving, weapons drawn. Their eyes swept the ridge like predators. Terrella lay dead in the sand, a victim of shrapnel.

Then came movement.

Kiln charged first, feet hammering the ground. Philips was seconds behind. The chase snapped into motion, a pursuit without words, only breath and gunmetal.

They cleared the ridge, swallowed by the dark beyond. The desert closed in with the sound of the wind carrying away every footfall, every breath.

DeWalt turned his head slowly, eyes fixed on the horizon. He keyed his radio and spoke with icy clarity. "Bring me one alive."

The order was enough.

Gunfire ripped across the night in short, savage bursts. Jones staggered, pitched forward, and his face struck the sand. Clinton fired back, wild, and frantic, muzzle flashes cutting bright streaks through the dark. Kiln's reply was cold and exact. His shot hit clean. Clinton spun once and dropped without a sound.

Kiln moved two steps before a red bloom spread across his chest. He stumbled backwards and collapsed, the desert swallowing him as if it had been waiting.

Philips reached Clinton's body in seconds. His hands worked fast, pulling open pouches, stripping encrypted tags from the belt, stuffing them into his vest. Then he turned to Jones, dragging him upright. Jones was dazed and bleeding, but alive.

Kiln's body lay where it had fallen. Dust already drifted over him like a shroud. Philips spared no glance. He would recover the dead before leaving, but now only the living mattered. "Alive?" DeWalt asked.

Philps nod was curt, a soldier's acknowledgement.

"Good," DeWalt replied, voice flat as stone. "Bring him in. We need the name."

Hours later, a helicopter swept low over the desert, its rotors scything the air. Searchlights flared across the sand before the craft banked east toward Jordan. The cargo door yawned open. Jones was thrown inside, wrists bound, hood over his head.

The engines howled, drowning the world. Jones sat hunched, shuddering in the strobe of red light from the instrument panel. He didn't move, didn't resist. The silence stretched, heavy and suffocating, until he spoke.

By dawn, the helicopter had crossed into Jordan. The safe site awaited, a place chosen for one purpose: interrogation without limit. Concrete walls. Bolted doors. Rooms that swallowed sound.

Jones was dragged down a narrow corridor, his boots scraping across the floor. He tried once to resist, a twist of his shoulder, but Philps slammed him forward until his knees buckled. The guards shackled him to a chair, leather straps biting into his wrists. The hood was pulled away. His eyes, bloodshot and furious, blinked against the strip light above.

DeWalt entered last. He stood in front of him, arms folded, the silence stretched until it pressed like weight on the chest.

"You will tell me," DeWalt said, his voice low and even. "One way or another, you will tell me who gave the order to erase Abu Simbel and kill us all."

Jones swallowed hard, the cords in his neck taut. His silence was brave, but fragile. The fight was still in him.

DeWalt leaned closer, his shadow long across the floor. "And when you do," he whispered, "the world will know who really pulled the trigger."

chapter 48:
Science and Superstition

Studio lights burned like a small sun. New York stretched beyond the glass in a slate skyline, the city held at bay by soundproof walls and the hum of air con. Max Keeper sat on the edge of his chair, mic clipped, notes closed, eyes steady. The lower third on the screen read: SCIENCE AND SUPERSTITION.

"Max, thank you for joining us," the anchor said. "Millions are watching events on La Palma. Give us the bottom line."

"The bottom line's risk," Max said. "The western flank of Cumbre Vieja's unstable. My models show a live fault. Best case, a bit of slippage. Worst, a big chunk goes into the Atlantic. If that happens, the eastern seaboard'll have about twenty, twenty-four hours before a serious wave hits."

"Significant meaning…?"

"Meaning it's not a surfer's wave," Max said. "It means evacuations for low-lying areas, coastal systems down, saltwater driven inland. I'm not saying the world's ending. I'm saying get ready."

"Has the White House engaged?"

Max exhaled. "No. Some governors are standing up to the White House and making their own plans. From the top, there's no real strategy. This's a science problem, and it needs a science answer."

The anchor looked down at her notes, then lifted her eyes. "Yesterday President Hope said again, you're scaremongering, that you and your team are trying to undermine the Bible and his good work."

The words settled like weight on the room. Max drew a slow breath before speaking.

"Faith's passed me by, but I respect it," he said. "Let's be clear though, we're not here to argue with scripture. We deal in evidence. And the evidence says if that volcano's flank gives way, it could be five hundred years, or it could be tomorrow. We don't get to pick when."

He looked round the room, his voice steady. "All I'm askin' is that we've got plans ready if it does happen. Tide-gate checks, hospital surge capacity, evacuation routes, clear communication. That's not heresy, that's survival. President Hope can pray if he wants, but he should act as well."

A graphic flickered behind them: ABU SIMBEL. The anchor seized the pivot.

"Separately," she pressed, "your colleagues in Egypt, Professor Lex Mullin's team, have been working with the Cairo Museum. We're hearing they went there in secret and made real progress. What can you tell us?"

Max's jaw tightened. Behind his calm reply, he carried the weight of what only a few suspected, that Hope himself believed Mullin's discoveries threatened scripture, that he had set wheels in motion to silence them. No one in the studio knew it yet. Not the anchor. Not the viewers. Only Max felt the chill of the truth creeping in, a truth he wasn't ready to say aloud.

"I can't give details till Cairo speaks," Max said, keeping his tone calm. "But I can tell you this, what the team's found isn't myth, and it's not made up. It's evidence. Proof that links monuments, records, and the sky itself. And when people start fearing evidence, it's because it matters."

The anchor tilted her head. "Feared by whom?"

Max paused, choosing his words. "By anyone who thinks truth should be trimmed to fit belief. Science doesn't bow to scripture. It just shows what's there."

"And the La Palma cavern? Critics still say it's a hoax."

"They've never stood inside it," Max said. "And they're not listening to what's being confirmed on site."

The anchor leaned in. "Viewers keep asking the same thing. Is this about natural forces or human interference?"

"Natural forces," Max said. "Measured, repeatable, testable. The fault under Cumbre Vieja runs deeper and longer than most believed. In the cavern we traced cracks showing centuries of movement, each one tied to pressure building under the ridge. It's not guesswork. It's evidence."

"A lot of people will hear that and think disaster waiting to happen," the anchor said.

Max gave a faint smile, though his eyes stayed firm. "Volcanoes and oceans follow their own rules. What we're showing isn't prophecy, and it's not panic. It's science. Geology. And the sooner people take that in, the sooner we can be ready."

The anchor nodded, then went for the question everyone else had been circling. "Sources in Washington say President Hope and several religious leaders asked Egypt to restrict access to the site. Is that true?"

Max weighed the camera for a quiet beat. "I'm not involved in access decisions. I'm a data guy. If you're asking whether power tries to get ahead of truth, always. Whether science should bend to that, never."

A producer's hand lifted behind the glass. Two fingers. Wrap soon. The anchor pressed one more time.

"If you had thirty seconds to address anyone living in a coastal floodplain tonight, what would you say?"

"Have a bag ready," Max said. "Charge your phone, keep your car fuelled. Know your route inland. Tell your neighbour if they don't know theirs. If nothing happens, you wasted an hour. If something happens, you bought a life."

They cut to commercial. The studio dropped a register. Someone unclipped Max's mic. He stayed seated, watching the skyline turn from steel to glass as clouds shifted. The anchor crossed to him with a producer in tow, eyes on her phone. The producer's face had gone sheet white.

"Max," the anchor said, voice low now, not for air. "We need you to sit tight."

"What's new?"

The producer swallowed. "We're confirming an attack at Abu Simbel."

He felt the words as a physical thing. "Say again."

"Drone strike," she said, her voice unsteady. "Multiple hits. Abu Simbel's been bombed, wiped out. Two of DeWalt's men, three local guards... all dead. The cameraman's missing. The footage, everything, is gone."

Max's mouth went dry. "Lex?"

"Alive," she said. "Esme Miller too."

He swallowed hard. "And Dr Zahid?"

The anchor laid a hand on his forearm. "Max... Dr Zahid was hit by debris. The report says she's fighting for her sight."

"Who did this?" he asked.

"We don't know yet," the producer said. "We're about to go back live. We want you to relay the story, the facts are on that screen over there. If you don't want to—"

"No," Max said. His voice returned, clipped and cold. "We go live."

The floor manager was already counting down. Three. Two. One.

The red light burned again.

"We interrupt programming with breaking news," the anchor said, her tone measured but tense. "Reports are coming in of an attack at the Abu Simbel site in southern Egypt. Early accounts confirm multiple fatalities and extensive damage to the temple complex. We have images, no sound at this stage. Joining us is Dr Max Keeper, who has been working closely with the Cairo team."

She paused, listening to her earpiece, then turned back to camera. "We're hearing confirmed reports of a drone strike, major damage to the inner chamber and the statue, multiple casualties, including Egyptian guards." She turned to him. "Dr Keeper, what can you tell us?"

Max looked straight into the lens. There was no training for this, no script that could hold what he felt.

"First," he said quietly, "to the families of the guards and crew, there's no words that'll ever be enough."

He took a slow breath before going on. "Second, to anyone already twisting this into politics, religion, or whatever else, just stop. This wasn't that. This was an attack on a heritage site, on the people keeping it safe. It was an attack on evidence. It was an attack on history."

The anchor's voice softened. "Do you know the status of your colleagues?" she asked, as silent images of the shattered temple filled the screen behind him.

"From what I've just been told, Professor Mullin and Esme are alive," Max said. "Your producer's told me Dr Amirah Zahid's suffered terrible injuries to her sight. She's the bravest scientist I know. She's carried more truth in her notebook than some governments keep in their archives. She deserves the world's protection now."

The anchor blinked hard and stayed with him. "If this was an attempt to destroy the record, can anything be recovered?"

"Yes," Max said. "Fragments, backups, copies kept off site. Destruction's never as complete as the one who orders it thinks. The past's stubborn."

"Max," she said, her voice tight, "we are hearing unconfirmed reports that a drone was involved."

Max leaned forward, his face set. "That shows desperation. Someone, or some group, was willing to use military precision to wipe out evidence. A drone strike means skill, training, access. And I'll tell you this, whoever gave that order isn't daft enough to use a weapon that leaves a trail back to them."

The studio went still.

He held the pause, then steadied his tone. "But science does not stop because someone is afraid of it. Evidence has a way of crawling out from under rubble. And while we fight the threats in the dark, people must prepare for the risks they can see."

The anchor swallowed, then shifted into her closing cadence, carrying the words as if they were glass. "We will continue to follow this developing story. Dr. Max Keeper, thank you."

The footage rolled without sound, only the ghostly shimmer of dust and flame. The once-majestic façade of Abu Simbel lay fractured, the colossal, seated figures of Ramesses torn open, their faces split by jagged light. Smoke coiled where the inner chambers had been, rising through the carved hollows like a spirit unwilling to leave. Debris drifted across the sand, glinting faintly in the sun, broken fragments of history scattered in slow motion. A torn flag clung to a fallen scaffold. No movement, no voices, just the heavy stillness of ruin, a monument to eternity brought to its knees in seconds.

The red light above the camera died. The studio noise returned in a rush, shoes on the floor, a cough in the corner, the rustle of paper.

The Rose Garden lay thick with late summer heat, lanterns throwing soft light over hedges trimmed with surgical precision. From the White House windows came the muffled spill of laughter and music from a dinner Hope had long abandoned. Out here, beyond the colonnade and the polite circle of Secret Service, the President and his fixer walked in tight arcs, their words pitched for no ears but their own.

President Hope tugged at his cuffs, jerky, restless. His gaze flicked to the trees as though he half-expected microphones in the leaves.

"You're sure they can't hear us out here?" he snapped.

Riley's hands stayed clasped behind his back, his calm practiced, professional. "They've swept it. We're clear."

Hope's voice cracked, then dropped to a rasp. "Clear? Nothing is clear. Not after today." He thrust a hand westward, to where the desert smouldered in his imagination. "Abu Simbel! We didn't just silence them. We burned three thousand years of history onto every television on Earth. That doesn't hide us. That paints a bloody target."

Riley's voice was steady. "You gave the order because you understood the stakes. Mullin's team was digging too deep. They weren't just rewriting history, they were tearing out the foundation. If their story holds, Genesis doesn't. Exodus doesn't. Your base doesn't. The Bible goes. And if the Bible goes, so do you."

Hope stopped dead. His shoes ground into gravel, breath harsh. "Yes, I said end it. I wanted it stopped. But not like this. A drone strike on a world heritage site? A scar so big even schoolchildren will talk about it. You don't silence with fire, Riley, you invite the hunt."

Riley stepped closer, his words low, controlled. "No one can tie it to us. The drone was deniable. No trail back."

Hope rubbed at his temple. "You don't see it. Every scholar, every Egyptian politician is baying for blood. My enemies already whisper the word criminal. And I can't step in front of a podium and tell the truth. I can't say, 'Yes, I ordered it, because they were about to dig holes in the Bible.' If people believe Khamariti's story, they'll burn me alive."

Silence stretched, broken only by the drone of cicadas. Riley read the tremor in the President's voice, the hairline cracks in his armour of certainty.

Then Riley spoke, sharper now. "Clinton's dead. Jones... Jones is missing. I don't know if he's lying in the sand, in Egyptian custody, or already in DeWalt's pocket. That's the loose end we watch. If Jones talks, he's the thread that unravels the whole fabric."

Hope's head snapped up. "And you let this happen?"

"I control what can be controlled," Riley said evenly. "If Egypt has him, they'll squeeze him. If DeWalt does, he'll use him as a bargaining chip. Either way, I'll know before it hits daylight. But the trail still doesn't reach here. You're insulated."

Hope gave a bitter laugh. "Insulated. You keep saying that word as if it's a shield. Can insulation hold when the whole house is on fire? Because that's what this feels like, Riley, smoke everywhere, and everyone sniffing for the source."

Riley's smile was thin. "Then we make sure the smoke points elsewhere. Cairo is unstable. We can seed stories, rival factions, Saudis, Israelis, pick your villain. And if that doesn't hold, we twist Clinton's final words into a confession. Egypt will publish whatever clears them and damns someone else. They want a scapegoat. We'll hand them one."

Hope stood stiff, roses pale around him in the dark. Finally, he nodded. "Do it. Make them believe it wasn't us. Make them believe it was anyone but us. I don't care if it sets the Middle East on fire. Better there than here."

Riley inclined his head. "Consider it done."

Hope's eyes gleamed in the low light, cold and unblinking. "But hear me. If this comes back to me, if Abu Simbel traces to this garden, then it won't just be monuments that fall. It will be me. And when I fall, you fall with me."

Riley met his stare without flinching. "Then we make sure you don't fall, Mr President. Because if you do, we all go down together."

The night pressed heavy around them. At the edge of the colonnade, agents shifted in the lamplight, unaware that half a world away, the blast still echoed in stone and sand. And in the dark heart of the Rose Garden, two men stood bound by ruin, by faith weaponised, and by a secret that could bury them both.

When Hope had gone back inside, Riley lingered among the roses, phone in hand, its glow hidden in his palm. He dialled a number without a name, the kind of line that never showed on records. "Jones," he said flatly. "Find him. Alive or dead. If the Egyptians have him, I want to know. If DeWalt has him, I want leverage. If he's in the ground, I want proof."

The voice on the other end gave a short reply, no promise, only acknowledgement. Riley ended the call, staring into the dark hedge line. Somewhere, Jones was either a corpse, a prisoner, or a bargaining chip. And whichever it was, Riley knew the truth would decide whether President Hope remained untouchable. Or whether Abu Simbel would come roaring back to bury them both.

chapter 49:
Crossing Thresholds

The sirens were gone, but the sound lived on in Esme's skull. A high whine under everything. The smell of stone dust clung to her hair no matter how many times the nurses washed it out. When the ward lights dimmed, she saw the statue fall again, the face shattering, the rush of air as the chamber collapsed and the world turned to grit and thunder.

Max had flown straight to Cairo, chasing the same midnight corridors that carried Lex and Esme to the hospital. Now he sat hunched in a brittle plastic chair beside her bed, the hum of machines filling the silence.

Esme lay motionless except for her hands. They clenched and unclenched against the sheets, fists waging battles with enemies that no longer stood in the room. Her face twitched as if fighting echoes only she could see.

Max whispered the things a scientist is meant to say when reason is all he has to offer. Words about adrenaline, shock, neural pathways sparking after trauma. He spoke of chemicals, of patterns, of how the storm would fade.

But the words fell like dust. None of it reached her. None of it helped. When she woke, she stared at the ceiling for a long time before she trusted it to stay where it was. Cairo General was an old hospital trying to be new. White paint over older white paint. Clean floors. A window that let in a square of pale sky above the city's soft roar. She turned her head and found Max with two coffees and a notebook that looked like it had not left his hand all night.

"How long?" she said.

"Thirty hours," Max said with a grin. "You slept, you swore, you tried to stand up and forgot to bring your feet. Then you went back to sleep again."

"Lex?"

"Bruised. Angry. Alive."

"And DR Zahid?" The name caught in her throat.

Max set the coffee down, no soft edges in his tone. "The surgeons did what they could. The optic nerve's badly damaged. They don't know if she'll see shapes, or even light. But they do know she's still herself."

Esme closed her eyes. The floor rolled and steadied. She breathed until the room agreed to stay still. She opened her eyes again and forced them to focus on Max. "Tell me the bad and then tell me the worse."

"The bad news," Max said, "is the press already knows there was a strike. They know guards died, a camera crew too, and a world treasure's been smashed. What they don't know's who did it. So, they'll start guessing."

"And the worse?"

"The worse is DeWalt."

"Of course it is," she said, and her mouth made a shape that was not a smile.

""He's called three times," Max said. "Says he can help, says his place is secure. Reckons he can get us out of Cairo quiet and into Luxembourg." He glanced out the window as if Luxembourg might just be there on the horizon. "Says we shouldn't waste time."

Esme pushed herself upright, wincing as the stitches in her scalp pulled tight. "He doesn't just want the discovery. He wants to own it. To own us. I saw it at Abu Simbel, how he manipulated Dr Zahid, how he manoeuvred around us. He travels with his own private army, Max. Why? Because he wants to be the man at the microphone when the rest of us are too broken to speak." She rubbed her eyes hard with the heel of her hand.

Max leaned in, his voice low. "Someone's hacked our databanks. Not clumsy, not amateur, proper surgical, beyond anything I've seen. I traced what I could. The trail's buried deep, but I'm sure it was DeWalt. He's the only one who knew exactly where we kept the files. I've spoken to Lex. He agrees."

"Good," Esme said sharply. Her gaze hardened. "Tell him I agree. DeWalt is up to something. And Thea, she's been gone for weeks. But in the dust, in the chaos at Abu Simbel… I swear I saw her."

"I already told him," Max said, handing her a paper cup of water. "Now drink, then eat. After that, we're getting you out of this bed before it starts charging you rent."

She took the cup. The water tasted like copper. She drank all of it.

A nurse came and checked her pulse and her oxygen and said all the things nurses say when they need you to believe the day is ordinary. When she went away again, Max pulled his chair close and lowered his voice.

"There is more," he said. "Two men loitered in the corridor at dawn. Not DeWalt's. Not police. They had the look of watchers."

"From where?"

"Pick a flag," Max said. "Or pick none."

Esme looked at her hands. They shook a little. She set them flat on the sheet until they stopped. "I will not spend the rest of my life behind a door."

Max's phone vibrated. The name on the screen made his jaw tighten. He showed it to her. DeWalt.

"Answer it," Esme said. "Put him on speaker."

"Max," DeWalt said, smooth, warm, as if they were resuming a conversation in a restaurant that did not know it was on fire. "How is she."

"Alive."

"Good," DeWalt said. "Then we move. The window is short, and the storm is building. I have a jet at Cairo West. We take off in two hours. By tonight we are in Luxembourg. There I have doctors and engineers I trust. No leaks. We can continue the work. We can keep the proof safe."

Esme looked up at the ceiling and said nothing.

"Cairo," Max said, "Zahid, the museum is our partner."

"Partners love discoveries," DeWalt said, his tone smooth. "They love the headlines, the applause, the front row. But they also love safety. And you have none." He leaned closer. "They did not even protect Dr Zahid. Do you think they will protect you? People are already moving against you, and against the museum. Stay in the open and you will be struck again. Come with me, and you will be protected."

"Like Abu Simbel was protected?" Esme asked.

The line went cold. "I do not run Egypt," DeWalt said at last. "And I did not push that button, no matter what your grief tells you. Come. Get out of the line of fire. Then decide if you hate me in person."

"Not today," Esme said. She reached for the phone. "Not this week. Not while Dr Zahid lies in the dark and I can't say her name without crying." She tapped the red circle and ended the call.

Max waited for the room to erupt. It did not. The world outside kept moving. A siren wailed far off. A car horn blared. A street seller shouted into the air.

"Eat," he said. "Lex will be here soon."

Lex came in with a limp, more bandage than pride. He dropped into the chair beside Esme and breathed out like he had been holding it too long.

"You look rough," he said quietly.

"You look worse," she answered, and they almost smiled.

Lex pulled a small case from his satchel and opened it. Inside was a plain phone, nothing fancy, no apps, no camera. He set it down on the blanket.

"When we leave," he said, "we do it quietly. The museum wants us in a safe house near Zamalek until they work out how to handle the press. But I want us out of this city before another drone decides to take a shot at us."

He paused, his eyes dark. "And one more thing. I had no idea DeWalt would bring his own private army. It is just as well he did, or we would all be dead. But the real question is this, he knew we would need them, and he never told us."

Esme nodded. "Let's go to Zamalek."

Max stood and reached for Esme's bag. His hand shook once before he steadied it on the strap. He looked toward the door and froze.

A man in a beige suit leaned on the frame as if he had been there all along. Ordinary yet not. His shoes shone, his tie was neat but quiet, and his face was the kind you forget at once which is why you remember it. He smiled, but his eyes stayed cold.

"I am from the embassy," he said, his voice smooth, carrying no warmth.

Lex's stance did not shift. "I didn't request an embassy car."

"No," the man said agreeably. "Your museum did. There is a lot of... interest in your movements. We would prefer you not be a target twice." He held up a badge. It could have been real. It could have been a very good lie. "If you are ready, I have a vehicle behind the service block."

"What is your name?" Max asked.

The man's smile widened a fraction. "Smith," he said.

"Smith, yes, had to be" quipped Max.

"We'll take the museum car," Lex said.

"Very well," Smith replied smoothly. "I'll trail you to the gate, then peel away. If anyone is watching, they'll chase me instead."

Lex studied him. The story was too neat. Whether they agreed or not, Smith would walk away with something. Lex gave him nothing.

Smith's smile did not move. "Two minutes," he said quietly. "After that, people will shift, and we will all pretend it was planned." He turned and slipped down the corridor.

Max looked at Esme. Her face was pale, her fingers tight on the blanket.

"Not him," she whispered. "Anyone but him."

"Okay," Lex said, firm.

They moved quickly. Papers signed. IVs pulled. A nurse wished them a good day. The lift carried them down to the lobby. Lex scanned the street through the glass, then led them out a side door into a narrow lane.

The museum driver was waiting, his elbow on the window of a tired old car. His shirt was creased, his face plain. He flicked his chin in greeting. Lex nodded and guided Esme into the back seat. Max followed. The driver pulled out, sliding into traffic like any other man on his way home.

They made it three blocks.

The traffic bunched. A delivery scooter toppled ahead. Boxes of bread spilled in a spray across the road. The driver braked hard. Hands reached to help the fallen rider. Shouts rose. A horn blared. Then came a tap at the back window, urgent and apologetic, eyes wide in excuse. The driver swore and reached for the door handle.

"Don't," Lex said.

Too late. The driver pushed the door open. A figure slid through with quick ease. Smith. He smiled at Esme as if he had brought a gift from next door.

"Forgive me," he said, and something cold kissed her wrist.

The world shrank to a single point of light, then it slipped away into darkness.

Max lunged. The door on his side burst open and a second man leaned in. The syringe struck fast into his arm. Max's breath caught, his eyes wide, then the light snapped shut.

Lex had time to grab Smith's hand and twist it the wrong way before another grip caught his neck. The pinch was precise, professional. Darkness rose fast and certain, as if it had been waiting.

The bread was gathered. The scooter rider climbed on and rode away. The lane breathed and reopened. The car door closed. The car rolled forward as if it had never stopped.

When Esme came back, the room was the opposite of Cairo General. Quiet. Cold. The air smelled of money and stone polished too often. Light pooled on silk drapes. Someone had thought about every angle a camera would love. The bed under her felt expensive enough to own a passport.

She did not move right away. She listened. The hum of a ventilation system that never let a window decide your air. The faint tick of a hidden clock. No sirens. No calls to prayer. No Cairo.

The door opened on soft hinges. A man stepped in, tall, dressed like a banker whose hobbies were risk and wind. At first Esme did not recognise him, the sedative still clouding her sight. He set a glass of water on the table and kept his hands clear. When he spoke, his voice was a precise instrument.

"Good morning, Esme. You are safe."

She pushed herself to sitting. The room kept its promise and did not move. "Where is Lex and Max?"

"In the building," he said. "Sleeping. It was necessary to bring you here. Cairo is no longer a place where your work can survive."

She looked at his face. It was a face she had seen on magazine covers attached to companies that did not like being seen. "DeWalt."

He inclined his head as if they had just met at a wedding. "Welcome back to Luxembourg."

"You cannot just kidnap us," Esme shot back. Her voice was sharper than she expected. Anger steadied her. "We work with you, yes. But you do not own us. You have no right."

DeWalt's smile did not move. "Kidnapping is an ugly word. I prefer to think of it as protection. You needed a place where drones cannot reach you. Now you have one."

Esme's jaw tightened. "And what else do I have? A locked room, a guard outside the door, and no choice?"

"You do have a choice," he said smoothly. "I will show you what I have built. You decide if you want to use it."

He nodded toward the wall. A hidden camera shifted. The door opened. Thea stepped in. She looked pale, drawn, smaller than Esme remembered, and harder.

Esme's breath caught. "You."

Thea did not step back. "Yes. M-me."

"You set this up."

Thea shook her head, breath catching as she tried to hold herself steady. "S-smith did," she said. "I told him not to, but he n-never listens to me." Her voice wavered, the stutter tightening with emotion. "I'm not innocent, I know that. But I wanted you safe in Cairo, even if you hated me. N-not here… not like this."

Her jaw trembled; the muscles in her throat were tight, every word a battle. Stress had always made it worse, breath shallow, timing lost, her mind racing ahead while her voice fought to keep up. She pressed a fist to her lips, eyes burning with frustration, willing her speech to obey her heart.

Esme gave a thin smile. "Then we both lost."

A knock. The door opened again. Another man entered. His face was ordinary, forgettable. New clothes, same emptiness. Smith. He set down a tray and folded his hands, waiting.

Esme rose to her feet. She did not look at Smith. "Take me to them," she said.

They moved through a corridor built for wealth. Glass. Wood. Paintings that cost as much as towns. Doors that closed without sound.

Max waited in a room that looked like a gallery. He sat upright on a sofa that had never known a stain. When he saw Esme, he stood, and the science fell off his face and left the friend. They held each other too tight, then too long, then not long enough. Lex came through another door with a bandage and a scowl, and the hug became three people trying to solve the same physics problem with arms.

"Like the decor?" Max said, because one of them had to be the one who could still make a sentence that might scrape the edge of normal.

"It screams hostage," Lex said.

"Prison with a wine list," Esme said.

Thea watched them and looked as if each word pressed on something sharp inside her.

DeWalt did not hurry. He let the reunion breathe. He waited until the anger finished its first lap. Then he gestured to a panel in the wall, and it slid aside, revealing a window into a space that did not belong in a city. A hangar carved out of rock and money. White light. Black floors. Machines that were not yet machines. Tables of glass with the past dismantled on top of them.

"You asked what you have," DeWalt said.

DeWalt led them through a biometric door and into a suspended glass corridor. The air hissed as they passed, filtered and cold. At the far end another set of doors opened onto a balcony that overlooked a subterranean hangar.

The sight froze them.

Below, under banks of floodlights, sat a craft. Black, wingless, its surface curved like liquid stone. Strange symbols shimmered faintly across its hull. Scaffolding climbed around it like ribs. Beyond, laboratories buzzed with scientists in clean suits working in silence.

On one wall, full scale replicas of cartouches from Nefertari's statue gleamed under white light. On another, a quarter scale reconstruction of the La Palma cavern glowed with embedded LEDs.

Esme stood by the railing, pale but upright, Thea at her side. Her eyes darted to Lex and Max. Relief, guilt, defiance, all in one glance.

DeWalt spread his arms wide, his smile cutting like glass. "You see it now," he said. "This is part of the complex you haven't seen, the piece that changes everything. History isn't just a story, it's a door. And I'll be the one to open it."

Lex stared down, his voice tight. "Impossible."

DeWalt turned, eyes bright. "We found the drawings in Abu Simbel. It has only been a week, but this is a mock-up my engineers put together for the shell. It will take more data, more interpretation of the scrolls before the real work can begin. But this shows what is coming."

Behind him stood the model, an ancient vision rendered in alloy and light. Its hull curved like a scarab's shell, inscribed with the same geometries that lined the temple walls. Fused bronze ribs spiralled into a crystalline core that pulsed faintly, as if alive. The propulsion vents resembled lotus petals, each etched with glyphs that caught and refracted the glow of the chamber lights. It was neither ancient nor modern, but something between, a bridge of lost knowledge that defied time itself.

Max shook his head, half laughing. "How'd you move this fast? You got teleport privileges I don't know about?"

"Determination," DeWalt said. His voice dropped. "And theft."

The smile left DeWalt's face. His voice hardened, the warmth gone. "None of you is saying what you really believe," he said, scanning their faces. "You want to, but you can't. Because as scientists, everything for you must be verified, peer-reviewed, repeatable. You hide behind data even when the truth is standing right in front of you."

Lex's tone was cold. "And if we walk away?"

He stepped closer to the glowing mock-up, the reflection of its light cutting across his face. "Then you watch the future without me," he said quietly. "And by the time you land back home, you'll already be irrelevant.

" He took a step closer, lowering his tone so they had to listen. "Do you think the universities will take you back after this? Do you think the journals will print your names? Without me you face nothing but ridicule. You will be branded liars, heretics, frauds. Locked out of archives, stripped of grants, barred from every hall that once welcomed you. A lifetime of exile from the very world you fought to serve."

His eyes swept over them, hard as glass. "With me you have protection, resources, and history itself in your hands. Without me you have nothing. Only shame and silence."

Dinner was laid in a chamber lined with glass walls. Beyond them, the laboratories glowed sterile white. In the centre, on obsidian stone, lay scrolls, fragile papyri, their ink faded, their meaning buried.

Esme turned on Thea, her voice sharp with betrayal. "You went behind our backs. You worked with him while we fought to keep the truth alive. How could you?"

DeWalt cut in before Thea could answer. "Because family matters. I put her through university. I paid for her future when no one else would. Do not be shocked she stands with me now."

Thea's eyes dropped. She did not deny it. "I-I'm s-sorry," she whispered, the words trembling out of her. "I d-didn't want this. I had no choice."

Her hands shook as she unfurled a fragile sheet of papyri, each movement measured, careful against the tremor in her fingers. "Th-these were taken from Nefertari's statue," she said, her voice low but urgent, struggling to stay steady. "Esme cracked the first layer. The rest... I c-couldn't."

The stress had tightened everything, her breath shallow, her jaw rigid, her thoughts outrunning her words. The stutter came harder now, each syllable fought for, her determination the only thing holding her voice together.

Esme stepped forward. Her fingers shook, not from fear but from the weight of the scroll. She bent close, eyes racing across the lines. At first it looked like ritual, but then the shapes began to shift. Patterns formed. Rules appeared. Some failed, some held, and her mind kept moving, testing, and fitting each piece.

"This is not prayer," she whispered. "It is a system. Instructions. Whoever wrote this wanted to teach. This is not worship, it is a manual."

Max leaned closer, eyes narrowing at the symbols. "You're right. These aren't prayers. They're notes, proper technical ones. Instructions for builders and engineers."

The words struck the room like an explosion.

Lex straightened, his voice edged with fury. "I abhor everything about this. The way you dragged us here, the way you threatened us with exclusion from our work, as if our lives are pawns you can move at will." He turned to Max and Esme, his tone heavy. "I think DeWalt has us in check."

DeWalt's smile sharpened. "Not check, Professor. Checkmate."

The silence cut deep. The glow from the scrolls lit their faces, but none of them spoke.

At last Thea stepped forward, her voice quiet but trembling. "I want to be part of this t-team. Whatever you think of me, I b-belong with you."

Esme's eyes flicked to her, then away. Max said nothing, his jaw locked tight. Lex gave no answer.

The glow on the wall grew brighter, but the shadows between them only deepened. There was no trust for DeWalt. And for Thea, only doubt.

chapter 50:
Revelations

The boardroom felt more like a vault than a meeting space. Walls of glass looked out across Luxembourg City, the skyline sharp against the night. Office lights glowed like watchful eyes beyond the dark.

At the centre stood a long black table polished to a mirror shine. Screens lined the walls, half asleep, the rest humming faint blue, waiting for orders.

At the head of the table sat DeWalt. His posture was composed, hands folded, eyes fixed on the spread of scrolls laid out on white cloth. They were fragile, cracked with age, yet the ink still seemed alive under the lights.

Lex leaned forward, one hand gripping the edge of the table. His pulse was uneven. The weight of centuries hung between them all.

Silence pressed down on the room.

Max broke it.

"It's incredible," Max said, his voice lifting with excitement. His pen hovered over the parchment like a scalpel. "Look at this. What I said before about the magnetic lines being a power source? It's confirmed. These aren't just alignments, they're conduits. The geometry's not symbolic, it's functional. And Khamariti drew them. He knew how to harvest the planet itself. The glyphs aren't scattered. They run in sequence, joined by lines cut in patterns that can't be random. In Egypt alone one node's the Great Pyramid of Giza. Another runs south to Abu Simbel. A third curves north to Pi Ramesses."

Esme leaned forward, her eyes wide.

"They are not monuments," she said. "They are aligned. Every one of them."

Lex asked the question that burned in all of them.

"Aligned with what?"

Esme traced the edge of the scroll with her finger. "This is not decoration. It is the same lattice we saw inside the orb. These lines have purpose. They are functional."

Max typed at speed, entering coordinates into his laptop. Blue light spread across his face. He overlaid the lines onto modern maps.

The wall screens came alive.

Lines stretched across continents. Every monument matched.

Max shoved his chair back, his voice shaking.

"It fits, all of it," Max said. "This isn't myth. This's engineering, way beyond Bronze Age precision."

Esme pointed to the parchment's edge.

"The lines do not stop.

Lex gripped the table tighter. "Not just the Nile. The entire grid. Built for something larger."

Max swallowed hard.

"He's saying Earth's a reservoir, a cell. This scroll Thea gave us says the grid keeps two planets going."

Lex's voice cut like steel. "If the grid fails, the planet fractures."

Esme steadied herself. "I saw this before. Another scroll. Two spheres. At first, I thought one was Earth and the other the underworld. But it was not myth. One sphere was Earth. The other was called A'tharan in the scrolls. Between them ran a lattice binding them together. If that lattice breaks, both worlds fall."

Thea's whisper carried across the room.

"A covenant i-in stone."

DeWalt leaned forward, calculation replacing awe.

"Exactly. Khamariti built a failsafe, beyond the reach of priests and pharaohs. And now, we hold the instructions."

Thea's voice rose, sharp with urgency. "P-philips stole s-spheres from Abu Simbel.

DeWalt's tone grew tighter. "Shut up."

Thea rose abruptly, her chair scraping against the floor. She returned moments later with a hard case. Inside were the two orbs. She set them on the table.

"The s-spheres."

DeWalt's smile thinned, his voice repeating the warning. "Dangerous things."

Esme lifted the spheres. They locked together with a soft click. She turned them once. Twice. Paused. Turned them again.

Light pulsed. A glow spread slowly across the walls, as if the room itself had begun to breathe.

Esme's voice cut through the tension. "I remember. At Abu Simbel there were carvings of these spheres. Not fixed. Turning. Each panel showed a different position, as if recording a sequence. At the time I thought it was ritual. Now I see it was instruction. The movements are the code."

Esme twisted the sphere several times with movements from memory. The light grew stronger. A beam swept the walls. She froze.

The walls blazed with fire. Earth and A'tharan circled together, their rhythm not the pulse of something living, but the measured beat of a machine.

Thea's hand covered her mouth. Max stood frozen, pen still in his hand. Esme stared into the light, her mind racing through every translation she had ever made. Lex gripped the table as though it could anchor him against the weight of centuries.

DeWalt broke the silence. His voice was calm, almost gentle, but it carried like steel through the air. "Then we are not guessing anymore. The record is clear. Earth is not only a home. It is a designed power source. A vast cell, created to sustain another world."

The projection casted its soft glow across the chamber. Earth spun slowly in the centre of the display, ringed by mathematical arcs. Beside it, another sphere ignited, smaller, dusky, its surface scored with ancient scars.

A'tharan.

Lines of orbit lit the space between them, a gravitational dance locked in precision. Around the edges, glyphs flickered and rearranged into equations, not in hieroglyphs or cuneiform, but in Greek notation. Golden ratios. Elliptical paths. Axial drift. Celestial mechanics no civilisation on Earth should have known.

Max stepped closer, drawn to the projection like iron to a lodestone. The light from the rotating spheres painted his face in gold and blue as he squinted at the orbital arcs now spinning through the air.

He didn't speak straight away.

Instead, he dropped to one knee, pulled his laptop from his rucksack, and flipped it open. His fingers moved fast. No hesitation. Just focus. Lines of astronomical code filled the screen. Axial shifts. Gravitational vectors. Orbital decay.

"Hold on," he muttered. "Let me check something..."

The room quietened. Only the hum of the projection and the soft clack of keys broke the silence.

Max angled the laptop screen so the others could see. "I'm modelling the approach vector based on what the projection shows. Cross-referencing known anomalies in Earth's magnetic field and geological disruptions. It won't be perfect."

He stopped. Froze.

Then he sat back and gave a low, humourless laugh.

"There it is."

Lex stepped forward. "What are we looking at?"

Max turned the screen. It now showed a jagged wave, peaks marked with dates.

"Every twelve hundred years, like a heartbeat.

"Next cycle is due... right now. Between 2050 and 2052. Give or take a few months depending on solar wind drag.

Esme stepped forward, staring at the wave. "You're serious."

Max nodded, voice tight.

"I think we've just caught the start of it coming back," Max said. "A'tharans not just drifting out there. It's locked to us. Not orbiting like a moon but visiting, like a capacitor coming back for a recharge."

He turned to the others, eyes sharp now.

"We're not just looking at archaeology. This is a twelve-century power cycle. A system. A circuit."

And then, from the edge of the projection, the twin spheres reappeared, Earth and A'tharan, glowing, turning, meeting again on a collision of influence rather than contact.

Max nodded. "Roughly. Twelve hundred before the birth of Christ puts us around twelve hundred BCE. Massive upheavals. The collapse of the Late Bronze Age. Civilisations fell like dominos, Mycenae, Hatti,

Ugarit, even Egypt trembled. Earthquakes, drought, mass migrations. It was like something tore through the world."

Lex stared at the orbits projected from the spheres. "And then... the bright star," he said, barely a whisper.

They looked at him.

He swallowed. "In the Gospel of Matthew. The Magi followed a light. A star that moved against the sky. Scholars have debated it for centuries, a supernova, a comet, an alignment. But what if it was something else? What if it was this? A planetary body passing close enough to reflect solar light in ways no one had seen before?"

Esme's voice was taut. "You're saying the Star of Bethlehem... was A'tharan?"

Max did not flinch.

"And twelve hundred years after that?" Max said, still facing the glowing orbits. "Around 1200 AD? The Crusades. The Great Famine. Earthquakes across Europe. The Mongol rise in the East. Entire dynasties collapsed. Cities burned. The climate dipped. Whole empires broke and shifted."

He exhaled slowly. "It's always there. Just beyond the reach of reason."

The sphere above them pulsed and reconfigured. A soft metallic tone echoed, and a second scroll uncoiled within the projection, this one older, darker, edged with symbols that flickered and rearranged as Esme stepped beneath it.

She raised her hand, casting a shadow across the glyphs. Her voice steadied.

"These aren't prayers or warnings," Esme said, her voice low but charged. "They're records, technical logs. Khamariti documented every energy cycle, every fluctuation, every failure." She stepped closer to the projection, the shifting light reflecting in her eyes. "Look here, the notation changes. Different syntax, different glyph pressure. Someone kept recording long after his death. Either his successors... or the system itself."

Max frowned. "You mean these spheres are still writing?"

Esme nodded slowly. "Updating, just like we update software. Each new generation refining the last, learning from every collapse. It's not ritual—it's maintenance. A living archive, still trying to stabilise a grid-built thousands of years ago."

Lex stared at the glowing symbols, the enormity of it sinking in.

"So, the Earth's most ancient artefacts," he said softly, "are still running diagnostics."

Esme stepped closer to the shifting projection as a low hum filled the chamber. A new spiral rotated into view, its glyphs older than any before, angular, deeply etched, and scorched in places, as if burned into memory.

She traced the pattern with her hand. "This is the earliest record. A foundational failure."

Max peered over her shoulder. "What year?"

Esme took a moment, eyes moving line by line.

"Circa twelve fifty BCE. Khamariti's lifetime. The Ramesside era."

Lex leaned in. "That's the time of the plagues."

Esme gave a slow nod. "And this spiral confirms it."

She began to translate, her voice steady.

"The western gate ruptured," Esme read aloud, tracing the faded symbols with her fingertip. "The water rose. The fault cracked where the sea touches fire. The island groaned. The circuit failed."

She looked up, her face pale. "This isn't just a record of disaster. It's an engineering log. When the western gate failed, Pi-Rameses was lost, not just to flood or plague, but because a major node in their energy network collapsed. The A'tharan device stopped charging properly. The excess power had nowhere to go, so it stayed in the earth."

Max leaned in. "And that would mean earthquakes, eruptions, storms, whatever."

"Everything," Esme said. "Life itself only began because they once controlled that flow. When they lost it, chaos followed."

Max stepped back, disbelief in his voice. "La Palma's landslide flooded the Nile, set off the plagues, and knocked out Khamariti's power source. Just hold on a second, we're saying Khamariti was an alien, yeah?"

The projection darkened. A spiral of glyphs turned slowly into view, scorched and uneven, more like a wound than writing.

Esme stepped beneath it, lips moving as she translated. Then she spoke aloud.

"Khamariti's account," Esme said quietly. "Not a record, an eyewitness history."

Silence gripped the room.

Lex looked up, stunned. "The royal capital."

Esme nodded. "More than that. The glyph calls it the mouth of power. It sat at the Delta junction, where the Nile split into seven arms. Khamariti built it as a primary conductor for the southern energy circuit. When the landslide struck La Palma, the wave raced east. It reached Egypt. The monument collapsed. Foundations split. Stone cracked. And the current meant to flow west was thrown back into the grid."

Max's voice was tight. "A feedback loop."

Esme's eyes stayed on the light. "It broke the pattern. The energy bounced. The glyph says the earth groaned and the air turned sour."

Lex frowned. "And that triggered the plagues."

She pointed to the next sequence. "Blood in the river, the Nile turned red from chemical bloom. Frogs fled the banks and filled the streets. Insects hatched out of season. Disease spread. Crops failed. The sequence was exact. Not random. Not divine punishment. System collapse."

She looked from Lex to Max. "This wasn't a malfunction. It was a total collapse. It damaged the Earth, and it damaged A'tharan. And yes," she added, her voice steady now, "I think we're past verification. He was an alien."

DeWalt looked stunned. "Were any other sites affected?"

Esme nodded. "The Temple of Dendera. The glyph calls it the sky mirror. It was aligned with the rising of Sirius. The ceiling fractured during the surge. Its resonance failed. The circuit broke again."

She moved along the spiral.

"Henu Platform west of Abu Simbel. A stabilising terrace over a buried chamber. The glyph reads, the chamber hummed, then screamed. Pressure built beneath it. The flood burst through. The whole platform was swallowed. Lost beneath the river."

Lex narrowed his eyes. "Henu Platform? That's not on any map."

"Because it is buried under what is now Lake Nasser," she said. "We built a dam over it. But Khamariti placed it there first, as a pressure release. A failsafe. Even that failed."

She paused.

"One more. Sa Maat. The Lighthouse of Justice. A tower of rose granite, seventy cubits high. A relay for energy into the western horizon. The glyph says, its fire turned black. It tried to absorb the charge. Then it imploded."

Max blinked. "That tower never existed."

Esme met his gaze. "That is what history says. But the glyphs say otherwise. If the ancients saw it fall, they would have erased it. Or turned it into myth."

Lex stepped forward, looking at the spirals as the system unravelled.

"All of it... collapsed. A chain of failures. Pi Rameses. Dendera. Henu. Sa Maat."

Esme nodded. "Khamariti was too late. He could not finish the grid before the collapse. The flood struck. The monuments failed. The circuit reversed."

Max looked up at the orbiting spheres. "What about A'tharan?"

Thea stepped forward for the first time. She had been staring at the projection of the second planet, silent until now.

"It does not behave like a natural object," she said. "It does not drift. It adjusts. It corrects. It follows a programmed path."

Lex turned to her. "You're the engineer. You think it is a machine?"

She nodded. "More machine than planet. Something built to orbit Earth. To draw power. To sync with our planet every twelve centuries."

The projection flickered, then shifted again. A new spiral unfurled across the chamber wall, this one etched deeper, more chaotic, the strokes like scars. The glyphs moved differently here, stuttering, breaking, reassembling as if even the data had been damaged.

The glyphs pulsed. The next line appeared, stark and violent.

The winds vanished. The skin of the world cracked. Heat replaced air. Ice turned to poison. The fire spread.

Esme's voice dropped.

"It says the A'tharan climate collapsed. Entire biomes failed. The atmosphere was stripped. Clouds stopped forming. The only elements that remained were fire and water. It happened around the time Homo sapiens first emerged, when the world was still learning how to breathe. And now it needs power again, to create and cleanse water, to rebuild an atmosphere, to restore the very foundations of life itself."

She moved to the final glyph, smaller, almost hidden beneath the curve of the spiral.

Lex stepped forward, slowly, eyes fixed on the spiralling projection, his face lit by the turning spheres above, Earth and A'tharan, locked in their impossible dance.

His voice was quiet, but there was no hesitation.

"Khamariti was not one of us, that's obvious."

Lex kept going.

"He wasn't human. Not fully. He came here for a reason, to build, yes. But as an engineer, a builder. Not as a servant of Pharaohs."

He gestured to the glyphs.

He paused.

"And he was obviously not alone."

Max's mouth opened, but no words came.

Esme turned back to the projection. The meaning now hung in the air, unavoidable.

The monuments, the grid, the planetary cycles, none of it had been random. Earth had been chosen. A'tharan had come here not by accident, but by design. And Khamariti had walked among mortals, shaping stone with tools no dynasty had forged, protecting a system older than any kingdom, answering to forces no scribe ever recorded.

Thea stepped closer, her voice unsteady.

"Then all of this... the plagues, the collapses, the temples, it was never about gods or punishment."

Lex nodded. "It was about systems. Balance. Recharge."

"And when the grid failed," Esme added, "A'tharan suffered, how bad we just don't know"

The projection flared again. The second planet no longer looked stable. It pulsed faintly, heat signatures rippling across its surface-like veins. Not a world at peace.

A machine trying to survive.

Lex spoke again, this time more to himself than the others.

Lex stared at the projection. The spirals had faded now, but the images lingered, Earth and A'tharan, locked together in their long orbit, both marked by heat, instability, collapse.

His voice was quieter now, more thought than statement.

"Khamariti knew the Earth's collapse would echo home. He built the grid to protect both planets. But maybe it was never enough."

The room held still.

He looked up at the flickering model of Earth. It pulsed with rising heat signatures. Deep red blooms glowed across the equator. Sea levels edged higher along every coast.

Lex's jaw tightened.

"Look at us. Rising temperatures. Shifting storms. Floods. Crops failing. Cities drowning. Earth is following the same path A'tharan did around two hundred thousand years ago, when the first Homo sapiens began to walk the earth. Climate stripped. Systems overwhelmed. A planet turning on itself."

He turned slowly, eyes scanning the chamber.

Lex's fists clenched. "If the grid fails, both planets die."

His voice hardened. "This was why he went to the Canary Islands. He had to find what threatened his energy nodes hidden as temples, pyramids, monuments worshipped by the world without knowing their true purpose."

DeWalt's eyes burned. "Then I will control it. Limitless energy. Nations begging for power. My company at the centre of civilisation."

Thea's voice lashed. "You would ri- risk millions for profit?"

"Technology will stabilise the planet," DeWalt shot back, eyes alight. "And if there's even a chance Khamariti lived long enough to keep updating those spheres, then I want what he had, the formula, the process, whatever it is. Eternal life isn't myth. It's engineering."

"You're mad," Max said, his voice shaking. "He's been dead for millennia."

DeWalt's gaze cut to him, sharp and cold. "Is he?" he said.

chapter 51:
The Breaking Point

Philips dragged Jones into the concrete room in cuffs. The man's face was streaked with sand and blood, his lip split. He carried himself with the rigid posture of a soldier. An ex-Navy SEAL. Men like him did not break easily.

DeWalt sat at the table, the low light cutting sharp edges across the room. To his right, Philips watched in silence, his hands clasped, his expression unreadable. Opposite them, a man with the stillness of a blade, General Hamdi of Egyptian Intelligence, leaned against the wall.

His uniform bore no medals tonight, only grief disguised as restraint. Abu Simbel had been more than an attack; it had been desecration. His men, his responsibility, reduced to ash beneath a heritage that should have stood for eternity. The photographs, the charred stone, the echo of their last transmission, all burned behind his eyes.

Now, across the table, Jones sat breathing, alive, while Hamdi's soldiers were names on a report. Every second that man drew breath was a deeper twist of the knife.

DeWalt placed a clear folder on the table. He did not open it. The photographs inside pressed against the plastic. Wreckage. Dead faces. Three thousand years broken in one night. He let the images bleed into the air without showing them fully.

"You know where you are," DeWalt said.

Jones kept his eyes straight ahead. "A room."

DeWalt's mouth curved slightly. "A room in Jordan. No consulate. No lawyers. But there is a camera. What you say here will outlast us. That can save you or bury you."

Jones glanced once at the lens in the corner. Its red light burned steady. "You think I will break. I won't."

DeWalt's tone did not change. "We have the truth. And time."

A cup of tea was set in front of Jones. He ignored it. His eyes never left the folder.

DeWalt leaned across the table until the edge pressed against his palms. The room was still, the air thick with the stale scent of coffee and sweat. His voice came low, precise, each word landing like a drop of acid.

"Your name is Jack Jones. You worked with a man called Rod Clinton. He is dead. You piloted a drone, an old model, smuggled in under diplomatic clearance. That drone carried a missiles from a third country, with enough payload to level Abu Simbel and turn a monument of eternity into dust. My sound guess would be orders from Rotheram at the CIA, or Riley himself. Orders that began in the office of the Chief of Staff, passed straight to President Hope."

He paused, letting the names hang between them like weights. "You will tell me everything, on camera. Then you will sign a confession. And after that, perhaps, you will breathe easier."

Jones stared back without a word. His eyes were cold, his jaw tight, the flicker of defiance buried deep.

For three days he gave nothing. No plea. No denial. No hint of the man beneath the silence. The guards changed, the light shifted from dawn to dusk, but Jones remained a statue in chains, his silence the only weapon he had left.

By the third night even DeWalt began to feel it, the unnerving certainty that somewhere inside that silence, Jack Jones was still winning.

They kept him cuffed to the chair in the bare concrete room. No sleep. No light except the strip overhead. No food, just water forced into his hands until he swallowed. His body sagged, but the will inside him did not crack. Pain, hunger, exhaustion. He had faced them all before.

DeWalt never raised his voice. He never struck. He sat in silence, waiting. The Egyptians pressed harder, snarling questions, slamming the table, but Jones's face stayed like stone.

On the morning of the fourth day, the door opened without a word. One of DeWalt's investigators stepped in, placed a thick folder on the table, and left as silently as he had come.

DeWalt waited until the latch clicked shut. Then, with deliberate care, he drew the folder closer and set it before Jones. The paper inside was worn at the edges, the tabs marked in red. Evidence. Names. Coordinates. Images taken from satellites and intercepted calls.

"This," DeWalt said, his voice almost calm, "is the story you thought we would never find."

He opened the file, page by page. Photographs of the drone wreckage. Fragments of coded transmissions. Bank transfers routed through shell accounts in Dubai and Cyprus and Thailand.

DeWalt looked up. "Four days of silence buys you nothing, Jack. Every secret you kept has already spoken."

Jones's eyes flickered for the first time. Not fear, recognition. And DeWalt saw it. The smallest crack in the wall

Inside was a single photograph. A young Thai woman held a baby in her arms. Chiang Rai. A street market blurred in the background, but the faces were sharp. Hers, wary but proud. The child's, a year old at most.

DeWalt slid the picture until it touched Jones's cuffed hands. His voice was quiet. "Three days without a word. You held the line. Impressive. But here is the truth. You broke the rule the moment you left her behind. You made a commitment. A woman. A child. A weakness."

Jones's head snapped up. His eyes narrowed.

DeWalt unlocked his phone and turned the screen. A live feed filled it. The market in Chiang Rai. The same woman. The same child. Moving through the stalls. A man with a camera followed a few paces behind. Patient. Close enough.

DeWalt's voice stayed calm. "You, see? I do not deal in threats. I deal in facts. They are there. They are real. They are within reach."

He tapped the photo with a finger. "You know what will happen if you stay silent. In your world, family is leverage. A baby is a target. Do you think your enemies will not find them? Do you think they will not use them? You put them in the crosshairs the moment you made them yours."

For the first time Jones's mask cracked. His lips pressed tight. His breath quickened.

DeWalt leaned close. "You can hold your silence and watch them vanish. Or you can speak here, now, on camera. Make it public. Make it loud. Put the truth in the air where no one can touch them. That confession is the only shield you have left. For you. For them."

Jones stared at the photograph. His eyes burned. His chest rose and fell with uneven force. He had endured drown proofing, starvation, cages. He had held against pain and cold. But this was the fracture.

His voice came at last, rough as gravel and heavy with defeat.

"My name is Jack Jones. I piloted the drone that struck Abu Simbel. The order came from Mike Rotherham. Rotherham's order came from Riley. Riley said it came from the top."

The camera light blinked, a small red pulse marking every word as it entered the record. The silence that followed was unbearable.

General Hamdi exhaled through his nose, a sound closer to a growl than breath. The weight of his fury filled the room, a heat that seemed to draw every particle of air toward him. His men dead, his temple desecrated, and now the truth, ugly, undeniable, had a voice.

DeWalt gathered the photographs with careful precision, sliding each one back into the folder. His expression never shifted. "Good," he said quietly. "Now your family live. And the world will hear you."

He snapped the folder shut, the sound sharp as a gunshot. "When they do, it will not be you on trial. It will be Hope."

He turned to the general. "General Hamdi, he is all yours."

As DeWalt reached the door, he paused and looked back once, his tone almost casual. "I don't think we will be seeing each other again."

Then he was gone, leaving the echo of his words behind, an aftershock that promised the storm had only begun.

The Oval Office was silent. President Hope stood at the window with his hands behind his back. Outside the gates, cameras crowded the lawn. His name was on every screen, bound now to Abu Simbel by a soldier's confession.

Jack Jones's voice was everywhere. "The name on that channel was Hope." No context. No defence. Just his name tied to ruin.

The next week was torrid.

Chief of Staff Riley paced the carpet. "Mr President, you have to face this. The Senate are drafting articles of impeachment. If you do not act, you will be crushed."

Hope turned, his eyes cold. "You want me to confess to something I did not consent to do?"

Riley stayed silent. The room felt airless.

Rotherham stood near the window, the city lights reflected in the glass behind him. His jaw was locked, his posture brittle.

Hope leaned forward across the desk. "Take the blame, one for the team. Keep Riley out of this. I do not want anything leading back to my office."

Rotherham turned, anger breaking through his composure. "Mr President, the Egyptians will be screaming for my deportation before morning. They want someone to hang."

Hope's reply was cold, measured. "Forget what the Egyptians want. There will be a trial. You will do a little time, maybe not if you appeal. When I leave office, I will pardon you and ensure a good pension. That is how this stays contained."

Rotherham stared at him, disbelief flickering into fear. "Not a chance?" he said quietly.

Hope held his gaze. "You survive. You take the fall, serve the story, and when the time is right, I make it disappear. That is the price of loyalty. Anything else is prison time, lots of prison time."

Rotherham's voice cracked. "That is not much of an option. I could take you down with me."

Hope straightened, his expression hardening to marble. His voice dropped to a cold certainty.

"It is the only one you are getting. And as for me, yes, I would be disgraced. But let us be clear, Rotherham… the American people will never put a former President in prison."

He let the words hang in the air, heavy with the arrogance of power and the certainty of history.

By afternoon, the cameras were in place and the seal of state glowed behind him. Hope sat before the Senate committee and the questions fell like hunting knives. Each answer he gave was a small, calculated deflection and a promise at once. The room leaned in. Outside, the world waited to see which way the first gust would blow. "Did you authorise the strike on Abu Simbel?"

"No."

"Did you discuss Egypt with Riley or Rotherham?"

"I did not."

Hope gripped the table. "This was a set up. Someone used my name to destroy me."

But the faces before him were already fixed.

By nightfall, impeachment articles were written. Abuse of power. Obstruction of justice. Misconduct.

Late in the night Riley came to him. "They will cut you loose. Everyone. The party. The donors. They will sacrifice you."

"And you?" Hope asked.

"I served the office," Riley said. His voice was thin.

Hope laughed, a bitter, hollow sound that filled the room like cold rain.

"Then you will fall on your sword," he said, each word measured and inevitable. "You will say you acted alone. That I knew nothing. Protect your President."

The next morning Hope stood at a podium. Cameras flashed.

"My fellow Americans. I had no part in Abu Simbel. Those who acted did so without my knowledge. Chief of Staff Riley and CIA Director Rotherham have resigned. They will answer for their actions. I will face the Senate. And I will tell the truth."

Reporters shouted questions. He turned away.

Hours later the House voted. The articles of impeachment passed with ease.

Hope watched the tally in silence. His allies gone. His name stained. Alone in the Oval Office.

Impeached.

The word echoed like a sentence. A trial in the Senate waited. His fate no longer in his hands.

chapter 52:
Meeting of Minds

They met four months later in Liverpool, in a small hotel near Sefton Park. Dawn rain swept the streets outside, a fine drizzle clinging to the trees. The world had moved on since Abu Simbel, but none of them could shake the echo of stone breaking and history burning.

Esme and Max had flown in from Cairo. In a quiet ward there, Dr Zahid had passed them photographs of new fragments lifted from the rubble, her sight partly restored by careful surgery. Her eyes were fragile, but her voice had been strong when she pressed the folder into Esme's hands. DeWalt must not know.

Thea came from Luxembourg. She had survived inside DeWalt's headquarters as little more than a pair of hands. She endured suspicion and silence, but all the while she observed, remembered, and found hidden ways to report back to Lex.

Lex arrived from America. His skin was pale, his voice hoarse. Weeks before he had testified before the Senate, forced to recount what had happened in Egypt. He had spoken under the hot lights while cameras burned his face into memory. His words had carried the weight of empires. They had also carried the name Hope into ruin.

Max had arranged their meeting. He had called in favours from old friends, men who owed him debts from university days and research contracts. They set decoys, swapped cars, and cut off any watchers that might have followed. By the time, the four of them stepped into the hotel's conference room, the trails behind them were smoke.

The room was plain. A projector, a narrow table, four chairs. Rain tapped the glass.

Max opened his notes. His face was pale, the glow of the screen painting shadows under his eyes. He spoke slowly, each word weighed.

"I've finished the last calculations," he said, his voice low but full of awe. "A'tharan doesn't just pass near us, it slips between Earth and

341

the Moon, twice the Moon's size but hidden in plain sight. For weeks, sometimes months, it holds its orbit, feeding on the same solar currents that drive our storms."

He paused, eyes locked on the holographic model spinning before them.

"But how," Thea whispered, "can something t-that massive not tear the tides apart? The gravity a-alone—"

"It should," he cut in. "By every law we know, it should. But it doesn't. Because A'tharan bends its own field. It balances its pull using the same energy it harvests, gravity folding back on itself like a mirrored wave. The oceans hardly move, the instruments stay quiet, and the world sleeps through its passing."

Lex stepped forward, his tone slicing through the hum of the projection. "We know the next recharge is in twenty plus years. The question is, does the grid still function? And where is the new hub?"

Max exhaled through his nose, the sound sharp with frustration. "I can't say yet. The data's incomplete. The grid's fractured. To find the hub, I need to track its resonance during the next cycle. That won't happen until 2050."

The words dropped into the room like stones. The spheres above them turned in silence, Earth glowing faintly red, A'tharan a darker shadow.

Thea spoke at last, her voice like a blade. "So, until t-then we don't know if the planets are safe or n-not?"

Max gave a single nod. "Yes. Somewhere out there's the key, I hope. A living hub built with the same precision as the pyramids. Until we find it, we can't know if the bond between Earth and A'tharan still holds or if it's already starting to fail."

Thea's eyes narrowed, calm but intent. "L-look at the world around us," she said. "Rising seas. Droughts. Floods. Pandemics. If the plagues returned, they're not waiting. They're here now."

Lex stared at the projection, its twin worlds turning in their endless dance. "Then we are already inside the next cycle," he said softly. "And we have no idea if we can stop it."

"I have a plan," he said at last. "Not something to debate now, but with what we've uncovered, and the theodolite, I think there's a way forward. It's not strictly scientific, so I'll keep it to myself for now. But if I'm right, it could change everything."

He drew a breath, steadying his tone. "For the moment, let's turn to Esme, she's uncovered some extraordinary new details about Khamariti."

Esme spread the photographs across the table. The projector lit the wall. Symbols burst into shape, glyphs twisting into visions.

Esme's hand trembled as she opened another folder. Photographs slid out. They showed a stone panel lifted whole from Abu Simbel's ruin. She placed them under the projector.

"This," she said, "is the record Dr Zahid allowed me to photograph. It traces Khamariti after La Palma. DeWalt knows nothing of this."

Esme's voice steadied as the projection filled the wall, the chamber bathed in shifting gold and blue. "Watch carefully," she said. "This was carved to be read in light."

The image glowed brighter. At first, it seemed simple, a man standing at the edge of the Nile, arms bound tightly at his sides, one foot brushing the water. "It looks calm," Esme continued, "but it isn't. When the illumination deepens, the shadows in the grooves start to tell the truth."

The man's form sharpened. "He was not the high priest's servant. This is Khamariti, the was the high priest's sacrifice." Her words came slow, measured. "The ropes on his wrists are not for punishment but for ritual. See the symbols? Glyphs of damnation. At his waist, a granite weight, judgment itself, chained to him."

The projection widened. Behind the bound man, figures raised their arms to the heavens, frozen in invocation. "The priests call to gods who no longer answer," Esme said. "And here, look at the barge. It tilts east, toward the rising sun. Toward rebirth, or annihilation."

A hush filled the room as the final sequence appeared. "This was an execution by decree of pharaoh," she said. "It was a sacrifice the pharaoh was forced into by Ankhwennefer."

Then she stopped. The light shifted again, revealing new lines that had been hidden in the glare. Esme leaned closer, tracing the glyphs with her finger as she read them aloud. "Here, the name. Ankhwennefer."

She drew a breath. "It was he who forced Khamariti down, the high priest in the leopard sash." Her eyes lifted to the next panel.

"And there… Pharaoh himself, watching."

The screen dimmed to reveal the final carving: the cracked Eye of Horus, faint but unyielding. Beside it, a kneeling scribe etched in miniature. "Nebit," Esme said. "He recorded it all."

Esme drew in a breath. "He saw it. He wrote it down. He left this as a warning."

Max's voice hardened, the memory slicing through him like a blade. "Then he's brown bread, dead. He said it himself, only fire and water could end him. I remember every word."

The chamber seemed to press in on them. The cracked Eye flickered with reflected light, as though the scribe's final message had not been carved for his own age, but for theirs.

Esme did not turn from the wall. Her voice was low, measured. "Thea pulled this from under DeWalt's nose. The carving Philips smuggled out of Abu Simbel. At first it looked finished. Final. But look again."

She unwrapped a linen cloth and laid a papyrus flat. She tapped her tablet. An infrared overlay lit the screen. Faint glyphs surfaced beneath the carving.

"Nebit took an older panel and carved over it," Esme said. "He plastered the first image, pressed it into the grooves, then carved the false death on top. To the eye of his time, it looked flawless. But the old lines hid beneath. Waiting."

She tapped again, and hidden shapes came to life beneath the light.

"We could never have seen this a century ago," she said. "With multispectral imaging, the layer beneath becomes clear. It's as if Nebit carved this for people who would come long after him."

Lex leaned in, his tone sharp. "So, it wasn't just history, it was a disguise."

"Not a disguise alone," Esme replied. "A message."

She followed the glowing lines with her finger, her voice hushed as if afraid to break the spell. "Nebit wrote that he and Imbu built a chamber beneath the river itself. A sanctuary hidden from gods and men. They wove its frame from reeds and papyrus, light but strong, coated every joint in clay and pitch until no drop could enter."

She paused, enlarging the image. The faint strokes of Nebit's stylus appeared clearer now, blue lines layered over brown, like veins beneath skin. "Here," she said softly. "They drove hollow stalks through the riverbed, narrow as a man's wrist, disguised among the rushes. From above, no one would ever see them. But below, those tubes became breath, their link to the world above. The river moved over them, but the chamber breathed."

Esme looked up, her eyes bright in the shifting light. "Nebit called it the second womb of the Nile. A place where death was swallowed and remade. Khamariti's descent wasn't an end, it was the beginning of something he planned all along."

The sequence shifted. Khamariti sank into the Nile, stones tied to his chest, eyes open, arms bound. Then Imbu appeared, strong, sure, pulling him down, not to die, but to survive.

The next panel showed a dome beneath the current. Reeds bent into arches, sealed with resin. Hollow stalks rose to the surface, hidden in the rushes. A lung beneath the river.

Thea's breath caught. "A-amazing."

Esme nodded slowly, her eyes fixed on the faint carving. "Nebit learned from Khamariti himself. He was taught the art of subterfuge, how to hide the truth beneath the lie. He carved it certain that no one in his own age would see it, but also certain that someone, one day, would."

She glanced back at the spiral of glyphs. "I have seen the same technique on another scroll. A surface story for the unworthy, and a deeper thread for those who were meant to understand."

The cracked Eye glimmered again in the shifting light, as if daring them to look beyond what seemed obvious.

Esme pointed to another line etched into the spiral. The glyphs were faint, as if deliberately softened, a record written in the margins of history.

"Here," she said quietly. "Pharaoh granted Khamariti time. The Ramesseum drawings to be finished under his name, but in truth they were a mask. While the plans were being drafted in the open, Nebit and Imbu were building in secret. The chamber was raised beneath the stone. Not a tomb. A refuge."

Esme raised her gaze. "Nebit hid the truth inside the lie. Khamariti did not die. He endured. Waiting beneath the river until the moment he could disappear."

She let her hand hover over the glyphs.

Esme traced the symbols with her hand. "Pharaoh must have known. No building escaped his notice. But this was not one of Khamariti's grand designs. It was a temporary structure, raised quickly, fragile by choice. The Nile would change course. The floods would wear it down. Within a generation it would vanish."

She looked at Lex. "Perhaps Pharaoh chose to look away. Perhaps he understood more than the priests ever admitted. Maybe he sensed Khamariti was building something that would outlast stone, memory. Not a monument of praise, but something hidden beneath it."

Lex followed the curve of the symbols. "A chamber, under the Nile, ingenious."

Esme nodded. "That was the trick. A shelter from the water."

The light from the projection caught the cracked Eye on the wall, as if to remind them that Khamariti's greatest works were always disguised.

Esme tapped another image, her voice steady but edged with awe. "The High Priest drowned that day. Not Khamariti."

The carving shifted under the projection's light, its lines harsh, almost violent. The final panel showed the dome, its curves intact. Outside its safety, a single figure thrashed in the river. The inscription named him, Ankhwennefer. His arms were flung wide, his head forced beneath the current.

A crocodile loomed close, jaws yawning open, teeth carved with such precision they seemed ready to snap shut. The water itself was cut with deep grooves, not waves of nature but deliberate strokes to show its violence.

The message could not be mistaken. The river had taken the high priest, not the architect.

"Yes," Esme said. "No one knew the truth. Not the priests, not the court. Only Imbu, Zarah, Nebit… and perhaps Ramesses himself.

But Nebit left the record for us. He hid it where only the future could find it."

Max finally spoke, his voice thick with frustration. "Khamariti could do all this, had the know-how to build grids that powered planets, so why'd he let the world stumble in darkness? Why'd we have to wait two thousand years for the industrial revolution? Why let us waste centuries with fire and bronze when he could've given us everything?"

"Because he knew what men like DeWalt would do with it. He understood ambition. He understood greed. Give technology too soon and it becomes a weapon, not a gift. He held it back so that power could not be stolen by a few who would use it to raise themselves at the cost of everyone else."

Esme stepped forward, holding another scroll that had unfolded within the projection.

She read slowly, her voice carrying the weight of the ancient script.

"He wrote that humanity needed its childhood, its youth, its turbulent teenage years. Civilisation had to grow before it could be trusted. To give too much knowledge too early would be to unbalance the world."

She paused, glancing at the next lines.

"He feared what he had already seen on A'tharan, a society stripped of its nature, its oceans gone, its forests turned to ash and fuel. A world where fire and water could kill without thought, and even those were twisted into tools of power."

Max gave a low whistle. "Sounds like we've already hit the teenage rebellion stage, phones, politics, and setting fire to the planet for fun."

Esme gave a thin smile and continued.

"He warned that if humanity was given the same path too soon, the same few would seize it, and they would drain the Earth as his own people had drained theirs."

She lowered the scroll, her eyes unsettled. "He gave us time. He forced us to learn how to live before learning how to command."

Max shook his head. "Well, I think he gave it to us too early. Just look at DeWalt"

Lex's gaze stayed on the spheres. "Or he might have had no choice. The technology may be the only way left to build a new grid and protect both planets."

Lex turned to the window. Rain streaked the glass in slow threads. He spoke without turning. "We cannot break from DeWalt yet. He controls money and access. If we walk, we lose everything. We stay close. We give him progress. Enough to keep him calm. Work that looks real. But never the heart."

Thea frowned, her voice unsteady but her gaze clear. "So… we k-keep w-working for my u-uncle?" she asked, the words catching slightly as she forced them out.

She drew a slow breath, steadying herself before the truth came. "He r-raised me after the accident," she said quietly. "Not out of love. He wanted the picture, the great man taking in his brother's orphaned daughter. Papers loved it. Sponsors loved it." Her jaw tightened, eyes fixed on the floor. "But I was never family. I was an asset. A way to p-polish his name."

She looked up, voice low but sure. "And now I see it for what it was. Trusting him again would be a mistake.

"Yes, I know." Lex said. "For now, we stay inside his circle, but we give him the minimum."

Max leaned forward. "That's your best plan?"

"It is the only plan for now, unless you have something better," Lex said.

He pulled a folded page from his jacket. He placed it on the table and pushed it forward.

"I wasn't going to show you this, but we need his funding for this" Lex said, his tone caught between hesitation and resolve. "It's the plan I talked about earlier, one that, after what we've just heard, feels less scientific and more like science fiction. But I think it's time you saw it. It sounds absurd… but you need to see."

Esme opened it. Her eyes moved across his notebook. She looked up, her face pale. "You are serious."

Lex nodded. "I am going to Switzerland. Whatever is waiting there ties all of this together. The grid. The monuments. Technology. A'tharan."

348

"The A-alps?" Thea asked. "What could be there?"

Lex's gaze stayed fixed on the table, his voice low, almost reverent. "Maybe it's what Max couldn't find," he said. "Or maybe something far greater."

He drew a breath, his hand resting near the projection controls. "It was the theodolite, the one recovered at Abu Simbel. That, and the slide show Esme showed me the other day and has now shared with you, convinced me. The instrument is centuries ahead of its time. It predates Djoser's pyramid, yet it measures with the precision of a modern laser scope. It shouldn't exist... but it does."

The room held its breath.

"Khamariti survived that execution," Lex went on. "He said only fire and water could end him. The craft hidden in DeWalt's vault, the cavern on La Palma, the chamber beneath Nefertari's tomb, it all connects. It's as if Khamariti was expecting us, leaving a trail across millennia. Leading us to something he wanted found."

He looked up at them, the weight of it clear in his eyes. "And whatever it is, we have to see it through to the end."

The room fell still. Outside, the rain thickened, striking the glass in relentless waves. Inside, the weight of discovery settled over them, the truth of ages lying quiet on the table between them.

Esme's voice broke the silence, soft but certain. "I think he's calling to us too."

Max gave a faint, tired smile. "He could have just sent a text," he said. "Would've saved us one hell of a trip."

Thea glanced at him, a spark of irony in her eyes. "He did," she said. "Only b-back then, they called t-them hieroglyphs."

epilogue:
Crossing into the Unknown

Six months had passed since the Senate had voted to impeach. A month since President Hope, shamed and disgraced, had resigned. True to his word, he had pardoned Rotherham and Riley before stepping down. But the pardon did little to save them. Egypt had issued international arrest warrants for all three, their names printed beneath the word fugitive in papers across the world.

Washington tried to steady itself, to draw a breath after the chaos. Yet far out in the Atlantic, beyond the noise of politics and blame, another storm was gathering, older, deeper, and far more dangerous.

Night covered the ocean. From the depths came a groan that travelled for miles. On La Palma the western flank of Cumbre Vieja split open, a mile of fine fissures glowing faintly under the moon. Villagers said the ridge whispered like a choir of stones. Instruments told a harsher truth. The slope was moving. Not by harmless centimetres. This was the beginning of a fall too vast to stop.

In Washington, the new president sat alone in a small, windowless room, no cameras, no aides, only the cold hum of machines. Before him lay Max Keeper's models, a map of dread rendered in light. The curves told no lies. If the volcanic flank gave way, the ocean itself would rise in vengeance.

He stared at the projection, the silence around him broken only by the distant echo of hurried footsteps in the corridor. Orders had already gone out. Along the eastern seaboard, governors had stopped waiting for confirmation. Convoys rolled, sirens wailed, and cities began to empty. The first tremors had reached the sensors. The countdown had begun.

Buses rolled inland without pause. Trains ran night and day, their carriages crammed. Highways turned into rivers of steel under sirens and flares. Stadiums filled with cots. School gyms became shelters. Warehouses became supply depots. Hospitals cleared their wards, sending the stable home so the weak and frail could be taken in. A nation waited, braced, counting hours until the mountain gave way.

La Palma answered.

Deep inside Cumbre Vieja, DeWalt drove his team through a narrow throat of rock that stank of sulphur and old fire. He had bribed men in Madrid, signed forbidden papers, broken seals wiser hands had left in place. His lamp cut thin blades of light through the dust. Every groan from the ridge made the walls shiver. The mountain was unstable. The earth warned them with each tremor. But DeWalt would not stop.

Thea had told him of a scroll hidden in the cavern, linked to the orbs. She said it carried the code, the sequence to unlock them, the process Khamariti had used to stretch his life. A path to immortality.

It was a lie. Thea had invented it to keep herself useful, to make DeWalt believe she was still valuable. But he believed her. The idea consumed him. If the scroll was real, he could master the orb. He could live far beyond the years of other men. That thought silenced caution. It drowned out reason.

The scroll meant life, long life which meant power. The scroll meant he would be the most powerful man on the planet. For that promise, true or not, DeWalt was ready to gamble everything.

"Search," he commanded. His voice bounced from the stone and came back harder. "Every wall. Every crack. He left it here. I want it."

A geologist tried to protest. "The slope is slipping. We need to—"

"No one leaves," DeWalt snapped. "Not until I have it."

Pebbles fell like dry rain. A worker pointed to a snake faded on the wall, half buried in rubble. DeWalt rushed forward, clawing at it with bare hands, lips drawn back, eyes alight.

"Here!" he cried. "I told you! Here!"

He was wrong.

The ground shifted beneath them, rolling like the deck of a ship in a storm. Dust rained from the ceiling. A sharp crack ripped through the chamber above their heads. Lamps swung in wide arcs, shadows leaping across the carvings.

DeWalt's eyes fixed on a panel of stone newly exposed by the trembling wall. In the flicker of the lamps, the image came alive. It was no record of the past but a warning. The carving showed the cavern itself, walls collapsing, the sea surging inward, the ridge breaking loose and sliding into the abyss. Khamariti had foreseen it, or dreaded it, and had carved the vision for those who refused to heed his words.

The floor lurched again. Outside, the mountain gave way. The first hundred metres of slope slid into the ocean, slow enough to hold its shape for a breath, then breaking apart in a roar of spray and stone. Eight hundred metres followed, the land folding in on itself, the ridge tearing free.

Inside the cavern, the walls split down the middle. The forbidden vault shuddered and cracked. DeWalt had only a heartbeat to register what he was seeing, prophecy becoming reality, before the ceiling tore open and the floor pitched away beneath him.

The cavern sheared from the mountain and plunged into the Atlantic. DeWalt and his men were swallowed in the collapse, vanishing with the chamber that should never have been reopened.

Thea, without realising it, had just become the sole surviving heir to the DeWalt companies.

The impact struck the Atlantic like a hammer on a drum. The ocean rose. A wall of black water stood, immense, and began to run west.

Across the world, screens turned red. Satellites traced the surge tearing across the basin at the speed of a jet. Buoys screamed until they went silent. Graphs climbed until they broke their scales.

In San Juan church bells rang as the sea withdrew. Fishermen stared at the harbour floor, suddenly bare, boats resting on mud where water should have been. Children chased fish that flopped in puddles, laughing until their parents screamed for them to run. On the horizon a line of darkness grew. It became a ridge. It became a wall. The sound came next, a roar deeper than thunder, the voice of the ocean itself. Then the wave struck. Streets that had held footsteps for four centuries drowned in one minute. Bells were silenced mid-peal. A saint's wooden hand floated through a window and was gone.

In the Bahamas, airports disappeared under white water. Resorts shattered like toys. Palm groves vanished in a single sweep. Pilots radioed frantic messages as their runways disappeared below the surge. A single sentence cut across the airwaves, "We have no land left." Then silence.

Florida waited under sirens and helicopter rotors. Miami watched the ocean pull back, exposing sandbanks littered with wrecks that had not seen air in a century. Tourists filmed it on phones until police screamed at them to flee. Parents dragged children by the hand, running for towers that would not be high enough. The wave struck with a force that bent steel. Skyscrapers swayed, their windows exploding in cascades of glass. Cars were lifted like leaves. Streets became rivers that ran against the earth. The city that had danced on the edge of the Atlantic for a hundred years was swallowed in one breath.

The Carolinas saw their low islands vanish first. Charleston's bells fell silent as salt water tore through the old quarter. Wooden houses lifted from their foundations and sailed into the marsh. Bridges folded like cards. Families clung to rooftops, their cries swept into the roar. The sea wrote its name across the land in a single stroke.

New York braced with all the strength it could muster. Subways emptied, their last trains rolling out through tunnels already leaking brine. Police shouted until their throats were raw. Firefighters carried children up stairwells that shook with the sound of approaching water.

In Battery Park crowds watched the river drain away, exposing ribs of old ships, the bones of centuries. Then they saw the horizon climb. The wave came in silence at first, too big to understand. When the roar reached them, it was already too late. The charging bull of Wall Street disappeared under white foam, horns last. Lights went out across downtown, flicker by flicker, as if the city had closed its eyes.

Boston fought. Seawalls slowed the first blow, breaking the crest but not the mass behind it. The second wave climbed over, higher, heavier. Boats were carried across streets, mast tips knocking out windows as they passed. People waded through water that rose to their chests, dragging neighbours toward higher ground. In Portland, a man carried his dog up a stairwell that had turned into a well, the water chasing his steps.

From space the white seam looked like a torn stitch running along a continent.

When the roar passed, silence fell. It was worse than the wave. In that silence came smaller sounds. A siren that belonged to nothing. A dog barking on a floating door. A child calling a name that would not answer.

Dawn spread a thin light over a new map. Helicopters thudded above steaming cities. Boats nosed past rooftops. Rescue workers waded through streets that no longer had names.

The new president spoke from a plain lectern. He made no promises that could not be kept. He spoke of the dead and the living, of the work that lay ahead. The coast, he said, would be rebuilt where it could, abandoned where it could not. He thanked Max Keeper by name, saying his models had saved hundreds of thousands. He did not name those who could not be saved; their absence was written everywhere.

What he could not say was what came next—the unseen consequence, the new plagues the wave had awakened, spreading quietly through water, soil, and breath.

Max did not watch the president's speech. He sat with Esme in the corner of a converted gym in Liverpool, now a shelter, the basketball hoops still hanging above rows of seats. Lex had tasked them with tracing the first landslip that could have drowned Atlantis. The black shard recovered months ago from the Campbells' overturned yacht had been carbon dated, its age confirming what legend only hinted at. Lex, though consumed by Khamariti's trail, had never let Atlantis slip from view.

Outside, Liverpool stood shaken but alive. The Atlantic wave had hit America first, tearing its coast apart, but the sea's force had not stopped there. It rolled northward, its energy curving with the ocean itself. By the time it reached Britain, the surge had weakened, yet still it struck hard enough to scar streets and break lives.

Crosby's beaches disappeared beneath a sheet of grey water. Along the Mersey, the docks tore open, cranes twisted like toys. Streets near the river drowned in salt and silt. Across the Wirral, in New Brighton, West Kirby, Moreton, and Hoylake, boats lay on their sides in car parks and gardens, tossed inland like driftwood.

The Irish Sea had never risen so fast. Warnings had cleared many homes, but not all. Some people clung to rooftops until helicopters reached them. Others were taken out by lifeboats, ferried through streets where pubs, schools, and shops now lay under brown water.

The gym smelled of damp clothes and diesel from the generators outside. Voices murmured in low tones. Families huddled under donated blankets. Volunteers carried trays of tea as if the act could hold back despair.

But Lex was not in Liverpool. He had left in the night. In his small case he carried the brass wand, a camera, the pumice stone, Imbu's statue, and a sealed vial of ash. He travelled like a man who never looked back but always did.

Paris blurred past. Then the Jura, snow clinging to the fields. Geneva rose, its streets polished, its air sharp with science and wealth.

Lex and Thea, their trust restored, had spent months buried in archives, chasing a trail that seemed to vanish, only to resurface centuries later. Cathedrals. Canals. Railways. Dams. Bridges. The pattern repeated itself across ages and continents. In the dust of old records one name kept appearing. Never the same twice, never the same face, but always the same hand. Each alias, each signature, each record resolved into a single anagram.

In Florence, as Brunelleschi's dome began to crown the skyline, a draftsman's neat signature appeared in the ledgers, Ami Kharit.

In Paris, during the construction of the Pont Neuf, a mason scrawled his mark on a payroll slip, Ira Thamk.

In the archives of the Panama Canal, buried deep among lists of forgotten consultants, one name surfaced, Hiram Tak Tak.

At Hoover Dam, amid hundreds of engineers, a single entry stood out, Tari Khim.

In Alexandria, a shipwright's blueprint bore the initials I.K. in a style centuries too advanced for its time.

In Kyoto, during the Edo period, temple plans were found signed Arik Ham.

Different names. Different eras. Different continents.

But every stroke, every angle, every calculation, belonged to the same impossible hand.

Khamariti had always been there, where earth was cut, where stone was lifted, where rivers were forced into new beds. He was always there when the world was reshaped. And always gone when the work was done.

Then the trail went dark. For the last hundred years there was silence. No trace in the Channel Tunnel. None in the files of the Three

Gorges Dam. None in the towers of Dubai or the Petronas Towers in Kuala Lumpa or London Dome.

Had Khamariti finally died? Or had he chosen to disappear, letting the world stumble forward without his design, blind to what it had lost?

Lex carried the question with him as the taxi wound through the grey streets. Years before, in a forgotten archive, he had found a draft buried among routine plans. At first glance it seemed trivial, some assistant's idle sketch. But in the margin, beneath a layer of dust and ink bleed, he had seen them: numbers, ratios, drawn with effortless precision. Ratios too exact to be chance.

The same geometry that shaped Abu Simbel.

And beside it, in a faded script almost swallowed by time, a signature: K. Arimith.

The memory had never left him. Perhaps Khamariti had not vanished at all. Perhaps he had left his mark here, hidden in plain sight, waiting.

The taxi slowed. Lex stepped out into air that stung with cold and the taste of snow. Ahead stretched a campus, its roads bending in deliberate arcs, its buildings arranged with intent. At first glance it was modern order. But as he traced the pattern with his eyes, his chest tightened. The angles were not random. The curves linked like the strokes of an ancient glyph. He had seen the shape before, on the walls of a temple, buried in dust.

He understood then. Even the grounds were part of the design. The campus itself was a code.

He followed the fence, obeying the warnings posted in three languages, while his eyes sought a weakness. Ahead, a narrow service path cut into the verge. A small door waited, its lock gleaming in the half light.

Movement froze him. Two figures stepped from the line of firs.

The first was vast, his frame blocking the pale glow, shoulders squared like stone. His skin caught the winter sun, a black sheen that gleamed against the frost. Each step pressed weight into the earth.

The second was smaller, sharper. A long coat hung loose across his frame, his eyes veiled in shadow. He did not need to move. The air seemed to bend toward him.

The giant stopped ten paces away, tall as a monument, dressed in black that swallowed detail.

Lex's breath caught. The likeness was unmistakable. His grip tightened on the case. "You look like the statue," he said quietly. "You must be Imbu."

The giant gave no reply.

Behind him, the second figure shifted, just enough for the fading light to catch his eyes. They were old, impossibly old, filled with centuries of weight. Lex's chest tightened. This was no attendant. This was Khamariti.

The figure spoke at last, his voice low, resonant, heavy with time itself.

"And you," he said, "are Professor Lex Mullin."

In that instant Lex understood. The story had never ended. Every path, every clue, had led him here, to CERN, the European Organisation for Nuclear Research. Its foundations were not only concrete and steel but geometry, marked with the unmistakable ratios of Khamariti's hand. This was not the end of the mystery. It was the beginning.

www.ingramcontent.com/pod-product-compliance
Lightning Source LLC
Chambersburg PA
CBHW060224030726
47499CB00004B/1176